a SNAPshot novel

FREEZE
frame

by

FREYA BARKER
& KT Dove

Freeze Frame
a novel

Copyright © 2017 Freya Barker & KT Dove

All rights reserved.

No part of this publication may be reproduced, distributed, or transmitted in any form or by any means, including photocopying, recording, or by other electronic or mechanical methods, without the prior written permission of the author or publisher, except in the case of brief quotations embodied in used critical reviews and certain other non-commercial uses as permitted by copyright law. For permission requests, write to the author, mentioning in the subject line: "Reproduction Request" at the address below:
freyabarker.writes@gmail.com

This book is a work of fiction and any resemblance to any person or persons, living or dead, any event, occurrence, or incident is purely coincidental. The characters and story lines are created and thought up from the author's imagination or are used fictitiously.

ISBN: 978-1-988733-02-9

Cover Design:
RE&D - Margreet Asselbergs

Editing:
Karen Hrdlicka
Joanne Thompson

DEDICATION

To those able to find beauty anywhere through the lens of their camera.

"Needed a piece of you. Something to remind me that through your eyes, there's beauty everywhere. That getting to know you allowed me a glimpse too, even if all I've seen for years is an ugly world."

Before you start…

It is highly recommended you read Shutter Speed, the prequel Snapshot novella, prior to reading Freeze Frame!

CHAPTER 1

Isla

"Mmmm…"

Ben groans as he rolls over on his back the moment I slip my arm from around his waist.

The soft light of an early sun is coming through the small window opposite the bed, as I untangle myself from the sheets and slip into the bathroom to relieve myself.

He's still softly snoring when I get back. A quick peek at the clock, on the nightstand, shows only six in the morning. To get up or crawl back under the covers, that is the question. After reacquainting myself with all Ben is able to do to my body last night—making up for lost time—I could probably do with another hour, maybe two. I'm still tired, and not just a little sore from last night's thorough workout.

Ben's face is lined with deep grooves, mapping out the hard life he's led. Every line a witness to the decade or more he's spent working undercover for the DEA, living side by side with some of the most depraved and vile criminals. It marks a man. It's marked Ben, but every line and every wrinkle he wears just adds to his appeal. His heavily fringed eyelids fan across his cheeks, his full lips slack with sleep.

Beauty in contrast. Something I have an eye for, being a photographer. Everything about Ben is both soft and hard; it wasn't difficult to fall for him.

I slide back underneath the sheets and my body automatically seeks his warmth, curling up against his side.

"Mmmmm, babe..." he mumbles sleepily, curving his arm around me and tugging me closer. "It's early."

"I know. Go back to sleep," I whisper.

I try practicing what I preach. My eyes drift shut, but the soft circular strokes of Ben's calloused fingertips on my neck at the hairline, keep me from drifting off. My skin is sensitized to the point that I almost anticipate the path of his touch. When his fingers change course and brush along my spine, all the way down to my ass, my skin buzzes with electricity and all hope of sleep disappears.

"You're not sleeping," I mutter, only slightly accusingly into his chest, as I trail my fingers through the hair there. His chuckle rumbles under my ear.

"Neither are you," he says, his big hand sliding down to cup my ass. Well, half of my ass, seeing as even his shovel-sized paws can't cover all my real estate.

"Mmmm, you sure you can manage after last night, old man?" His hand squeezes as he rolls me on top of him. My knees drop on either side of his hips and it is immediately evident how well he'll be able to manage. No words are needed; his solid erection rubbing along my slick core is plenty of proof.

"Isla," he growls, his hands settling firmly on my hips, holding me in place. "We have to talk."

Ignoring him, I lean forward, nipping his full bottom lip with my teeth,

"Later," I mumble against his mouth before sliding my tongue inside.

One of his hands slips back over my ass, while the other comes up to cup the back of my head. In one move, he sits up on his knees and has me on my back, my legs draped wide over his thighs. I shiver when his hand slips around to the front where he leaves it curved around my neck, the light pressure keeping me still as he bends forward and takes my nipple between his lips. The light bite, followed by the wet heat of his mouth, has my hips lift up, eager for friction.

"Easy," he whispers against my skin. "Lift your arms over your head and keep them there." I don't question him and do as he tells me. Not because I don't have a mind of my own, but because he's already proved to me that he knows better than I do how to make me feel good. My expertise is mostly reserved to the number of settings on my vibrator. Any sex with another person involved was long ago and barely memorable.

Ben is memorable. Has been since the first time we slept together, a couple of months ago. My body had been played to perfection, much like he is making it sing now. Both of his palms are scraping slowly over my sensitized nipples, dragging down over the soft swell of my stomach to the junction of my thighs. His thumbs play lazily through the wetness gathering there, brushing lightly through my folds. His eyes are focused on his hands—on my body—before he lifts them up to mine.

"Pretty." Is all he says before he grabs me by the hips, lifts, and with forceful precision, fills me in one powerful stroke.

My body arches off the mattress, my mouth falling open in a long drawn out groan. "Oh..."

"Eyes open." His gruffly voiced order penetrates my mindless state. I'm not even aware I have them closed. Blinking, I clear my vision, focusing on Ben's large form moving between my legs.

-

"Are you done in there?" Ben asks when I step out of the tiny bathroom, a towel wrapped around me. It would've been nice to take a shower together, but there's no way; Ben can barely fit by himself.

"Have at it." I step aside when he squeezes past me, dropping a kiss on my lips. I try hard not to giggle when I watch him work his shoulders through the door sideways, swearing under his breath. "I'll just get coffee going."

Tucking the towel in between my breasts, I step into the kitchen, thankful for the Keurig sitting on the little counter.

I'm just adding some cream and sugar to mine when the door opens behind me.

"Are you done already?" I ask, turning around with the mug already to my lips. I promptly drop my mug, spilling hot coffee all down my front. "Fuck, *ahh*!" I swing back toward the sink, pulling the soaked towel away from my skin.

"Jesus, girl," my Uncle Al says, moving up behind me.

"What's wrong?" I hear behind us, as the bathroom door slams open. I turn my head in tandem with my uncle, as a buck naked Ben rushes out.

"Son of a bitch," Uncle Al bites off before he looks at me, at Ben, and marches straight back out the door. "I'll wait outside," he barks, pulling the door to the trailer shut behind him.

Wonderful.

Ben

"So that's how it is?" Al Ferris says when I walk outside, two coffees in hand.

"Black okay?" I hand him one, taking a deep breath before sitting down across from him at the picnic table.

I just spent ten minutes trying to calm Isla down while icing down her chest, which was burned bright red. She's getting dressed as we speak, and I don't want her to walk out here to her uncle and me going at it. So I take a sip of coffee and make sure I'm calm when I answer.

"We're together," I say simply.

"I gathered as much. For how long is what I'd like to know? Until the next assignment comes along?"

I understand his concerns. I told him as much the first time I spoke to him about his niece. It's the only reason I'm able to keep my cool.

"Al—with all due respect—I've barely had a chance to talk with Isla about the future. What I'm willing to tell you is that I care for your niece, and I have no intention to up and leave. I won't have to; I'm retired." I hold his glare until he gives his head a brisk shake and lowers his eyes.

"It complicates things," he finally says, snorting. "I came to make her an offer, but now..." His voice trails off.

"Now what?" Isla walks up and slips onto the bench beside me. "You know I can hear every word in there, right?" My hand finds her knee under the table and I give her a light squeeze.

"I forgot," Al admits, a bit contrite.

"So what brings you out here, Uncle Al? Is Ginnie okay?" The old man lifts his hand and covers Isla's.

"Ginnie is fine. Do you remember Henry Carmichael?" he asks her.

"Of course. You went to the academy together. He was at your retirement, wasn't he?"

"Yeah," Al sighs, looking down at his own fingers tracing the woodgrain in the table. I have a feeling what comes next won't be good news. "He's also the one who said that just because I was retired from the force didn't mean I should sit on my ass, twiddling my thumbs." He barks out a sharp, regretful laugh. "Sitting idle would kill me," Al said. "This is his property, you know?"

I feel Isla startle beside me.

"His? I didn't know that."

"Yup. He bought it as an investment property when he handed in his badge a few years before me. Ran the place for a few years, and then decided a campground on a mountain wasn't gonna help him get laid."

I had to chuckle at that. I've spent enough time living from a small trailer to know that is the damn truth. Although I got lucky in the end. Al lifts his head and grins at me.

"Never got married. No kids. He was always looking for his next conquest. Damn, I swear he got worse the older he got."

The smile disappears from my face. *Was.* Which means he's dead. The small nod Al gives me is confirmation, before he lays it all out.

"I got a call last week from a lawyer in St. Petersburg, Florida, who'd been trying to reach me. Henry died from a massive heart attack, while cruising the Caribbean." This time it's Isla who reaches out and grabs her uncle's hand.

"I'm sorry," she softly says. "You've lost more than your share in this lifetime."

"Oh, baby girl—that happens when you get to be my age." The old man smiles at her. "I just prefer to think of it as being lucky I had all of them in my life: your mom, your Aunt Kate, Henry."

"Still sorry for your loss, Al," I offer my regrets, earning a hesitant smile.

"Thanks, son, but that's not why I brought Henry up." He turns his attention back to Isla, whose hand finds mine in her lap. "The lawyer who called is handling his estate. The damn bastard left me the campground. Lock, stock and barrel. Took me a bit to get my head around that. Even with Ginnie in a care facility, I don't want to be too far away. Thought about selling it." Al doesn't notice Isla going rigid beside me and forges on. "Would probably make a pretty penny, but what am I gonna do with that? My life is fine the way it is. And then there's you." He lifts his eyes to Isla. "Anyway, I had the guy send the papers I was to sign to my lawyer in Cortez and went to see him yesterday." He pulls a folded document from his inside pocket and slaps it on the table. "It's up to you, baby girl, but I had him draw these up. Figured since you seem to have found your legs here, you might want a say in this."

Trembling, Isla slips her hand from mine and draws the papers toward her. My eyes slide over her bowed head to her uncle, who gives me a slight shrug before turning his attention back on his niece.

"I don't know what to say," Isla finally mutters, shoving the papers back across the table. "It's too much."

"Bullcrap," Al reacts instantly. "It's not enough. Trust me on that. You've made my life rich, baby girl. Richer and more fulfilled than I could ever have dreamed of. You're as much mine as you were my sister's. My blood. My *only* blood. And don't think for a second you haven't brought color to Kate and Ginnie's lives, too." He sniffs loudly before letting out a hoarse chuckle. "Besides, you'll be the one doing all the work. We may both hold ownership, but you're driving the bus. That is, if you want it?"

CHAPTER 2

Isla

"Only one more."

My uncle's lawyer, Nicholas Flynn, all done up in his Armani suit and Ferragamo shoes, seems utterly out of place here in Cortez. Hell, he'd look lost anywhere in Colorado but perhaps Denver. You'd be hard pressed to find another suit in this town, which is why my eyes had darted to my uncle for reassurance when we walked in.

"He's a good man," Al whispered behind me, as we followed the tall, very bald, and impeccably dressed man into his office. "Don't let the fancy threads fool you; he knows how to get down and dirty when a situation demands it."

It almost seems too easy. Just signing a few papers and I'm suddenly a landowner. Feels like I should at least be made to take a test, some kind of exam to establish my suitability. I don't think my brain has caught up to what is happening yet, and Ben was no help. He just shoved me into my uncle's old Cadillac DeVille, telling me he'd take the golf cart and do my morning round of garbage pickup. Something I would, at any other time, have paid good money to see. The big, burly, and rather ferocious looking biker put-putting around on a battery driven senior's version of a four-wheeler.

I chuckle at the thought as I sign the last sheet of paper with great flourish, before putting the pen down, and looking up at my uncle.

"Now we go to the bank," he says, grabbing my hand and almost pulling me out of the chair. I barely have a chance to say goodbye to Nicholas before I'm ushered out of the office and into Al's car.

"What's the rush?"

"Loaded baked potato," he says, looking at me like he can't believe I don't get it. "If we don't get to Once Upon A Sandwich before noon, there won't be any tables left. I miss those potatoes."

Once Upon A Sandwich is a small restaurant at the back of a Main Street bar. The lunch menu features large baked potatoes, topped with just about anything you can imagine. One of Al's favorite hangouts.

"What about Ben?" I want to know. Oh, I'm sure Ben can fend for himself when it comes to lunch, or anything else for that matter, but it just doesn't seem right.

Yesterday I thought I was finally finding some solid ground and today I feel like I'm spinning out of control. So much has happened in less than twenty-four hours. Ben and I still haven't had a chance to talk about anything and now the campground—it's all a bit much.

I can feel my uncle's eyes on me as he turns into the parking lot behind the bank.

"We can call in an order, take it back to the trailer, if you like," he says, pulling into an open spot and turning off the engine. "Of course, it'll be cold by the time we get there..." His blatant guilt trip makes me laugh. And it's working. The restaurant is not much to look at but the atmosphere is great. Feels like you're sitting in someone's kitchen and that is half the experience.

"Nah...we can bring him back something," I concede,

smiling broadly at the twinkle in Al's eye. The old coot knows exactly how to get his way.

-

It's three hours after we left, before we get back to the campground. I was duly added as a signatory to the business accounts. Uncle Al had been eager to head off for lunch as we walked out of the bank, when I spotted the awning for SouthWest Printing across the road. With everything that happened since yesterday afternoon, I'd almost forgotten I had a few more prints to pick up for the coffee shop. They hadn't been ready the last time I was here.

I just saw Jen, the owner of The Pony Express, yesterday and was surprised to find she'd sold every last one of my prints she had on display. She warned me that the five new ones I brought with me wouldn't last long.

"I just have to pop across the street," I announced, before dashing off, Al grumbling behind me, but he was easily soothed twenty minutes later when we sat down for lunch.

There is no sign of Ben or his bike when Al pulls around the trailer.

"He better hurry, or his spud will be stone cold," Al mumbles as I get out of the car, the paper bag with lunch for Ben in my hand. I try to ignore the small niggle of doubt as I walk in the door. Maybe we should've talked first and fucked later. At least I would've known where his head was at before Uncle Al dropped his bombshell.

The first thing I see is a note in the middle of the kitchen counter.

Pixie,

Picking up my truck and things in Durango. Don't count on me for dinner.

Ben
907 741 4348

He's not exactly forthcoming, and the note could've been written to anyone, but it's the content that puts a smile on my face. He's getting his stuff and bringing it back here.

Uncle Al leans in and shamelessly reads over my shoulder.

"Perfect," he mumbles, grabbing a knife and fork out of the drawer. Before I can stop him, he snatches the brown paper bag off the counter, sits down on the couch, and starts eating.

"Hey!"

"What?" he says, his mouth full of potato. "He's not here, he's not gonna be here anytime soon. You want me to let this food go to waste?"

"Do you know how many calories are in one of those? Let alone two?" I try to get through to him but he just waves his fork at me. "It's not healthy. Didn't your doctor tell you to eat healthier after you had that last scare?"

"Bullshit," he spits out. Literally—potato crumbs go flying. "That snotnosed quack. He knows nothing."

Exasperating: the same old discussion with the same predictable outcome.

"You die from a stroke or a heart attack, that you could've prevented, I'll never forgive you, Uncle Al." My voice is rough with an emotion I'm trying hard to hold back. He doesn't even notice; he's too busy wolfing down Ben's lunch. Stubborn old fart.

"Have you seen that spot I started clear-cutting on the ridge, just off the gate?" he asks me, tossing the empty bag in the trash underneath the sink.

"You mean the lookout point?" I'm pretty sure he's referring to a spot I used to love hanging out on. Just a quarter of a mile up the mountain behind us, there's a small clearing with a rocky outcrop from which you can see the entire reservoir.

"Yup. Planned on building there before Ginnie got sick. Was getting tired of the trailer. All damn summer having to take a crap with the bathroom door open was gettin' old." And just like that he has me snicker and he knows it, too. His eyes sparkle with humor as he tilts his head to the door. "Come on. I'll show you. Maybe you should build there."

I wordlessly follow him outside, a new sense of excitement settling in.

Ben

"Already?"

Damian walks up behind me as I toss the last of my bags into the bed of the truck. After working together on more than a few cases, FBI Agent Damian Gomez and I have become good friends. When I'd needed a place to get my shit in order, he'd offered to let me park my stuff with him; a nice chunk of land just north of Durango, right along the Animas River. The past month, I spent most of my time here; giving Isla the space she needed, while tying up the loose ends of my employment with the DEA. There aren't many people I can talk to, but Damian is one. By now he knows exactly what went down with my last assignment. And with Isla.

"Yup." I turn around with a smile on my face. "Already."

"Didn't take much then to convince her?" Damian grins back.

"Just my usual charm."

He barks out a laugh before his eyes turn serious.

"This is what you want?" he asks, scrutinizing my face.

"I have no idea what the future looks like, if that's what you mean. I sure as hell don't want to be sitting around doing nothing, but all of that is secondary." I run my hand through my hair, sorting through my thoughts. Thoughts that haven't shut down since waking up this morning in Isla's trailer. I hadn't considered much beyond getting her back when I drove down there yesterday, but her uncle showing up had given some direction at least. A starting point. "I want her," I tell him simply. "I don't have a foothold anywhere. No roots to return to at this point, no real place that's mine to claim, like you have here." I turn toward the fast flowing river and the mountains beyond. "But she does." I look back at Damian. "I can figure out what I wanna do with the rest of my life anywhere—and I want to do it where she is."

"Fair enough," he says, clapping me on the shoulder. "Do you want take that piece of crap with you?" He tilts his head in the direction of an old trailer, just off the side of the driveway. One Damian had stayed in while working on his house. "You could fix it up a little, maybe rent it out."

I hadn't planned on taking on another trailer. In fact I'd been glad to be rid of the constant reminder of my old life, but an idea started forming at the sight of the aged mobile home. Maybe I could make some use of it at the campground. A bed should I need it, or least it would give me something to do—fixing it up. The structure is still decent, albeit dated, so maybe there are still some miles left on the thing. With a bit of elbow grease, I could give it new purpose. Much as I'm doing with my life.

Damian helps me tie the bike down in the truck bed and hitch the trailer in place, before he grabs me in a brotherly hug.

"Stay in touch," he orders when I get behind the wheel. I roll down the window and lean my elbow out.

"Will do," I promise. "Be easier now that I won't have any more assignments coming."

"Right," he says and slaps the roof of the cab. "And if you get bored, remember to give Gus Flemming a call. His outfit is based out of Cedar Tree, only forty minutes or so from Dolores, and he's always looking for good men. Keep it in mind."

"I will."

"And bring that woman next time you head this way. Would love to know who turned you into such a pussy," Damian says wearing a big smirk.

"You're an asshole," I tell him. Starting the truck, I listen to him laugh as I slowly drive away.

-

It's dark when I finally pull through the gates of the campground.

She must've been on the lookout, because the moment I pull onto the vacant lot beside Isla's place, she's already running in my direction.

"What's this?" she asks when I get out, running her fingers along the side of the old trailer as she walks around it. "Your new home?" There is veiled uncertainty in her question. I come up behind her, grab her shoulders, and turn her to face me.

"It could be, for now. You need some space—some time—to wrap your head around what is happening here? The extra bed could provide that, but mostly it's just a project I want to work on," I offer her, brushing her bangs from her forehead as her mouth twitches into a soft smile, and her pretty hazel eyes glance up at me.

"A project?"

"Something to keep my hands busy. Refinish it and maybe rent it out? It's big enough for four adults." Isla nods her head and I let her go, opening the door for her. The inside is worn, old, but the paneling is a nice, real wood veneer that can be brought back to life with a little help. The upholstery has to be replaced, as does the carpeting, and the chipped counter, but a lot of what's there just needs a little lift. The big work is in the electrical and the water pump. The propane lines need replacing too, and I'm pretty sure the bathroom should be completely overhauled. I need some time to inventory everything.

"So..." Isla leans back, her hands braced against the small kitchen counter. "What exactly is happening here?" The hesitant hope in her eyes when she asks the question has me put my hands on her hips and tug her a little closer.

"What's happening is you're adjusting to some new

realities, but so am I. The two are not mutually exclusive, though. Instead of just finding my way, I'd much prefer to find my way to you. This is a start. For whatever we choose to make it."

The hesitant hope on her face is transforming into a radiant smile. It's all she has to do; this woman's smile hits me square in the gut every time. Her hands sneak up until they rest on my chest and her head is tilted back. An invitation if I ever saw one, so I don't make her wait, I lean in and slant my mouth over hers.

Losing the ability to think clearly is inevitable, when I have her tongue in my mouth and her taste on my lips.

"I like that," she mumbles when I finally come up for air. "And I like this idea of restoring classic trailers and renting them out."

"One," I correct her. "One classic trailer."

"Yes," she says, a twinkle in her eyes. "One for now, but think about it; we could probably pick up some real beauties for next to nothing and restore them. Make them permanent fixtures on the campground; each maybe with a different theme, and all in a prime location, of course. Private and unique." Her eyes drift around the interior and as she did on the outside, she trails her fingers along the surfaces in here, her mind clearly spinning.

"Big plans already," I tease her with a smile. Truth is, I actually quite like the idea. "Come on. Let's get this damn thing unhooked and stabilized. We'll get a better look tomorrow, in the daylight."

It doesn't take us long. I leave my truck there, and walk my bike over to Isla's trailer, an overnight bag hanging off the handlebars.

"Did you eat?" Isla asks when she dives into the small

fridge to grab us a beer.

"Grabbed a burger at the drive-thru in Cortez. I'm good." That earns me a stern look before she turns back to the fridge and pulls out half a meatloaf, lettuce, a tomato, mustard, and a jar of mayonnaise. I'm not even going to try and argue. I've come to recognize that stubborn set of her chin. "Where is Al?" I ask, suddenly realizing he's missing.

"Motel in Dolores. He was going to meet up with some old cronies of his and play some poker tonight. He's heading back to Flagstaff tomorrow, but said he'd be back in the morning before hitting the road." I watch as she expertly puts together an impressive sandwich.

"Everything go alright today?" I ask, as she walks over, two beers in one hand and a plate in the other. Sitting down beside me on the couch, she hands me the plate and sets the beers on the small coffee table. While I scarf down the sandwich, she fills me in on her day.

I'm just licking the last crumbs off my fingers when she tells me about the plot on the mountain.

"You want to build there?" I ask her, even though I already know the answer. It's clear as day on her face.

"It's perfect," she gushes, sitting on the edge of her seat, her hands waving around as she describes the location. I don't have the heart to tell her I've seen it. I stumbled on it in the spring, when I was scouting out the area. "From the point you can see for miles. And it's beautiful this time of year, with some of the trees changing color and the chill keeping the air clear. It's stunning. We should go up tomorrow."

I try to recall the details of the clearing, but I'd been so focused on what was going on in the campground below, I hadn't given myself a chance to enjoy the views. The thought of building a house up there, putting down some permanent roots, that idea appealed to me, even though it's not my land or my call to make. Not yet anyway.

"Then that's what we'll do." I smile at her enthusiasm. I'll follow her up that mountain in a heartbeat.

Fuck, I'd follow her anywhere.

CHAPTER 3

Ben

"You gonna stick around?"

I look up at the old man coming toward me. When Isla's uncle arrived this morning, I'd already been out here, working on the trailer. I wanted to check out the propane lines first, since I'd noticed the faint smell of gas when I was inside last night. I'm not about to start any kind of work when there is even the slightest chance of a leak. One single spark could blow the tank.

Al looks over my shoulder, where I have the compartment for the propane hook up open.

"Not sure what you're going to do with this old thing, but I suggest you change out that propane adapter and all of those hoses. I could smell the damn gas when I came outside." I tuck my chin down to hide my grin.

"Probably because I've had the valve open. Don't want to work on it with the propane tank half full." I turn to look at him over my shoulder before I continue. "And as for your question; yes, I will be sticking around." I focus back on what I'm doing.

"You'll get bored," he says after an extended silence.

"Be hard with Isla around. Your niece is not boring, Al."

"Don't be a smartass," he snaps. "You know what I mean. Guys like you, you need your adrenaline fix or you wouldn't have been able to do what you did for so long."

I drop the wrench I was holding with a loud clang,

into the opened toolbox at my feet, before I turn around. As much as I appreciate his concern for his girl, his mistrust stings.

"Here's the deal; I left the DEA for a reason. You, of all people, should be able to appreciate the fact that a life like the one I lived erodes a person. When your job has to trump everything you care about, everyone you love, or it leaves you dead. I was trying to cut loose long before I met Isla, but she was the clearest sign of why I had to. You'll get no promises or guarantees from me, old man—but that's only because I'm not the only one who decides how this will come out. What I can tell you is this; I know where I want this to end up, and I'm finding my way to get there."

I'm not backing down from the glare he shoots me. When he realizes I can't be intimidated, he drops his eyes and rubs the back of his neck, mumbling a profanity.

"What are you fixing this up for?" he finally asks, and I take it as the white flag it is intended as.

"It's a classic," I explain, bending down to grab my tools again. "She's a little worn, but could make a nice little, permanent rental trailer with a bit of TLC."

"1958 Deville," Al mumbles, clearly knowing his stuff. "I remember growing up, our neighbors had one in the driveway. Pink thing. Ugly damn color, but we had so damn much fun in it." He falls quiet, lost to his memories for a bit. "She have the original wood paneling?"

"Sure does, and the Formica table and countertops. Go on in, have a look." I wave to the door. "It's not locked."

Without another word, Al goes inside, while I try to vent off the remaining gas. By the time he steps back outside, I'm disconnecting the old hoses from the couplings.

"I've got a buddy in town, Phil McCracken. He's got a place off Merritt Way, on the south side of town. Easy to spot, looks like a damn junkyard, but he's got a couple of old Airstreams sitting in the field on blocks. I'll leave Isla the number." With that he walks off.

-

"Well, that didn't take long," Isla says as we trudge up the mountain.

"What?"

"Uncle Al. I was by the window, ready to pull him off you if things got too bloody, but I never expected him to come back with a smile on his face. What did you tell him?"

"Nothing I didn't tell you first," I state, as I watch her face soften into a smile.

"He likes your ideas," she says, swinging around to block my path.

"Yours," I tell her firmly. "I didn't think beyond that one old trailer. You're the one who came up with turning it into a theme. Clearly the apple doesn't fall far from the tree, since your uncle's mind took much the same route."

Isla goes up on tiptoes and slips her arms around my neck, the camera around her neck poking my stomach. It doesn't stop me from wrapping her up even closer and dipping my head for a kiss. She tastes like the cool, fresh, fall air. Breaking the kiss, she pulls away from my hold, grabbing onto my hand.

"Not much farther," she says cheerfully, leading the way up the path.

When we break through the tree line into an open space, littered with young growth, the view hits me like a fist in my gut. Unbelievable that I never noticed the raw beauty of this place before. Months I'd spent at the reservoir, but I'd never really *seen* it. At this elevation the air is clear, much crisper than down in the valleys and on the surrounding mesas. The surface of the reservoir, stretching from one end of the view to the other, is a shiny blue-gray mirror, reflecting the light of the midday sun.

Unlike fall in the New England states, where the reds would be dominant, the colors here are limited to golds and yellows offset against the evergreens, but the effect is no less stunning.

Isla lets go of my hand and grabs her camera, while I walk out on the rock jutting over the view below. There have been places I've been in my lifetime that I thought might make a nice home one day, but they were forgotten the moment a new assignment came and I was on the move again. This place, it stayed with me the past month. How much of that has to do with location, and how much with Isla, I don't know. And it doesn't really matter.

This excitement at the prospect of building something here, with her, is a feeling even more powerful than the thrill and danger of a new operation. The ability to look ahead—a day, a month, even years—is something new. Gratifying.

The whiz of Isla's camera draws my attention away from the view. She's climbed up on a tree stump, balancing precariously, as she snaps away at our surroundings.

"Don't fall," I caution, making my way over to her.

"You know," she says, dropping the camera from her face and jumping down, completely ignoring my warning. "First thing we should do is put a proper road in." She points at the path we just walked up. "It'll make bringing up the heavy machinery a lot easier. I'm thinking if we can even just put in the road and level the plot before the frost hits, we'll be able to break ground the first sign of spring."

I'm normally a man of few words, but am always able to find one or two. Right now I'm dumbfounded. Two days ago, I was prepared to fight for just a chance, and today she is casually planning ahead for next spring, not a question in her openly excited face whether I'll be here or not. The blind trust a gift I'm not even sure myself I deserve.

"I..." I have to clear the frog from my throat before I try again. "I think that sounds like a plan."

"Awesome," she chirps, clapping her hands with the excitement of a little girl. "Let me take a few more shots from the rock, and maybe we can go into town and get some of the prints enlarged? It'll help planning the layout of the house, and I'd love to do a series showing all the steps in the process."

I patiently wait until she has all she wants, and listen to her chatter all the way back down the mountain, her small hand firmly tucked in mine. She's so excited she doesn't notice I'm not responding to a thing she says.

I'm too busy processing it all.

Isla

I think I may have scared him.

The entire way back to the campground, he was quiet,

his face a passive mask. Trust me to jump light-years ahead, instead of letting things follow their natural course. *Stupid.*

Once at the trailer, he kisses me almost chastely and heads toward the Deville.

"Hey!" I call after him. "It'll take me only ten minutes or so to download these. Aren't you coming with me?" He stops and turns, a slight tilt to his lips.

"Figured if we're going to Cortez, we might as well stop at that building supply store coming into town. I'm just gonna make a quick list," he says before disappearing inside.

So it takes me a little longer than ten minutes, but only because one of the shots caught my eye. An image of Ben on the rock, hands in his pockets, and a pensive look on his face. The picture is slightly overexposed, and I quickly edit it in a dramatically contrasted black and white effect, before adding it to my USB drive.

Ben is waiting outside in his truck, the engine already running.

"Hope you don't mind the truck," he says when I climb in. "Because there's no way in hell I'm driving that thing." He points at my little black Beetle and I bite back a grin. He'd have to fold his legs in his neck to get into the front seat.

"Don't insult my trusted little steed," I scold him. He snorts loudly as we pull out.

"Wouldn't trust that thing through the first real snowfall. We're gonna need some proper wheels, and some other things. I want to check in town to see if any of it needs to be ordered in."

Snowfall. *Yikes*, I hadn't even thought of that. We're

going to be up on this mountain through the winter. Or at least that's what it looks like.

"What other things?" I ask, a little worried about finances. I haven't done too badly with the sale of my prints, and the company account Uncle Al showed me has a healthy balance, but still. The numbers I'd crunched in my head, for the road and groundwork on the plot, did not include any additional expenses.

"We need a generator, for when the power goes off."

"There is one in the shed by the trailer. Occasionally losing power is not uncommon up here," I inform him.

"Good. We'll just have to make sure we have plenty of fuel to keep it and the vehicles going, and a separate shed to store it in. But we're also gonna need some snow fencing to protect the trailer from drifts coming up off the reservoir. I'd like to order a plow blade for this truck and we'll need some shovels."

"Wow. That sounds like a bit of an expense. I'll have to work out a budget," I offer carefully. Ben turns to me with a big smile, like he didn't just drop what has to be at least a couple of thousand dollars worth of *necessities.*

"Yeah, we can work that out later," he says easily. "But they are investments. Even when the house is built, we'll still need to get through our winters. Besides, I was thinking, maybe your uncle's friend has an old but serviceable blade, sitting in his field somewhere, we can get for a steal."

The entire drive to Cortez I try to wrap my head around what it means to live in a trailer through the winter. Luckily Dolores is only a short ten-minute drive, although that might be a little longer in the snow. The small town is good for basic necessities but Cortez, which is twenty minutes farther, is better for everything else.

As much as overwintering up here makes me nervous, I'm also excited about the photographic opportunities it'll offer. By the time we pull up to the print shop, I've already planned a whole new winter series, making mental notes of the kinds of shots I'd like to take.

"I'll just be a sec," I call over my shoulder as I hop out of the truck. Ben just lifts his fingers off the wheel in acknowledgement. Fortunately there's no one else in the store, so it doesn't take long to explain what I'd like. With a promise I can pick up my prints in a couple of days, I'm climbing back in the passenger seat. "Okay. What's next?"

I turn my head to find Ben looking at me slack-jawed.

"What?"

"Usually when a woman says she won't be long, I know I should settle in with the newspaper because it'll be a while." He shakes his head, turning the key in the ignition. "You're a new surprise every day, Pixie," he mumbles under his breath. I have to smile at that but one thing sticks in my mind.

"How usual is it to have a woman ask you to wait?" I try for aloof, but of course with a question like that, there's no hiding the hint of green. Ben keeps his eyes on the road but a shit-eating grin spreads over his face.

"I have a sister," he says, surprising the shit out of me.

"You have a sister? I thought…" I'm still thinking, wondering whether he's actually ever said he didn't have family. "I thought you told me your teammate that got killed was the only family you had?" I remember something he told me only days ago.

"My family wasn't a fan of my career choice. My sister was only four when I went off to college. My grandfather was a lawyer, my dad was a lawyer, and the expectation was I'd be a lawyer as well, joining the family practice after college. Instead, I chose criminal justice, following my dream of law enforcement. It didn't go over well." I want to say something sympathetic, but his broad hand lands on my knee, giving it a cautioning squeeze, so I press my lips together. Part of me instinctively understands it's not easy for him to share this. "When my parents died, I didn't find out until after their funeral. And only because my father's secretary thought letting me know was the right thing to do. My parents left me a dollar in their will." Ben chuckles harshly at my sharp intake of breath. "Apparently it was their way to ensure I'd never be able to contest the will. And my grandparents weren't much better. My sister Anastasia, Stacie, was fourteen at that time, and when I tried to contact her, I was told in no uncertain terms that no contact would be allowed. I lost myself in my work after that. Took on one assignment after another." He sighs deeply as he turns into the parking lot of the building supply store, pulls into an empty space, and turns to face me. "Nine years ago she contacted me. She'd just finished college—studying law—and found herself pregnant. When she refused to abort, my grandparents shut her out. I was able to help her find a place in Albuquerque, and a job with the Public Defender's Office."

"The baby?" I ask, grabbing his hand. I'm relieved to see a gentle smile on his face.

"Mak, a feisty little thing."

"So you stayed in touch."

"Yeah. As much as my work would allow. Stacie has a good life in the city. Great career, friends, good schools for Mak."

"And your grandparents?"

"Both gone now." He looks unseeingly out the windshield before turning his gaze back on me. "Come on. Enough about that," he cuts off any further discussion.

For now, I mentally add, still teeming with questions. There are many more layers to this man than I'd imagined.

-

My head is spinning by the time we drive back into Dolores.

I have a creative mind. Ideas come to me fast and furious, but I'm much less courageous when it comes to execution. It takes me a while to organize my ideas to a point where I'm ready to act on them. Ben, on the other hand, is much more practical—hands on. I'm amazed at the methodical way he is able to mark things off his mental checklist.

We have four large fuel containers, a prefab shed, insulating panels, two snow shovels, and a roll of snow fencing in the truck bed. He even noted down prices on plow blades. All that was before he drove us to a car dealership, where he put a deposit on a brand new Toyota Land Cruiser. He'd be able to pick it up in two weeks.

Just. Like. That.

I tried to argue that maybe he needed to think about it a little longer, but all he said was, "What's there to think about? My bike's no good in the winter, and who knows how long the truck will last. And I'm not even going to mention that toy you call a car. We need some way to get around."

It shut me up.

Mostly because he was right, but also because what he

said meant something. Buying that car, preparing for a long winter—even asking for reputable contractors, like he did at the building supply store—all of it meant a whole lot. As much as I made a statement when we were up on the mountain, talking about joined plans as if it was a foregone fact; Ben's actions were an even louder statement.

He wasn't just talking about it—he was making it happen.

CHAPTER 4

Ben

"Wow. I didn't think you'd get it up this fast."

I grin and lift my eyes to find Isla leaning over me.

This morning I woke up to her head under the sheets, leisurely licking her way up my thighs. Before my eyes even opened, she had me engulfed in the slick heat of her mouth, and I had to struggle not to come down her throat. All it took was a tug on her short hair, and she was sliding her body up mine until her core was poised over my cock. There was nothing more glorious than to see her sturdy hips sink down until I was buried deep inside her. It was slow, even lazy, the way she took what she wanted from me, and I'd been happy to lie there and let her have it all. She'd been playful and would bring me to the edge before easing the pace, only to do it again. Only so much playing a guy can take before he takes matters in his own hands, and finally I flipped us, so Isla was on her back and I was taking us all the way.

Later, as I was twisting this way and that, cleaning up in the tiny shower, I promised myself we'd have to invest in a large bathroom in the new house. Big enough for the two of us. When I stepped out, wrapping a towel around my hips, Isla was already perched on a stool at the counter, her laptop open in front of her. Engrossed in her edits, I got dressed, kissed her neck in passing, and went to build a shed.

"Watch it, Pixie," I growl into her smiling face. "You're enough to give a man a complex with those old man barbs you throw out."

"I was talking about the shed, you perv," she says, shaking her head but grinning as she did it. She moves back a step and takes in the small building. It hadn't taken much to level the floor and put the walls up. These prefab kits come mostly preassembled, so as long as you keep your angles plumb, they basically just snap together. The only things left are the insulation panels and the roof, and last comes hanging the door.

"How come you're so good at this?"

"Worked construction on weekends and during the summer breaks to pay for college," I admit on a shrug. "Found out I'm good with my hands."

"I'll say." Her cheeky smile matches the twinkle in her eyes when I glance over, before she turns serious. "I know you shouldn't speak ill of the dead, but your parents sucked." I throw my head back and laugh at her unexpected venom.

"Yes, they did. But I came out with an added skill set that sure comes in handy now, doesn't it?" The only response is a grumble. I get up from my knees and pull her into my arms. "Hey. It's done. Been done for a long time and I'm okay with it." When the frown is still on her face, I lean down to kiss it away. "We'll have to have Stacie come visit here sometime. I'd like you to meet her. She and Mak would love it here." I change the subject and that perks her right up.

"Do you think they could come before the snow hits?"

"I'll give her a call this week."

"Awesome." Her voice is breathy but her smile is big.

"I have to run into Dolores to drop off a few prints at Jen's and pick up something for dinner. Anything in particular you like or don't like?"

"Depends," I answer. "Are you gonna cook it?" I watch as she rolls her eyes. *Cute.*

"Was planning to," she finally concedes.

"Good, then I'll like anything. Word of warning; I can feed myself, but I'm a shit cook. All I'm good at is meat. Grilling it that is." Now she's grinning.

"Is that your way of telling me I'll be the cook in the family?" she teases.

"Seems fair," I shoot right back, hooking her around the waist. "I'll build shit and you cook."

"Whatever," she mumbles against my mouth as I give her a hard kiss, before letting her go.

"Drive safe," I call after her.

She keeps walking, giving me a thumbs-up over her shoulder.

-

A couple of hours later, I step back to admire my handiwork.

Looks pretty good.

The roof went on smooth, the hard foam insulation panels were easy to cut to size and install, but I had to use shims to hang the damn door. That part took longer than I expected.

Tossing my tools back in the toolbox, I hear a truck start up on one of the camp spots along the water's edge. Out of the fifty or so sites, there were only about eighteen taken, and that would likely become fewer over the weeks to come. I expect that numbers will pick up over the weekends, but with summer over and kids back to school, it's pretty quiet during the week. Most of the current campers are likely fishers or hunters, and there'd be more of those coming in. Hunting season opens early September. Mostly elk and deer, maybe black bear in these regions. It's a whole different breed of campers.

The truck pulling out now, with the large chest freezer strapped down in the bed, belongs to a couple of guys who'd been a bit rowdy last night. Celebrating maybe, since they obviously pulled up stakes and are heading home this morning.

I was never one much for hunting. I like game as well as the next guy, but I guess when hunting bad guys is what you do for a living, there's not much thrill in hunting down animals. I might go out at some point. See if Damian is interested in coming down for a weekend; maybe see if we can tag an elk. It would give us enough meat for both our freezers.

Thinking of freezers, I should check to see if the generator is in good working order. Isla mentioned there is a chest freezer in there as well. The door to the big shed is padlocked, so I head inside to see if I can find a key that fits. On a hook just inside the trailer door, I find a bunch, most of them with tags. It doesn't take long to locate the one for the shed.

The key turns smoothly in the padlock and I pull open the double doors. I'm pleased to find the generator is not as old as I thought it might be. Looks like a 10,000-watt unit, which is plenty big enough to sustain a house, let alone a trailer.

Lifting the lid on the freezer, I find it maybe a third full. Ice has frosted the inside of the walls and lid. It's an older one, but could probably handle one more winter. It just needs cleaning out. Next I turn to the generator, checking the fuel gauge. When I try to fire it up with the electric starter, it kicks on immediately. Not exactly without noise, but it isn't that bad. I let it run for a bit, while I scan the rest of the shed's contents.

Gardening tools, some lumber, and a shelving unit with bathroom and cleaning supplies. I presume those are for the public showers and toilets. Then I notice a tall narrow safe tucked on the far side of the shelves. A gun safe. Wonder if Al left his guns behind. Of course the safe is locked, this one not with a key, but a numeric pad. I should give him a call and find out the code.

"Three, seven, three, four, one, zero, eight, three, four."

I whirl around, my hand automatically reaching for the gun I'm not carrying.

Isla

"Ah, you brought me the rest!" Jen cries enthusiastically, when she spots me coming in the door to The Pony Express.

"I did. And I'm already working on more," I respond, lifting the large tote with the heavy frames onto the counter. "I shot some of the colors yesterday and am trying something new with the edits. I worked on it all morning. Want to see?" I pull out my phone where I've saved a few of this morning's edits to show her. Some of them shots I took yesterday, everything in gray tones, except for the golden yellow and deep green of the trees.

"Oh my God, these are stunning!" Jen flips through the images. "These will be perfect," she says, looking up from the small screen of my phone.

"Perfect for what?"

"You missed him by about twenty minutes. I was gonna call you, but I just got a late lunch rush in. This guy walks in, an older man, a bit too distinguished looking for these parts," she muses, a little smile on her face, before looking back at me. "Anyway, he ordered coffee and a sandwich and sat down there." Jen points at a small table against the wall on the other side of the coffee shop. "Had a perfect view of your prints from there and spent most of his time scrutinizing them and taking notes in his phone while he was eating. When he brought his dishes to the counter, he wanted to know who the artist was. I didn't want to just give out your name, so I hope you don't mind I asked him why he wanted to know." The excitement is clear on her face as she claps her hands together. "Have you hear of Colorado In View? That new gallery in Durango?" When I shake my head, she explains. "It's fabulous. I think it opened some time last year. I was there in the spring. Sculptures, paintings, tapestries, pottery, and photography. The one common theme of all; the art on display is Colorado through the eyes of the artist. He owns the place. The guy who was here. He wants to do an exhibition of your work." Her last words come out as one, as if she's barely able to contain herself.

"Seriously?" Is all I manage to get out, as my eyes drift to my prints on the wall. Jen nods eagerly.

"Yup. And he left a card. His name is Ryan DeGroot. Wants you to call him and set up an appointment."

"Can you do it? Organize it?" I immediately ask, my

glance shooting back to her. I'm suddenly scared. Selling pictures from a small local coffee shop is one thing, but taking a huge step closer to my dream like this, is a whole different kettle of fish. What if he sees me for the hobbyist I am? I mean, I was a professional newspaper photographer, but that doesn't qualify me as an artist. I do better staying behind the camera, where I'm comfortable.

"Me?" Jen asks. "You want me to set this up?"

"Yes," I nod. "I do. I want you to act as my agent. You're poised, you're professional, you know how to handle people, and you know my work well." I lean over the counter and cover her hand with mine. "I trust you more than I trust myself with this," I give her the truth.

Slowly her face brightens with a smile as she sandwiches my hand in both of hers.

"How fast can you get me an online gallery set up? Make sure you watermark everything you upload." Jen is suddenly all business, pulling a pad and paper toward her and jotting down notes. "This new series. Call it Colorado Gold, it sounds lush, just like the shots. The prints should go on board, no more than a quarter inch, no frame. Just a hint of wrap around. I'll find out if SouthWest can do the job. If not, I'll find someone. Do you have twelve prints? He wants to start with twelve prints to fit one long wall in the gallery."

She's writing furiously while I'm standing there, gasping for air like a fish on dry land, barely able to contain everything she's telling me.

"How fast, Isla?" The repeat of the question breaks through my apathy and my mind scrambles to catch up.

"Three days to finish up the edits and set up the online gallery. SouthWest does the board mounting. I was just there and ordered one done like that. When you call them, ask for Nate. Tell him it's for me." I'm already mentally flipping through all the images I could use, while pulling the prints I brought with me from the tote bag.

"I'll call Ryan tomorrow, if not this afternoon. Find out what his commission is and work out any details. I'll call you," she adds quickly, as I'm already moving to the door.

"Sounds good." I wave and let the door slam shut behind me.

I'm almost halfway up the mountain when I realize I didn't stop to pick up food. I'm eager to get home, but I remind myself I'm not alone. Not anymore. A little reluctantly, I turn around and head back to town.

-

I realize he didn't hear me come up over the din of the generator, when I see him whip around, his body immediately in a defensive position.

"Sorry," I mouth, quickly switching off the noise. "I didn't realize you couldn't hear me."

Ben bends down, his hands braced on his knees and head hanging low.

I just got back and dumped the bottle of wine, the steaks, and the rest of the groceries in the trailer, before going in search of Ben and finding him at the gun safe.

"Uncle Al left two hunting rifles and a hand gun in there. Just in case. He has me keep a shotgun in the trailer too, but I don't know how much good that'll do, I won't be able to shoot it. I promised him I'd practice, but I haven't yet. Not sure my stomach can take aiming at anything. Even a coke can," I ramble, feeling guilty for scaring him.

"Where's the shotgun?" he asks, his head still down.

"I stuck it in the back of the closet. The box of shells are in there, too," I admit, watching as he shakes his head.

"I'll teach you," he finally says.

"Okay. Sorry if I scared you."

"Good thing I have my gun in the glove compartment in the truck," he mutters, before straightening up. I walk straight into his arms, burying my face in the middle of his chest.

"My pictures are going up in a real gallery," I mumble.

"Say what?" he asks, loosening his grip and taking a step back.

"An art gallery in Durango wants to exhibit my work," I say a little louder, unable to keep the smug grin off my face.

"No shit?"

"No shit," I shoot back at him.

"Fuck, that's amazing." I love the way small lines appear at the corners of his eyes when he smiles big. His light eyes warm and his face is unusually open. He's normally quite grim looking, but when he looks at me I can see his whole face soften. He reaches out his hand and I entwine my fingers with his. "Tell me about it."

"Are you done here? Then come inside with me, I'll tell you while I get dinner going."

Instead of starting dinner, we end up cuddled on the couch, each with a beer in hand, while I give him all the details.

"I'd better get those potatoes in foil or they won't be done in time," I finally say, casting a longing glance at my laptop, before getting up.

"What's for dinner?" Ben asks, getting up right behind me.

"Baked potato, bagged salad, and steak, which I should probably marinate for a bit. I also brought home wine to celebrate."

Ben slips his arms around me from behind, while I scrape the potatoes clean under the tap.

"Leave dinner to me," he mumbles, with his lips brushing the shell of my ear.

"But you said…" I start protesting, when he tilts my head back and cuts me off with a hard kiss.

"I can handle baked potatoes and salad from a bag. I told you I can do meat." His wicked grin gets my skin tingling; for a second I'm considering forfeiting my laptop *and* dinner to have my way with Ben instead. "Go," he growls, plunging his face in my neck. "Before I take you up on those dirty thoughts spinning through your head."

I feel his teeth graze the tender skin at the base of my neck, before he reaches around and turns off the tap, pressing a towel in my hand. I turn around as I dry my hands and smile up at him.

"Thank you," I tell him softly, lifting up on tiptoes to kiss his scruffy jaw.

"Go," he says again, giving me a tap on my butt when I walk past him.

CHAPTER 5

Ben

"Should we go up there?"

Isla stares up the mountain, where as of this morning, work on the roadway to the clearing above has begun. Heavy equipment rolled in earlier, and Jim Bayfield, the local contractor, came knocking on the trailer door.

It has been a busy week. The first few days, I left Isla alone with her camera and her laptop, while I looked after the grounds and worked on the Deville. I had to pry her away from the computer at night and force her into bed. Since her selection of pictures was finalized and sent off, she had nowhere to go with her nervous energy, and when I suggested putting together a budget for the house, she dove straight into that.

I was pleased to see her uncle had amassed quite a decent contingency fund; one that could easily handle the groundwork for the house. It had been the start of an interesting conversation about money. Uncomfortable, as I would've expected, since the moment I laid out my financial condition and suggested she add my savings to the house budget, she was up in arms. What finally got her to give in was when I explained that it was simply an investment. I'd done well over the years. Had a financial advisor handle my savings, since I didn't have time to dick around with that, and the guy had made me some nice change. Of course I've had virtually no living expenses.

"I'm a couple of years away from fifty. It's about time

I spent some on me. And if it makes you feel more comfortable, we can have that lawyer in Cortez draw up some kind of agreement."

I know she's worried about what might happen if things go south between us. Turning this into a business agreement just takes that stress out of the equation.

Jim Bayfield was recommended by Nicholas Flynn, Al's lawyer, and I guess now Isla's as well. I wasn't too sure about that guy at first glance. Looked a little too soft and pretty, until he shook my hand. Rough calluses lined his grip and his eyes were unwavering. Smart guy, too.

Bayfield is a general contractor, who is clearly well connected; he has a crew and equipment ready to go within a week.

"Let them get some work done. We'll get some coffee up there when they break," I suggest, smiling as Isla almost has her nose pressed against the small window. "Want to help me rip up some carpet?" That gets her attention. She turns around wearing a big grin.

"Yesss—demolition," she says, channeling her inner Schwarzenegger, as she slips by me.

"Renovation!" I call after her, just as she disappears out the door.

-

By the time lunchtime comes around, both of us are grungy, but the old carpet is piled up outside the trailer. Isla had pulled the padded backing off the banquette seats as well, deeming them unfit for reupholstering. She's outside jotting down measurements for the replacements, while I scrape away at the old glue on the floor with a putty knife.

"I'm going to put on some coffee," she says, sticking

her head in the door. "I think they're taking a break." I lift my head to listen. It's quiet out there. All morning the sound of heavy engines could be heard, but now I can only hear the crunch of gravel under Isla's feet as she makes her way over to the other trailer.

Putting the putty knife down, I step out of the trailer and breathe in deep, trying to clear the dust from my nose. It's a clear day. The campground is quiet, only twelve sites rented out and all, but one older couple, hunters. During the summer you can hear the constant buzz of engines on the water, but now the reservoir is still. Only an occasional fishing boat puttering by.

I load up the old carpet in the wheelbarrow from the shed and roll it over to the garbage dumpster, tossing it in. By the time I get back to the site, Isla is already coming out of the trailer, a large tote in her hands and her camera around her neck.

"You coming?" she calls out when she sees me.

"Need a second to wash my hands," I mumble against her ear when I reach her, giving her hip a squeeze before slipping inside. A quick splash of water on my face to clear the worst of the dust, and I'm back outside.

"Give me that," I order, grabbing the tote from her and slinging it over my shoulder. I take her hand as we walk over to where the trucks are parked at the base of the path.

"Not much to see yet." Jim's clearly seen us coming. Five guys, plus Jim, are sitting at a picnic table they must've hauled up here from one of the empty sites. "Hope you don't mind," he says when he catches me looking.

"Of course not," Isla answers first. "Whatever you

guys need, just let us know. We brought some coffee." I put the bag on the table and Isla starts pulling out not just a large thermos and Styrofoam cups, but a container of brownies. Were the hell she got that from on such short notice, I have no idea.

Under approving grunts and words of thanks, the guys attack both coffee and sweets like a bunch of locusts.

"Did you at least save me a brownie?" I whisper in her ear, and she elbows me in the stomach in return.

"That's a dangerous precedent you're setting, young lady." Jim smiles at her. "Now these Neanderthals will expect to be fed every day."

"Haha, that would be a no," she says with a smile. "First day on the job gratitude only, I'm afraid." She sits down beside Jim, who moves over a little to give her room, and plants her elbows on the table. "So, who's scared to have their picture taken?"

In minutes, she has the gruff looking crew of guys eating from her hand, with her ready smiles and quick wit. I cross my arms and lean against the fender of a truck, watching her magic at work. When there's nothing but a stray crumb or two left in the container, and the last drop of coffee is gone, she coaxes the lot to pose in front of the massive bulldozer. I stay where I am, scrolling through my phone to kill time while she takes shot after shot, until Jim calls a stop to it, citing a need to get some more work done before day's end.

The air fills with the sound of engines, and I sit down at the table, putting my phone facedown as Isla and Jim approach.

"What are the chances of pouring a foundation and getting up framing before winter hits?" I ask when they sit down. Isla looks surprised, but I keep my eyes on Jim, who's scratching his chin.

"Middle of September now," he says pensively. "Doesn't leave a lot of time. It would have to be in by the end of October. Six weeks, give or take. Do you have plans drawn up?"

"Maybe," I answer tentatively, since it all depends on Isla. "We've been looking at some pre-fab homes. There's one we both like and we have the option of doing interior finishes ourselves."

"But the guy we talked to said it would be anywhere from four to six months to get the modules built," Isla pipes up.

"I know," I confirm, as I flip over my phone and swipe the screen before shoving it in her direction. "But things change."

I watch as understanding hits her and a big grin almost splits her face.

"We can have it as fast as it'll take the trucks to get it here," I tell a confused Jim. "Someone walked away from their contract, and the sales guy will let us have the components, as is, at seventy percent, provided he can have it out of their warehouse before winter. He attached the plans to the email."

"Oh my God," Isla gasps beside me. "I can't believe our luck."

"Before we celebrate, let Jim have a look at the plans."

"Can you print those off?" He points at my phone.

"Yes!" Isla jumps up, shoving everything on the table in the bag and slinging it over her shoulder. "I'll be right back," she says as she starts walking. "Are you coming?"

She throws me an impatient look over her shoulder that has Jim chuckle.

"Looks like you've got a live one there," he guffaws as I stand up.

"You have no idea," I tell him as I take off after her.

But I do it wearing a grin.

Isla

"She's coming?" I beam at Ben when he hangs up the phone and gets in the truck.

"We're going there," he says, smiling back. "She's up to her eyeballs in court cases, but has booked the Thanksgiving weekend off. She's excited to meet you, though," he quickly adds when my face falls.

We're on our way to pick up the Toyota and have an appointment at the bank to get our finances sorted. Feels like everything is suddenly moving forward at a breathtaking speed, when my life before coming to Dolores seemed to have been stuck in second gear. Thinking about Ben's sister visiting would have been a welcome distraction from the near overwhelming changes.

"That's not until November," I point out, pouting a little.

"We'll drive to Albuquerque and make a trip of it," he promises, squeezing my knee before turning out of the gates. "We'll be busy once Jim gives us the go ahead on those plans. Besides, I've got a trailer to finish first or they won't even have a place to sleep." Just like that my smile is back and my fingers are crossed.

"We," I correct him. "*We* have a trailer to finish."

"Of course." Ben tags me around the neck and pulls me close to plant a kiss on my head. Snuggling into his side, a thought occurs to me.

"We should go shopping in Albuquerque. We need furniture." The responding growl is a clear indicator Ben, like most men, does not like shopping. Not that I particularly enjoy shopping for clothes, or just for the hell of it, but shopping with a purpose? That I enjoy.

"Not going shopping."

"But, Ben, we're gonna have a whole house to furnish and decorate. I can't make all those decisions on my own."

"Pixie," he says with barely subdued impatience. "I don't shop. I also don't care much beyond having walls to keep us dry and warm, a bed to sleep in, and a fucking shower, big enough to fit us both. Other than that, the only requirement I have is you." Any irritation I feel fades at his sentiments. "If you don't like shopping alone, take Stacie; she's got a masters in bargain hunting."

-

The bank manager is doing his best to sell us on a mortgage when we explain what we're there for, but Ben is adamant he doesn't want to lock in to anything that we can't control ourselves. All we want is some emergency financing, something we can access on the spot if we were to run into trouble. In the end, they compromise on a small line of credit that we can access, or pay off, at any time.

Ben is still grumpy when we leave the bank.

"Patronizing son of a bitch," he mumbles under his breath. I stop him with a hand on his arm.

"He's an idiot," I concur. "Which by now I'm sure he

realizes, since we walked out of there with exactly what we came for, and *not* what he wanted to sell us. So chill." I wind my arms around his neck when he glares at me. "That may intimidate him in there—" I nudge my head in the direction of the bank, "—but your scowl doesn't scare me at all." I watch as the corner of his mouth twitches and his eyes soften.

"No?"

"Not even a bit," I tease. Ben's arms come around me, lifting me clear off the ground as he takes my mouth in a toe-curling kiss. When he sets me down again, I'm grateful for his hands on my hips to steady me. My legs are far from steady.

"We've got a car to pick up," he says, leading me to where the truck is parked.

When we pull into the dealership, I tell Ben to go ahead, that I'll be right in. I wait until I see him walk into the office before pulling out my phone.

"Is this Phil?" I ask when a man answers.

"Who wants to know?"

"It's Isla Ferris, Al's niece. He gave me your number." I explain why I'm calling, and after a brief conversation, I end the call and hop out of the cab of the truck to follow Ben inside.

"Wanna drive the truck or the Toyota?" Ben asks half an hour later, when we're back outside.

"Is that a trick question? Like I'd dare get between a man and his new wheels," I joke, holding my hand out for the keys. "Better follow me," I call over my shoulder as I walk toward the truck and open the door. "We've gotta make one stop on the way home."

Before he has a chance to ask questions, I'm in the

truck, start the engine, and drive off, leaving him glaring after me.

Dolores isn't big and Merritt Way is easy to find. And Phil McCracken's place is impossible to miss. The fields around his doublewide trailer are littered with car carcasses. I pull into the driveway and watch in the rearview mirror to see Ben pull his shiny, new car in right behind me. I'm already out of the truck by the time he ambles up.

"Al's buddy?" he asks, just as the trailer home's storm door squeaks open, and a small, stooped, old man, dressed in overalls and a ball cap, steps out.

"Phil McCracken, in the flesh," I confirm, walking ahead to where the old man is waiting. "I'm Isla, Al's niece," I call out when I spot the shotgun casually held alongside a leg. "And this is Ben." I point over my shoulder, where I'm sure he is somewhere right behind me.

"Come round back," Phil says without a greeting, as he makes his way around his house. I start following when I feel Ben's hand slip in mine.

"If someone starts playing the banjo, we're hauling ass," he leans down to whisper in my ear, and I fight to keep the snicker bubbling up in check.

The urge to laugh disappears the moment we get a good look at what's hidden behind the house. Shielded from the road by a strip of trees and underbrush on one side and a barn on the other, are two neat rows of tarp covered cars. About eight of them. In places where the tarp has shifted, gleaming chrome and bright paint can be seen. Classics. From what I can see, either restored or very well maintained.

"This way," Phil calls out when he looks back to find us stopped in our tracks. I can feel Ben's heat right behind me.

Phil points to the other side, where right along the barn sits what Uncle Al used to call a silver Twinkie. A large Airstream, propped up on blocks.

"Son of a bitch," Ben mumbles, as he suddenly takes the lead and is already running his fingers over the silver panels by the time I catch up.

"1952 Cruiser," Phil says, no small amount of pride in his voice. "Varmint got in, tore up the inside. Spent five years working on it, almost had the inside done when the wife got sick. Time I got back to it, after Maisy passed, damn critters had damn near ate through the floorboards. Ain't had the heart to give her another go. She's waistin' away. Damn shame."

"Sorry about Maisy," I say, stepping closer and covering his gnarled, wrinkled hand with mine.

"Been a while," he says, almost dismissively, but his weathered voice cracks. "Damn near eight years. Long damn time for a man to cook his own damn meals."

-

Two hours later, we drive off in the new Toyota, leaving the old truck to be fitted with an equally old blade Phil had in the barn and offered for a measly hundred bucks. The brittle man is still standing in front of his house, watching us drive off in our *'cheap, foreign, dinky-toy,'* according to him. He promised to have the truck done before first snowfall, which is vague enough to be a little worrisome.

"My boys'll come 'n give me a hand," he said, when Ben carefully asked whether he'd need a hand with the heavy plow.

The Airstream had been a little trickier to negotiate, but Ben is not a stupid man. As soon as he clued in that as much as Phil didn't want to let it go, he also wanted to see his project finished. In the end, it was as simple as an offer to come check out progress at any time—lend a hand even, if he wanted—and the promise of a hot, home-cooked meal at the end of each visit.

"Long fucking day," Ben says, picking my hand off my knee and slipping his fingers between mine. "But a very productive one. Thanks for this, Pixie." I watch his profile as he drives with a barely there smile on his face. Happy, though—he looks happy.

"Don't thank me," I tell him. "I just found my next project."

"Phil?" He throws me a quick glance before focusing on the road again.

"An American Garden of Classics. That's gonna be the name. Images of Phil's cars through the seasons."

"Bet that would tickle him," he says on a yawn, which of course triggers one of my own.

"Let's pick up something easy in town," I suggest. "I don't feel like cooking."

Ben lifts my hand to his mouth and kisses the palm.

"Good idea," he says with a cocky grin. "That leaves more time for dessert."

CHAPTER 6

Ben

It's amazing what can be accomplished in short order, when your timing is lucky and your people are right.

It's been only a week since Jim gave us the go ahead on the house. His crew is willing to work extra hours and weekends to get the foundation in, especially if brownies are part of the deal. That had made Isla blush, which was kind of cute, since she doesn't seem to embarrass easily.

The road will be asphalted today and excavation should start up top. If not for the preparatory work Al did to have the site cleared, there may not have been enough time. It is touch and go as it is, but Jim seems hopeful.

The noise of the heavy machinery started when the sun was barely up. Good thing the eight remaining campsites house just hunters. All of them were out this morning, well before the sun rose.

"I'm sorry." Isla's voice is sleepy, her face pressed against my neck.

"For what?" I ask, lazily running my fingers through her short tresses.

"Making you come into Durango today."

"Not a hardship, Pixie," I respond on a chuckle. "You do your thing at that gallery, and I'll keep myself busy. There's a few places I want to hit up for trailer parts, and I can always drop in on Damian."

"You sure?" she asks, lifting her head to look me in

the eye.

"Babe." I lift her face between my hands and kiss her to convey my message, before I pull the covers off us. "You grab a shower first, I'll get coffee going."

Reluctantly she swings her legs over the side, gets up, and pads in the direction of the bathroom. Her short hair is standing up in random directions, her cheek is creased with sleep lines, and the old shirt of mine she's wearing is twisted around her waist, leaving one juicy butt cheek hanging out.

"I can feel you ogling me," she complains, as she whips the shirt over her head and ducks into the bathroom.

"Appreciating, you mean," I call after her, sitting up and tagging my jeans off the floor.

"Save it for when I don't look like I just got zapped by ten thousand volts," she yells back, and screeches the next moment when I duck my head through the door.

"You're beautiful," I assure her, before shutting the door and setting my mind to some coffee. A naked Isla is way too distracting and the fucking bathroom is way too small.

A bit of a purist when it comes to my coffee, normally preferring the old-fashioned brewing techniques, I'm getting quite attached to Isla's Keurig. It's all in the timing. I have my coffee ready by the time I've finished rubbing the morning crap from my eyes. Scratching my stomach, and mug in hand, I stick my head out the door.

The morning air is chilly and I quickly grab a sweater off the back of the door and tug it on. I take a seat on the picnic table, my feet on the bench, and look at the water. A light mist is coming off the reservoir, its temperature's warmer still than the air. That will change over the next few weeks, I'm sure.

I look to my left, where the Deville is almost completely gutted. We've taken out what could be removed, and what is left are raw floorboards and the wood paneling that needs to be sanded and refinished next. Right behind it is the Airstream that Phil's son hauled up the mountain the day before yesterday. That'll be project number two. For now, it's a good place to store the stuff we've pulled from the smaller trailer.

I'm still getting used to the fact I don't constantly have to look over my shoulder. The job is so ingrained, that I find myself making mental notes of whatever I see around me. For instance, I can recite the license plate of every vehicle on this mountain. I can describe every camper and every man on Jim's crew. Observing and being watchful has become second nature, and it's not something you can just turn off.

But when my hands are busy, my mind stills. Restoring something to its former glory is a process that is addictive and easy to get lost in. First you strip everything down to the bare, ugly bones, before building it back up, layer by improved layer.

I turn when I hear the trailer door open behind me, and there's Isla, who is her own brand of distraction and addiction, all rolled in one.

"Your turn," she says, sitting down on the bench between my feet, wrapping her arm around my leg.

We sit like this for a few minutes, in companionable silence, sipping our coffee, and staring out on the water, before I get up and head inside for my shower.

-

"What's wrong?"

It's not the first time I've heard Isla hiss between her teeth since we passed Mancos.

"It's nothing," she says quickly. "Probably just something I ate." I'm not buying it. She had a damn piece of toast for breakfast, didn't want anything else. I glance at her and catch her watching me. Her face is pale and her eyes look pained.

"Try again," I say, before focusing back on the road.

"Fine," she spits out, and I can almost *hear* the eye roll. "I'm probably getting my period. It can get bad."

Of course. I'm not oblivious to what happens, but frankly I don't usually give it much thought. Never have that is, until now. With Isla it's different. There were a few times I've been a bit lax with the protection, but she's assured me she's taken care of. Not even sure what the hell I'm thinking. My mind has no business going there, but the thought of planting something inside her wouldn't be a horrible thing.

"This is the first time you've had one," I point out.

"I'm irregular, always have been. Even on the pill."

"Do you want me to turn back home?" I ask as we drive into Durango.

"Hell, no. Best to muscle through it, I'll be fine. If you could just stop at Walgreens, so I can pick up some stuff."

Curious, I trail into the drugstore behind her.

"What are you doing?" she hisses, when I follow her down the aisle with feminine products. I have to admit, not a place I've ever found myself before.

"Learning," I explain, stopping her with a hand on her shoulder. "I wasn't around when my sister hit her teenage years, and I sure as hell wouldn't have learned anything from my mother. My job didn't really allow for any kind of relationship outside of my assignment, so consider me uneducated on the subject." I chuckle at the look of disbelief on her face.

"Why?" she asks, obviously puzzled.

"So next time, you can keep your ass in bed, where you belong, and I'll get you what you need." I shrug when her mouth drops open.

"I'm not sure if I should hug you or kick your shin right now," she huffs, but she does it smiling, which I'm hoping means my shins are safe. I hook her around the neck and give her noogies. "Watch your shins," she growls in warning.

I'm taking note of everything she dumps in the basket, including the bag of mini Reese's Pieces. Mainly because she holds it up before dropping it in, saying; "Chocolate is an imperative part of the cure." I take that to mean, don't ever come home without it.

When I drop her off in front of the gallery, she looks a little better, but I make her promise to call me if she wants to go home. I wait until she disappears through the door before I drive off to find the parts place.

It's not easy leaving her, when I know she's nervous as hell about meeting this Ryan DeGroot guy and having her stuff on display, not to mention when she's already feeling ill. Not easy, but it's important. This is something she has to own completely.

The back of the Land Cruiser is packed, with replacement wood paneling for the few pieces that were damaged, a new sink and counter, and a variety of hoses, clips, odds and ends. I'm about to head over to the small FBI field office on Rock Point Drive, to see Damian, when my phone rings.

"Hey, Pixie," I answer when I see her on the call display. "You done already?"

"Can you please come?"

I don't like the sound of her voice—at all.

With a screech of tires, I whip the SUV around in a U-turn and head back to the gallery.

―――――― ⌘ ――――――

Isla

Part of me wants to call after Ben—get him to come in with me—but instead I try to ignore the sharp cramps low in my stomach, straighten my shoulders, and march into the place like I belong there.

"You're Isla," the well-groomed, handsome gentleman behind the counter says, offering his hand.

"I am." I put my hand in his and notice immediately how smooth his palm feels against mine. So different from Ben's callused ones. His shake is firm enough and his appeal is obvious, I can see what had Jen a little flustered when she spoke of him.

"Let me show you the space," he says with warm smile. "The mounts all arrived yesterday, and I have to say, your guy does great work." My guy, meaning Nate at SouthWest.

"I'll be sure to tell him, I'm sure he'll get a kick out of it."

I follow him around a narrow floating wall, which breaks the long space into sections without cutting it up. You can pass easily on either side to reach the back gallery. Where the front section is an assortment of eclectic art from ultra modern to classic, this back section is like one, big, blank canvass. Gray washed floors, eggshell walls, and minimalistic halogen lighting designed to draw attention to the space, not the fixture. A perfect backdrop to my images. The only color in the space will be the golden yellow I've left in the photographs.

Time gets away from me as I help Ryan first set out the prints, in the order I see them, before hanging them. There is an easy atmosphere in the gallery, only interrupted a few times when he has to go tend to a customer. I stay in my anonymous bubble behind the floating wall.

He seemed understanding that I prefer to keep a low profile. It's mostly for self-protection. What if people hate my pictures? I know they've sold at The Pony Express, but most of those folks are locals and just buying a pretty picture. Here they're supposed to represent art, and I still can't get over myself as just someone who likes to take pretty pictures. Never could quite figure out what art was supposed to look like.

The prints are beautiful, if I say so myself. The stark black and white images, with only the changing leaves of fall standing out in color, look perfect in this space. My name, I. Ferris, is printed in my digitalized signature on the bottom right-hand corner of each image. Ryan has adjusted the focus of the light fixtures, so that the light appears to bounce off the gold in the prints.

I'm pleased. I'm more than pleased, and part of me wants to be a fly on the wall tonight, when the exhibition officially launches. Jen is going to be here in my place, though. It's better: I'm not big on crowds or mingling with strangers. Besides, now that the rush of getting the gallery ready is gone, my stomach is really making itself known.

"Are you okay?" Ryan asks, putting a hand on my back when a particularly nasty cramp has me doubled over. "Would you like to sit down?" I shake my head and reach for my purse.

"I'm fine. It'll pass," I lie, grinding my teeth as I throw a fake smile. "I'm just going to call my ride and be off."

Gentleman that he is, Ryan turns away and busies himself at the counter, giving me the privacy to make a call.

"Can you please come?" I have to fight not to sob, when another wave of cramps steals my breath.

"On my way, babe. Five minutes tops."

The familiar rasp of Ben's voice instantly soothes, but a moment later I'm doubled over again. I barely notice being guided to the small love seat on the other side of the counter, or the hand that slips the phone from mine.

"Hello? Yes, this is Ryan. I own the gallery? She's not looking too good—Okay, I'll bring her out." The next thing I know, I'm on my feet again, being shuffled out the door, where a pair of strong, familiar arms scoop me up and put me in a vehicle. I vaguely register Ben's voice as he tries to put a seat belt on me, and all I can do is slap at his hands.

"Fine," I hear him mutter. "We'll do without."

A door slams shut, and then we're moving. It feels like something is tearing at my insides, trying to claw its way out, and every bump and rut in the road aggravates it. I just concentrate on breathing.

I'm not sure how much time has passed when the door opens beside me; arms lift me and carry me into an unfamiliar building.

"Hospital," Ben says reassuringly in my ear, when I try to ask him. Not much more than a pathetic whimper comes out. "Acute abdominal cramping," I hear him say. If I weren't in so much agony, I might have giggled at his officious tone.

-

"Is this the first time you've had this happen?"

The fresh-faced doctor moves the cold wand of the ultrasound over my stomach.

Not sure what they gave me, but I feel a lot better than when Ben first carried me in. He's sitting like a growling bear beside me, refusing to be removed from my side. Not that I want him to go.

"I've never been what you call regular and sometimes get sharp cramps a few days before I get my period, but nothing like this, no."

He puts the wand away, and carefully wipes at my stomach with a towel to clear off the gel, before he sits on the edge of the bed. I squeeze Ben's hand when I see him glare at the doctor, who seems oblivious and starts explaining.

"I suspect you have something called Polycystic Ovary Syndrome, or PCOS for short. We'll do a few more tests to confirm, but it's clear from the ultrasound that there are a number of cysts on your ovaries. What you've experienced is a ruptured cyst. It can be very painful, but most of the time is not something worrisome. It tends to resolve itself, within a few days, as your body reabsorbs the tissues. What I'd like to do is send you home with some painkillers to get you through the next few days and make an appointment to see you soon, so we can get going on a treatment plan."

"Is there someone a bit closer to home?" Ben pipes up, and the doctor looks his way with an eyebrow raised. "No offense to you, Doc, but with winter coming, I'd feel a lot better if my girl had someone looking after her in Cortez. Someone who is not a two hour drive away, on the best of days."

"Fair enough," he says, smiling first at Ben and then at me. "Cortez? I can refer you to someone there."

"What about kids?" I blurt out, shocking myself. I've heard of PCOS, heard of people having a hard time getting pregnant. Not that I was necessarily looking to have kids, but it would be good to know if I could. If I wanted one. Maybe.

I already suspect the answer when I see the doctor glance uncomfortably from Ben to me. "That's something we perhaps should address when we've confirmed with testing?"

Ben's hand pulls mine closer, and he rests them against his chest, looking at me before he says to the younger man, "Just answer the question, Doc."

"When it's diagnosed early and treated, the chances are better. Age comes into play, level of damage done to the ovaries. I think it's fair to say the odds are slim."

I close my eyes. The answer doesn't really surprise me, but the reality of what he's saying is poignant, especially since I'm holding hands with the first man to ever put the thought of kids in my mind. I force the burning tears back, but I guess one slips underneath my eyelid. I don't notice it until the rasp of Ben's thumb wipes it away.

"Not something we've had a chance to even consider,

and already the option is gone," I whisper into the palm he presses to my face.

"Shhh," he hushes and I open my eyes. The doctor must have snuck out because it's just Ben and me. "I never thought about kids before. Never had reason to. I do now. But I also know jumping the gun does no one any good, so let's make sure all the information is in before you declare your option gone." I warm at the smile in his eyes, and watch as they start to twinkle. "There's more ways to skin a cat." I haul back and punch his shoulder.

"We're talking cute little babies and you bring up skinning cats? What's wrong with you?" I scold him, not quite able to keep the grin off my face at his attempt to lighten the mood, which was clearly successful.

He leans over the bed, wipes the hair off my forehead before pressing a kiss there, on the tip of my nose, and finally to my lips.

"I just needed to see that smile, Pixie."

CHAPTER 7

Ben

"Mornin'!"

Jim is standing at the edge of the large hole, waving me over. I just followed the big concrete trucks up the new road when I saw them come by.

"Everything ready?" I ask, when I join him on the edge of where the foundation is going to be poured.

"Pretty much," he says, "boys are just bracing the wall on the south side. The framing shifted a little overnight." I follow the direction of his finger, where a couple of guys are working on the wooden boards that hold back the dirt on the edge of the hole. "Soon as they're done, we'll start pouring."

"Gonna run and grab Isla then. Be right back."

She told me this morning she was feeling a lot better, and this might lift her spirits. The physical pain she was in, she seemed to able to manage, but I'm not so sure about the rest. The past days she's mostly stayed in the trailer, only occasionally coming outside to sit at the picnic table and stare out at the water. She's not talking much, and I don't know how to make her—or if I even should. All I know is that I miss her almost constant smile.

I find her in the trailer, watching YouTube videos of cute animals. Again.

"Enough." Her head shoots up at my stern voice. "You're coming with me. Get some shoes on."

"I'd rather..." she starts, her eyes drifting back to the screen.

"You'd rather watch video clips that make you miserable? That's not you. We're going to talk about this giant fucking elephant sharing the trailer with us, but first you're coming with me." I reach past her and close her laptop. Then I grab her hands and pull her out of the chair; ignoring the dirty look she throws me. Cupping her face, I tilt her head back a little and lean my forehead against hers. "Our future is being built out there. You're missing it."

Her eyes are swimming as she stares up at me, but finally she gives a sharp nod before turning to grab her shoes.

"You'll need something other than flip-flops or those Converse for the winter. Some good boots," I point out.

"I've got a pair of UGGs somewhere."

"Those are not boots, those are confused slippers."

"They're warm," she counters, biting back a little smile.

"Not for long if you wear them outside."

The tension disappears with the lighthearted bickering, and Isla is smiling by the time I have her loaded in the golf cart. I hand her the camera that is normally fused to her body, but has been gathering dust for days now. There's a flash of guilt in her eyes, but she takes it from me and fits the strap over her head. I get in beside her, even though it still goes against my religion to drive the senior wheels, but I don't want her having to walk up. I swear we have to rock back and forth to get it the last fifty feet up the mountain.

"Not gonna get ya very far when the snow hits." Jim

chuckles heartily as I climb out of the damn thing. "Would've thought an ATV would've been more your speed," he adds for good measure, before he walks off with Isla.

Tomorrow. Tomorrow I'm going into town and buying an ATV. *Fuck*. Don't know why I didn't think of that before. I hurry to catch up with them, and throw my arm around Isla, as we watch our foundation being poured.

The modules of the house are scheduled to arrive in a little over a week, and Jim and his crew will be back to install them. We had the option of adding on a garage, which we did. It'll come in handy over the winter. Set back into the tree line, Jim has also framed in a large shed to move the generator into and for storage.

At this rate, we could be in by Christmas. That is, if I can get the interior work done by then.

"Are you guys going to be a while?" Isla asks Jim, fitting the cap on the lens of the camera. She's been snapping pictures the entire time.

"Most of the day, probably, why?"

"Don't let anyone leave before stopping by the trailer," she says, before grabbing my hand and pulling me toward the golf cart.

"Where are we going?"

"Town. I need groceries."

I throw occasional glances in Isla's direction as we make our way down to the trailer. She seems focused and more alert than she has been the past few days.

"Are you gonna fill me in on the plan that is clearly taking shape in your head?"

"Chili and cornbread, I think. And we'll need beer.

Lots of beer."

"You're gonna feed everyone," I conclude, remembering how she'd made friends, when she first got here, by driving this damn golf cart all over the campground, delivering breakfast.

"Of course," she says, turning a shocked glare my way. "The guys worked their asses off to get that foundation in on time. We should celebrate."

"Of course," I echo through a smile. I'm glad to see her hands folded protectively around her camera and some fire back in those eyes. Today we celebrate; tonight we talk.

-

It's pretty chilly when I walk the garbage bag to the locked container. I keep my eye out for that momma bear and cub that have been spotted. Isla had an encounter in the summer, and I want to bet it's the same bear who has been seen by some of the hunters, hanging around the dumpster in the early mornings.

No bears tonight though, just a quiet night with a bright moon shining off the water.

The crew left a while ago. Isla had charmed every last one of them. She'd been waiting with a huge pot of chili, two pans of cornbread, and cold beer, by the time they shut down for the day. Something that clearly was appreciated by all the guys, since they hung around until it was dark outside and there was nothing left in the pot.

I'm just glad to have the Isla back who can work a smile from the most cantankerous guy with her sharp little tongue, quick wit, and playfulness.

She's outside when I walk back up to the trailer. Tossing paper plates and napkins into the fire pit along with a few logs. A couple of beers sit on the picnic table.

"Nice night for a bonfire." She turns at the sound of my voice and smiles.

"I thought so," she says. "It's still pretty cold though, would you mind grabbing the quilt off the couch?"

When I come back out, flames are already shooting up from the pit, and she's pulling two folding chairs side by side, facing the fire and the reservoir beyond. Settling in for a cozy night.

Too bad I'm going to ruin it by talking.

Isla

"We need to talk."

I look over at Ben, who sits down beside me, looking like he just ran over someone's puppy.

"I know," I confirm with an encouraging smile.

Hiding is not exactly my style. I'd rather face what's heading my way, and I knew this was coming. Ben's tiptoed around me this past week. I can't blame him, I've not exactly been Shirley fucking Temple, but part of me knew he'd be done with it at some point. I honestly don't know where he's at with this PCOS thing, but I guess I'm about to find out.

He covers us both with the blanket and tucks me under his arm. I wish we had a couch out here, so I could curl up against him, but this'll have to do.

"That was nice," he starts. "What you did for the guys. Smart too, making sure they won't likely forget us while we wait for the house to get here."

Not the opening I was expecting, but it's a nice way to head, and I let his words warm me nonetheless.

"Thank you for dragging me up there. I would've hated missing that."

"I know," he rumbles, and we fall quiet again, just staring into the flames.

"I guess I needed a little kick in the butt," I offer, carefully opening up the floor.

"You were sick. You needed some time, I get that, but it's not like you to hole up inside while life passes by. So I nudged." I feel him shrug beside me.

"With a sledgehammer," I add and he chuckles.

"A calculated risk," he says. "Big stuff is happening. Unless we both have our heads and our hearts in it, we might lose track of what's important."

"What *is* important to you?" I ask honestly, turning my head to look at him.

"You are. My sister and Mak are. What we're building here is," he answers, his face relaxed with a little smile tugging the corner of his mouth. "I'm kinda finding it out as I go. I had few expectations six months ago, but my dreams grow as possibilities present themselves."

"What about kids?" I have to force the words from my throat. Ben reaches over and runs the back of his fingers along my cheek. An almost innocent gesture, but it shows me he feels the weight of my question.

"Kids were never really on the radar for me. Not with my job. Not with that life." He takes in a deep breath and blows it out between pursed lips before he continues. "Kids with you? With this life? The one we're building? Fuck yes—I'd be lying if I said the thought hasn't crossed my mind once or twice. If that opportunity had come along, I'd have built dreams around that, too."

"I did dream," I confess quietly. "In the back of my mind, I guess I always hoped one day… But it was never an urge so strong it was choking me, until this week, now the choice is taken away. That is the hardest part for me."

Ben is quiet beside me, stroking his thumb in the palm of my hand. Not saying a word, just being there—hearing me. We sit and watch as the flames slowly die down.

"We should go inside," I suggest. I flip back the quilt and am halfway out of my chair when Ben pulls me down—onto his lap. "We're gonna break the chair," I protest, but he ignores me.

"I have something to say." His voice is gruff and I twist around so I can see him. "I didn't fall for a dream. Not for the promise of a house on a mountain, or a meal every day. I didn't fall for fancy galleries or classic trailers." His mouth pulls in a lopsided grin. "What I fell for is a tomboy, in the ugliest pair of cutoff jeans I've ever seen, covered in mosquito netting, sharing an egg sandwich with me on a dock…"

"You stole that sandwich," I interrupt, ignoring the tears tracking down my cheek. Ben grins bigger and continues as if I never said a word.

"Who taught me how to see the beauty in a simple night sky."

"You fell?" I slip my arms around his neck and bring my face close enough so our noses touch.

He gently rubs his along mine, before he whispers, "I think it's safe to say I've fallen."

-

The sound of a gunshot has me sitting up straight in

bed.

"Son of a bitch," Ben grumbles beside me, swinging his legs over the side and tugging his jeans on.

"Where are you going?"

"Middle of the night and some asshole is shooting a gun, babe. Gonna check it out."

"I'm coming with you," I announce, jumping out of bed myself.

"Pixie," Ben says in his *I'm-trying-hard-to-be-patient* voice.

"Ben," I return a lot firmer. "I'm not letting you go out there alone."

"I'm law enforcement. This is what I do," he argues, pulling his shirt down and grabbing his gun from the shelf above the bed.

"Not any more, you're not," I counter, making a grab for the shotgun still stored in the small closet. If I didn't know any better, I'd swear he was biting down a grin when I turn around with the gun in my hands.

"May wanna take your finger off the trigger until you've got something in your sights. You trip like that and you're bound to shoot your foot off."

"Fine," I grumble, none too graciously. I'm ignoring the fact I have no clue what to do with the gun in my hands, or that I have no clue how to shoot the thing if it came to that. For now, holding it makes me feel better as I follow Ben outside.

"Do me a favor," Ben says, stopping me right outside the trailer door and shoving a large flashlight in my hands. "Stay here? Aim this at the dumpster?"

Before I have a chance to protest, he disappears into the dark. I fumble one-handedly, and almost drop the light when another shot rings out and loud yelling ensues. Finally locating the switch with my thumb, I aim the bright swatch of light in the general direction of the noise. I don't see anything at first, but then the beam catches on some movement right by the garbage bin. Two men, one of them Ben, clearly arguing about something.

My hand is shaking as I try to lift the flashlight higher, and I lose my grip. The beam hits the dark in an erratic pattern as the light crashes to the ground, before it goes dark completely. The sudden dark is blinding and I dive down, my hand frantically searching around. The sound of gravel crunching has me look up, but I can't see beyond the subdued circle of light filtering from the trailer window. I abandon my search for the light and straighten up, lifting the shotgun I've been clinging to in my other hand, and aiming it in the direction of the sound. My heart is almost beating out of my chest when a voice comes from the dark.

"It's just me, Pixie."

Ben steps from the shadows and I immediately drop down the barrel.

"*Jesus!*" I exclaim, bending over to catch the breath that is lodged in my throat.

"One of the guys on thirty-four thought it was a good idea to try and shoot at the bear he found by the dumpster. Second time he shot was at me. Stupid fuck," Ben grumbles, as he bends down to pick up the flashlight that had rolled under the steps.

"I almost shot at you, too," I confess, mortified.

"Nah, not a chance," he says, grinning ear to ear. "Be hard to do with an unloaded weapon."

"What?" I look at the shotgun before my eyes find

Ben again. "What if it wasn't you? What if someone had—"

My protests are cut off when he tags me behind the neck and kisses me quiet. Very damn effective.

"I…" I start back in when he allows me to draw a breath but he talks over me.

"Wouldn't have happened. I wouldn't have let it happen," he says, as he walks past me into the trailer.

I follow behind but instead of moving right, into the living space, I take an immediate left. I dump the shotgun on the floor beside the bed, strip my clothes, and crawl under the covers in a snit, my back turned to the door.

It's not long after Ben crawls in—ignores my rigid back, curves his long body behind me, with one large hand splayed comfortingly on my stomach—that I finally fall asleep.

CHAPTER 8

Isla

"Finally!" Jen calls out when she sees me coming in. "I was this close to venturing up on that mountain of yours, even though I'm desperately unsuited to outdoor life."

I snicker at her dramatics as I grab a stool on the side of the counter.

"Hit me up with a no-fat-skimmed, full calorie, double shots of caramel, macchiato. Easy on the coffee and heavy on the whipped cream." I grin at her raised eyebrows.

"We celebrating?" she wants to know. "Cause if we are, I'm in."

Before waiting for an answer, she turns to her prized espresso maker. The gleaming copper monstrosity looks more like it belongs in an old steam locomotive, instead of a coffee shop, but it produces sheer bliss in a cup.

I glance up at the wall to where my prints are displayed and see two are missing.

"You sold some already?"

Jen glances over her shoulder up to see where I'm looking. "Oh, yeah, one of the things I wanted to tell you about. A couple of women came in earlier this week. One is the owner of an old diner, just south of Cortez, who is looking to upgrade. Someone had sent them here to see what I was doing with local artists. Had a nice chat with them and they ended up taking two of your prints. She may call to see if you're interested in displaying in her place. Arlene's Diner, I think it's called."

"Kinda cool that we're being talked about," I tell Jen, when she sets down a huge mug with whipping cream sliding down the sides.

"You're being talked about," she states pointedly. "In fact, that's why I've been trying to reach you all week. Already this exhibition is creating all kinds of attention."

"I'm sorry. I haven't been well," I apologize, but Jen waves it off.

"I know. Ben told me."

"You talked to Ben?" I'm surprised; he never mentioned anything.

"I called him when I couldn't get through to you. He explained what happened; said you might need a friend at some point, but that you needed a little time. Don't be mad at him," she adds quickly when she sees my lips press together. "I made him tell."

I snort at that, and just like that, the tears that threatened dry up. No one could make Ben do anything he didn't want to give freely.

"Not at all," I assure Jen. "Maybe we can carve out some time to chat, but I'm just starting to wrap my head around it." Jen pushes off the counter and raises a hand, palm out.

"I get it. I'm here when you're ready," she promises, before she changes topics. "Okay, so let me grab what I was going to show you."

She disappears into the small office off the back, and I use the break to take a sip from my rich indulgence.

"Here," Jen says, when she comes back out, tossing a napkin in my direction, and I immediately lick at the cream on my bottom lip. Wiping it would be a waste.

"Ryan sent me this. It was in the paper, the day after the exhibition opened." She slides a newspaper to me. *The Durango Herald*. "Front page of the Arts & Entertainment section."

Pride blooms in my chest when I see one of my pictures taking up half the page with the header:

Colorado In View features Ferris
A bright new light in Colorado's art scene!

Underneath the picture of Ben overlooking McPhee Reservoir is the caption:

Only one example of the dramatic and emotive images currently on display at Colorado In View Gallery. Gallery is open daily from noon until 8 PM—closed Sundays.

"Can you order more copies?" I know I'm grinning like a fool when I look up at Jen.

"Already done. Actually, Ryan did. He's got a box at the gallery. This one's yours." She points at the newspaper in front of me. "He says it's been a good draw. The article helped."

"I'm stumped."

"I'm not," Jen counters. "Your work is beautiful: simple, unpretentious, and unmistakable. I'm not surprised it appeals to a larger audience."

"All I wanted was a coffee table book," I mutter, a little shell-shocked.

"I'd say you might set your goals a little loftier," Jen

chuckles. "Maybe more than one coffee table book?"

I take another sip of my macchiato as I let my mind run away with me.

"I have all these ideas," I share. "Everywhere I look, I see possibilities. I've been recording the progress of the build, which I'm planning to follow till it's done. I have another project I'm working on, trying to record seasonal changes on a few subjects. And I just had an idea for another one, earlier this week." Jen is leaning with her elbows on the counter and her chin resting on her hands.

"Well, go on then," she urges. "The suspense is killing me."

"Whatever." I roll my eyes at her. "Anyway, so you know Ben's been working on these old trailers? I thought those might look good too; all gleaming chrome and pastel colors. I can do a retro edit on the images. I'm not sure, they're just thoughts."

"Good thoughts," Jen says, straightening up after a pregnant pause. "Keep thinking them. In the meantime, I have some research to do on the cost of printing. Oh," she interrupts herself as if just remembering something. "That's right, too, I was going to tell you. Ryan's been fielding quite a few phone calls at the gallery and is sending them through to me. Mostly, people wanting to know where else they can find your work. One lady was quite persistent about needing to speak with you directly about your photos. I gave her your email. You may want to check. I'm thinking you should consider getting a proper website designed, where people can order your prints from wherever they are."

"My head is spinning," I admit, barely able to absorb all this information, and frankly, more than a bit overwhelmed.

"I'll jot stuff down. Send it to you in an email instead," Jen says with a pat on my shoulder. "More coffee?"

-

I find Ben sitting at the picnic table, sanding what looks like drawer fronts. My head is almost exploding with new ideas, and he immediately notices I'm distracted when I barely kiss him hello on my way into the trailer.

"Everything okay?" he asks.

"My head is full," I explain, although I'm not so sure that is sufficient. For Ben it might be, since he watches me silently as I rush inside, dump my purse, and grab my camera before leaping out of the trailer, missing the steps entirely. "I'll be back," I promise him in passing.

"I know," I can hear him say, but I don't see the grin from ear to ear that accompanies his words.

Ben

I hate sanding.

I especially hate sanding by hand, but it's the only way to do these kitchen drawers. That's why I'm tackling them first; get it over with.

Jim called earlier to let us know delivery would be on time, which means we have a week before the modules arrive. Not really enough time for me to pull the paneling down in the Deville, sand and stain them, and then reinstall them. I don't want to start anything I can't finish. Once the house goes up, I'll be tied up in there.

Luckily, I closed the gate on the last of the hunters this morning. I'll probably spend a few days cleaning up the sites and shutting the bathrooms down for the winter. The water supply to all the buildings has to be turned off or the pipes will freeze. There's also some brush on the sites along the water I want to clear. General maintenance, which will be so much easier with the new toys that will be delivered around five this afternoon.

A grin slides into place as I watch Isla skip off with the camera around her neck. I'll probably catch some flack, but it'll be worth it. Wait until she gets her first ride in, I bet she'll be sold.

I reach for my phone when it starts buzzing.

"Damian." His name popped up on the screen.

"Are you bored yet?" he teases, making me laugh.

"Hardly," I correct him. "Been keeping busy."

"Damn. I was hoping you were eager for some work."

"Like what?"

"Nothing specific. Flemming is still trolling for new blood."

"Yeah, I'm thinking that won't happen any time soon. Things are busy here. Trying to get the house up before the real cold hits will take up all my time."

"You know what they say, right?" Damian pokes at me. "All work and no play, makes Jack a dull boy."

"Don't think that's gonna be a problem," I inform him. "I'm planning on some serious play time as soon as my toys get here."

"Toys?"

"Isla's been driving around the place in this old golf cart. I hate the damn thing. I bought two gently used ATVs and a small trailer." I smile when I hear Damian burst out laughing.

"Does she know?" he asks, snickering.

"She will soon." That only makes him laugh harder.

"You poor sap," he mocks. "I wish you well."

"She's a smart woman. She'll get that it makes much more sense for the winter. Besides, Isla is the adventurous kind."

"She must be," he fires back. "To get tangled up with the likes of you. So when am I gonna meet this girl?"

"Actually...how would you like to come play with some really big blocks a week from today? They're dropping the modules off next Saturday morning."

"Sounds like fun. If work allows, I'll drive down. Do I bring a tent?" he jokes.

"No need. We'll find you a bed."

I end the call after he promises to let me know sometime next week. I can probably get the mattress back in the Deville. It'll be just like home for him.

-

"Get this," Isla points at her computer screen.

She's been almost like herself since coming back from Jen's. Excited, high on life and bustling with ideas. She was gone for three hours this afternoon with her camera. I almost went to look for her when she came back, dragging her ass but smiling wide.

It was a mild afternoon, so I'd already pulled out a few pork chops from the freezer to throw on the grill with some vegetables. Isla disappeared inside before emerging with her laptop and camera. She's been working at the picnic table, while I've been throwing together dinner.

I abandon the grill and peek over her shoulder at the screen.

"What am I looking at?" I ask, seeing only the body of an email that has a picture of me attached.

"This woman is looking for someone. *The Durango Herald* ran an article about my exhibit and included that shot I took of you on the outlook point. She apparently saw it, and thinks you may be someone she knows." Isla turns sideways in her seat to look at me, as I peek at the name at the bottom of the screen. *Julie Wilton.* I've never heard of her and I tell Isla as much.

"Not a clue who that is. Who is she looking for?"

"She doesn't give a name, she just says she lost track of *him* and has some important information to pass on."

"Sounds fishy to me," I casually share, but years of well-honed instinct have my antennae twitching. "How did she get your email, anyway? I thought you were letting Jen handle this kind of thing?"

I sit down beside her and turn the laptop a little my way. *JW_1978 at gmail dot com.* A pretty generic web-based email.

"I was, I am," Isla answers. "But Jen gave this woman my email when she insisted she needed to talk to me."

"I don't like it," I caution her. "Let Jen tell her you can't help her."

"Do you think you're being a little paranoid?" she mutters, and I lean in so we're face to face.

"Perhaps," I admit. "But I've stayed alive and well for over two decades because I've listened to my gut. And my gut tells me there's something fishy about this. Humor me."

I watch a struggle play out over Isla's expressive face that finally settles on surrender.

"Fine, but just so you know, I'm really curious to

know what her story is," she says, pouting.

"Then ask Jen to find out." I smile when she sticks out her tongue. "And by the way," I swiftly change tracks. "Congrats on making the newspaper." Her face morphs into that wide smile I love.

"I know!" she squeals, punching my shoulder for good measure. "Isn't it awesome? I almost fainted when Jen showed me. I'm sorry I didn't tell you right away, but I got so overwhelmed with…well, with everything happening, I just needed some time," she prattles on, while I give her shoulder a squeeze and get up to flip the chops.

Just an occasional "Mmmm" or "Right" is required, and half of what she says admittedly leaks out the other ear, but I'm smiling. *Man,* it's good to see her this animated and energetic.

While we eat, I tell her about Damian's call, and she starts talking about how she needs to find a sewing machine, so she can put up some curtains in the Deville to give him *privacy*. I don't have the heart to tell her that Damian would probably be comfortable sleeping on the picnic table, he's had worse, but if it makes her happy to make curtains, I'm not going stop her.

Isla just took our plates inside, when I hear the rumble of a heavy engine, coming up the road. I take off on a run to open the gate, waving Phil McCracken Jr. through. When he dropped off the Airstream, he mentioned he sells some used vehicles at his repair shop. He managed to get a line on the ATVs and I had him get them in prime working order.

"What is this?" Isla comes up behind me as Phil pulls to a stop.

"These are our new wheels. Yours and mine," I tell her proudly, before helping Phil unload them. I fully expect her to balk, but she stays surprisingly quiet.

"Headlights work?" she casually asks Phil, who smirks and nods in response. Then she holds out her hand. "Keys?"

Phil barks out a laugh and fishes a set from his pocket, dropping them in her hand.

She climbs on the hunter green one, starts the engine, and with her ass up out of the seat, floors it down the path, leaving me gaping after her in stunned silence. I turn to Phil, just in time to see a second set of keys flying through the air.

"Better go get the girl," he says, still grinning ear to ear. "I'll close the gate behind me."

I take off in the same direction, going mostly by sound, since she disappeared between the trees. Clearly she's driven an ATV before, judging by the expert way she handles the machine at a respectable clip. She darts in and out of the trees, leading me through and around the campground. I'm happy just to follow, feeling the cold breeze on my face, and smiling at the occasional peal of her laughter ringing out over the noise of the engines.

Finally she scoots around the gate and hightails it up the new road to the building site. That's where I finally catch up.

"You're a very smart man," she says, smiling big. "Nothing promises a sure thing like the wind in a girl's hair and the purr of a fast engine between her legs."

Holy fuck. I almost swallow my tongue at the heavy innuendo. I'm not twenty anymore, so I managed all right, giving her time to heal these past two weeks, but I'm drooling like a damn puppy dog now.

"Pixie," I growl in warning, not hiding the fact I'm adjusting my painfully hard cock. Before I have my hand back on the handlebars, she takes off down the mountain.

I have to stand for comfort as I tear off after her, following her down to the trailer, where she jumps off the ATV, and disappears inside.

I take a minute to make sure the fire is out and the four-wheelers are secured, before I head in after her, pulling my sweater off as I go. She's giggling softly as she hops on one leg beside the bed, trying to pull the other free from the tangle of her pants. I stand, just inside the door, as I strip down jeans, boxers, and pull off socks, watching her do much the same before she tumbles on the mattress. So fucking beautiful, with her open smile and welcoming curves.

"Yesssss," she hisses, when I approach the bed and set one knee down on the mattress beside her.

"You sure?"

"I'm so ready," she pants breathlessly, opening her legs in invitation. I lower myself in between, suppressing a shiver when she runs her fingertips through the hair on my chest, flicking a nail on my nipple.

"Christ, Isla—" I choke out, when my hips drop in the cradle of hers and I feel how wet she is. I involuntarily rock my hips to slide my cock along her heat. "So wet."

"I need you in me," she whispers against my skin, right before she marks me with her little sharp teeth.

I make sure to check her first with my fingers, sliding first one, and then two fingers inside her. Her pussy easily yields as she tilts her hips, hungry for more.

"Watch me," I tell her, grabbing the base of my cock

and poising it at her entrance. In one strong thrust, I drive balls deep inside her, watching her eyelids flutter and her mouth fall open. Her nails are digging at the back of my neck, where she's holding on for purchase.

"Keep your eyes on me, Pixie, and watch me love you."

CHAPTER 9

Isla

It's been a great week.

With the campground empty, we've been able to clear away any remaining garbage, fix a few broken picnic tables, and clear out any dead brush. Ben shut off the water valve to the showers and bathrooms, after I spent a couple of mornings scrubbing them as clean as I could get them. There was only one leaking tap that Ben fixed easily. All the bathrooms are padlocked now for the winter.

I have to say it's been a breeze with the four-wheelers. As much as I loved puttering around in my uncle's golf cart—and as economical, and environmentally friendly, as it was to run—I get a kick out of riding the ATV. Nothing wrong with feeling that power underneath you. Plus, Ben is right, with the wide, deep-treaded tires, they'll be much easier to handle on the snow. Heck, if need be, we can drive these things clear down the mountain into Dolores, and that is peace of mind for when we get hit with big snow.

Funny how he expected me to be pissed that he'd bought them behind my back. Sure, I argued a bit about dividing the cost, but not hard. Growing up with Uncle Al, who's basically cut from the same cloth, I know it's important for him to feel he's got me taken care of.

"Excited?" Jen asks me, as she sets two large

thermoses of coffee on the picnic table. She just showed up, out of the blue, the back of her car loaded with vast amounts of coffee and a stack of boxes, with what smells like cinnamon rolls fresh from the oven. It's barely eight in the morning.

"For the guys," she explains, looking over at the water. "It's been years since I've been here. Couldn't pass up the chance to see what you guys are up to." She dives back in the trunk and loads the boxes in my arms before pulling out a grocery bag with creamers and sugar packets. "The promise of a whole crew of working men, who know what to do with their hands, helps." She grins as she throws me a wink. "Not many eligible men in Dolores; I couldn't pass up on the opportunity."

She's shameless, and I love it. I throw my head back and laugh.

"What's this?" A deep voice sounds behind me and I turn around, a smile still on my face.

"My friend, Jen, who apparently feels the need to feed the masses. She owns the coffee shop in town."

Damian, Ben's friend, who arrived last night and bunked in what turns out to be his old trailer, reaches past me and lifts the lid of one of the boxes.

"Thought I smelled cinnamon buns. Damn, are those still warm?" he directs at Jen, who is standing there slack-jawed.

Oh, I get it. Damian is beyond handsome with his smoldering Latino good looks. Something Jen's clearly noticed.

"They are," I quickly jump in when Jen doesn't answer. "Where is Ben?"

He rolled out of bed while it was still pitch-dark

outside. I'd still been half-asleep and vaguely remember him saying something about getting the site ready. I haven't seen him since.

"He's going over the plans with Jim," Damian says, lifting a sticky pastry from the box and looking at Jen for approval. Still struck dumb, she just nods sharply and watches as Damian shoves half of the cinnamon roll in his mouth, biting it in two with strong white teeth. "They're really just killing time," he mumbles around his mouthful. "The trucks won't be here for another half-hour or so."

I grab my phone and give Ben a call.

"Jen just showed up with fresh coffee and warm pastries. Enough to feed an army."

"Be right there," is the only answer I get before the call is ended, but just moments later, I hear the sound of engines. Ben, on his four-wheeler, is leading a pickup truck with four or five guys in the back, straight up to the trailer. Three more come out of the cab of the truck. Ben saunters over with a grin, tagging me around the neck, and pressing his mouth to mine in a hard kiss.

"Jen," he turns to my friend, before they zoom in on the pastries. "You're a sight for sore eyes."

"*Suck up*," Damian coughs out.

The rest of the crew ambles up to the table, and I get busy pouring everyone coffee, while Jen does the rounds with the boxes. I manage to secure a coffee for Jen and me, and motion for her to join me on the trailer steps. I take a bite of the roll she hands me and enjoy the banter around me. There's quite a bit of good-natured ribbing going on between the guys, which Jen seems to get as much of a kick out of as I do.

"They're here," Jim announces, standing up. The

rumble of voices instantly dies down, and then we hear the sound of truck engines.

In a matter of seconds, everyone is up, mumbling their thanks and hustling back to their vehicles. Ben lingers to kiss Jen's cheek and my lips.

"You coming up?" he asks, excitement dancing in his eyes. He's like a kid on Christmas morning with a new box of Lego bricks.

"I'll just clean up and grab my camera. Be right there," I promise, waving him off.

"God," Jen sighs, a little breathlessly, when we watch as Damian gets on the ATV behind Ben and they hurry off behind the rest. "That was an overwhelming infusion of testosterone. How do you survive?" She turns to me with her eyebrows lifted high. I shake my head and chuckle.

"I just concentrate on the one that's in my bed every night." I shrug, and Jen's eyes narrow to slits.

"Lucky bitch," she mutters, gathering the empty paper cups and tossing them in the fire pit.

"You should come up more often," I suggest, nudging her with my elbow.

"Are *they* gonna be here?" She tilts her head in the direction the guys disappeared.

"Maybe not—but I will."

"Oh, all right then," she concedes with a wink.

We've got the now empty coffee containers loaded back in Jen's car, and she's standing with the door open.

"Did you ever talk to that woman? The one I gave your email address to?"

"I got an email, she's looking for some guy and thought she recognized Ben in that picture."

"Good to know," Jen says, surprising me. "She called

again to make sure I gave her the right email address.

"I haven't sent anything back," I admit. "Ben was a little freaked out and asked me not to. I promised him I'd let you handle it. I should've called you."

"Not to worry," she says, waving her hand. "Just shoot me a copy of her email when you have a chance. I'll take care of it. You go enjoy the view." She grins, pointing up at the lookout point where the arm of a big crane is visible.

"You're not coming up?"

"Nah. I get one look at men getting sweaty; I'll never leave. I've got a business to run." She gives me a one-armed hug before getting in the car.

I give her a wave as she drives off and rush inside to grab my camera.

Time to see my house come together.

Ben

"Wow," Damian says behind me.

The sun is going down fast as last of the trucks is just rumbling down the mountain. Jim and his crew are packing up for the night, and I just told them to take tomorrow, off.

That was a hard fucking day of work. Six crew from the builder, plus Jim and his crew of seven, Damian and myself, and I am looking at our new house.

"No shit," I respond.

Nowhere near done, but the shell is there, complete with windows, outside doors, and a roof. Monday, the guys will start with the hookups: plumbing, heating, and electrical. Jim put in the rough-ins, according to the plans the builder supplied, before pouring the foundation, but it all still has to be connected. Jim cautioned it would likely be another three weeks, two if he pushed it, before it would be anywhere near habitable.

It looks bigger than I thought it would be.

"I should head back home," Damian says, clapping a hand on my shoulder. "Just got a message one of our cases is heating up." I turn and clasp his hand.

"Thanks for your help, man. Appreciate it." I pull him in a man hug, pounding him on his back a few times, before stepping back.

"Whatever," he scoffs. "I owed you; you spent enough hours on my place." He starts walking toward the ATV.

"No bite before you head out?" I ask, following him. Isla left about thirty minutes ago to throw some dinner together. She'd been up here most of the day as well, only heading back to the trailer every so often to download the massive number of pictures she was snapping all day.

"Nah, I'll hit a drive-thru in Cortez."

I swing my leg over the seat and scoot forward to make room for him.

"Don't tell Isla, she'll be pissed if she finds out you're blowing off her dinner for Taco Bell," I warn him when he climbs on behind me.

"Wouldn't dream of it," he promises with a chuckle, before his tone gets serious. "You know you hit the jackpot, don't you? You deserve it, man. Despite what you might think."

"I know," I finally answer, my voice rough, as I start the engine.

Isla is disappointed when Damian announces he has to leave, as I expected, but she gives him a big hug and a kiss on the cheek.

"Next time you come, you won't recognize your Deville," she promises. "It'll be ready for you whenever you want to get away."

"Sounds good. And tell that old man of yours to bring you up to see me, if not before the winter, then in the spring. I'll take you out rafting on the Animas River." With a last wave at her, he turns to his vehicle, where I'm waiting. "Jackpot," he says again. "Lucky bastard."

"You'll hit yours," I tell him as he climbs behind the wheel.

"Nah. Thought I did once, turned out to be someone else's quarter."

Before I have a chance to say anything, he drives off. I watch until his taillights disappear through the gates before heading inside.

"Isn't it awesome?" Isla smiles big, turning her head when I come in. I walk up behind her, slip my arms around her waist, and lean my chin on her shoulder.

"Pretty amazing," I agree. "What's for dinner?"

"Potato ham soup and grilled cheese. Easy, stick to the bones kinda food."

"Sounds good," I mumble against the side of her neck, before closing my mouth over the tender skin and sucking. "Do I have time for a quick shower?" I ask, stepping back to put some distance between us before it's more than just the grilled cheese burning up.

"Tease," she hisses, throwing me a dirty look. "Yes, there's time."

After dinner Isla pats the spot next to her on the couch.

"Come have a look."

She has her laptop open to a sleek looking website.

"*I. Ferris Snapshots*? I like," I comment when I see the heading. "This looks good. Who did this so fast?"

"It's only temporary," she says, a little flush to her skin. "Until I can get a proper website designed."

"You did this?" I ask, pulling the laptop closer so I can get a better look. I'm impressed; I wouldn't know where to start. "It's really good. Doesn't look temporary to me."

"Anyway," she says, pretending not to have a pleased little smirk on her face that makes me chuckle. "I wanted to show you this." She takes back the laptop and clicks a few keys. "Have a look."

A slideshow of pictures, taken from the exact same spot, from the first time she took me up to the clearing until this afternoon, with the sun already setting. Like a time-lapse video, you can see the entire evolution from the first breaking of ground, to the roof lifted onto our house. A black frame with a single word in white ends the sequence.

HOME

My eyes move away from the screen and brush over her face. My fingers trail lazily behind.

"Home?"

"Feels like it," she whispers, self-consciously shrugging her shoulders.

"It does," I agree. "Wasn't sure I'd ever be able to remember what that felt like."

"The last time I remember feeling home, was walking in the door after school and having Mom putzing around the kitchen, while asking me all about my day." I watch as Isla swallows hard before adding, "Don't get me wrong, Uncle Al and Aunt Kate were amazing—and later Ginnie, too—but living with them always felt more like an extended stay than a home. Maybe because I remember Mom so vividly, it would've felt like a betrayal."

She turns her attention back to the screen, her fingers flying over the keyboard.

"What are you up to now?"

She logs off and shuts down the computer before glancing at me.

"I just went live with my new website," she says with a grin.

I've never seen someone adapt and adjust to whatever life throws her way, and come out the other end with that infectious smile on her face.

"You're amazing," I tell her honestly, because she is. "You're like the gift that keeps on giving."

"That's sweet," she says, setting the laptop on the table before she climbs in my lap and slides her hands along the scruff on my jaw. "But I think that's the jelly of the month club."

"It's not sweet if it's the truth, and why are you quoting *National Lampoon's Christmas Vacation?*"

"Hush," she giggles, tilts my head back, and makes me forget everything but her filling my senses.

It's him.

Twelve years and I've finally found him.

Mine.

It wasn't the right time then, but it is now. I can feel it.

The images roll over the screen and I freeze the frame when his face appears. The lines familiar, albeit a little deeper with age. It looks good on him.

When I read the caption at the end of the slideshow, my vision blurs and a sharp pain hits me square in the chest.

That bitch.

CHAPTER 10

Ben

"Stacie," I say in greeting, when Isla hands me the phone.

Those two have been planning out our Thanksgiving trip to Albuquerque in minute detail. It's giving me a headache. It's my own fault; Isla had been getting increasingly anxious about meeting my sister, and I thought it would be easier to break the ice over the phone. I didn't count on those two hitting it off so well. They talk at least once a day, mostly about color schemes and furniture. Isla had taken some photos of the interior of the house to give Stacie a sense of the space, and now the two of them are decorating. Making lists that make my head spin.

"Ben, you should rent a trailer when you come down. It would be so much cheaper than having everything shipped." I must've groaned out loud, because my sister's hearty laugh sounds in my ear. "Don't be dramatic, brother dear. I'm just trying to be practical." I don't even try to hide my incredulous snort.

"Practical is a bed, a couch, a TV—that's it."

"What would you sleep under? Where would you eat? You need a coffee table, chairs, linens, china, cutlery, pots, hand towels…the list is so long."

"Stacie," I press the bridge of my nose with my fingers. "You're calling at seven in the morning, waking us up, to talk about fucking hand towels?" Isla chuckles as she slips out of bed, and tugs on sweats, before padding to the kitchen.

"You're sleeping?" My sister feigns innocence, but I don't buy it for a second.

"I was, and now my bed is getting cold because you got my girl all fired up about fucking hand towels. *Jesus.*"

"That's a dollar for my swear jar, Uncle Ben." I groan louder. That conniving brat put her kid on the phone.

"Hey, kiddo, what happened to a quarter? You'll have me in the poor house at these rates," I tease; smiling despite the gray hairs my little sister is giving me. Her kid is the bomb.

"I'm saving up for a dog. It'll go faster with dollars."

"Smart," I manage, chuckling at Mak's irrefutable logic. "I'll pay my dues next week when we get there, kid. Put your mom back on?"

There's some rustling on the line and a mumbled, "Grab your backpack," before Stacie comes back on the line.

"I've gotta run, Ben," she says. "Gotta get the kid to daycare and get to the office."

"So Mak wants a dog?" I ignore her plea, going in for a little payback.

"Yup. Not gonna happen," she says in a low conspiratory voice. "I may have carefully suggested a Bernese Mountain dog, knowing they're pricy and almost impossible to find in New Mexico."

"I don't know," I argue. "Shouldn't be that hard here in Colorado, and it would make a perfect uncle gift for Christmas, don't you think?"

"Don't you dare," Stacie hisses, making me laugh,

because I have her just where I want her.

"Think about that next time you can't wait to discuss fucking hand towels and chase Isla from my bed."

"You're evil," she spits out.

"You bet," I counter. "But you love me anyway. We'll see you guys Wednesday."

"I do, even though you're the biggest pain in my ass. See you Wednesday, and don't forget, Isla's ass is mine for some Black Friday shopping fun!"

I toss the phone on the bed beside me, fold my arms behind my neck, and watch as Isla comes sauntering in, two steaming mugs in her hands. Gray sweats hanging off her hips, an old big tank barely covering her tits, and hair sticking out everywhere, she's the best part of every morning.

Even more so when bringing coffee.

She hands me mine and balances the remaining mug, while climbing back in bed, snuggling in beside me.

"Morning," she mumbles with a sweet smile.

"Hmmm," I growl, bending down for a kiss. I prefer show to tell, especially before caffeine. Isla's lips smile against mine.

"Sorry we woke you."

"You, I don't mind," I assure her. "My sister? Other story."

"I like her." Isla takes a sip of her coffee and looks at me from under her sleep heavy eyelids.

"That's good. I'm pretty sure the feeling is mutual, seeing as she's calling you at the butt crack of fucking dawn," I complain, making her chuckle. "You morning people are deviants. It's unnatural."

-

It's freezing cold.

My fingers are icicles, with the wind making the air feel much colder than the forty degrees showing on the thermometer outside the trailer door. I should've grabbed an extra pair of gloves.

Isla's taken to making hot lunches for the crew. Something she wanted to do to keep her busy until all the structural and electrical work is done, and we can have some heat at the house. We'll need it before we start painting and putting in floors. We, meaning Isla and me; our way to make the house a bit more ours.

Hard to believe Jim and his guys will be gone after we get back from Albuquerque. Jim's going to meet us on Monday, to officially hand everything over, but the work should be done. Isla and I have already agreed we'll throw a big barbecue in the spring, when we've got the inside all done and I have the deck built.

But for today, it's a big pot of goulash and fresh biscuits on the menu.

She's already got the fire going for some heat when I drive up. Since there's no way we all fit in the trailer, she dragged two more picnic tables to our site and set them up around the fire pit. I head inside, where she's just pulling a tray of biscuits from the small oven, and I press a kiss to the top of her head.

"Need me to do anything?"

"Just take the pot out when you're done?" she says, tilting her face back and offering me a soft smile.

"Yup."

I shrug out of my heavy coat before stepping into the bathroom. I won't fit with it on; I tried, to Isla's great hilarity. Damn bathroom. I can't wait until we've got the water running hot in the new house. Now *that's* a bathroom, with a separate shower stall, large enough for me plus one. I'm not one for baths, but the two person Jacuzzi thing Isla wanted in there is definitely something I wouldn't mind trying, as long as she's in there with me. Not much longer.

I wash my hands, struggle back into my coat, and grab the massive pot taking up two burners on the stove, and carry it outside. Isla's already greeting the guys and has hot coffee and bottles of water on the tables. Before long everyone is chowing down.

"Anybody happen to know where I can get my hands on a Bernese Mountain dog?"

Isla

I haven't said a word.

Ben didn't offer and I didn't ask. Not when he brought up the subject of a dog, and not when the guys spent the rest of the meal discussing the drawbacks and merits of one dog breed versus another. He'd just winked at me, and although I should probably still feel a little left out of whatever he has going on in his mind, by the time the guys head back to work, I'm already getting used to the idea of a dog. So when he follows me inside to kiss me goodbye, and tells me he'll explain later, I don't make a fuss and just let him go.

After cleaning dishes, getting rid of the garbage, and sorting the leftovers, I'm curled up on the couch with my laptop on my knees, Googling the hell out of the breed he mentioned. Big hairy beasts, but the puppies are adorable. They don't stay small like that, though. My mind immediately starts working on a new idea for a series. Discovering the world through the eyes of a dog, or something like that. Images shot from a puppy's eye level as it grows and learns. Furniture, trees, people, other creatures.

I'm jotting down notes and ideas when a ping announces the arrival of a new email. Expecting one from Nate at SouthWest Printing, who was supposed to send me a quote on handling my online print orders, I quickly click on my mail server. Not from Nate.

The email isn't long, just a handful of words and a picture, but its impact is lasting.

The image is of a boy, maybe eleven or twelve, with a shock of dark hair falling into his eyes, which are an eerily familiar ice blue color. The boy is smiling at the camera, his straight white teeth framed by full lips and a strong jaw, unusual for a child. It's the caption that has me toss aside my laptop and rush into the bathroom, puking up my lunch in the small chemical toilet.

-

I hear the crunch of feet coming down the path to the dock.

I'm not sure how long I've been out here, but daylight is almost gone and with it the temperature has dipped. I'm bundled up, though. The insulated sleeping bag has kept me mostly warm, except perhaps my face, even though I have my beanie pulled down over my eyebrows.

"What are you doing out here?" Ben sounds curious and perhaps a little concerned, but I can't bring myself to answer. Not even when he drops down beside me. "Pixie?" His gloved hand tilts my head his way and his eyes roam my face. "Are you upset about the dog? I should probably explain what brought that about; I should've probably done that before I threw you for a loop. It's for Mak, and Stacie. Well, technically it's not for Stacie, she doesn't want a dog but Mak does, and I thought—"

"Did you look at my laptop?" I cut him off, my voice raspy with cold. I've never heard Ben talk that fast before and I find it slightly unnerving. I can't help but wonder if it's guilt that has him ramble. The startled look on his face seems genuine, though.

"Laptop? Why? Did I miss something?" He sounds sincere in his confusion. "Whatever it is, can we get out of the cold to deal with it?"

My legs are stiff from being folded under me, for however long it's been, and Ben's hand shoots out to steady me.

"What the fuck?" he bites off, noticing my involuntary flinch at his touch.

"I..." I start to apologize but my head is such a mess, I can't even find the right words. So I shake my head, pull the sleeping bag tight around me, and lead the way to the trailer.

Once inside, I fold the sleeping bag, attempting to calm myself while buying time. But Ben doesn't wait; he goes straight for the laptop, which is still lying where I tossed it on the couch. He sits down and perches the computer on his knees, while he pulls off his gloves with his strong, white teeth.

Blowing some heat on one hand, he uses the other to

open the laptop. I'm afraid to move and observe his reaction closely, looking for the truth in his face.

"What the hell? Who is this kid?" he asks, looking up at me puzzled.

"I was hoping you could tell me." I try to be strong but my voice betrays me. Ben immediately looks back at the image, a little closer now; his eyebrows draw together.

"Is this some kind of joke? *Did you know he has a son?*—is that kid supposed to be mine?"

"Is it?" I counter, looking into his now angry eyes.

"You think maybe I would've told you if I had a kid?" he snaps, before looking back at the screen. "This the same woman who wrote you before. I told you I don't know any Julie Winton."

"What are you doing?" I ask when he starts two-finger typing furiously.

"Getting to the bottom of this," he growls when he's done. He puts the laptop aside and pulls out his phone.

"I have a favor to ask. I just forwarded two emails to you. They were sent to Isla. Can you see if you can find out where they're coming from, and who the fuck that is? Much obliged." Without another word he ends the call and tosses his phone on the table.

Guilt is starting to eat at me when he throws me a look of disbelief. Is it possible I jumped to conclusions?

"Ben..." I start, reaching out, but he pushes my hand away.

"Not now, Isla. Not fucking now."

I watch as he grabs a couple of beers from the fridge, walks right by me, and heads outside, slamming the door shut behind him. The impact snaps something inside me, and for the first time this afternoon, I let the tears come.

I've never felt anger like this from Ben before. The look on his face, like he's almost disgusted to be in the same space with me. It hurts. Everything hurts.

-

I hear the squeak of the spring on the door.

I'm not sure how long I've been lying here in the dark, but long enough to have my body shudder with every breath from all the crying. I kicked off my boots, and my pants at some point, and curled up on my side, the blankets coiled up around my ear.

"Shit, Pixie," I hear his deep voice say, full of regret, before I feel the mattress shift and his large warm body shape itself to mine. "Christ, baby. Don't cry. You're killing me."

Clearly that only makes me cry harder.

"I was so mad you'd think I'd keep something like that from you, I didn't stop to consider what it looked like from your side." He slides his hand over my belly. "*I'm sorry.*"

The softly whispered words trigger me to turn around and wrap myself around him.

"That's my line," I tell him, still struggling to get my tears under control. "He just looks so much like you."

"I know," he mumbles in my hair. "I don't know what this is about, but I promise you, I'll find out. That was Damian on the phone. He's got a guy who's good at this stuff."

Ben pushes up on his elbow, brushing aside the hair stuck to my wet face.

"I'm sorry," I offer when I notice the pained look on his face. "So much good stuff is happening, it's been easy to lull myself into thinking I've processed it. Guess I haven't," I turn my face away, but Ben turns it back, his thumb stroking my cheek.

"Wish I could make it easier, but I can't. Trust me, though, that I would never do anything to make it more difficult. I have no secrets from you. I have no reason to lie to you, especially about something as major as having a kid." He lies back down and pulls my head down on his shoulder. "We're bound to run into rough spots here and there, right? We've just gotta trust we'll struggle through together."

For a man who would get by using only the bare minimum of words needed, he sure has a way with them. Whether it's the meaning of the words he uses, or the fact he's taking the time to say them at all, I'm touched deeply.

So deeply I don't even try to stop as my feelings slip from my mouth.

"Lying here, feeling your heat, hearing the steady beat of your heart—knowing I'll get to wake up tomorrow morning to the same thing—it means everything. I want to freeze the moment, frame it, so whenever I get lost I can use it to find my way home."

"*Jesus*, Isla…" His voice is hoarse as his arms tighten around me.

"I love you, Ben."

CHAPTER 11

Ben

I'd rather stay under the blankets with Isla a little longer, but the incessant buzzing of my phone, somewhere in the pile of clothes on the floor, compels me to get out.

"Hang on," I answer in a hushed voice, trying to pull up my jeans and yanking a sweater from the pile. Sticking my bare feet into boots and tagging my coat from the back of the door, I slip out of the trailer. *Fuck, it's freezing.*

A thin, shimmery layer of frost covers everything; the first strands of early morning light bouncing off it like silver. My breath comes out in thick cloud when I talk.

"What've you got?" I ask Damian, whose name shows on my call display.

"Jasper just had time to have a quick look at the image," he says, referring to his tech guy. "It's fake. The original picture is actually a stock photo, available on several sites, so that doesn't help much."

"It looked more like a grainy snapshot," I interject, remembering the substandard quality.

"Made to look," Damian corrects me. "The image was modified from the original. Eye color, jaw line, cheekbones. Jas was gonna send it to a friend of his, who knows more about image modification, while he gets on the email itself, but the guy won't be able to get to it right away. I thought maybe your girl could have a closer look."

I curb my instinctive reaction to shut him down.

Perhaps I should leave the decision to Isla, whether she wants to have a look or not.

"Okay. Yeah, I'll ask her. I'm more interested in figuring out who sent it, though. Obviously someone who knows me, but dammit, that could be a fucking long list of people."

"I'd focus on women. I know we can't go by the name on the email, but this kind of thing screams disgruntled female to me."

"Only women, other than a handful of flings from my early twenties, were part of one or another undercover assignment. Part of the job. They wouldn't even know my name."

"She wouldn't need to," Damian points out. "She clearly knows what you look like." He's right. And she knows it well enough to recognize me as a mostly shadowed figure in a picture. "It might help to try and remember some names," he adds.

The light flicks on in the trailer.

"I'll work on it. I've gotta go," I tell Damian. "Appreciate the help. We'll be in touch." I end the call and head back to the warmth of the trailer.

"Hey," Isla greets from her favorite perch by the coffee machine when I step inside, quickly shutting the door behind me to keep out the cold. Instead of telling her, I walk right up in her space and show her how glad I am to see her. "God, you're cold," she mumbles against my lips.

"We had frost overnight." I shrug out of my coat and kick off my boots. Damn, I'll be glad when we can move into the house. As much as I enjoy close quarters with Isla, this trailer is too damn small to hold big winter coats and boots for both of us. There's no room to move.

I drop down on the couch and catch Isla peeking through the small window over the sink.

"It's pretty," she says, grabbing the cup she was hoarding from under the Keurig and bringing it to me.

"Why do you do that?" I ask her, when I take the coffee from her. She looks at me puzzled, so I explain. "Every morning, you give me the first cup." A small smile tugs at her mouth.

"It makes me feel less guilty about disturbing your morning grump with my cheery disposition."

"Morning grump?" I growl, quickly setting my coffee on the table, before pulling her down on my lap.

"You should see your face when someone says more than two words to you before you've had your coffee," she teases. "It's downright scary."

"You're not scared," I point out, tucking her head under my chin.

"Nope," she confirms. "But I was last night. Not that you'd ever hurt me," she quickly adds, when she notices me freeze up at her words. "You were so angry, I was afraid maybe you'd leave."

"I'm here."

"I know," she says, snuggling a little closer. "One of the last things my Aunt Kate told me was that if I kept my chin up and a smile on my face, troubles would bounce off. I've lived that, you know; the harder the hits, the bigger the smile."

"Hmmm," I hum encouragingly, with my chin resting on her head.

"First time I let down that shield was with you," she says, putting a hand over my chest. I brace myself, because I know this, and I know what happened after.

"And I lied to you," I finish for her.

"And you lied to me," she confirms, wistfully. "I guess it was closer to the surface than I thought. Stupid, because I get why it was necessary, intellectually. Emotionally is clearly a whole different ball game."

"Anything happens, you come to me first. Okay?" I urge her. "Doesn't fucking matter what it is, you come find me." She tilts back her head and smiles up at me.

"I will." She pushes off my lap, bends over to give me a quick peck on the lips, and hands me my coffee, before turning back to the kitchen. "I need coffee."

So while she waits for hers to brew, I tell her about my conversation with Damian. By the time I'm ready to head up to the building site, she's already completely immersed in Photoshop.

-

"Jim says the final electrical hookups can be done before the weekend," I tell Isla, when I enter the trailer later that day.

"Seriously? That's amazing. Does that mean we can get in there and start painting?"

"If we can get some space heaters going, then I guess. They still have to finish installing some of the plumbing hardware and hook up the furnace and air, but that won't be done until the weekend. The guys have been pushing to get it signed off before Thanksgiving. They want to get home."

"I can't blame them. They've been here virtually nonstop for the past month and a half," she points out. "You know what that means, right?" Her face lights up and I can't help smile back. "We need to go paint shopping."

She snickers when I dramatically roll my eyes.

"Fine. Grab your coat; we'll go now. Get it over with."

Isla slaps the lid down on her laptop and jumps up with a squeal.

"Grab the color chips," she waves her hand at the counter. "I've marked them all with sticky notes of what goes where." I grab the binder and follow her as she bounces out the door.

Like a kid.

Isla

I'm excited to go out.

I spent most of the day cooped up inside, dividing my time between photo edits, my search for a Bernese Mountain dog, and trying to make some sense of the image of the boy. The first two were fun; the latter gave me a headache and filled me with foreboding.

I'd found the stock image and used it as a guideline to lift off the segments that were altered on the emailed file. Eyes, hairline, lips and chin; those were different. I isolated them on a new layer, and pulled up a snapshot I took of Ben a while back. Just a quick picture taken one morning at the picnic table, but his face was fully turned to the camera. Then I started comparing details, and by the time I got to the eyes and found the same small gold fleck in the ice blue on the left side, I pretty much knew whoever it is used an actual picture of Ben.

Looking for puppies was a pretty good distraction

after that.

"All set?" Ben asks, climbing in behind the wheel.

"I've got them all," I tell him, waving the paint chips in his face. "Every room, and all the sizes marked."

I've stayed away from the house for the most part, not wanting to get underfoot and maybe slowing things down, but I can't wait to get in there and start doing something. Putting my own mark on it. I'm doing that with color.

"Any luck with the picture?" Ben asks, as we pull on to the road.

"Yeah. Some picture of you was used to alter the original. I created a separate file with all the parts; eyes, lips—the only thing that threw me was the chin, it was clean-shaven. When was the last time you shaved smooth?" Ben's hand comes up as if by rote, scratching at the scruff he maintains there now.

"Can't remember off hand. I'll think about it. We should probably send that file to Damian's guy. See if he can do anything with it."

"Do you think we're overreacting?" I ask carefully, but Ben still reacts sternly and instantly.

"No. Absolutely not," he says, his hand squeezing my leg to underscore his words. "First and most importantly, whatever the fuck is going on, they're picking on you. I don't like that." I shouldn't smile, but I can't help myself, it's cute when he gets all protective and growly. "Next thing to consider is that over the last twenty some years, I've not exactly made good friends in some levels of society. Someone may have decided to get some payback. You never know."

Well, that wipes the smile clear off my face. I don't really have details on any of the work he's done over the years, but judging by my involvement in his last undercover case, right here at the campground, it's not without violence.

"Oh." The single syllable comes out on a sigh and I can feel Ben's eyes on my profile.

"Right," he confirms, his hand finally easing up on my knee and now gently rubbing up and down my leg. "I'm not easy to find. We're pretty much off the radar where we are," he reassures me, but what he says raises another question.

"Is that why you were so eager to build there?"

He's quiet at first, and when I look at him, his eyes are focused on the road but I can almost feel the wheels turning.

"In part," he finally admits, casting a quick glance my way. "Don't get me wrong, anywhere *with you* would've been good for me. But when the opportunity came along to put down stakes right there on the mountain, I wasn't gonna let any grass grow under my feet. Living in a trailer during the summer is easy. In the winter, not so much."

"True," I concede, a little disappointed at the practical considerations, but I shake it off.

The rest of the drive is silent, although I can feel Ben glancing over every so often. When he pulls into a parking spot, around the corner from the hardware store, he turns off the engine and twists his body to face me.

"Not sure what thoughts are going around in there," he says, tapping a finger to my forehead. "But fit this one in there; you are far from a convenience."

"So now I'm an inconvenience?" I say, turning my head away. I'm not sure where that comes from, but it's out before I can stop it. Petty, stress-induced word games.

It's childish and I'm immediately ashamed, but when I turn back, Ben's already getting out of the car. "Ben..." I plead, scrambling to get out on my side when he throws his door shut.

I have to run to catch up with his long strides and manage to grab his arm right before he turns the corner.

"Stop. Hold on a sec."

He turns around and I try to read his eyes, but his expression is impassive.

"That was just a dumb thing to say. I..."

"Ya think?" he counters with a snort, before grabbing my upper arms and pushing me with my back against the brick wall. "Trust, Isla," he bites off between clenched teeth, his forehead almost touching mine. "You've gotta trust that what comes out of my mouth is exactly what I mean. No more, no less. Don't project *your* insecurities on *my* intentions." He lets go of my arms and takes a step back. "That's a battle I can't win for you."

"Wait," I call out, rushing after him when he starts walking away. My heart is in my throat and my stomach is doing flips, but that doesn't stop me from launching myself at him, hanging on to his neck and burying my face there.

His arms catch me, just as I knew they would.

"I'm sorry. Please, let me be sorry," I whisper in his ear like a mantra, ignoring the odd looks we're getting in the middle of the sidewalk.

"Babe," he rumbles, letting me slide down and peeling my arms from around his neck. "It's fine."

"It's not fine, Ben. I don't know why I say shit like that," I admit, close to tears.

"Stress," he says, tagging me behind my neck and

pulling my head into his chest, leaning his chin on top. "Both of us. We need to slow down."

"Yes," I mumble. His hand finds mine clenched in his jacket next to my face, and carefully untangles it, slipping his fingers between mine.

"Let's get some paint," he says, gently tugging me along.

Forty-five minutes later, we have twelve gallons of paint loaded in the back of the Toyota. Not enough, but a good start.

"Can we stop at the print shop?" I ask when Ben pulls out of the parking spot. "I need to pick up some new memory cards for the camera, and I want see if Nate has those prints ready I want to give the guys."

It had been Ben's idea, actually; when I mentioned wanting to do something for the guys as a thank you for their hard work, he'd suggested getting a print done for each of them. I ended up with pictures of each of the guys at work on the house. Some I already had, and some I went out and shot specifically. I sent the files over to Nate last week.

"Sure," Ben says casually. "I'll pick up something quick for dinner. Fast food okay?" I chuckle. From what he tells me, he existed on fast food most of his life, and gets a craving every now and then.

"Wendy's is around the corner," I point out.

"I know." He turns to me with a grin before turning east on Main Street. "I'll pick you up around the corner," he says a few minutes later, dropping me off in front of Southwest.

Nate is busy with a customer when I walk in, so I have a look at the display of memory cards on the far counter. I have my selection made when I hear the door close and Nate walks up.

"They're not done. The color wasn't right," he says by way of hello. "I'm running the print again tonight, after I close up, and will have them for you tomorrow afternoon. That okay?"

"Yeah, sure. I'll pop in tomorrow or the day after. We were just in the neighborhood, I thought I'd take a chance," I explain, handing him the memory cards to ring up. "What do you think of the website?" I ask, following him to the cash register.

"Not bad," he says. "It could do with a bit of tightening up, but you've got a bit of traffic going over it already."

"Seriously?" I'm pleased as hell. I didn't expect anyone to look unless I told them to. "How did they find it?"

"I made it a little more visible. Checked with Jen to see if we could link it to her website, and she checked with the gallery. Your link is up on both. People who visit the coffee shop, or the gallery, can easily find your work now." He shrugs, like it's nothing.

"Thank you so much. I never got that far."

"I'll get my buddy to look at the site itself. See if he can't put a few moving graphics and some music on. Make it a bit more interactive. It'll take off," he says, handing me my change.

"I appreciate it, Nate. Why don't you give me a call when the prints are ready?"

"Yup," he answers, lifting just two fingers when I walk out the door.

I don't expect Ben to be back yet, so I turn down

Beech Street to pick up a bunch of large padded envelopes for the guys' prints. I'm having them mounted the same way Nate did the prints for the gallery, on thin rigid board.

The post office isn't that busy. I'm in and out pretty fast and walk back toward Main Street, keeping an eye out for Ben.

I'm just crossing the alley that runs parallel to the main thoroughfare, all along the downtown, when an engine revs to my left. All I see is a flash of white from the corner of my eye, and I instinctively throw myself forward, landing hard on my hands and knees. Behind me there's a screech of tires, and when I turn my head, I can just see the back of a white sedan turning the corner at the post office.

"Are you okay?" An older man comes walking out of the barbershop and helps me to my feet, collecting the envelopes that flew from my hands when I fell.

"I'm okay," I assure him. "I wasn't looking where I was going." He looks at me oddly as he hands me the envelopes.

"Not sure it was on you," he says. "Saw that car speed off, they sure were in a hurry to get out of here."

Of course Ben picks this moment to pull up beside us. I quickly thank the man and climb into the passenger seat.

"What happened?" he asks right away.

"I fell. Well, technically, I almost got hit by a car." I can immediately feel the charge in the car as Ben's eyes turn to slits.

"What?"

"I wasn't looking," I quickly explain. "All I saw was a white blur and I jumped. Nothing happened. The old guy came to help me up, that's all." Ben grabs for my hands and turns them over. My palms are a little scraped but nothing major.

"Anywhere else?" he snarls, sounding almost mad at me.

"I may have bruises on my knees tomorrow, but really, it's no big deal," I try to reassure him.

"You get hurt, it's a big deal to me," he grumbles, turning the key in the ignition.

"Smells good. Did you get fries?" Ben glares at me for a moment, before reaching into the back seat and pulling out a brown paper Wendy's bag.

"Eat. But don't think for one minute you're distracting me."

CHAPTER 12

Ben

"You won't need the space heaters," Jim says, when I find him in the master bath, installing the showerhead. "Furnace is up and running." He turns to me with a big grin on his face.

The guys have been working like mad these last couple of days, running lights along with their power tools off of the generator, so they could keep working into the night.

"No shit?"

"We're out of here tonight. I'll leave the furnace running overnight to get the chill from the house, and I'll come back around noon tomorrow to do a last walk-through with you; make sure everything is working as it should. But other than that, we'll be out of your hair."

"Make sure you stop at the trailer before you head out. Isla's gonna be pissed if she doesn't get a chance to say goodbye."

"Will do."

She would be too. She picked up the prints a couple of days ago, signed and left a personal message on every one of them. I'm sure the guys will get a kick out of them. I asked her to pick up a bottle of scotch for each of them as well, my way of saying thanks. For nearly two months, we've seen these guys every day, ate with them, worked side by side with them—it's going to be quiet when they're gone.

I get the feeling winters are going to be long up here. Not sure how we would've fared if we'd had to wait for spring to build, but I'm glad we don't need to find out. As it is, it's been a little tense with Isla and me.

They say purchasing a house, or in our case building one, can make for the most stressful times in a relationship. I don't really have much experience to draw from, but I'd have to say it certainly doesn't help. Nor does the fact that we're no closer to figuring out who sent that picture. I wish we could brush it off, but it's too damn personal for that. It hit Isla right where it hurts, and it has me racking my brain to come up with a person I can attach to it. Other than that I agree with Damian, it's got to be a woman, I'm no further on that front.

Then this morning, when I popped back into the trailer to grab my phone I'd forgotten, Isla startled and slammed her laptop shut. Not sure what that was all about, but it sure as fuck made for an awkward moment. She's hiding something, and although I'm tempted to sneak onto her computer to find out, I can't do it. Not when I've been preaching trust to her. It's messing with my head.

Tomorrow is Sunday. We'll have three days to get painting started, and then Wednesday morning; we leave for Albuquerque. I'm hoping that trip will be good. Get away for a bit. Besides, it's been too damn long since I've seen Stacie and Mak, who's probably grown another foot.

I leave Jim in the bathroom and walk-through the master suite and down the short hall into the living area: a big, open living/dining space, with the kitchen on the other side of it. The master bedroom, the great room, and the kitchen are all at the front, facing the reservoir. The roof over the center of the house has a steep peak over the great room, making for high cathedral ceilings inside and massive windows that showcase a fantastic view. The entire house is one level with three bedrooms, or in our case, two bedrooms and one study. The spare and the study plus the second bath are on the backside of the house. There's a main entrance behind the kitchen, off the side of the house. We opted for a small basement, just below the kitchen, with a set of stairs leading down beside the main entrance. The furnace and water heater are down there, as is a cold storage room. Laundry is on the main level, on the backside of the house, with a door from the main entrance.

It's not huge, but it feels big because of the high ceilings in the center of the house. I'm planning to build a deck in front of the big windows of the living room and a small porch off the master bedroom. All plans for the spring.

I slip outside through one of the doors on either side of the living room windows. Pretty sure tonight will be another frosty one, the air is cool and crisp on my face as I make my way to the four-wheeler, but I can smell evidence of Isla's cooking from the trailer below.

"How much did you make?" I ask her, when I step into the trailer a few minutes later. She turns from the stove to face me, a curious smile on her face.

"Why? Are you hungry?"

"That," I admit, "and I told Jim to stop by before they take off. They're done."

Isla's smile breaks wide open.

"For real?"

"Jim's gonna come back to walk us around tomorrow

and sign off on the job. Looks like we'll be painting." I chuckle when she starts jumping up and down. Suddenly she stops and her face falls.

"I'm going to need more garlic bread from the freezer." She turns her back and starts pulling things from the fridge and cupboards, her movements rushed and slightly frantic.

"All of them?" I ask.

A sharp nod and a mumbled "Uhhuh" is the only response I get.

By the time the wheels of the two pickup trucks crunch over the gravel path, there's a fire burning in the fire pit. The venison stew Isla was making has been expanded with potatoes and vegetables, and the last of the garlic bread is coming out of the oven. Grudgingly, I dive into my beer stash on Isla's instructions, to grab a twenty-four for the guys, just as they come sauntering up to the picnic tables.

Despite the fact everyone is tired, the mood is celebratory and it isn't until we're well into my second case of beer that Jim gets up and calls it a night.

"Wait!" Isla jumps up from where she's been huddled under a quilt by the fire, listening to the guys talk, and surreptitiously snapping a picture here or there. "Give me a hand, Ben?" I follow her inside and grab the tote with bottles before letting her load me up with a couple of her prints. She carries the rest outside herself.

After handing out the scotch, shaking hands, and slapping shoulders, I stand off to the side and watch Isla as she says her goodbyes. If these guys didn't love her already, they certainly would after tonight. She knows something about every one of them—the name of a spouse, a sick parent, a child's performance—she has them all eating from her hand. The prints are a big hit and every last one of the guys promises to come back during the summer and bring their families.

"You good?" I ask; slipping my arm around her as we watch the trucks drive off.

"Gonna be quiet," she says, tilting her head back, giving me a watery smile.

"I know," I acknowledge. "But we're gonna be too busy to notice," I remind her. "We've got a house to paint and floors to lay."

-

"Ben?" Isla's fingers trail through my chest hair, drawing lazy patterns.

I'm almost asleep after she rode me hard and fast, my hands holding onto her hips, and my mouth on her perky tits. What little energy I had drained away with every spurt of my cum inside her.

"Hmmm."

"Do you really want a dog?"

Isla

I flinch at the loud gurgle of my Keurig when I hit the button for my coffee.

I was up early and left Ben snoring in bed. I'm eager to get this day started; head up to the house and slap some paint on those walls, but he's been working hard—seven days a week, ever since the house went up, so I figure he deserves to sleep in for once. The paint will wait till he gets up. My need for caffeine has run out of patience.

When my cup is brewed, I peek around the corner, fingers crossed he's still sleeping, otherwise I'll have to hand off my coffee. Satisfied he's still down for the count, I take my cup and snuggle in the corner of the couch, my laptop within reach.

He'd laughed last night when I asked him if he was serious about a dog. At first, I was worried he'd changed his mind, but then he told me that he wouldn't mind one, if that's what I wanted.

I flip open my laptop and look at the picture I'd found when I was searching the breed he'd mentioned. Bernese Mountain dog. It popped up, a shelter in Farmington, where a seven-month-old male had been put up for adoption. A black face with soulful liquid eyes, and little tan patches for eyebrows, the narrow strip of white fur running between and ending in a white snout. His name is listed as *Atsa*.

I called the shelter yesterday. The lady who answered was very friendly. She told me he'd been there for a month already, the owners had given him up when they discovered he was getting too big for their apartment. It pisses me off when people don't think ahead when they see a cute little puppy. In the end, it's the dog that gets hurt. Just like those dumb people who buy kittens or puppies for Christmas, only to discover that they don't stay that cute forever. Ugh. I confessed to her I was interested but that it wasn't just up to me.

"What has you smiling?" My head snaps up at Ben's raspy voice, and my hand is already poised to slap the laptop shut. A frown appears between his eyes when he notices my movement, so I drop my hand back in my lap.

"This," I say instead, turning the screen toward him. The frown smoothes out and a little smile lifts the corner of his mouth.

"Who's that?" he asks, making his way and sitting down next to me, pulling the laptop closer.

"His name is Atsa, he's seven months old and the rescue shelter in Farmington is looking for a permanent home for him." Ben turns his head and looks at me with his eyebrows raised.

"Yeah?"

"Yup." The P pops between my lips, drawing his gaze down, before his eyes drift back up to my eyes, humor shining in them.

He reaches out and taps his index finger on my nose.

"And it just so happens, we'll pass close to Farmington on our way to Albuquerque," he points out.

"So it would seem," I admit, feigning innocence, which doesn't fool him for one second, judging by the growing smirk on his face.

"Manipulated already, and I haven't even had my coffee yet."

I jump up and rush to jab a mug under the Keurig—but I'm smiling big.

-

"I can't believe how toasty it is in here."

I strip off the big sweater I'm wearing and toss it on the kitchen counter, next to the trays and rollers I just brought in, along with a can of paint.

"Yeah, Jim really cranked it up, trying to get the chill out. Let me adjust the thermostat," Ben says, as he follows me into the kitchen, carrying six cans of paint. Show-off.

"What time was he going to be here?" I call after him

when he walks out of the kitchen.

"Noon," he calls back.

It's just past nine now, so we have plenty of time to tackle one of the rooms before he gets here.

"Which one first?" I ask Ben when he reappears.

"Master," he says without hesitation. "Get the bedroom ready first so we can sleep here and then move out from there."

"We don't even have a bed," I point out.

"We'll bring the mattress up," he says with a grin. "Not gonna squeeze in that damn shower any longer than I have to. Besides, that dog will need the room."

We'd discussed Atsa over breakfast and Ben called the shelter himself with some questions. We're going to stop by the shelter on the way to his sister's, and if we click with the dog, we're going to have their vet neuter him before we pick him up on our way home after the weekend.

The kitchen floor is tiled with a deep gray slate, matching the beautiful concrete countertop Jim's guys put in. The stainless steel appliances are enough to make me drool: the fridge, about five times the size of what we have in the trailer, and the gas stove is almost industrial sized. The bathrooms have similar floors but the counters are a lighter gray composite. It is odd, moving through the house when most of the flooring is missing and only a layer of primer covers the walls. Very stark, until you look out the humongous ceiling to floor windows and all the beauty of the outdoors is right there.

It's one of the reasons why we decided on a fairly neutral palette inside, just a selection of warm gray tones for the walls and floors. I'd wanted real wood floors, but

Jim had convinced us to go with a high-end laminate that looks like old barn boards. The subtle differences in color and ridging detail makes it look like real wood, but with the convenience of being scratch resistant and easy to clean. Something I'm sure we'll appreciate now that it looks like we'll have a dog.

-

I'm up on a stepladder, cutting in the top edge of the wall with an angled brush, when Jim walks in.

"Wow," he says, looking around at the walls, which already sport one coat of the odorless, fast drying paint. "Ben wasn't kidding when he said you were hustling."

"He wants to sleep here tomorrow night, so the walls have to get done today, and the floor has to go in tomorrow."

"Ambitious," Jim mumbles, grinning.

"You doubt we can do it?" I challenge him with a smile of my own, to which he vehemently shakes his head.

"Oh, hell no, I don't doubt you can do anything you put your mind to."

"She sure can," Ben pipes up, from where he leans against the doorpost, smiling at me. "Got a minute to do a walk-through with us?"

"Sure."

It doesn't take long before we're waving as Jim's truck rattles down the brand new road, and we are alone. When I walk into the kitchen and see the stack of paperwork and manuals, along with a pile of keys, lying on the counter, the full impact hits me.

"We have a home." I slap my hands over my mouth to hold back the semi-hysterical giggle bubbling up as I turn to face Ben, who is right on my heels.

"That was the plan, right?" His lopsided grin belies the dry tone of his voice. He's excited too; he's just too much of a *guy* to show it.

That was her.

I can't believe the gall.

Right in the middle of Main Street, she's putting her lips on my goddamn man. I spotted him right away, pushing the greedy bitch away from him, right outside the hardware store. But then seconds later, she is wrapped around him, his arms lifting her up like she belongs there. Not if I have anything to say about that.

It was a stroke of luck, which brought me to Cortez at that exact moment. Divine intervention, if you will.

Yesterday I finally had enough money to buy that picture she took of him. The flashy guy at the gallery wasn't very forthcoming about her, but he willingly gave me the name of the printer. That's where I was headed, when I saw him. I almost ran into the car in front of me. I panicked, there'd been nowhere to park, and traffic was thick, so I pulled around the block. By the time I got back where I'd seen them, they were gone. I waited thirty minutes on that corner but they never showed up. Sure that I'd lost him again; I drove to the printer and found parking in the alley across the street.

I'd barely said hello to the young guy behind the counter when SHE walked in. I can't remember exactly what I said, but I made some excuse and hurried back to my car. My heart was pounding in my chest. What are the odds?

No sign of him, so when she crossed, right in front of me, I reacted.

Stupid. That had been stupid. I have to be more careful, but she was taunting me.

Touching what belongs to ME.

The father of my child.

CHAPTER 13

Ben

"Isn't he amazing?"

It's not the first time I've heard that in the past hour, so instead of answering—again—I just give her knee a squeeze.

We stopped in Farmington, of course. The woman at the shelter knew who we were, or rather who Isla was, the moment we walked in. Not surprising, since she's been 'checking up' on Atsa daily. The two women greeted each other like they were old friends.

The moment the door to the small waiting room opened and the big furball was brought in, Isla was on her knees, with her arms around the big lug's neck. I tried cautioning her about putting her face in such close proximity to the dog's much bigger head, but it fell to deaf ears.

He's a beautiful dog, already big, but with more growth in those big paws ahead of him. Great demeanor too, since he allowed Isla to coo and cuddle while he silently endured. Despite the laid back attitude, his eyes were sharp, not missing a thing. With his big snout resting on Isla's shoulder, he threw me a look that said: *I've got this*. I got the distinct feeling he might already be protective of Isla and that's fine by me.

If not for the promise of picking him up on our way home in four days, and the prospect of meeting my family, it would've been impossible to drag her away from the shelter.

But now I'm in a car, and will be for another couple of hours, with an overexcited Isla.

Only one coffee so far today, and already too many words; I'm going to need more reinforcement.

"I need more coffee."

"Oh, perfect," Isla chirps. "I need to pee."

I'm already sipping the bucket-sized coffee, when she comes bouncing out of the gas station, carrying a bottle of wine and a stuffed animal.

"What's that?" I ask her, when she dumps both on the backseat.

"Can't come with empty hands. The wine is for Stacie and the toy is for Mak," she says, climbing into the car. I tamp down a smile, she is in for a bit of a surprise when she meets Mak and Stacie.

Bolstered by the added caffeine, the rest of the drive is manageable. Isla chatters about the dog, the fact that it's her first visit to Albuquerque, and the furniture we need for the house. It's a little bit confusing, at times, to try and keep track of what she's referring to now, but judging by her reaction to my occasional monosyllabic responses, I've done okay.

Truth is, I'm pretty excited about seeing those two as well. I won't lie, sleeping in a real bed for once, is probably the thing I look forward to most. I've spent long enough in small trailer beds or on floors.

My plan to drag a mattress up the mountain, so we could sleep in the house, never materialized. We worked our asses off these past few days. Bedrooms, bathrooms, hallway, and kitchen are all painted, courtesy of Isla, mostly. The great room still needs to be done, since I'll need some ladders to reach the ceiling. I'd planned to wait to lay the flooring until each room was painted, but it was more practical to keep going once I started it.

The days and nights had been long to get the place this far, so at night we just rolled down the mountain and into bed. And in the mornings, I'd curse myself when I hit my elbow or my head in that joke of a shower.

Stacie offered for us to stay with her on the air mattress in her office, where I'd usually sleep, but I declined this time. She lives right around the corner from a nice Holiday Inn & Suites, so I booked a room there: with a king-sized bed and a walk-in shower. *Fuckin' A*.

"Are we going to your sister's first or the hotel?"

"Hotel," I answer, knowing that if we head to Stacie's first, we wouldn't get out of there again. I want to get a feel for that mattress first, so I can spend the rest of the day looking forward to it. "I might want a quick shower," I add, and Isla bursts out laughing.

"You get in that shower, you won't be alone," she says, taunting me. "And that will mean we won't be coming out of the room again today. So let's save the shower for later. Much, much later."

"Spoilsport," I mumble, as I pull the Toyota up to the front of the hotel.

We only have two small bags, which I easily toss over my shoulder as I reach out and tag Isla, before she runs off without me. My hand rests casually on the back of her neck and I'm suddenly struck by our reflection in the automatic doors as they slide open. The top of her head just barely reaches my chin and the shadow of my much bigger body dwarfs her. Our contrasts are undeniable, and yet we fit. She is strong and resilient, and matches me step for step when it comes to hard work and focus. I think I knew the first time I saw her that there was a hell of a lot packed into that small package.

I keep my hand on her neck as we walk up to the desk, and while the clerk puts our information into the computer, I lean down and put my lips against her ear.

"Love you."

I can feel her startle under my hand, before she slowly leans the weight of her body into me.

"Here are your keys," the young girl chimes, sliding a small folder over the counter. "You'll find the Wi-Fi login information inside, and the complimentary breakfast buffet is setup in the restaurant between seven and ten. Your room is just down this hall and there should be parking right outside your door. Hope you have a nice stay."

"Thank you," Isla says, and I just nod, using my hand on her neck to guide her down the hallway to our room.

I let her open the door to a decent space, probably a little bigger than the trailer, with a large bed, two chairs and a sofa, plus a TV. To my immediate left, the bathroom with a large walk-in shower. *Hell yes*.

Isla stops in the middle of the room and turns to me. I drop the bags on a chair and take a step so our fronts are touching. My eyes are focused on her shiny ones as I pull my phone from my pocket.

"Stace?"

"Yay!" my sister squeals in my ear. "Are you here yet?"

"Yeah, we're in town," I tell her, my eyes focused on Isla's face. "Listen, can't wait to see you, we'll be there by dinnertime." I don't wait for an answer, just end the call and toss my phone on the bed.

Isla's hands come up and brush up over my stomach to my chest, where they still. I lift my fingers and stroke them along her jaw, tilting her face while lowering mine. My mouth brushes her lips and they easily open for me, but I don't deepen the kiss. Instead I duck down, and flip her over my shoulder in a fireman's hold. She squeals and slaps at my ass, as I walk her straight into the shower, a big grin on my face.

Isla

"Ben..."

My clothes are in a pile on the floor, I'm desperately hanging on to the shower door with one hand, and the soap dish with the other, gasping for air as Ben's eyes burn into mine from between my legs. On his knees in front of me, he has one of my legs over his shoulder while the other one buckles; his mouth seems the only thing holding me up.

"Ben..."

I'm not sure if I'm begging him to stop or pleading for him to break the protracted pleasure he's building with his lips and tongue. He hums against my pussy and I can feel the vibrations on my clit.

"Please..."

His hand slides over my thigh and between my legs, where his thumb finds the tender bundle of nerves with devastating accuracy, as his tongue penetrates and fucks me.

I know I must have screamed loud when I see Ben's shit-eating grin through blurry eyes. My own ears are still ringing.

"Always wanted to do that," he growls, getting to his feet.

I'm still limp from that eruptive orgasm when he pulls me against his wet body, kissing my mouth with equal passion and dexterity. There is something so intimate about wet flesh rubbing wet flesh, my taste on his lips, and his need for me clear, in the press of his hard cock against my stomach.

Still completely pliable, Ben turns me around, bending himself over my back.

"Hold on tight," he rasps against my skin, as he helps me brace against the glass of the shower door. I feel his hard length slide along my ass, as he widens his stance, going through his knees. His hands tighten on my hips as he helps me tilt my ass up and feel the crown slide through my folds. "Watch," he rumbles from behind me. I lift my eyes, catching our reflection in the mirror straight ahead, the shower door blurred by droplets and condensation. My palms are flat against the glass and Ben's large shape, even less defined, is looming over mine.

His cock teases at my opening.

"Are you watching?" he asks, keeping me once again in suspension as one of his hands slides from my belly, up between my breasts, and curves around my neck.

"I am," I whisper, just as he drives up with force, stealing what little breath I have.

His pace is furious and I can't tear my eyes away from our reflection. Ben's head is down, his attention on the furious piston of his hips, and yet the touch of his hand on my neck stays gentle in contrast. A dichotomy, much like the man. Soft and hard in equal measure.

"Get there, baby," he breathes from behind me, his plunges even deeper but less controlled. He slides his fingers over my clit and presses down as his thrusts about lift me off my feet. "*Please...*"

His urgent plea pushes me over the edge, and Ben is right behind me, bucking his release. His jerky movements still, until all that remains are the two of us, plastered together back to front, still connected.

"Love you, too," I finally say, my cheek plastered to the glass and my mouth barely moving.

Ben's arms band around me and lift me upright, as he slips free of my body, turning me to face him.

"Thought you heard me," he says, his eyes warm. "The words are a little rusty—don't use them often and then just with my sister, or Mak." I slip my arms around his neck and tilt my head back.

"I'm grateful for the words, but even without them, I already knew." I watch as one side of his mouth lifts. "You show me every day."

-

It's two hours later that we are finally standing in front of the door of a cute little bungalow, in a nice residential neighborhood. Now that we're here, I'm getting a little nervous and my hands are getting slippery around the bottle of wine and the stuffed animal I'm holding. Ben's hand is calming in the small of my back.

"Relax," he mutters under his breath, and I whip my head around to glare at him.

"Easy for you to say," I hiss, just as the door opens,

revealing a striking woman.

Before I can fully take her in, a blur streaks past me, yelling, "Uncle Ben!" almost bowling him over.

CHAPTER 14

Ben

"Uncle Ben!"

Before I even have a chance to say anything, my niece is dangling around my neck, like the monkey that she is.

"Makenna," I mutter in greeting.

"*Mak*, Uncle Ben. Makenna is a girl's name."

"I'm sure they told me that's what you were, when you came out of me already screaming, Makenna," my sister scolds her daughter. "A girl."

I snicker at the disgruntled snort emerging from the lanky girl in my arms. I tilt her back a little so I can have a good look. Still with the short hair, but her pale blue eyes—like the rest of the family—are fringed by beautiful dark lashes and her face gets prettier every time I see her. Sadly, Mak is unmistakable as a girl, despite the short haircut and the aversion to girly clothes.

"Can I at least tell you you're growing like a very pretty weed?" I ask her teasingly.

"Am I gonna be big and strong like you?" she asks, her little hands on my cheeks.

"You sure are," I tell her before adding, "and prettier than your mom."

"Alright," Stacie interrupts, untangling Mak's arms from around my neck and setting her on her feet. "Give me a chance to say hello?" I give my sister a hug, lifting her off her feet.

My sister is slender and tall, but still a fair bit shorter than I am. Aside from our height and the telltale light blue eyes, we have little in common. There's the substantial age difference, but in addition to that, my sister is a true blonde—unlike me—a legacy to our Scandinavian heritage. She is also one of the most put-together women I know, with never a nail chipped or a hair out of place. This is why it so funny to me that she has Mak as a daughter. Seems like some kind of divine joke that the girliest girl I know, would give birth to the biggest tomboy on two legs.

It's not until Stacie steps back that I notice Isla trying to disappear in the background. Mak is standing right in front of her, with her arms crossed over her little chest and a scowl on her face. *Uh oh*.

"Stace, this is…"

"Isla! I'm so sorry, we're being rude." My sister steps up and pulls the slightly shell shocked Isla in for a hug. "This is my daughter, Makenna, who, as I'm sure you've picked up on, prefers to be called *Mak*." She grabs Isla's hand and tugs her into the living room. I follow behind, hooking my arm around Mak's neck and giving her a noogie, while dragging her with me.

"She's your girlfriend?" Mak asks, when I drop her on the couch, as Stacie and Isla disappear into the kitchen.

"She is," I confirm, following Mak's suspicious gaze in Isla's direction.

"She looks like a tomboy," Mak observes and I chuckle.

"She is that, too," I admit and she turns her gaze to me. "It's part of what I like about her. She likes to ride on her four-wheeler and can build the best campfires." I see interest spark on my niece's expressive face. "She's a photographer and can cook the best meatloaf you've ever tasted."

"Lucky," she whispers with a wink. Our little secret; my sister is not a particularly talented cook, and she insists on making me meatloaf. My favorite. It is, but not Stacie's version. I just don't have the heart to tell her.

"What are we having for dinner?" I whisper back, leaning conspiratorially close to Mak.

"I thought we could order in," Stacie's voice sounds behind me. I roll my eyes and blow out my relief, making Mak giggle. "I'll be in the kitchen most of tomorrow," she adds by way of explanation.

Overcome by hilarity, my niece rolls off the couch, and I can barely keep a straight face at her antics.

"What?" Stacie wants to know, her eyes suspicious slits.

"I can help you cook," Isla offers innocently, looking from one to the other.

-

How I got roped into this, I have no idea.

Fucking Ikea, on Black Friday. If man invented hell, it would look like this.

I can barely keep track of Isla and my sister, who are somewhere in front of me, amid the throng of shoppers looking for the best sales. I have Mak's hand in mine, and despite her dislike for girly things, she's got the shopping thing down pat. She yanks me to a stop at every new display we pass to check out a fluffy throw, or shiny bauble, along this torturous maze of fake rooms.

The girls insisted I come, arguing that if I was going to sleep on it, I needed to be there to test the mattresses.

Oh, and they needed the muscle. Apparently Ikea is carry-out. My point that no mattress worth spending time on would be able to fit in the Toyota, fell on deaf ears. I was told, in no uncertain terms, the Swedes make the best beds. Whatever. After a day of overindulgence in alcohol and food—which, thanks to Isla's assistance in the kitchen, had all been tasty—I'd been too tired to object too much.

I'm regretting my easy capitulation now.

"There they are," Mak chirps, as we round yet another corner of the maze, finding my sister and Isla in the middle of a sea of beds.

"Ben," Isla calls, waving me over. "This is the one I was looking at online, remember?" She points at a bed that to me looks like any other. As for remembering, I've got nothing. She's pointed out things to me for weeks, and I've smiled and nodded to make her happy, but even a photographic memory wouldn't have helped me recall it all. Or any.

I don't mind the bed, with a plain dark gray fabric headboard and simple lines. And I like the fact that it doesn't require a fucking ladder to get into.

Mak lets go of my hand and hops on.

"It's comfy," she concludes, patting the mattress beside her in invitation.

"It's too small," I say as I lie down beside her, trying not to think about how many bodies have been on here before me.

"They have it king-sized as well," my sister, ever practical, points out as she flips through the catalogue she's been toting around.

I have to admit, I much prefer this construction of

wooden slats and firm mattress to the often too soft and ridiculously high box spring sets.

"You try, Isla," Mak offers, getting up to make room.

She's warmed up to Isla quite a bit. Especially after tasting the turkey yesterday afternoon, knowing full well we'd be chewing on turkey jerky if my sister had been left to her own devices. For dessert, my girl had whipped up that awesome cheesecake she made me once before, and if the turkey hadn't done it yet, for sure that would've won my niece's approval.

Isla lies down beside me, her hand searching for mine on the mattress.

"What do you think?"

I turn my head to look at her. "I like it," I let on. "I'm just not sure about this whole carry-out thing. We still have a dog to pick up," I remind her, whispering so only Isla hears. We haven't mentioned anything about Atsa yet, hoping to keep it a surprise for Mak and a tease for Stacie, when the two come up for Christmas.

"It'll fit." She smiles confidently.

And it does, as I find out another hour and a half later. Although with Stacie and Mak in the backseat, the only way to fit it is with the gate open and everything tied down. They roll their damn mattresses up and vacu-seal those suckers. Still, even with the backseats down, the boxes with the bed, which apparently will require *some* assembly, as well as the rolled up mattress, it will be too long for the gate to close.

Not looking forward to driving home with an eye on my rearview mirror, to make sure I don't lose my load, I make our next stop a trailer place, right off the interstate. I tell myself, and convince Isla, it'll be handy hauling stuff around the campground, like picnic tables and garbage bins. Luckily, I had the foresight to have a trailer hitch installed on the Land Cruiser.

I feel much better when I turn onto the road, everything properly loaded and tied down in the new utility trailer, instead of hanging half out of the back gate of the SUV.

"That's so cool, Uncle Ben," Mak pipes up behind me. "You've got room for more stuff now." My face must show my feelings on that because both Stacie and Isla start laughing.

"No way. Anything else we get delivered." I shut that down right away, ignoring the lingering chuckles from the women.

Isla

"Poor baby."

We left early this morning after an exhausting but fun weekend of food, bonding, and shopping. Ben's sister is amazing. I have to admit; I hadn't known what to think when I first saw her. I was a little intimidated to say the least. I mean, not only is she a lawyer and does super important work, but also she looks like she just stepped out of a magazine. I might have turned on my heels and beelined it out of there, if Mak hadn't picked that moment to come barreling out of the house, throwing herself without abandon into Ben's waiting arms.

The contrast between Stacie and her daughter was startling. If I hadn't seen the obvious affection between the two, I would've ventured to guess these were some volatile teenage years coming up. As it is, I'm sure Mak will give Stacie a run for her money, but at least there will be a solid love at the base of it.

Ironically, Ben's sister was immediately warm and accepting of me, whereas Mak, whose appearance and unconventional demeanor is more like me, was obviously reluctant. Having observed her with Ben all weekend, I understand why. He's amazing with her. By the time we said goodbye this morning, a still sleepy Mak had wrapped herself around me, with arms and legs clinging like a monkey, as I'd seen her do with Ben, just days before.

"I don't want you to go," she'd mumbled in my neck. It made me emotional and I had to swallow a lump as I looked over her shoulder at Ben, who just smiled.

"Three weeks, honey. Just three short weeks and Christmas break starts. You'll love it up there. We can go ride the four-wheelers through the woods, and build campfires every night. Have you ever had s'mores?" I prattled along, reminding her of the plans we'd made this weekend, while Stacie tried to dislodge her daughter from my body. "You'll have to find your mom some jeans to wear, though," I tease. "I wouldn't recommend the pencil skirt and heels when we go cut down our Christmas tree." With a giggle Mak finally let go of my neck.

The drive had been easy. Not many folks on the road at seven on a Sunday morning, but Ben had insisted on an early start, reminding me quietly that we would have a stop to make, and that he had a bed to put together this afternoon.

"You poor, poor baby," I mutter again, wrapping my

arms around poor Atsa's neck, to which a large white cone had been attached. "Does he have to wear this thing?" I ask the woman who brought him out of the kennel.

"He was licking the incision and we can't keep a constant eye on him here. The worry is the closing of the wound, which goes fast when he doesn't lick it open. His stitches are dissolvable, so those you don't have to worry about, but unless you can keep an eye on him, I suggest keeping that cone on for a few more days."

Atsa seems only a little more subdued than he had been a few days ago and happily trots to the car, alongside Ben, on his new leash. It was Ben's suggestion to stop at a Walmart before heading to the shelter, to pick up some necessities. Food bowls, leash, toys, giant dog bed, and a gigantic bag of food, recommended by the shelter. All of it packed in the back of the car.

"Aren't you glad we got that trailer?" Ben teases me, as he bends down to lift Atsa into the backseat.

"If I recall correctly," I point out. "That was originally your sister's idea. One that you yourself laughed at, at the time."

"Renting one is laughable," he defends himself. "Buying makes sense."

I just roll my eyes when I get into the Land Cruiser, twisting in my seat to see the dog rolled up on the backseat, comfortable as can be.

"Ready to go home? Sleep in your new bed tonight?" Atsa's ears perk up at my chatter, but as soon as I'm quiet, his eyes close.

"Give the pooch a break." Ben climbs in behind the wheel. "He just had his balls removed," he whispers dramatically, and I snicker at the expression of horror on his face. "Still don't know how I had you women talk me into that." It's true, it had taken both the volunteer at the shelter and myself to convince Ben it was the best thing for everyone. He clearly was still not entirely on board, but it's too late now.

"Can we stop at Jen's?" I ask him when we're close to Dolores. "I'm really craving one of her lattes."

The dog has been sleeping most of the way. I'm happy he clearly doesn't mind car rides. He doesn't even wake up when Ben pulls up outside of The Pony Express. Cranking the window open a bit, we leave Atsa in the car and head inside.

"Look at you guys!" Jen calls out when we walk in the door. "Have a look," she says, smiling as she gestures at the gallery wall, which is almost empty. Again.

"Seriously?" I blurt out. "Where are all these people coming from?"

"We had a busy weekend here," she says. "Families coming in from out of town. Weekend travelers passing through. There was even someone who had seen your display at Colorado In View and wanted to see more, so Ryan sent her here."

"That's great," Ben rumbles behind me. "I'm thinking maybe you should consider upping your prices a little," he suggests.

"Yes," Jen agrees readily. "Twenty-five percent on top. That's what I'd do." Ben nods in agreement when I turn around to gauge his reaction.

It's hard, figuring out what your work is worth. I never really thought I'd be in the position to consider pricing on any of my pictures, but here I am.

"Okay," I give in. "But only on new material. No

changing price tags on what's already out there. And I want to do that book, in the spring."

"Sounds like a plan to me," Jen is of the same mind. "Now, what can I make you?"

With our orders in, she works that machine of hers while we catch up on each other's Thanksgiving. Jen's apparently was spent visiting her elderly mother in Cortez and keeping the coffee shop going. A little depressing, but when I told her about the dog, she insisted on coming outside to meet him.

"He's beautiful," she coos, reaching into the cone to scratch behind his ears. Something he clearly enjoys, judging by the way his eyelids droop down and his tongue lazily licks the inside of her arm. "Next time, I'll make sure I have treats for you." She straightens up as Ben takes Atsa for a pee, off to the side of the parking lot. "That's weird?" she says, looking over my shoulder, but I don't notice anything.

"What?" I ask, turning back around.

"I could've sworn that car that just came out of the road up to your place, is the same car that woman was driving," she mutters, almost to herself.

"What woman?" Ben asks, as he lifts the dog back in the car.

"The one Ryan sent over. She bought a second print from here. The night sky over the reservoir. She was asking directions to get to the reservoir, just the other day." Jen shakes her head sharply.

"What kind of car?" Ben asks.

"A white Chrysler sedan, looked new."

Ben slowly looks around him and points at a car in the parking lot next door. "Like that one?" Jen nods.

"I think so."

"And what about that one?" He points out another similar car across the road at the gas station.

"Right," Jen says grudgingly. "Point made. Guess she just gave me the willies."

"The customer?"

"Yeah." She nods at me. "Seemed a bit intense. Maybe it was me. I'm tired. I need a break."

I lean into the car to set my latte in the cup holder, before turning back to Jen and wrapping her in a hug.

"Then you take a break," I instruct her. "Let me know if there's anything I can do in the meantime. We'll have you up soon for dinner. As soon as we have our furniture."

"I'd like that," she says, smiling as I climb into my seat.

I'm about to close the door when Ben, who was already behind the wheel leans over me and calls out to Jen, who is walking away.

"Hey, Jen? You mentioned something about it being the second print she bought? What was the first one?"

"Oh, that was one of the ones at Colorado In View. The one with you taking in the view from the rock."

CHAPTER 15

Ben

"Do me a favor?" I ask Isla. "Stay in the car."

I'm not sure what made me ask Jen about the picture, but something was nagging at me. When she mentioned the picture of me, that unsettled feeling only grew. I suddenly felt the need to get up the mountain quickly.

"What's going on?" she asks me, a hint of worry on her face.

"I just want to have a quick look," I tell her, pulling the gun from under my seat, where I'd stored it. Isla's eyes go big, but before she can object I lean in for a kiss. "Just professional paranoia. Lock the doors." I close the door and wait until I hear the click of the central lock engage before I turn to the house, glancing sideways at the tracks I spotted in the dirt when we drove up to the house.

I smell it the moment I unlock the door and push it open. *Urine*. The heavy pungent odor clinging to the air particles and masking any remaining paint fumes that may have lingered. To my left, the door to the laundry room stands open. A door I'm pretty sure I closed before leaving the house on Wednesday. I slip inside and notice a smudge on top of the dryer. Part of a shoe print. My eyes immediately fly up to the window, which appears to be closed. On closer inspection, I notice the safety bar that braces the slider in place, is not engaged. I'm trying to remember if I'd checked the window closely enough on leaving. Apparently not. Complacency is a dangerous thing; I should know that. I've lived on the edge and vigilant most of my adult life. It was simply a matter of survival. Somewhere in the past couple of months, though, I've clearly become too relaxed.

I click the safety bar in place and move slowly past the kitchen on my right. Nothing appears out of place there, but when I move further down the hall along the back of the great room, the smell of piss gets stronger. A quick peek into the smaller bedrooms reveals nothing, and I know in my gut whatever I'll find will be in the master suite. I almost have to gasp for air when I step into the bedroom. In the midday sun, it is easy to see the wet marks on the new floor and the freshly painted walls. Everywhere. Like someone took a hose to it. The stains go as high up as the ceiling.

I don't want to walk through the mess in here, but I have no choice, it's the only way into the bathroom and something draws me in that direction.

REMEMBER THIS COLOR ?
LOOKED BEST AROUND YOUR COCK !

The deep red writing on the mirror stirs a memory, as does the silver lipstick lying on the wet counter. Everything in here is sprayed as well. A woman. Most definitely a woman. I pull my phone out of my back pocket.

"Damian? I've got a problem."

-

"But why can't I see?"

Isla hasn't let up since I drove us down to the trailer.

The poor dog is barely able to move in here, but he seems to have settled in on our bed. It's Isla who is restless.

"Not much to see. We've got to wait for law enforcement do their thing first," I tell her again. That wasn't necessarily my choice, but Damian insisted I back the fuck out of the house and handle this by the rules.

"Sorry man," he'd said on the phone earlier. "Things have been nuts here and what with Thanksgiving and everything, we haven't really had a chance to look at those emails yet. Think it's the same chick?"

"Hope to fuck so," I told him. "One is enough."

"Any thoughts on who it might be? Names?"

Truth is, I hadn't until I saw that message today. A woman I'd associated with during the course of an investigation about ten, maybe twelve years, ago. A club owner in Tulsa, with ties to a Columbian drug lord, was suspected of using his exclusive club for more than just pussy. The woman was one of the bartenders and provided an easy way in for me. I remembered the club was called *Orquidea*, and the girl…

"Jahnee." The name finally came to me.

"How do I spell that?"

I told him everything I remembered, which wasn't necessarily a whole lot. My interest had only been access to the club, which I accomplished by fucking her a few times, not sharing life histories with her. I don't even remember her last name. Not something I'm proud of, and certainly not information I want to share with Isla.

"Just please tell me there weren't dead animals in there or something."

Isla's worried voice drags me back to the present. I guess not giving her details, so I don't upset her, only sends her imagination in overdrive. I reach over and pull her to me.

"No, nothing dead. Someone came in through the laundry room window and vandalized the master suite," I explain, stroking my hand over her head, hoping it's enough.

"Vandalized how?" she demands to know, tilting her head back to look me in the eye. "Holes in the wall? Windows broken? What?" The deep sigh slips out before I can check it. *Not enough then.*

"Nothing broken, and nothing that we can't get rid of with a good scrubbing—urine." Her confusion is visible on her face. "And lipstick," I add, and that gets her attention. Her eyes close to slits and her perfect lips press into a straight line.

"A *woman*," Isla hisses, pulling from my hold. She turns around, braces herself on the small sink, and drops her head down.

I've got to admit, I'm at a bit of a loss what to expect here, so I settle for putting a hand on her back.

"That woman!" she yells, as she swings around, knocking my hand away. I take a cautionary step back and watch as my little pixie changes into a snarling fury. "What was the message?" she spits out, catching me of guard. "Oh, don't look so surprised, it's not quantum physics. It's clear what she's trying to do."

Isla doesn't even blink when I tell her what's written on the bathroom mirror.

"God, how cliché," she mutters dismissively.

The next moment, I hear the crunch of tires on the

path—the cavalry has arrived.

═══════════════ ∞ ═══════════════

Isla

The sound of the approaching car has got Atsa up and off the bed in a flash.

I barely manage to grab him by the collar as he tries to squeeze by Ben, when he steps out of the trailer.

"Not without a leash, buddy." I grab my coat where I tossed it on the couch and find his leash underneath. The dog is at the door, his nose pressing against the seal, and a low growl coming from his throat. "Easy, puppy," I whisper at him, as I clip the lead to his collar and take it in a strong grip before opening the door.

Good thing too, since his head is already pushing through the narrow opening.

"Hold on, boy."

Outside, Ben is talking to a tall, lanky man in uniform. Both heads turn my way, as I struggle to control the dog, and all conversation stills. That pisses me off.

"What's the plan?" I snap, inserting myself in whatever it is they were discussing.

"Isla," Ben mumbles, his voice low and warning, before he sighs and indicates the other man. "This is Drew Carmel, Montezuma County Sheriff. Sheriff, this is Isla Ferris."

"Sorry to meet under these circumstances." The man offers his hand, which Atsa doesn't seem to approve of, if his low guttural growl is any indication.

"It's okay," I tell the dog as I take the handshake. "Sheriff." I nod with a tight smile. "Now, what was I interrupting?" I push, when neither man gives any indication of volunteering any information.

"I was just about to head up to the house and wait for my deputy," Sheriff Carmel says with a nod, and quickly retreats to his patrol car, leaving Ben and I to watch him drive away.

"You scared him off."

I whip around, my temper flaring.

"I don't care," I snap, fired up. I don't give a shit if I'm being unreasonable. "Why is it, I get the feeling that even after I had to drag what little information I have out of you, I still get the sense you're holding back? Oh, wait, maybe it's because the big boys stop whispering the moment I'm within earshot?" Ben opens his mouth to speak, but I flick my hand in front of his face to cut him off. I'm on a rant. "I had plans, Ben. Plans that involved that big new bathtub up there, and our new king-sized bed, in our brand-spanking new house. I'm tired, and I'm pi-hi...pissed," I sob, hysteria finally catching up with me.

I hate feeling out of control.

I hate that there may be things I don't know about Ben.

I hate thinking it means something when he tries to hide things.

I hate feeling unhinged.

More than anything else, I hate that someone is messing with a really, really good fucking thing.

Ben

I'm clearly clueless as to how this works.

The one thing I was trying to avoid, is the one thing I managed to accomplish; upset Isla. *Shit*—and not just a little. Who knew that anger and tears go together? I sure as fuck didn't.

So I stop thinking and do what comes naturally; wrap her in my arms and in a hushed voice start talking.

"I think her name is Jahnee..." I start, and proceed to tell her exactly what I told Damian and Sheriff Carmel, holding nothing back this time.

By the time I'm done, her sniffles have slowed down, and she takes a swipe at her nose with her sleeve.

"How did you leave it with her?" she asks.

"Not sure what you mean."

"How did you end the relationship? Was it amicable? Was she upset?"

"Babe, there was no relationship," I point out. "I got the information we needed, we shut down the operation, and I moved on to the next assignment." That earns me a punch to my shoulder.

"But did she know that? You just disappeared without a word, didn't you? And clearly that message didn't get across if she still carries a torch," Isla mumbles those last words, shaking her head. "Although she has a weird way of showing it."

I did disappear without a word. I never told her my real name. I think I was Brent Kaiser for that one. I used that alias a few times. My focus was always on getting the job done, by whatever means necessary, and I didn't spend a lot of time worrying about the players—or the innocent bystanders. At least not until my last assignment brought me to McPhee Reservoir. And Isla.

-

The sun is going down by the time the police cars finally leave and I lock up the house. We'll deal with the mess tomorrow.

Isla is on her way back down to the trailer. She came up with me when the evidence technician arrived. We'd left Atsa in the trailer and he was making a ruckus, wanting to tag along. I was surprised Isla was more curious than anything else.

She'd brought her camera and offered to take pictures of anything worth noting. I ended up simply observing, as Isla tagged along behind the other woman as they moved from laundry room, to bedroom, and finally into the bathroom. By then Isla was so focused on getting the exact shots the tech asked for, she barely seemed to register the message.

I watch from the rock as she parks the ATV and opens the trailer door, removing the cumbersome collar from an excited Atsa, before letting him run free. Young as he is, he already seems protective of her. He was leery of the sheriff and seemed restless with the arrival of the other cars. He hasn't even had a chance to get used to all the sounds and smells. Despite his obvious excitement, he doesn't seem to venture very far from Isla as she walks down toward the water's edge, returning to her side before loping off to investigate another trail his nose picks up.

I'm covering the utility trailer, which is still housing the bed, with a tarp, when they come back from their walk.

"There should be bleach in the shed on the shelves,"

she says, holding down the corner as I pull the strap tight. "Come hell or high water, tomorrow night I want my bath, and my bed." I look up and smile at the determined look on her face.

"Damn right," I confirm, earning a little smile back.

"Sandwiches okay?" she asks over her shoulder, as she walks to the trailer, slapping her thigh to call the dog.

"Sounds good to me."

With the tarp tied down, I head into the shed to look for the bleach. Two bottles are sitting on the supply shelves and I pull them down. I grab some other things I think we might need, along with a couple of buckets, and set them close to the door so it's easy to pick up tomorrow. Then I pull out my phone and dial Damian.

"And?"

"They just left."

"How's your girl doing?"

"Good, all things considering. Surprisingly well, actually." Damian chuckles at that.

"She doesn't seem the type to suck her thumb in a corner," he offers.

"Not exactly. So have you had any luck?"

Damian was going to try and see what he could find out about the woman, with only her first name and her place of employment, give or take a decade ago.

"You'd think with a name spelled like that, there wouldn't be many around," he complains. "Two hundred and thirteen popped up in the system. Can you believe it? That's only the ones who've been witness to or perpetrated a crime. You can always check with your old boss, see if the DEA is willing to share what they have."

I know they'd have a record. I also know that my old

boss didn't always agree on the way I got the job done. After Isla's reaction earlier, I'm starting to see why.

"I will, if you can't dig anything up," I concede.

"Now what about security? Gus Flemming is right there, maybe twenty minutes away, if you decide you need some help."

"Appreciated. I think we'll be okay. Just a middle-aged woman on a rampage, right? We should be able to manage," I jokingly assure him.

I don't let on that this whole situation unnerves me.

I close the shed door and look around the deserted campground, the only light from the two street lamps on the other side of the gate, and that coming through the windows of the trailer.

It's silent, without the sound of frogs at the edge of the water, or the lowing of the cattle grazing the mountain in the summer. The hair on the back of my neck stands up, but nothing is moving.

The noise of the tap running inside the trailer pulls me from my trance. I head inside, where the dog lifts his head from his perch on the couch, and the woman looks up from the plate to greet me with a smile.

Home isn't a place.

CHAPTER 16

Isla

"That one goes in the great room."

I point the delivery guy in the right direction. This is the third delivery today. The huge horseshoe-shaped sectional couch was delivered this morning, along with the twin dressers and nightstands we picked from the same place in Albuquerque. Those were in a spare bedroom for now. The second delivery of furniture was a collection of smaller items: stools, bookshelves, and a desk and chair for the office, as well as some high-end pots and pans I can't wait to put to use.

This last one is the one I know Ben's been waiting for; the big screen TV. We don't have cable up here, but apparently Ben knows a guy who installs satellite, and he's scheduled to come in sometime this week.

"I have years of football to catch up on," he said with a grin, making me groan out loud.

We scrubbed everything yesterday. More than once, but the smell still lingered. Ben insisted he wasn't going to have me sleep in the stench of his old life. I was going to argue, but when I saw his face, I decided against it. This morning he was already here, scrubbing the floor again, by the time I walked up with Atsa.

Now the windows are open in the master suite, to get rid of the chlorine fumes, and Ben is out with the dog to find some firewood for the fireplace that bisects the large picture windows.

I close the door behind the delivery guy, who left the huge box propped against the wall, and head back to the kitchen, where I was washing the new plates and glassware that were packed in the trailer with the bed. The new pots are already done and hanging from the massive pot rack, dangling over the island.

For now, we're going to make do with stools at the counter, instead of a dining room table, because Ben really wants to make one. I worry a bit, with all the projects he's got lined up, that he'll get bored when he runs out of things to do. Is he worried about that?

"Hang on, boy." I can hear Ben mutter to the dog when they come in. "Let me clean your paws."

Makes me smile. Yesterday he'd laughed when I put an old towel by the door for Atsa's muddy or wet feet. Today he's using it without prompting. And they say you can't teach an old dog new tricks.

"I've got some deadwood that needs cutting, but I don't want to do it with the dog outside," Ben says, walking into the kitchen stocking footed. He gives my neck a kiss in passing, before opening the double door refrigerator and pulling out a beer. "The TV's here?"

"Just arrived."

I watch as he grabs his bottle and goes straight for the big box. I sigh when I think about the boxes holding the pieces of our bed in the master suite.

I dry and put away the last of the glassware and head down the hallway to our bedroom, leaving Ben to play with his new toy. I don't need him to put together a bed.

-

"I'm putting that together," Ben says twenty minutes

later, when he finds me sitting on the bedroom floor, boxes opened all around me, reading the instructions carefully. "And we don't need this." He plucks the sheet of paper from my hands and tosses it over his shoulder. Then he hands me my phone. "You've got it on vibrate. I found it almost buzzing off the kitchen counter. It's Al, I just missed him."

"You sure you can manage?" I ask him, taking the phone and scrambling to my feet. I know I'm poking the bear, but it's fun to see his eyes narrow on me. "I mean, I did already read the instructions and all."

"Out," he growls, which I ignore as I lift on tiptoes and kiss his scruffy jaw.

"If you're sure..."

"Pixie."

"Oh, okay. I'll just give Uncle Al a call then."

"That'd be good."

I'm already dialing as I walk inside the great room. I sink down on the new couch and feast my eyes on the view.

"How's my girl?" my uncle's smiling voice answers.

"I'm good. No, I'm great." I correct myself, smiling at his voice.

"How's that boy treating you?" I roll my eyes. My uncle never fails to call the big, husky man, currently wrestling our new bed, a boy.

"Uncle Al..." I chastise, as I always do and Al just chuckles.

"Gotta ask, girl. Especially since I've gotta call six times before you even give me a ring back."

"I'm sorry. Left the phone on the counter. I was working in the kitchen earlier."

"So how's the house coming along?"

I feel bad for my uncle. This was originally his idea, and he hasn't had a chance to see any of it yet, except through pictures.

"It's mostly done, just some cosmetic stuff now. We had some...a delay, but we're back on track now." I feel guilty not telling my uncle about the recent events, but he's had his hands full with Ginnie, whose health hasn't been great. That's the reason he hasn't been down yet, he didn't want to leave and then have something happen to her.

"How's Ginnie?"

"Much better," he chuckles after a brief pause. "For sure, I thought that was it for her, but that woman is indestructible. She doesn't know me at all anymore, after this last episode, though. Keeps asking me who I am. Every day I walk in, hoping I'll see some recognition, and she smiles pleasantly enough, but it's no different when she greets anyone else."

My heart is heavy for my uncle. Already he's had to say goodbye to one wife, and although Ginnie is apparently hanging in physically, it sounds like her mind is long gone, along with all their memories. It's heartbreaking.

"That's tough, honey," I say softly, knowing he won't want the tears filling my eyes anyway, or the words of sympathy I'm feeling.

"Yeah, kid. Tough is right. But she's happy, you know? She giggles at everything and her hands are always busy, she hasn't forgotten the knitting."

"Crocheting, Uncle Al," I gently correct him. Ginnie hated knitting, but always had a crocheting project in her purse she could pull out anywhere, like others carry rosary beads or something.

"Same damn thing," he responds, the same way he's done many times before, and it makes me smile. So much has changed, but when you look at the details, so little is different.

"So I'm thinking," he says casually. "Maybe I'll come down for a visit at some point, now that things with Ginnie have settled down. I'll stay at that Dolores Mountain Inn, always wanted to see what that's like."

"Nonsense," I interrupt. "We've got room. I won't have you staying anywhere else."

"Stubborn," I hear him mumble over the phone.

"I learned from the best," I fire back, making him laugh. "Look, how about getting away for Christmas? Or would you prefer to stay with Ginnie during the holidays?" He's quiet for a minute before he answers.

"I was dreading Christmas, to be honest," he says, the struggle with his emotions evident in his voice. "Last year she was still mostly there. We made some good memories. The thought of sitting across from someone I still love with all my heart, who has no idea who I am, or what Christmas is, is not something I want to have as my last memory."

"Understood." I struggle to swallow down the ache I feel at hearing his pain. "Come as soon as you feel you can get away," I forge on, not lingering on the sadness, which I know my uncle won't want. "You'll like the trailer we got from your old buddy here. It needs some work, though."

"Yeah? How's Phil? Did he try to shoot you off his property?" It's good to hear his chuckle. It'll be good for him to come and see his old buddies.

"It was close," I joke, glad to hear my uncle's mood lifted.

By the time I end the call, he's all geared up for his visit and excited to take Ben's niece exploring, like he used to do with me when I was a kid.

In the laundry room, I empty the dryer and quickly fold all the new bath towels on the nifty, fold-down shelf Ben apparently installed. It doubles as an ironing board. There are more dandy little touches he's added. A shallow knife drawer, right beside the stove. A drop down spice rack, underneath the upper cabinet. And in one of the bedrooms, he reconfigured the closet with storage slots for office supplies on the inside of the door.

One of the things I enjoyed about living in the trailer was the practical use of every nook and cranny. Everything had its place. Ben has brought a little of that into our new house.

With the stack of towels in my arms, I walk into the master bedroom, finding Ben sitting on the floor, in the middle of the bedframe, looking a bit confused at two large pieces of wood still lying unused, beside the rolls of slats, on the far side of the room. I struggle not to chuckle as I walk by, as if nothing is wrong, and quickly put away the towels in the bathroom.

"Looks good." I press my lips together and lean quasi-casually against the doorframe. From the slightly stormy look Ben sends me, I know he knows I'm laughing inside.

"We're gonna have to send this back. There's something wrong with it," he grumbles, waving his hand around.

Atsa, who was sleeping in his bed in the great room

earlier, saunters into the room, and nudges his big head against my knee.

"Need to go out, buddy?" From the enthusiastic wagging of his tail, I deduct he likes the sound of that. We haven't really let him go off alone without one of us being outside.

"I'll take him," Ben offers, pushing up off the floor. "I need a break before I take this piece of shit apart and ship it back. Son of a bitch," he swears under his breath as he walks out of the room, taking Atsa with him. Right before I hear the front door slam, he has one parting thought.

"But we're keeping that goddamn mattress!"

―――――― ⦵⦵⦵ ――――――

Ben

"Let's go, Atsa! I'm freezing."

My face is numb with the wind coming up off the water. The temperature is well below freezing, and I can see the system they were warning about coming in from the west. Eight to ten inches of snow expected at higher elevations. A bit early, not even quite December, but anything is possible in the mountains.

"Atsa!"

Some stumbling in the underbrush, and out comes the dog, trying to drag half a tree trunk with him.

"Buddy, that's not a stick." I chuckle when he proudly drops the thing and stands over it, looking mighty pleased with himself. I have to stop him when he makes a move to drag it toward the house. "You've got toys inside. Sticks are for outside."

We make it inside, me with a hand on his collar, while he struggles the entire way. I leave him whimpering at the door to kick off my boots and hang my coat. In the kitchen, I grab his bowl and fill it with kibble. In two seconds he's there, his tongue lolling and the tree trunk forgotten.

With the dog inhaling his food, and my mind a little clearer, I head back to the bedroom, determined to have another go at that frame. Maybe I'll have a quick peek at the instructions. I stop right inside the doorway.

"Come lie down with me." Isla smiles and pats the mattress next to her. "Help me flatten it." She's talking about the mattress. The mattress that is on the bed, that now looks to be complete. I throw a quick glance around the room. Nothing left. Not a single piece of wood, screw, bolt, or nut is left on the floor.

Isla's soft snicker draws my eyes back to her. On the bed, casually waving the instruction sheet between her fingers. *Fuck me*.

"I hate Ikea," I mutter, as I drop down on the mattress beside her. "But I love you." I reach over and pull her giggling on top.

"Ditto," she says, propping her chin on her hands folded on my chest. "On the second part, because I love Ikea, too."

"Whatever," I gripe, lifting my head to kiss her.

"You've got a cold nose."

"It's colder than a witch's tit out there," I inform her, rolling her off me, and swinging my feet to the floor. "I should build a fire. Grab some of the smaller pieces for tonight. I'll chop the rest tomorrow."

"You know we still have about half a cord left behind the trailer, right?" she points out, lying on her side propped up on her elbow. "Chopped and ready to go."

"Not the same," I tell her. "I'll need to chop a lot of wood to make up for my loss of manhood over this damn piece of Ikea crap." The peal of her laughter follows me all the way to the front door.

-

I check one last time, to make sure I have the flue open, before I strike a match to the kindling. Sitting back on my heels, I watch as the small flame slowly licks around the dry wood.

In the end, I drove down to raid the woodpile behind the trailer anyway. Whatever I'd dragged from the woods was either too big or too wet.

The chassis of the old truck almost hit some of the dips and bumps on the gravel path of the campground, with the load of the snow blade in front and the wood piled in the back weighing it down. I'd need a wheelbarrow to haul the rest of the wood onto the small overhang by the door, but for now, I just brought what I could carry.

The dog lifts his head when a piece of dry wood snaps in the flames, only to drop it back to his paws, his eyes already closing again. Isla's humming something in the kitchen as she throws together some dinner, and I grab an old paperback I found at the bottom of my duffel bag when I was unpacking.

Reading. For years it had been the only thing I could occasionally lose myself in, until it eventually became more about the exercise than it did the pleasure.

Now I want to read because I feel like it.

"Want to watch something on Netflix on my laptop?" Isla asks after dinner. Whatever Internet hookup she had at the trailer via HughesNet, works up here as well.

"Like what?" I ask, making room beside me on the couch.

"Have you ever seen *The Shining*?" she asks, spotting my old Stephen King book on the couch.

"If I have, I can't remember. I'm pretty sure I've read the book," I confess.

"Oh, you'd remember," she says, smiling. "You'll love it. It's all about this snowed in place up in the mountains. Jack Nicholson? I love him."

I listen to her rattle on about Jack Nicholson and what movies he was in, while she logs into her Netflix account on the laptop. From what I know about Jack Nicholson, he's a bit of an asshole.

The movie is pretty good. Especially since it would seem Isla is a bit jumpy and thus is plastered against me during most of it.

Just as Jack is trying to prove he's not a dull boy, by chopping down a bathroom door, a notification pops up on the screen, startling both of us. Without thinking, I reach over and click on it. Isla's email opens automatically to the last received message. A grainy image with lettering in the top left hand corner, circled in red.

"That's an ultrasound," Isla says, leaning forward to look closer before I hear her suck in a sharp breath. "Of a baby," she adds. "That woman's name is on there."

I lift the laptop from the table and enlarge the image. It takes me a second to process what I'm looking at, but when it sinks in, it feels like someone hit me upside the head with a sledgehammer.

Kaiser, Jahnee — 30, F
DIAGNOSTIC CENTER
E31579-05-08-31
GA:19w0d   31-08-2005

As if nothing happened.

I'd watched and waited, and then I'd finally got a break. I had to show her, she couldn't claim what was already mine. But now it looks like the message didn't get across.

Delivery trucks going up and coming down, but no sign of Brent, or that bitch. I don't understand. He'd know by now it's me. Surely there's no way he can stay with her when he knows I'm out here. His.

He's blinded by her.

Not even the decency to put drapes up. Cozy as can be, with her filthy hands all over him. The whole world can look in as she buries her face in his chest—MY chest—and he ruffles her hair with a smile.

That touch is mine.

That smile is mine.

Time to remind him for once and for all.

CHAPTER 17

Isla

I've never seen blood literally drain from someone's face before.

Ben's face is white, his jaw slack, and the sight of that scares me more than anything else ever has.

"*Jesus,*" he finally mutters, shoving the laptop aside and jumping to his feet. "*Son of a motherfucking bitch!*"

That's a bit louder and has the dog up, growling low. When it is followed by a fist through the newly painted wall to the hallway, Atsa barks sharply.

"Ben! What the fuck?"

I rush up behind him, and just manage to grab his arm on the backswing, when he reels back to punch another hole in the wall. Jerking his arm free, he swings around, making me jump back with my hands up defensively. Atsa slips between us, the hackles on his back up, and he's whimpering in confusion. I take another step back for some breathing room. Not that I'm scared of Ben, but I've never seen him actually angry before. Even when those drug peddlers threatened to hurt me, he never lost control.

"Christ, Pixie," he whispers in a pained voice, before looking down at the dog. I follow his gaze to his hand, which is dripping blood on the floor.

"You're bleeding," I point out the obvious, just because I don't really know what else to say. I'm as confused as the dog is. One minutes we're cuddled up on the couch, watching a movie, on our first night in the new house, all mellow and relaxed, and the next I've got a hole in the wall and a man who's bleeding.

Since my brain can't quite process it all, I do what seems like the first course of action: stop the bleeding. It's at least something I can concentrate on while the world resets itself on its axis.

I nudge aside Atsa, grab Ben's hand, and pull him along into our bathroom, where the first aid kit is shoved under the sink. Ben doesn't say a word, but he doesn't resist either.

I turn on the tap and hold his hand under the stream of water. He must've hit a stud or something, because a nice deep slice runs along the back of his middle finger and hand.

"You're gonna need some stitches," I tell him softly, looking up in the mirror to his reflection behind me. Turmoil, that's what I see on his face. When his eyes focus on mine, I see regret, and that hurts.

"Just tape it up."

While I clean his cut, I feel his body curve around me from behind, his head dropping in the curve of my neck.

"I'm sorry," he murmurs there.

I'm not sure what it means—what he's sorry for—but I have a feeling he's not talking about the hole in the wall, and I'm not about to ask. It doesn't matter how hard I try, I can't ignore the possible significance of that image.

He doesn't say anything else while I bandage his hand the best I can, and neither do I, but it doesn't help; the elephant in the room only grows as we try to ignore it's there.

"Go to bed," Ben finally says, as I clear away the

supplies. "I've got a few calls to make."

I open my mouth to protest, but his single finger raised ever so slightly, has me shut it again.

"I'll clean up," he adds, as he slips past me out of the bathroom.

I go through my nightly routine, trying not to focus on the fact he didn't kiss me, or that I didn't stop him from walking away. By the time I strip off my clothes and pull on my nightshirt, that last thing is bothering me.

I'm not a coward. Just because I might not like what I'm going to hear isn't reason enough to hide under the covers. Ben may not be ready to talk about why his earlier confidence there's no chance of him having a child, is suddenly so clearly wavering—but I am.

I can hear his low voice as I walk down the hall behind the great room. I lean against the opening, watching Ben's back, as he's outlined against the large picture window.

"She used my fucking last name, Damian. The name she knew me by. The dates on the image match. I've sent you the email. There's a file number on the attachment, see what you can come up with." I watch as he runs his fingers through his hair before resting his forehead in his hand. "Something tells me this one is not a fake. I want to know, Damian. If I have a kid out there somewhere, I want to fucking know."

I was right. I don't like what I'm hearing. In fact, it hurts like a sonofabitch. I slip back into the hallway and down to the bedroom, where I slip between the pretty new sheets that don't give me any of the pleasure I thought they might.

I don't sleep. I just lie there, trying to figure out what

is more painful; the possibility Ben has a child with someone else, or the fact that he clearly doesn't trust me enough to talk to me about it.

I'm not sure how long it is before I hear the front door open and close, but it's what finally triggers my tears.

Ben

That's fucked up.

I have so many questions but unless I can find that bitch, I won't have any answers.

Why start off with sending a fake picture? Why send anything at all after eleven fucking years? What does she want? Money? Fuck, all she had to do was let me know I had a kid. This, though? This is messed up.

What's most messed up is the fact that a small part of me was excited at the implications of that ultrasound. A kid. *My* kid. And that made me feel guilty.

Isla...*Jesus*...

You think everything is falling into place, and the road is clear ahead, when a fucking bomb goes off and suddenly you don't know where you are anymore.

I saw her, reflected in the window, when I was talking to Damian earlier. She looked so fucking lost. I wanted to go to her, rescue her, but what if I'm not a life preserver? What if I'm an anchor instead, just pulling her under?

"Come, Atsa," I call out for the dog, who's been a little leery of me since I put my fist through the damn wall. I'll have to fix that tomorrow.

Once inside, he heads straight for the bedroom, where I know he's checking up on Isla. I lock up, flick off the lights, and grab the dog bed along, so he can sleep with us—but on the floor.

She's on her side, her back to the middle of the bed and her body curled tight. Protective. Like she needs protection from me. I forfeit any bedtime routines and instead strip down to my skin, dumping my clothes in a pile and crawl in behind her, carefully molding myself against her back.

"Ben?" Her sleepy voice cracks, as she rolls onto her back and looks at me with eyes that no longer dance like they used to. That's on me. "I thought you left."

"I did. Took the dog out."

"No," she sighs, her eyes swollen with sleep, and the remnant of tears, and puts her small hand in the middle of my chest. "I thought you left…me."

Christ, she's killing me.

"Never," I grunt, cupping her face and pressing my forehead to hers. "Never gonna happen."

"Good," she mumbles, wrapping her arm around my waist and hitching her leg up on my hip, pinning me to the bed.

Everything I wanted to say dries up on my tongue when I hear the small, satisfied sigh from her lips before her breathing evens out with sleep. My thoughts keep me up until at some point, exhaustion wins.

-

The smell of coffee and soft voices wakes me up.

Before I have a chance to fling back the covers, the familiar soft padding of feet comes down the hallway. Isla's smile is tentative when she walks in carrying a mug, and I hate that I'm the cause of it.

"Morning," she says, too brightly. "It's actually almost afternoon. Guess you needed your sleep. Damian is here," she rambles. "He had a meeting in Cortez this morning and thought he'd drop in."

The moment she puts down the mug on the bedside table, I snag her wrist and pull her down on top of me, trapping her body with my arms.

"Love you, Pixie." I watch her eyes well up and before they have a chance to spill anything, I lift my mouth to hers and kiss her hard. "We're gonna talk later," I promise her when I pull back and release my hold on her. "But first I've gotta whiz and have a quick shower."

I smile at her dramatic eye roll. It's a fuckuvalot better than tears. I lift her off me and swing my legs from the bed. "Tell Damian I'll be right there."

"Ben," she hisses, when I slap her butt on the way to the bathroom.

Feeling better with some decent sleep under my belt, an empty bladder, and freshly showered, I walk into the kitchen ten minutes later.

"About bloody time," Damian ribs me.

"Miss me?" I smack the back of his head on my way to the Keurig. I need more coffee for this.

"Fuck no. Missed your girl's cooking though," he smiles, pointing at the empty plate in front of him.

"Yours is staying warm in the oven," Isla says. She's perched on a stool next to Damian, with her laptop open between them.

"I was just telling Isla that my IT specialist is tied up with a case that is heating up, as we speak, but he sent his files to GFI, Gus Flemming's outfit? Neil James is their techie and he's going to have a look at it."

"Is this your way to force my hand with Flemming?" I only half-joke.

"It's not," Damian responds with a serious look on his face. "But GFI isn't bound by the rules and regulations my office is limited by. I can't ask my guy to hack into a healthcare network without a warrant. It's one thing if he bends the rules to get some answers on one of our cases, but for something like this, he and I both could lose our jobs."

"Fuck, man. I'm sorry," I mumble around my first bite of Isla's spicy scrambled eggs and ham, which I just fished from the oven. "I'm so used to working without rules or guidelines, I didn't stop to think." Damian just shakes his head dismissively.

"I asked Neil to meet me here. He'll be putting some tracing software on the laptop and on your phones. He had to pick up a few things."

Atsa, who'd been lying beside Isla's stool suddenly lifted his head and let out a soft woof. More like a *humpf*. The dog clearly takes his cues from us. As agitated as he was last night when I lost it, he's alert, but almost casually so, now. He stretches his big body and walks to stand by the front door.

I have it open before the young guy standing on the other side can even knock.

"Nice place," the guy, who looks like a big kid, waves his arm at the view.

"Thanks," I grumble. "You must be Neil?"

"Neil James," he says, sticking his hand out and when I take it, his grip is sure.

"Ben Gustafson."

"So I hear," he says easily. His eyes, much older than the rest of him, slip over my shoulder.

"And you must be Isla."

I step aside when I feel a hand in my back, and she steps up beside me, her hand out.

"Nice to meet you," she says, smiling hesitantly. "Please come on in."

"Don't mind if I do," the guy says, a big grin on his face as he watches her turn to go in before following behind her.

I just want to rip out his balls, through his throat.

Isla

"Do you have a desktop unit?"

The hunky, blond surfer boy, who is far too pretty to be hiding out behind computer screens and motherboards, also has a voice like silk. Sexy. Not quite the same caliber as Ben's deep rasp, but sexy nonetheless.

"Nope, just the laptop," I answer, only vaguely aware of Ben, who is watching our interaction closely.

"I suggest you get a desktop to run your edits in Photoshop on. It takes up a lot of your disk space on the laptop, which causes it to get sluggish. If you want, I can hook you up with a decent refurbished unit that has enough RAM to support your needs." Neil's smile is shameless as he wiggles an eyebrow at his own blatant innuendo.

I almost laugh out loud when I hear Ben growl, before shooting from his seat, and stepping up behind my stool.

His arm slips possessively around the front of my chest, his hand cupping around my opposite shoulder, as he pulls me into his body.

"Almost done?" Ben snarls at the young pup, who seems to be having a great time rattling the older man's cage.

"I don't like to rush things," Neil drawls, winking at me and effectively taking his life in his own hands. I quickly grab Ben's arm, crossed in front of me. "I'm always thorough," he can't seem to resist adding.

I can't help it; I burst out laughing when I feel Ben go rigid behind me.

"You are incorrigible." I wag my finger at Neil. "And you," I direct at Ben, tilting my head back so I can see the flare of his nostrils. "You need to stand down. Or did you not hear the part where Neil was telling me about his lovely wife?"

"Not to worry," Neil interjects, aiming a grin at Ben. "All done. I'll get out of your hair."

Damian was already gone; he'd left, right after Neil got here, with the promise he'd be in touch. I like Damian. He looks all polished and proper, but underneath there's this whole smoldering Latino passion. The complete opposite of Neil, who could've stepped right out of the movie *Point Break*, looking like Patrick Swayze's younger brother, and is mischievous. A blatant flirt.

"Call me if you need me," he says suggestively, peering around Ben's broad shoulders when he's being ushered out the door.

I'm still chuckling when Ben slams the door and prowls toward me, bracketing me in with his hips between my legs and my back against the counter. The angry scowl on his face just makes me laugh harder. It's a welcome release after a tense day.

Apparently Ben's had enough of my hilarity, because he bends down, lifts me off the stool, and tosses me over his shoulder.

"Hey!" I protest, knowing exactly where he's taking me and what follows. "I thought we were going to talk?"

"Gonna fuck you first—then we can talk," he says, making clear there will be no argument on that.

I'm flipped, rather unceremoniously, on the mattress and Ben doesn't hesitate divesting me of my clothes. Every last thread.

Then he pauses, with his shirt halfway up his torso and his eyes on my body. He pulls the shirt over his head, slowly, much slower than the frantic pace he set earlier.

By the time he steps out of his jeans, I'm squirming on the bed, heated by just the touch of his eyes.

"Correction," he rumbles, sinking down on his knees and pulling my hips toward him.

"First, I'm going to worship you—then I'm going to fuck you. Then we'll talk—much, much later."

CHAPTER 18

Ben

"Aim for the largest part of the body and gently squeeze the trigger."

The loud reverberation of the gun travels and bounces off the mountains around us.

Then it's quiet again. Almost too quiet, the noise absorbed by the blanket of snow that fell yesterday. A good ten inches, not quite the several feet I've been told to expect, but a decent start anyway.

I should be glad things seem to have settled down, but instead it's making me uneasy.

It took Neil a few days to pull the information. The clinic in Tulsa, where the ultrasound was taken, had closed down since, but the files were digitally archived and stored in a central data bank. Harder to access, and apparently a maze of digital information to sort through, but he found her.

Jahnee Kaiser nee Wells, born March 13, 1973, in Amarillo, Texas. Except, there had been no record of any Mr. Kaiser. I could've told him there's no record to be found. Nor would there be a marriage license of such a union, since it never took place.

Bat-shit crazy.

The DEA would have some file on her—at least leading up to our sting in Tulsa—but no need to keep track after.

I'm more interested to find out where the fuck she is

now, I don't really give a shit where she's been. Except to find out what happened to that child she was clearly pregnant with. A kid, which by my calculations, could very well be mine.

Neil dug hard but found no record of any birth. What he did find was that Jahnee sent those emails from different IP addresses. He tried to explain that he knew she was sending from her phone and had a dynamic IP address assigned to her from the server, depending on where she was. The only conclusion he was comfortable drawing was that she'd been in or around Durango for the first one, and somewhere in central Montezuma County for the last one. That's a pretty decent chunk of real estate to cover.

"Can I go again?" Isla turns to me, the gun in her hand aimed at the ground and away from her body, like I instructed. The first time I took her up for target practice, I'd nearly crapped myself when she swung the damn thing toward me, barrel first.

She argued at first, but when I explained that unless she had an adequate alternative to protect herself, I'd have to handcuff her to my side, she relented. This is our third day shooting, and I'm pretty confident she'll be able to pull the trigger under extreme circumstances. I'm not sure what she would hit, hopefully not her own foot, but it would be enough to scare an attacker off.

"One more," I give in. "But then I want to head inside, see if my game is on."

Friday the guy was here installing the satellite and we mounted the TV in the great room. Today is Sunday and I'm ready for some damn NFL.

-

"*Jesus Christ*, Brady—throw the damn ball!"

The fucking guy always hangs on to the ball a little longer than is comfortable, or wise. I don't care if he's the winningest quarterback in the NFL; he likes playing with fire.

"Damn right you got sacked! *Dumbass*."

A soft hand slides down my chest and I lean my head back on the couch. Isla is standing behind me with a grin on her face.

"Should I be worried?" she asks, biting her lip. I'm instantly distracted by her little white teeth, biting into the plump pink flesh. "Ben?"

"About what?" I ask, blinking a few times.

"Your blood pressure, for one," she says sardonically. "My new furniture, for another." Her gaze focuses on the beer bottle I'm still holding clenched in a fist.

I pluck her hand from my chest and press my lips to her palm.

"Not to worry, baby. I'm good." I wink and bend forward to set my bottle on the table. My eyes naturally drift to the big screen, where Gronkowski can barely stay inbounds as he's barreling to the end zone. "Fucking time, too!" I yell at the screen, when I feel the couch depress beside me.

"If this is going to be my life, you better initiate me," Isla says, shrugging her shoulders. "First I want to know why that cutie, who keeps throwing the ball, is wearing the little white apron?"

It's eleven-thirty by the time the last whistle blows and Isla is fast asleep on my lap. Three back-to-back games is a bit much for a novice NFL fan, and Isla gave it her all. If possible, she ended up yelling at the screen louder than me.

Poor Atsa is exhausted too; every time Isla would jump up or raise her voice, he was on his feet and alert, ready to protect her. The dog's protective instinct actually makes me feel better than my Pixie's newfound fascination, with the gun, about leaving them for a couple of hours tomorrow.

It's a surprise for Isla. We've both been going a little stir-crazy up here in the past week. Isla, because I wouldn't let her go into town on her own, and me, because my once legendary patience is at an end. I need to actively do something to flush this crazy chick out or I'll go nuts. Besides, in another week my sister and niece will be here, and I'd feel a whole lot better if we have this woman located by then.

When I called her Uncle Al two days ago, he was ready to hop in his old car, but I convinced him to fly in. He's arriving tomorrow at noon in Durango, and I plan to pick him up, alone. He'll be pissed when he finds out what's been going on, and I don't want any of that blowing back on Isla. The two-hour drive back here will give him a chance to work out his inevitable anger on me.

I turn off the TV and slide out from under Isla's reclined form. Atsa scrambles to his feet and I know what he wants, but he's going to have to wait.

"In a minute, boy," I tell the dog, who's closely following my moves as I bend down and carefully lift a sleeping Isla up in my arms.

Other than a little groan of protest when I tug down her jeans and cover her with the blankets, she doesn't stir.

"Let's go."

Atsa is waiting by the door while I shove my feet into

boots and tug my coat on. He's out of the door before I have it opened properly, and bounds into the tree line. I follow in the same general direction at a much slower pace. When I hear him bark frantically somewhere in the woods, I break out in a run. It's a clear night, and the moonlight reflects blue off the snow-covered ground. I have no trouble seeing where I'm going until the trees get denser and less light filters through.

Atsa's barks are getting closer, which is my main source of navigation now. The gun I've taken to carrying on me again recently, is already in my hand when I break into a small clearing at the base of a large rock, not too far up from the house. The dog stands in the middle of the clearing, his body tight with tension, and his ears pulled back. His attention is entirely focused on the mountain lion on top of the rock.

The beautiful animal has its head hanging low between its shoulders, staring straight at Atsa, looking ready to pounce.

Isla

The second sharp crack has me shoot up straight in bed.

Gunshots. Away from the house, but not far.

"Ben?" I call out, but even as the sound travels through the house I know he's not here. He's out *there*.

Already I'm out of bed, tugging on the first pair of pants I encounter as I hop to the door. No Ben, and no Atsa, I confirm, peeking into the great room where the lights are already off.

From the shelf in the laundry room, I retrieve the small gun Ben has had me practice with. The thing is shaking in my hand as I try to jam my bare feet into my snow boots. I'm terrified and all I hear is my own panicked heartbeat.

I swing around, and lose my balance, when the door suddenly flies open.

"*Jesus*, woman!" Ben's angry growl is a welcome sound. He bends down, plucking the gun from my hand, just seconds before Atsa barrels in after him, landing almost in my lap. "Get off her, you big mutt." The dog is yanked off and Ben's large hand wraps around my upper arm, pulling me to my feet. "Are you alright?" *Other than my heart forcing its way up my esophagus?*

"Fine," I croak instead.

"Had to get between the dog and a mountain lion," he grumbles, still holding me with one hand on my arm, and the other wiping imaginary dust off my ass. I slap at his hand impatiently.

"Mountain lion?" My voice has gone from a croak to a squeal. "I didn't know we had those here? And aren't they supposed to be hibernating?"

Ben calmly turns to lock the door and shrugs out of his coat, kicking off his boots at the same time.

"They're around," he confirms, as he pulls me along down the hallway to the bedroom, where he leaves me by the side of the bed, so he can take off his clothes. "There's just not that many. They're generally shy. And no," he adds with a grin. "Mountain lions don't hibernate."

"Clearly this one wasn't shy," I grumble, ducking back under the covers, while Ben slips in on the other side.

"He's probably just checking out who moved into his territory," Ben explains, slipping his arm around my waist, and tugging my backside into the crook of his body.

"*His* territory? We're going to have to move," I announce, Ben's body shakes with laughter behind me. "I don't find anything about this even remotely funny." It's clear Ben disagrees with me.

I work hard to hang onto my snit, but eventually sleep, and the safe heat from his big body, gets the better of me.

-

"Do me a favor?"

I glance over my shoulder at Ben, who's waiting for his eggs to be done.

"Depends?" I say cautiously, not wanting to make promises blindly. Ben smirks and shakes his head, looking down in his cup.

"Stay inside this morning? Or at least within a few steps from the house? Atsa can fend for himself, and he'll listen to you."

"I'll be fine." I wave the spatula dismissively and turn back to the stove, doing my best to ignore the real concern I hear in his voice. He's heading to Durango for some important meeting with law enforcement there. Something about an old case that came up. I didn't really ask because he seemed reluctant to talk about it.

I ignore the scrape of the stool on the floor, and the footsteps coming around the island, but I can't ignore the arms that slip around my middle and the lips that find the back of my neck.

"Please?" I roll my eyes at his clear attempt at manipulation, with the use of his raspiest voice. He knows full well it makes me a little weak in the knees. "It'd make me feel better, Pixie, knowing you're safe. Otherwise, I'm just going to be worrying the entire time. My focus will be off, I might not even pay attention while driving, and—"

"Alright, alright. Enough already!" I twist around in his arms and shove against his chest. His grin splits from ear to ear. Cocky bastard was laying it on way too thick. "I think I liked you better when you weren't talking at all."

Half an hour later, I'm waving from the doorway as he drives off down the road.

Grabbing a fresh cup of coffee and snagging the remote off the table, I settle in for the Netflix binge I've been craving. I tried watching one episode of *Downton Abbey* with him, but he was providing nonstop, nonverbal commentary. Mostly in the form of snorts and grunts, but at some point he even laughed at the most inappropriate moments.

When he'd mentioned needing to go into Durango for a good chunk of the day, *Downton Abbey* was the first thing that popped in my head.

-

I'm almost through season two when I hear the crunch of wheels on the snow. Atsa beats me to the door and I have to shove him out of the way so I can pull it open. Just in time to see Uncle Al climb out of the SUV.

I don't notice the cold on my shoeless feet as I bolt out the door, straight into his arms.

"You crazy, girl?" he grumbles into my hair, lifting my feet high off the ground. "Came here for some good cooking, and how are ya gonna manage that if you're laid up with pneumonia?"

I squeeze his neck hard.

"Missed you so much," I mutter, fighting happy tears.

"Me too, girl. Me too. Come grab this crazy woman of yours, will ya?" he calls out to Ben, who walks up toting luggage. "I can carry my own damn bags."

I'm swung up into Ben's familiar arms and carried inside the house.

"Thank you." I smile at him when he finally sets me on my feet. "I should be pissed you lied to me, but I'm too happy right now."

"That's what I was going for," he grins. "And I didn't technically lie," he whispers in my ear, bending down. "I did have a meeting with law enforcement in Durango."

"He's retired," I point out, shoving at his shoulder.

"Semantics."

"Whatever." I shrug, grabbing one of my uncle's bags to put in one of the spare bedrooms.

Al is impressed, I can tell. Even though he's too stubborn to voice it, he can't hide the appreciation in his eyes. Ben lets me do the honors showing him around, while he takes the dog out for a run.

"You keeping things from me, little girl?" my uncle starts, when I hand him a hot chocolate.

"Ben tell you?"

"Uh-huh. Ticked at you but I'm right pissed with him. Knew that boy had trouble written all over him, right from the get go," he grumbles, his lips carefully testing the hot drink. My own temperature is rising at my uncle's remarks.

"You have no right," I spit out forcefully, and his eyes fly up at my evident anger. "If anyone should get the kind of sacrifices he's made his whole life, in an effort to uphold the law, it should be you. That man has been here, at my back, by my side, covering my front, every damn step of the way. He does not deserve what you're laying at his feet, and you don't even know the half of what's going on."

"I know enough," he says, his face hard and unforgiving. "He told me, girl—about the crazy bitch, about the child he might have, and about the pain it's causing you. He's hurting you, that's enough for me."

On a cerebral level I know he's concerned, he's worried about me, but my heart is so disappointed. I lean over the counter and let him see the tears in my eyes.

"You're the one hurting me," I hiss at my uncle, who's been at the center of my world for so long. "You're sitting in his kitchen, in the house that he spent the past few months building with me, and you dare tell me *he's* causing me pain?" Not even the flinch on his face at my words can stop me now. I grab the mug he just put down on the counter and dump the whole thing in the sink, shattering it on impact.

"Isla…" he starts, his tone conciliatory, and I don't want to hear it, but I do hear the rasp of Ben's voice.

"No, Pixie," he says, boxing me in from behind. I didn't hear him come in, but with his next words I can tell he's heard enough. "Your blood, baby. The man who took you in and raised you to be the incredible woman you are. Don't say what I fucking know you're going to regret, the second the words leave your mouth."

How does he know? *Get out.* Those were the words burning on my tongue. Just like my anger was burning in my veins. But Ben…God, Ben…he douses the flames with a touch, and a few words.

"What hurts, babe? It's the knowledge that some of

what he says is true. And you know it."

CHAPTER 19

Ben

"Need a hand?"

Isla stands in the doorway to the Deville, her face swollen and blotchy, looking like she's been crying for days.

I left her to talk with her uncle after she lost her shit. I know she's been carrying stuff around. Fuck, so have I. Things I'd like to be able to talk with her about, but can't, because it'd be too painful for her. It's just been easier for both of us to stay quiet.

I knew it couldn't last, that's why I talked Al into coming earlier than planned. I was just shocked it took her less than an hour to detonate.

I heard part of her tirade, and I can only guess at what Al said to validate such a response, but I'm pretty sure I know the gist. It wouldn't be much different from what he already subjected me to on the two-hour drive home from the airport.

Not much different from what I've been telling myself.

"Always," I tell her, holding out my hand. The moment I feel her fingers slide over my palm, I grab on and pull her further inside.

It's pretty cold in here, the space heaters doing only so much to warm up the uninsulated tuna can, but warm enough for what I'm doing. All the wood panels I could remove, I've brought up to the shed, where I have more room to sand and stain them. The rest I have to refinish in place.

Isla runs her fingers over the patch I was just sanding.

"Already looks so much better," she says, looking everywhere but at me.

"How was your talk with Al?"

Her eyes flick at me before going back to studying the wood.

"Hard," she admits. "But this'll be harder." I watch as a tear tracks down her cheek.

"No, it won't. You know why?" She finally turns her full gaze on me. "Because you already know what I'm struggling with, just as I know what you're thinking."

"But it's different saying out loud how angry I am at you," she finally blurts out. "And how guilty that makes me feel. You didn't ask for this, any more than I did; yet I still blame you. How fucked up is that?" I reach out to sweep some stray hairs from her face, but she brushes my hand away. "I don't want to feel this way. I love you, you know I do," she says, and yet she turns her back to me. "Uncle Al…he just tore the lid off the can, you know? A baby? Christ, Ben…I'm still reeling from the news that chances are good I'll never have kids of my own. I'm almost forty, six months ago, kids weren't even on my radar, but dammit…"

She sobs and leans her forehead against the bare wood. I want to touch her but I'm afraid if I do, she'll stop bleeding the wound clean. It's the only way it can heal without festering.

"And now," she continues. "Finding out there's a possibility there's kid out there somewhere, with your

DNA—some other woman who has a piece of you I'll never have—it hurts."

Fuck it. I turn her around and pull her into my arms. I rest my cheek on top of her hair and listen to her cry.

"My turn," I warn her, and I can feel her brace her body against my words. "I'm struggling. This whole situation is so fucked up; I don't know what I'm supposed to be feeling. For all we know the bitch is yanking our chain, and if there even is a kid, it may not even be mine. Still, I can't help wanting to know, which makes me feel guilty." Isla's suppressed sniffle tears at my heart but I can't stop now. "So I'll take your anger, but I'll be damned if I let her make you think she's got one over on you. The truth is, Pixie, you have a piece of me no one's ever had before."

-

"So good," Isla mumbles with a mouthful, juices dripping down her chin.

Fucking sloppy Joes.

I don't think I've had those since I was a kid, but it's what was waiting for us when we got back to the house. Al's version of comfort food, I'm guessing, based on Isla's reaction. With emotions already running high, she immediately teared up, seeing her uncle in the kitchen.

"She could eat four of those as a kid," Al explains. "Easiest damn fix for a bad mark, or a broken heart, was a pan of meat sauce and a couple of buns."

"Whatever," she interjects between bites.

I don't say much, happy to feel the ease slip back into the interaction between Isla and Al. He is still glaring at me from time to time, but I'll take that, too. He's entitled, and besides, he makes a mean sloppy Joe. I watch as Isla shovels down three in record time, while I eat my first two.

"So good," she says again, when she finally comes up for air, wiping sauce off her chin.

That, right there, is what I love about her: the ability to lose herself in the enjoyment of even the most mundane things. This is not a woman who needs fancy shit or expensive dinners. She's happy with her Ikea bed and meat on a bun.

The smile she habitually wears—the one that had worn off this past week in particular—is back in its full glory as she banters with her uncle. Things may still be a little tender between us, but at least she's got that back. The old man will look after her.

I haven't mentioned anything to her yet, but I'll be leaving her in his hands tomorrow. I wish I could wait for things to settle a little, but I already lost time waiting for Al to get here. He knows, I told him everything. I don't want to delay anymore. I want this shit sorted, sooner rather than later.

-

The old man opted to stay down below in his trailer.

He threw that out there after dinner and Isla had a conniption fit, but Al stayed firm. Said it'd been a happy place for him to come home to for plenty of years. Isla wasn't convinced until he added that he didn't want to run the risk walking in to anything that might upset his fragile constitution—then she laughed, and helped him with his bags. I knew the more likely reason, he didn't want to be anywhere near when I tell her what Neil found.

I moved one of the space heaters into the trailer and made sure there was enough propane to run the built-in heating unit, for a couple of days.

"Come on, boy," Isla calls for Atsa, who's rummaging around the campsite. She hooks her arm through mine as we walk up the road, leaving the four-wheeler for Al to use.

Atsa, who seems completely recovered from his flinch-worthy surgical emasculation, is loping around us before running ahead. I watch as he stops at the top of the ridge, his head high, and one of his front legs lifted up.

"What is it?" Isla whispers beside me, having noticed the dog stand to attention.

"Not sure. Hold on to the back of my jacket," I instruct her, pulling my gun at the same time.

Just as we get to the top of the ridge, Atsa takes off around the back of the house and I hustle Isla to the porch.

"Get inside." I give her a little shove in the direction of the door.

I start to follow Atsa's path around the house. Keeping my gun trained on the ground in front of me, and with a sharp eye on the tree line, where shadows move with the breeze. I briefly consider alerting Al, but quickly decide against it.

I'm about to slip into the trees when I stop to listen for any movement. I can't hear anything, so when the dog comes trotting out of the woods, not fifty yards from me, he startles me. It's the snow that sucks up any sound. The nights are so silent when it's snowed.

Atsa doesn't look any the worse for wear. Doesn't look alarmed at all anymore either, as he trots over to me and allows himself to be rubbed down.

"What was that, buddy?"

A rhetorical question, since I don't expect an answer,

but I wish he could give me one all the same.

"What was that?" Isla echoes, just minutes later, as she pulls open the door just as I'm reaching for the knob.

"Don't know. Wildlife?" I shrug. "Maybe that mountain lion again."

-

"I've got to head back to Durango tomorrow."

Isla stops in the doorway to the bathroom, looking at me suspiciously.

"Why?"

"Neil found a lead." I watch her absorb the information, with a slight jerk of her body, before pushing away from the doorpost and walking over to the bed. She sets a knee in the mattress and crawls closer.

"Tell me."

"Found an address in Tulsa listed to a Dorothy Wells—her mother. Took a while since apparently Dorothy got married in 2009, but he was able to trace her to Durango, where she's been living the past six years with her new husband. I want to try and talk to her."

Isla is quiet, apparently lost in thought, until finally she looks up at me and nods. I can guess what's going through her mind. She realizes what I might find out, what I might find.

"Okay," she whispers.

"Okay?"

"Yeah. You need to know." I reach out and tag her behind the neck, pulling her down beside me, her head on my shoulder.

"*We* need to know, but it's not just that, Pixie. I need some answers about her daughter. Stacie and Mak are gonna be here next week…"

Isla

"…I'd like to get this shit resolved before then."

I focus on the comforting rumble of Ben's voice under my ear, and not on the pinch of panic I feel. Part of me doesn't want to find out, but he's right, we need to know.

"A sane person doesn't do what she did in here, Pixie," he says gesturing around the room. "Next time, she may escalate to harming someone. I don't want anyone hurt."

The pinch becomes a steady throb at his words. She may have tried already. I'd convinced myself I was overreacting when I thought that white car was aiming straight for me. I didn't want to look like a fool so I didn't say anything. I'm not so sure now.

"She may have tried already," I voice what I was thinking just now.

In a fraction of a second, I find myself flat on my back, with Ben looming over me, his nose almost touching mine.

"I fucking knew it," he growls. "I should've gone with my gut and drilled you for the truth when you tried to distract me." He closes his eyes and drops his forehead to mine. "Fuck, woman, why didn't you say something?" The words come out exasperated.

"I wasn't sure. I—"

His mouth swallows my words as he kisses me forcefully. By rote, my hands slip around his neck and up in his hair, as my tongue tangles with his. By the time he releases my lips, I can't remember what we were talking about.

"Do you trust me?" His eyes burn into mine and I feel the weight of his question.

"With my life." My answer is firm and immediate.

"Then don't make it more difficult for me to prove that trust justified."

Right. That's what we were talking about.

"Okay, so in that case I should also probably mention that I think—I can't be a hundred-percent sure—that the car Jen was pointing out, coming down the mountain that day? I think it may have been the same one."

Ben drops his face in the pillow beside my head and groans, "I fucking know."

I slip out from under him, leaving him flat on his stomach. Throwing a leg over his body, I end up sitting on his butt. I stroke up his back, feeling the muscles tense and knotted under my hands. Leaning down, I cover his back with my front, smiling a little when I hear him groan again, but this time in appreciation.

"Just relax," I whisper, my lips brushing the shell of his ear.

With a strong touch, I start at his neck, massaging the taut muscles. I roll my thumbs over the knots with firm pressure, eliciting another groan from deep in his chest. Slowly I can feel his shoulders relax into the mattress, before I move my touch lower, pressing in along his spine and laving extra attention to his lower back.

"Isla…" he moans when my hands start kneading the tight globes of his ass, pulling down his boxers as I go.

"Shh," I hush him, scooting down so I have better access to his body. "Let me."

All it takes is a slight tensing of my hands on his hips for him to flip over. His eyes peer at me from under heavy lids, as I deftly lift the elastic of his boxers away from that beautifully erect cock.

His body presses down further into the mattress at the first touch of my tongue, and a light shiver runs down my spine at his taste.

"Mmmm," I hum, sliding my lips down on him, while my fist wraps around him at the root.

With my hand and mouth working in tandem—firm pressure followed by the gentle suction—his hips involuntarily buck up, and his fingers grab hold of my short hair, guiding my movements.

This is what I want—what I can give *him*.

This is what makes my heart swell in my chest—when he can no longer control his need for me.

CHAPTER 20

Ben

"Who are you?"

The older, rotund guy, opening the door, looks me up and down with a healthy dose of suspicion. I guess the sight of a rough-looking, leather-wearing, unkempt biker on his doorstep, is not one he's met with on a daily basis. Not in this high-end neighborhood of Durango. Should've worn fucking gloves or something, since the guy can't keep his eyes of the tattoos on the back of my hands.

"I'm looking for Dorothy Wells," I say, in my most polite voice. At least I think it is, but from the scowl on the guy's face, I don't think he notices.

"Only Dorothy here is my wife, which make her Dorothy Banks, not Wells," he snaps, and I feel my patience already waning. That didn't take long.

"It's important I speak to her, it's about her daughter."

"Geoffrey? What's this about Jahnee?" The wobbly woman's voice comes from somewhere behind the man, but instead of stepping aside, he leans right into my space.

"You upset my wife, you've got problems," he hisses, and I've got to give him props for having the balls to threaten me. I stand about a foot taller, and although he beats me out in mass, mine is of a muscular variety and I'd be surprised if this man has any of those left.

A sweet, but gaunt-looking, gray-haired lady pokes her head around her husband.

"You know where Jahnee is?" she says, deflating my hopes she might provide some answers. "Wait a minute!" She shoves at her husband, who rolls his eyes as he steps out of her way, and this time it's the woman getting in my face. "You're Brent!" she exclaims, clapping her hands together. "Oh my goodness—Jahnee's going to be over the moon. She said she was off to meet you! When did you come back from overseas?"

Something is seriously wrong here. Overseas?

"I'm not sure I understand," I start carefully, glancing at the man by her side, who is warning me with his eyes. "Could I perhaps come in and ask you a few questions about your daughter?"

"Of course." She hesitates, only for a second, before stepping back and letting me inside the house.

"Would you care for some coffee?"

The woman can barely stand on her feet, so I quickly but firmly decline, almost relieved when she takes a seat on the couch.

"I apologize," she says, smiling weakly. "I haven't been well. Jahnee moved here to look after me, just the end of the summer. Then a few weeks ago, she said she had to go. That she'd received news you'd be back from your deployment and was meeting you when you arrived back stateside. I've been waiting to meet you for years. Did you miss her? Have you talked to her?" I notice worry creeping into her voice as she starts realizing something is not computing.

"Ma'am," I carefully say, with a sideways glance to her husband, who looks ready to have a coronary with his wife getting upset. "I'm afraid, perhaps, there's been a misunderstanding. I'm a retired agent for the Drug

Enforcement Agency. I met your daughter ten or eleven years ago in Tulsa, while working on a case. My case concluded and I left. I haven't seen your daughter since."

"But I don't understand?" the poor woman mutters, grabbing the pendant hanging around her neck. "You were married right before you left for Afghanistan. She was devastated you would miss the birth of your baby. I remember she cried so hard when she found out you'd been captured."

Dorothy's husband wraps his arm around his wife's shoulders, rubbing her arm with brisk strokes. I see regret and genuine care on the man's face, as he looks almost apologetic at Dorothy.

"You warned me," she suddenly whispers, turning to her husband. "You never believed her, did you?"

"Sweetheart," he mumbles soothingly. "I don't want you upset. Why don't I help you lie down and I'll see if I can clear this up?"

The last is said with a stern look in my direction and I nod my consent. I'd rather deal with the angry, protective husband than with his emotional, and obviously unwell, wife.

As he gently leads her out of the room, I use the opportunity to have a look around. The mantel over the fireplace holds a large collection of photographs. I'm guessing children and grandchildren, but I only recognize the people in one picture. A large frame, behind a collection of smaller ones, which shows a newly married couple. Jahnee—much as I can recall her—in a wedding dress, holding onto a large bouquet of red roses in one arm, and a tall man in a Marine Corps uniform with the other. A much younger version of my face is sticking out of the high collar.

It's a bit surreal, looking at an image of yourself when you know for a fact that isn't you.

"I've always questioned her story." A defeated looking Geoffrey walks up behind me, taking the frame from my hands and placing it back on the mantel, behind the others. "At first I gave her the benefit of the doubt, even if her stories of you and what I knew about the military didn't exactly mesh." He walks heavily to the couch where he sits down, staring blankly out the window. "Dorothy was first diagnosed with cancer back in 2009. That's when we moved here. She'd always wanted the mountains, and I'd been too stubborn to move, but I was desperate to give her everything she wanted. At least while I could. I never thought she'd beat the first round." His red-rimmed eyes turn to me when I find my way back to the chair I was sitting in before. "This was a second marriage for both of us, and my children and Jahnee never mixed well," he explains. "It was a relief at first, being away from the tension…" His voice trails off before he shakes his head lightly as if to clear it. "But you're not here for that. It was probably 2014 when I knew something was up. Most of the troops stationed in Afghanistan at that time were brought home. Not that I believed all Jahnee's reasons for never having met you in the years she claimed to have been married to you. But I never started openly questioning her about it until the clear evidence of her lies was on the news every day, as troops flew home. That's when she gave her mother that picture." He points at the large frame. "Dorothy had just found out her cancer had spread, and I didn't have the heart to tell her the truth; that the picture was a fake and that there was no husband."

"My name is Ben Gustafson and I've never been married." I'm not sure why I feel the need to clarify that, but it feels right. The old man should know exactly who he's spilling his guts to.

"You were undercover," he concludes appropriately.

"I was. I'm not proud of using your stepdaughter to further my case." I snort. "Hell, I'm not proud of a lot things I've done in the name of one investigation or another, but it was always with the greater good in mind."

"I understand," he says, although I wonder if he really does, since I don't myself half the time. Too many years undercover tends to start blurring the lines of morality, and I'm pretty sure mine were nearly nonexistent, which is why I needed to get out. Besides, it clearly had some long-lasting effects on this family. "You know she was diagnosed with schizophrenia a few years ago? Jahnee?" he asks. I clearly didn't, but it doesn't come as a surprise. Not with what I've learned today. It makes it even more important to share what I know with this man.

"I have reason to believe that Jahnee may be behind some disturbing events that have occurred recently." Geoffrey's head lifts up, and he straightens his back like he's bracing for impact.

I spend the next fifteen minutes outlining the events as I know them and watch carefully for his reactions. He blinks a few times when I tell him about the first image she sent, before his eyes flick over to the wedding photo. He listens quietly through my recount of the white car, nodding every now and then.

"Could be hers," he volunteers.

When I tell him of the break-in of our house with

minimal detail, he flinches. It's when I describe the ultrasound picture that I get the biggest reaction. A great sadness settles on his features.

"It about killed Dorothy," he mutters. "We were still living in Tulsa and she went with Jahnee to every damn doctor's appointment. She was getting big as a house and at the end could barely fit behind the wheel."

I know what's coming. I'm expecting it; I'm braced for it, but it still hits me with the hot power of a bullet.

"Damn near broke my wife when she lost that baby, with one month left to go. I'm thinking that's what broke Jahnee's hold on reality."

Isla

"I'm off to see that old coot, McCracken," Uncle Al announces, walking into the kitchen where I'm cooking dinner.

Ben came home earlier, all moody, and didn't want to talk. "Later—I promise," he said and I didn't push. He took off down to the trailer on his four-wheeler after putting his work clothes on. I saw Uncle Al head over to the Deville a little later, and he stayed in there for a good hour before he made his way up here.

I just killed my time with edits and checking in with Jen and Nate via email.

"You're not staying for dinner?"

"Nope. I promised Phil a good steak, so that's what I'm gonna get him. Heading over to Shiloh's Steakhouse in Cortez. It's his favorite restaurant, but he never goes there because the bastard is too cheap. He don't seem to mind me payin' for it, though."

I smile, because despite the complaining and the bickering, it's clear my uncle cares for his buddy.

"Also, you need to be patient with your man. Have a mind. He'll tell ya, but don't you go throwing that temper of yours around," he says, his finger almost poking my eye as he's waving it in front of my face.

"Better stop pointing that thing at me then," I grit out. "Cause I'm *this* close to biting it off."

Wisely, my uncle tucks the offensive finger, and the rest of his hand, quickly in his pocket.

"And for your information, I don't lose my temper, I'm simply...spirited." I lift my chin as high as I can get it, while trying to look down my nose at him. He shakes his head, and with his big paw, grabs me by the back of the head, tagging me closer.

"Sweet girl," he says in that voice that makes me feel twelve years old again and believing in fairy tales and magic. "Do me a favor and just let the man talk."

I'm still grumbling quietly when Ben comes in twenty minutes later.

"Where's Al?" he asks, looking around.

"Off for a night on the town with Phil. Promises to be a rockin' time." I'm glad to see a grin break through the stoic mask he's been wearing today.

"As long as we're not called to come pick them up from the hospital because one of them breaks a hip line-dancing, I'm good with that," he shoots back, and now it's my turn to grin. "What's for dinner?" His expression straightens out, but his eyes are still smiling, so I smile back, with full-face involvement.

"Tamale pie. With ground elk instead of beef." I turn around to open the oven door. The cornbread topping on the meat is nice and golden, and I carefully lift the dish from the oven with a towel. "Al loves elk, I thought he'd enjoy."

"So do I, and I know I'll love it."

The pleasantries continue through dinner, which we enjoy at the new dining table we picked up right here in Dolores. "Temporary," Ben had said, since he still wants to build his own with wood from the property, but with his current project list already long enough to last him through to the spring, I wasn't going to wait. We've got Stacie and Mak coming, and we need a table for the holidays, something Ben wasn't going to argue with.

"I'll do dishes," Ben offers when I've put the leftovers away.

It's a rare treat, since he's not one for cooking or cleaning, but he makes up for it in many other ways. I pull out a stool and sit at the counter where I can watch him and enjoy.

"Decaf?" he asks grabbing a mug from the cupboard. He usually has a beer during or after dinner and I like a coffee. I just don't like the caffeine this time of day, since it has me up at three or four in the morning, wide-awake.

"Please."

I get the sense he's building up to talking about what he found out today, so I try not to chatter like I normally might. *Have a mind*. I can hear my uncle's voice in my head. And I keep having a mind, when Ben starts to tell me about his meeting with Mr. And Mrs. Banks.

Oh, there are times that I want express my anger at that sick bitch, with copious amounts of creativity, but I'm reeling it in. Mostly because I can see that however upset this has made Ben, it's not what upset him most.

It takes everything out of me to keep my mouth shut when I finally discover what really cut him today.

"I'm so much more responsible for this whole situation than I could've imagined," he says, with no small amount of defeat in his voice. That's what finally has me let go.

"That's crap," I spit, immediately defensive. I ignore his raised eyebrow and forge ahead. "Well, it is. Did you make any promises of any kind to her, while you were...intimately involved?" I flick my hand back and forth with a distaste I can't hide. One that Ben apparently finds amusing.

"Babe, it's not like we talked much."

"Alright, I could've done without that," I point out, even more worked up now. "My point is; how can you be held accountable for anything other than flawed judgment?"

"Flawed judgment?" he parrots back at me, his eyebrows still up in his hairline.

"Clearly. She wasn't wearing a sign that said, '*off my rocker, back away,*' now did she?" Ben closes his eyes, drops his head and shakes it slowly, but he does it grinning. "No way you could know she had a mental illness, if she didn't even know. And don't even get me started on the way she lied and manipulated her parents, her mom. That's just wrong. Afghanistan? Does she know they generally behead their prisoners, not keep them fed for fucking years, and then send them home with a pat on the back, and a *'Please, come again'?*"

By now Ben is full out laughing, and the sight of it

unravels the knot of tension I've had since last night when he told me his plans.

"Honey," I softly say, drawing his attention. "I know you like to take responsibility for all the wrongs in the world, make yourself accountable for every flaw and fail, but dammit—not everything is yours to carry."

I slip down the stool and walk around the island where he is perched on his own. I slip my hips between his legs and lay my hands along his jaw before I continue.

"And that baby? That little boy? I'm sorry that she lost it, and I'm sorry it may well have cracked her mind. I'm especially sorry that all of that is painful for you, but not even that is yours to carry. Truth is, knowing what you know now about her mental state, there's no way for you to be sure it was your child she was pregnant with."

"The timing fits," he counters, as his hands come up and circle my wrists.

"It may well," I'm quick to concede, before putting my point across. "But do you know for sure you were the only one? Did you vow to be exclusive?"

"None of that," he admits. "It was just a handful of hookups."

"Did you ever fuck her without a condom?"

"Fuck no. I'd never go unprotected, not until you anyway," he says with a cocky smile, before realization sets in.

I don't need to say anything else, I just watch his facial expressions while he processes.

CHAPTER 21

Isla

Not sure why I'm so nervous. It's not like I didn't just spend Thanksgiving with Stacie and her daughter. I think it's the idea of blending the families, as it were. It makes everything so much more…official?

I also can't deny that Stacie, in all her perfection—her immaculate home, her successful career, her flawless appearance—intimidated the shit out of me.

It's ridiculous, but I want everything to be perfect. Which is why I may have gone a little overboard on the cleaning, the decorating, and the Christmas baking. According to Uncle Al, it's not all I went overboard on; he's the one I dragged into Cortez to pick up a few necessities and ended up loaded down like a pack mule.

We'd agreed no gifts; we'd focus on having some quality family time, but I couldn't have an eight-year-old wake up Christmas morning without at least a few gifts under the tree. As for the rest of the stuff, that was just for their comfort: some nice bedding for the spare room, a few knick-knacks, and fresh towels for their bathroom. Those don't count as gifts.

"You know the dog was supposed to be the big surprise for Mak, right?" Ben pointed out last night, when he caught me wrapping gifts in the bedroom.

"Yes, but it's not like she can take Atsa home with her. He'll stay here and she can come visit anytime she wants, but she needs something to take home," I plead my case, which didn't go very far with Ben, who just raised an eyebrow.

This morning, I'm even nervous about the dog. What if Mak doesn't like Atsa? Or he reacts weird to them? I mean; he's been fine with Uncle Al, and even Jen, who came for a visit this week, but what if he doesn't like kids?

"You worry too much," Ben whispers in my ear as he stalks up behind me.

"She has that from her mother," Uncle Al volunteers, having clearly overheard. I turn my head to where he is deftly unwrapping Hershey's Kisses and pressing them into the balls of dough I'm rolling. At least that's what he's supposed to be doing, but I've already caught him popping a few in his mouth.

"Better not be eating all those," I threaten, but he just winks at Ben.

"My sister always said: Worry often gives a small thing..."

"...a big shadow," I finish for him. A smile forms on my lips because I can clearly hear her say the words. I never understood the meaning until long after she'd passed away. I glance at my uncle again and find him gently smiling back.

It's funny how the loss of a loved one, although once gut-wrenchingly painful, can become a lingering ache that at times feels almost comforting. Even though they're gone, you learn to feel blessed you had them in your life in the first place.

So when Ben flexes his arms around me, and mumbles, "I'm sorry." I turn so we are nose to nose before

I answer.

"I'm not sorry at all," I tell him. "She left me loved."

Ben opens his mouth to say something, but the low growl coming from the dog by the front door, has him snap it shut. We're all frozen in suspended animation, listening for what Atsa might be reacting to.

When the familiar sound of tires crunching on the snow becomes clearer, I jump into action. Or perhaps I should say, into panic.

"They're here," I yell at no one in particular, since everyone already knows, as I move mixing bowls into the sink, grab a rag and start wiping the counter. Again.

Which is why—when Ben calls from the hallway, "Pixie, get your ass over here and come say hello!"—I'm wearing my apron, covered in flour, and am holding a dishrag in my hand when he pulls the door open.

It doesn't even take a second before Mak squeals at seeing a nosey Atsa, who pushed his way past Ben's long legs. There's no time to caution, or even take in a breath, as she dives for the dog, landing on her knees on the floor, her lanky arms wrapping tightly around Atsa's neck.

"Mak!" Stacie scolds her daughter, who is blissed out with her face buried in the dog's fur. Luckily, Atsa sinks down on his butt and with arrogant resignation, lets himself be cuddled.

"Ben!" is Stacie's next admonition, punching her grinning brother in the shoulder.

"Chill, sis," he rumbles, pulling her into a hug. "The dog stays here, but he's Mak's all the same."

I can't hear what she mutters into his shirt, but whatever it is makes him chuckle. The moment she pushes out of her brother's arms and turns to me, I realize the state I'm in, but it's too late. Apparently unconcerned with the flour covering me, or the dirty dishrag still clasped in my hand, she wraps me in a bone-crushing hug.

"It's so beautiful here. The house is amazing! What is it I smell? Are you baking? I'm so jealous. I can't bake for shit. Cookies? Please tell me they're chocolate chip," she chatters, as she tucks her arm in mine and drags me into the house. "Ben, grab our bags from the car, will ya? Mak, get up off the floor and leave that dog alone. Why don't you give your uncle a hand?"

Just like that, she has everything and everyone organized. I haven't even formulated words yet.

"I already know I like you," Uncle Al says, when we walk into the kitchen, where he's waiting. "Anyone who manages to leave my niece stumped for words deserves my respect, at the very least." He holds out his hand at Stacie.

"You're Uncle Al," Stacie says, grinning as she pumps his hand a few times.

"And you are Ben's sister."

"Anastasia, but everyone calls me Stacie."

"Beautiful name for a lovely lady." I swear Uncle Al is swooning, but Stacie laughs it off.

"Heard lots about you already," she informs him.

"All good, I hope?"

"Nothing but the best," she confirms, making my uncle blush.

"Well, I'm sorry to be the one to tell you," Al says, and I brace myself for what might come out of his mouth. "But what I was told about you doesn't even come close to doing you justice." Then old coot winks at her, and I think I may have just groaned out loud.

My God, they're flirting. I don't know whether to giggle or hurl. It's equally funny and disturbing. I've never really seen my uncle so thrown off by anyone, but he clearly doesn't know whether he's coming or going now.

"Yay! Cookies."

Clearly Stacie is unaffected as she dives for the cookie tray.

As introductions go, these weren't anything like I could've imagined...but the result is a comfortable, familiar atmosphere by the time Ben walks in, followed by Mak and Atsa. Clearly the dog has already claimed the girl, as much as the girl has claimed him; he follows her everywhere. Traitor.

"Everything okay?" Ben asks a while later, when I slip his shepherd's pie in the oven. I'd wanted to make some nice mushroom and asparagus risotto with stuffed veal, but was met with protest from both men.

Uncle Al wanted chili, but I shivered at the thought of him lifting an ass cheek off his seat. His signal that those beans were making a return in gas form. I was well-trained to spot the signature move and make myself scarce before detonation. To my horror, Ben had discovered my uncle's propensity, just a few days ago. Instead of being equally horrified, he thought it was hilarious, adding music of his own. I vowed then never to make chili again. Or anything else with beans for that matter. Grown men, for Christ's sake.

Ben came up with the shepherd's pie, reminding me that although risotto and veal sounded pretty good, the simple potatoes and beef with a side of applesauce, might be something Mak would enjoy.

"Everything's fine," I assure him, pulling myself up on the counter so I was face-to-face. Of course, Ben would see it as an invitation to worm himself between my legs and with his hands on my ass, pull me closer to the edge, and his hips, or thereabouts.

Stacie and Mak were in their rooms. Something Stacie had initially protested against, claiming she could just as easily share with Mak, but my uncle assured her that he much preferred sleeping in his bed in the trailer. Ben showed them their rooms, and I had to smile at the girly squeals from Mak, who probably found the few things I left on her bed for her.

I keep looking around for Atsa, who is usually underfoot when I'm doing anything with food in the kitchen, but he's nowhere to be found. Although I'm pretty sure he's making himself comfortable in Mak's room, on Mak's bed.

Traitor.

Ben

"Are you ready to get a tree?"

Mak is smiling big as she nods at Al, who is helping her in her snowsuit.

"You need to hold on tight to Isla, okay?"

"Why aren't you coming?" my niece asks the old man.

"Who's going to make sure there is hot chocolate and a nice fire ready for when you come back frozen like icicles? Besides, Uncle Al is too old for shenanigans in the snow, I'll leave that up to you young 'uns." Al ruffles her hair before tugging her hood up.

"Uncle Ben is old, too." Mak shrugs innocently, and my sister, who is struggling to get her feet shoved into boots, snorts. I'm close enough to cuff the back of her head.

"Hey!" Stacie cries out, lifting her hand to her head. "I didn't say anything."

"But you were thinking about it."

"You guys, ready?" Isla comes in from outside, where she just picked up an armload of firewood.

"Yeah, daylight's wasting here, and there's a show starting in ten minutes I'd really like to see, so scram, you lot," Al says, taking Isla's load and carrying it inside.

The plan was for Mak to ride with me and Stacie to climb on the back of Isla's ATV, leveling it out weight-wise. A solid plan, or so I thought, until the girls got hold of it and my input was completely ignored as they rearranged it.

There isn't a whole lot of snow yet, so we should still be able to get around on the four-wheelers, for the most part. If it gets too deep at some point, we can always walk a ways.

With Stacie hanging on for dear life, I lead us up a narrow trail I flattened, the best I could, earlier in the week. The whine of Isla's engine sounds right behind us and the dog is trotting along beside her.

"This is so fun!" Stacie yells in my ear. "Can you teach me to ride one of these?"

"Nothing to it," I tell her, turning my head sideways so she can hear me. "Just need to learn to work a throttle."

"Cool." I can feel her shift as she looks behind us,

where both my niece and Isla are smiling wide. The next moment, she's back at my ear. "Can you teach me to shoot a gun?"

"Fuck no," is my knee-jerk response. It's already a challenge to try to teach Isla to hit a target. My sister, who is not particularly coordinated, on her best days—in anything but her outfit that is—would be a nightmare.

"I'll just ask Isla," she says, and I don't even need to look to know she's got a big shit-eating grin on her face. She's a fucking lawyer; she knows exactly how to manipulate. She went to law school for three goddamn years after her bachelor's, that's all they learn there. She knows damn well I wouldn't even consider letting Isla be the one to teach her. It would be like the blind leading the blind.

So I just shut my mouth and resign myself to the fact that I'll probably be taking Stacie for target practice before the end of the year. *Fuck me.*

-

"That one is nice," I point out a nice little tree, when we stop in a section with quite a few nicely-shaped pine trees.

"Too small," Isla shuts me down.

"Yeah, good shape, but you need much bigger for that ginormously high ceiling." My sister, of course, readily agrees.

"I think it's cute," Mak says, standing beside me, the sweet little girl face, currently reddened by the cold. *Cute.* Damn kid is as almost as good as her mother, pushing my buttons.

"You're right," I agree, knowing I've been overpowered, yet again. "Let's keep looking. *Cute* won't cut it."

If I had any doubts about Mak's premature, but already finely honed feminine wiles, the sneaky grin she throws the other two swiftly eliminates them.

The next tree, this one selected by the half pint, is massive, and I carefully explain we'll likely be wrecking the home of quite a few of the local wildlife, if we were to cut that one down. That doesn't sit well with Mak, so we're looking again. At this point, it's more me hanging back by the ATVs, keeping an eye on the rest of the group.

All of a sudden I notice the dog frozen and alert, his nose sniffing the air. I quickly track Isla's dark head with earmuffs, and off to her right is my sister, her blonde hair poking out of the blue knit hat she's wearing. But I can't find Mak's red hood.

The moment I start moving in the direction, where I thought I last saw her, Atsa takes off running, his head low and stretched out in front of him. My feet immediately pick up speed, and by the time I hear my name called, I'm full out running in the direction where Atsa disappeared in the brush.

"Ben! What's going on?" I vaguely register Isla's call, but I'm too focused on where I'm going, while instinctively reaching for my gun.

I'm noisy as I crash through the underbrush, but I can still hear loud growls and snarls to my left. I immediately shift toward the sound of animals fighting, firing a shot in the air in hopes of breaking it up.

I clear the trees, just as I see the mountain lion pin Atsa on his back, and without thinking about it, I aim and shoot again. This time to hit. The majestic animal slumps down on top of the dog, a good-sized hole in its side. I aim again when I see its body move, but it's just the dog crawling out from under the weight of the big cat.

"Atsa!" Isla exclaims as she bursts out of the trees, my sister right behind her.

"Mommy?"

The blood freezes in my veins when I see Mak's red hood poke up from the brush on the other side of the small clearing, right in my fucking line of fire.

-

"Hit me up with another," I tell Al, who is generously spiking the hot chocolate with dark rum.

He was coming through the woods when we were on our way back down, having heard the shots. I had him drive the ATV home and I walked the rest of the way. I needed the time to get my jitters under control. Clearly, I was only partially successful.

Luckily, other than a few spots where the cat pierced the skin with teeth or claws, the only injury Atsa bore was a small tear on his ear. Isla wanted to take him down to Dolores to find a vet, so he could get stitched up. The dog didn't look to be in pain, and there was barely any bleeding, once we had the mountain lion's blood washed off him and were able to get a good look at any injuries. It didn't look that bad and would heal on its own, with a bit of care.

Mak had wandered off a little when she spotted the big cat in the distance. She'd panicked and started moving to where she thought we were but ended up in the wrong direction. The animal had wasted no time closing in on the much smaller Mak. If not for Atsa, Mak may not be cuddled on the couch next to her still shaky mother.

Christ, I can't even think about that.

Isla got mad when I suggested perhaps Atsa deserved a battle scar or two, but my little niece intervened by saying, "That way I can't ever forget he saved me."

That resulted in a sobbing Isla in my arms. Arms that were still shaking.

Al insisted on coming back up with me, to drag the cat's carcass a little further away from the house. We also ended up cutting a tree, the only way to lift everyone's spirits.

That, and the rum in hot chocolate.

CHAPTER 22

Isla

Well, I got my Christmas.

The tree Ben and Uncle Al ended up dragging down the mountain, not quite as big as I would've liked, but it also wasn't as small as Ben initially suggested. We kept the decorations simple and Mak's enthusiasm made trimming the tree fun.

Compromise.

I'm pretty sure we'll see a lot of that.

My elaborate dinner suggestions had been voted down, in favor of deep fried turkey the guys planned to cook. Ben had taken Mak into Cortez to pick up groceries and came back three hours later with the back of his SUV loaded to the top. For a man who vows to hate shopping, he was awfully proficient at it.

"Wait until you see your present," Mak twitters, clapping her hands excitedly. She was describing every item being pulled from the Toyota by the two men.

"Pixie," Ben called, drawing my attention. "Got no place to hide this thing until tomorrow, so you're getting your gift early."

"We're not supposed to be doing gifts!" I protested, but Ben turned his glare on me.

"Yeah? So how come you're hiding shit in the back of the closet in our bedroom, and in the rafters of the shed out back?"

"I didn't put anything in the shed out back." My eye flicked to my uncle, who suddenly seemed very busy studying the big outdoor fryer Ben picked up as well.

"It's Christmas," Uncle Al finally muttered with a shrug when I stared him down.

In the end, it appeared we'd all caved. No lavish amounts of gifts under the tree, but thoughtful ones, every one of them.

The gift Ben got me is easily my favorite: a beautiful wooden bench. It apparently is an old church pew he found at a thrift store. The arms and backrest were ornately carved, albeit crude. The snout of a bear, a forest of pines, elk antlers, and what looked like a salmon, were all hewn out of the rustic wood, with just enough detail to recognize the image. It's weathered, and has a long crack running along the backrest that someone haphazardly braced by hammering a two-by-four to the back, but it fits perfectly out front, on the deck.

I'm sitting there now, bundled up against the chilly temperatures but unable to resist the first warm beams of the sun. They predicted a few days of warmer weather this coming week and I'm ready for it.

I take another sip of my coffee, listening to the relative silence around me. It's funny, in the early morning during the spring and summer, you can't miss the sounds of everything waking up around you, but in the winter you have to listen for it. The distant screech of an eagle looking for an early morning snack, the clucking of a chipmunk detecting the threat overhead, and the creaking of frozen limbs as the tops of trees sway in the breeze.

I grab my camera from the bench beside me and

quickly zoom in on the bird of prey, diving down and catching something on the campground below. I adjust my lens, sharpening the image of the eagle; its feathers gleaming in the morning sun, as it tears the head off a mouse or maybe it's the chipmunk I heard earlier. It's a swift death, the eagle's beak curved dangerously with edges sharp as a knife.

All I hear now is the whirr of the camera, a soft click of the shutter counting the images I take.

Brutal—but also beautifully raw. There is honesty in the wild—balance. A certain justifiable order in the way of things, in only taking what you need.

We, as humans, tend to take what we want and are rarely satisfied just having our needs met. There are times when I wish I could live off the grid, sustain myself only by taking what I need, but I'll be the first to admit; I like some of my comforts too much to give up.

I think the inherent difference, between man and animal, is that man has the capacity—or maybe the curse—to dream. We dream of better, bigger, more, and when we reach it, we simply create new dreams. The constant drive forward with an objective in mind.

Nothing quite as simple as a next meal or another day survived.

I lower the camera and lift my head at the soft thud of the front door and the crunch of boots on the snow. I'm expecting Ben, so it surprises me when Stacie steps onto the deck, carrying a steaming mug of her own.

"Am I interrupting?" she whispers, mindful of the peaceful morning.

"Not at all," I assure her with a smile. "Did you sleep okay?"

"It's unbelievable how well I sleep up here. The first couple of days I was a little headachy, but now I feel fantastic."

"Probably a touch of altitude sickness," I guess. "Isn't Albuquerque at about five thousand feet, on average? McPhee is at seven thousand. It may just be enough of a difference to make you feel it a bit."

"Possibly," she concedes. "I could live here, you know? If I could bring my job with me, I'd be here in a heartbeat. Mak loves it, too. I actually like the idea of her not growing up in the big city."

"I wouldn't complain." I give her hand a squeeze and smile. "And I can pretty much guarantee that Ben would be over the moon. It's food for thought," I add, carefully gauging the other woman.

This is one of those decisions you don't make in a day. Not if you have a complete life built somewhere else. It was different for me; I had more here in my uncle, and the familiar surroundings, than was left for me anywhere else.

"That it is. But for now I'm enjoying the sunshine on my face, and I've had enough of lazing about. I feel like doing something."

"Come fishing."

Both Stacie and I swivel our heads around to find Ben heading toward us.

"Not going fishing," Stacie says, making it sound like it's the most disgusting proposition she's ever heard. I bark out a laugh. She may be thinking about moving closer, but I'm afraid she'll never be an outdoorsy girl.

"Mak is," Ben returns, shrugging his shoulders.

"Of course she is," Stacie fires back. "She'd shovel poop if you told her it was the cool thing to do. You ask and my daughter jumps, but I ask her to pick up her dirty clothes; I don't even have to wait for the answer to know it'll be *no.*" She turns to me with an exasperated look on her face, and I have to bite my lip not to laugh. "I swear I thought I had years before puberty hit."

There's nothing for me to say. I don't even think she expects me to, so I just pat her knee, while Ben chuckles behind us.

"Morning," his voice is suddenly right by my ear and I tilt my head back.

"Hey," I whisper, as his hand slips around my neck and forces my chin even higher. His kiss is soft and sweet, and I could stay like that forever, if Mak didn't come barreling around the corner.

"Can we go now?" she chirps, bouncing up and down impatiently.

"Lord have mercy," Stacie groans.

"Right behind you, kid," Ben says, and with a wink at me, follows the skipping girl around the corner, only to turn back at the last minute.

"Sis," he calls to Stacie. "If you're looking for something to do, ask Isla to show you where the stain is for the Deville trailer."

Ben

Of course Mak hasn't eaten yet, or brushed her teeth, and it takes a little convincing to get her to sit down at the kitchen island and eat the oatmeal I made her.

"Why is oatmeal good for you?" she asks, right after I tell her that.

"I remember my mom making oatmeal every morning before school," I tell her. "I didn't like it much, but she called it *brain food*, explained that if I wanted to be smart and strong, I'd eat oatmeal every day of the week."

"Did you like it then?" I chuckle as she tentatively puts another spoonful in her mouth.

"Not right away, but I learned to love it."

"Well, I love Isla's pancakes best for breakfast. They're much better than oatmeal," she declares, her stubborn streak showing.

"That's easy," Isla says, as she walks into the kitchen, looking for a refill. "And you're so lucky." She taps Mak on the nose. "Because it just so happens you haven't even tried my best pancakes yet."

I chuckle at my niece's face, full of expectation as Isla takes her time filling her mug and doctoring it up the way she likes, before she turns back around.

"You'll never guess the secret ingredient for my *best* pancakes." Mak is not stupid. She knows exactly what's coming next as her face falls.

"Oatmeal," she says, a little defeated.

"You bet. I ground it real fine, mush in a banana, and add just a little milk and an egg. They're easy to make, I can teach you."

"Cool," the now widely smiling Mak breathes.

"I'll go grab some bananas and eggs later. We're running low on supplies anyway. Maybe we can make them tomorrow?" Isla winks at me, as I grab the vibrating phone from my pocket and slip into the hallway.

"Neil," I answer, when I see his name displayed.

"Hey, hope you had a good Christmas?"

"What's up?" I ask right away, dismissing with the pleasantries. The guy is probably nice enough, but he's too damn pretty and smooth, and his soft chuckle on the other end irritates the fuck out of me. I found out from Isla he's married to an older woman. Her age, Isla felt the need to inform me with a smile, which really pissed me off.

"Do you know if Isla's checked her emails recently?"

"No. I don't think she's touched her laptop since our family arrived. Why?"

"Good. If she does, I don't want her to worry. I've temporarily rerouted her emails."

"Why?" I ask again.

"There was a video this time. I'm pretty sure it wasn't you. At least I hope the fuck it wasn't, or I'll have to wash my eyes with goddamn bleach. Way too many hairy parts." He audibly shudders, and I feel rage bubbling up, as I realize that this fucking crazy bitch upped the game in trying to scare Isla off.

"Not me," I bite off.

"God, please don't tell me how you can know for sure. Knowing each other's grooming habits is way too fucking intimate."

"Did you pin her?" I want to know, ignoring his jabs.

"Back in the Durango area. It came in on Christmas Day. I noticed it hadn't been opened, downloaded it, and then deleted it from the server. That's when I rerouted any incoming emails. Figured you guys didn't need your holidays messed up."

I breathe in a small sigh of relief that Isla's not around the corner somewhere, but make a mental note to check back in with Geoffrey Banks after I take my niece fishing.

"Thanks," I tell Neil. "Appreciate it."

"Anything for that beautiful woman of yours." I can hear the smile in his voice as he fucking yanks my chain again. I'm about to tear into him when I hear a woman laugh in the background. *"Would you quit torturing the guy?"*

"Did you hear that?" he asks. "That's Kendra, my wife. Be assured she'd have me castrated, with my balls shoved down my throat so far, I'd need a surgical team to dislodge them, if she suspected, even for a second, that I was being serious." There's the sound of a bit of a scuffle, and then a woman's voice comes over the line.

"He's right. This is how he is, always the jokester—the tease. Just don't think for a second he's not deadly serious about his job, because he is. And once this mess is settled, you two should come over for dinner. We're not that far from Cortez."

"Thanks," I mumble, a little taken aback by the unexpected invitation.

"Well, now that my wife has ruined all my fun, I'll let you go. Anything moves on this, you'll be the first to know."

"Sounds good. I'll see if I can get anything out of the stepfather. I'll let you know."

I end the call and make my way back into the great room, where my sister is hoisting her grumbling daughter into a snowsuit.

"Ready, Freddy?"

-

"Why are we fishing for just that fish? Whatever that name is?"

Mak is standing at the edge of one of the two ponds

off the reservoir. She's still a little uneasy with the large rod in her hands, but over the past few hours, she's managed to pull a few little fish out of the water, even taking them off the hook herself.

We walked down here, Mak chatting excitedly the entire way, and Al following behind riding one of the ATVs, loaded with the gear.

"Kokanee salmon," Al answers for me. "Because you can only fish for it between September and the end of December. We only have two days left."

"Why?"

I bite back a smile at Mak's nonstop questions. Her curious nature is such a big part of why I love her to pieces, but from the look on Al's face, it's testing his patience.

"Salmon spawn in the spring. Here they run up the Dolores River and deposit their eggs..."

I walk away, letting Al do his best to explain the Kokanee salmon's propagation to my niece, while I answer my buzzing phone.

I'm surprised to see Neil calling again.

"Ben. Everything quiet up there?"

The hair on my neck stands up at the question.

Why?

Why do they force me to this?

My mother, she's so frail, so sick. I can already see death in her eyes. It's all moving too fast on one side and not moving at all on the other.

My nails score over my scalp, drawing blood, forcing

myself to feel. I've been numb—at the mercy of those pills for too long.

My mother is the only one who loves me, but I will win Brent's love back. I know I will. He'll understand why I had to shut him up. That disgusting, fat, nosey slime bucket, who just wanted my mother for himself. He was always in my face about everything. Asking questions he had no business asking. Embarrassing me in front of my mother.

The pain on her face. I just couldn't take it anymore. I had to make him stop.

"I'll be back for you," I'd whispered, with my lips against her forehead. "It'll all be alright."

And it will be. This cabin is perfect. It has no running water but there is enough snow up here to melt. The wood stove is enough to keep it warm and it was only temporary anyway. I can see the reservoir below and the sharply peaked roof of the house I will be living in soon, to my left.

I've been invisible to everyone. No one has seen me watching. No one has heard me move. No one knows I exist only in the darkness.

I'm tired of living in everyone's shadows. I want to step into the light.

There is just one person left standing in my path.

One person, who keeps me from claiming what's rightfully mine.

So I wait, and I watch for a time when their guards are down, and I can clear the final obstacle to him.

CHAPTER 23

Ben

"What's the matter?"

Al's head shoots up, like a good cop; he can hear the concern in my voice.

On the other end, Neil sighs deeply, not making me feel any better. The ominous feeling crawling under my skin only intensifies.

"Fucking talk, James!" I bark, startling Mak. So I smile and just shake my head, while Al does his best to distract her, without taking his eyes off me for long.

"Jesus, Ben. Did you talk to the parents at any time?"

"No. Was gonna call them later, why?"

"I had a BOLO pop up on my screen this morning, with a familiar car description. That's what drew me first. Took a closer look at the call, and it turns out it's connected to a violent attack on an older couple. The name and address are familiar, Ben."

I don't really need him to spell it out for me. The sick feeling in my gut tells me enough.

"Alive?" I manage to bite off, thinking about those poor people. There's no doubt in my mind who's responsible.

"She is, but barely. He was dead on arrival at the hospital."

"Can you smell smoke?" Al suddenly asks, drawing my attention. I take a good sniff and sure enough, I can smell it.

"Could be a bonfire somewhere?" I suggest, but I don't really believe it.

"The fuck is going on there, Ben? Fire? Do you have everyone with you?"

"I don't," I whisper, staring at the plume of smoke forming coming from the general direction of the house. "Gotta go."

I'm already moving when I end the call.

"Ben!" Al yells behind me.

"Stay here, and stick close to Mak!"

I'm running when I feel, before I hear, the vibrating rumble of a loud explosion. I don't stop. Even with my lungs empty and my heart stopped, my legs are still pumping, moving at full speed.

Isla

"Why are they in here when the Deville is down there?"

We're clambering about in the large shed, behind the house, to locate the stain for the trailer, hard to find in the leftover construction detritus strewn about. Anything that was still potentially useable was tossed in here, to be sorted through properly in the spring. Right now, I'm wishing for a dumpster while cursing Ben's frugal nature.

I was surprised when right after Ben and Mak left; Stacie turned to me and asked if I had any old clothes she could borrow. No way her five foot eight frame was going to fit into my ultra petite jeans, so I raided Ben's drawers instead. Better too big than too little, I figured.

She looks so out of character, in an old flannel shirt of mine, and Ben's old paint splattered jeans, rolled up at the bottom, and cinched in with a belt at the waist, so they don't end up around her ankles. Her hair is up underneath the bright blue beanie and suddenly she looks like a tomboy—just like her daughter—or like me.

"Temperature. We just turn on space heaters when working in there. The shed is heated, Ben insisted."

Stacie snorts. "Doesn't feel heated in here," she grumbles.

"Heat kicks in when it drops below forty degrees. Keeps stuff from freezing. Got them!" I call out, triumphantly pulling two cans from underneath a stack of drywall scraps. *Seriously*.

Stacie takes one and makes her way outside, where her SUV is idling. She'd insisted, because she has seat heaters. Whatever, for the short distance we had to go, I would've survived a frozen ass. I do it all the time.

"Wait," I stop her when she opens the tailgate and sets the cans inside. "I was just going to get you started and then hit the store."

"So?" she asks, shrugging her shoulders. "You take my car, at least your ass and hands will be warm." She slams the gate shut and moves to the driver's side, sliding behind the wheel. I get into my seat and am met with the most delicious glow heating my tush.

"Oh God," I groan, inadvertently closing my eyes before turning to face Stacie, who has a big grin on her face.

"Right? And touch this," she says indicating the steering wheel. "Just wrap your entire hand around it. No gloves."

"I need this," I blurt out, as I am introduced to a level of luxury no one here should have to go without. But it begs a question. "Why in the hell do you need it? Do you even get snow in Albuquerque?"

"It freezes, and yes, we've seen snow in Albuquerque," she says, starting up the car and pulling away from the shed. "Doesn't stay long if it falls, but I've seen it. Besides, it comes standard on this model. The seat was extra."

"What is it?"

"Subaru Forester, you should check them out. You can consider your trip to the store a test drive."

By the time we get to the Deville, I don't want to leave the comfort of the toasty seat and shiver against the cold when I get out. Forgot my damn earmuffs.

Stacie oohs and aahs over the improvements Ben has made so far. It's mostly invisible, for now just the bones and mechanics, but she clearly can see where he's planning to take it.

"This isn't all that needs to be stained," I tell her. "The cupboard doors and drawer fronts are in the Airstream, next door. Those have already had a coat." I slip around Stacie and lift the little space heater on the fold out table. "Electrical hookup is done." I show an outlet just underneath the hinges on the table. "Let's heat this place up. It won't take long but you need it warmer to be able to work with the stain. Wanna see the Airstream?"

"I'd love to spend some time here in the spring or summer," Stacie says as we step outside. I clap my hands over my ears to keep them warm. "Want my hat?"

"Nah, I'll be fine, it's just the wind."

Inside the slightly larger Airstream, Stacie takes stock of her surroundings, and like her brother, seems to have the uncanny ability to see beyond what is there to what it potentially could be.

For all my creative blood and my discerning eye, I see beauty in things that are tangible, whether physically or implied—things that evoke emotions from me. I don't have that creative talent to conjure something out of nothing.

"If I could take some extended time off, it sure would be a lot of fun to help with these," she says, as we close up the Airstream and make our way back to the smaller trailer. "I'm pretty sure I remember how to sew, I know I can handle a paintbrush and a hammer. And I have an extensive Pinterest collection you would be jealous of." I grin at her silly eyebrow waggle.

"I think I have maybe two boards started in there. Maybe I should follow you."

"You should, but remember; just look, don't touch," she says waving a finger at me.

"Isn't that the whole purpose of Pinterest? To raid other people's boards?"

"Other people's—yes." She stops on the first step and turns to face me. "But not mine."

Inside the trailer, it's already warmed up quite a bit, and I help Stacie find the rags and brushes.

"Go," she finally waves me out of the way. "Go take the car for a spin and get your groceries. Maybe bring me back a large macchiato from that coffee place?"

"That's your real reason for shoving me out the door, isn't it?" I tease, watching as she shrugs her shoulders, not looking in the least guilty.

"Here," she says, pulling the beanie off her head and tugging it down over my ears. "So you can stay warm while you fetch me my coffee."

"That's bribery."

"If it works…"

-

Stacie's car handles really smoothly, even on the snow. I like that I have decent visibility and can see over the steering wheel, despite the fact I'm short and get lost behind the wheel in Ben's Toyota, for instance.

A white flash draws my eyes to the left, where one of the many trails meets the road, but when I turn my head, the road takes another turn and I can't see. There are dozens of these cattle trails, called that because ranchers will drive trailers full of cattle up those small mountain paths to graze during the summer months.

Winter is pretty quiet in Dolores, compared to the summer. They still have some tourist traffic; mostly for the cross-country skiing trails around here, but most folks would rather head further into the mountains to places like Telluride for downhill skiing or maybe Ouray for the hot springs.

It's not hard to find a parking spot outside the grocery store, and with maybe four other customers, it doesn't take me long to pick up what I need.

The Pony Express is busier than I expected, quite a few people waiting in line to be served.

"Isla!" Jen calls, waving me over from the doorway to the kitchen and her little office. With an apologetic smile at the people lined up in front of me, I slip around the counter and through the door behind Jen.

"I just received the proof of your book from the

printer this morning. How's that for coincidence, right?" I quickly wipe my hands on my legs before accepting the beautifully bound, photo book, with the picture of my cow on the front, as well as my name in big letters. Surreal.

I end up spending much longer in the coffee shop than I intended. Ryan at the gallery in Durango has offered to sell my books at his place and Jen has apparently got a few other local merchants willing to try them out. But before we can put their orders through, we need to make sure the proof is flawless. Jen jots down a few minor points to take up with the printer and walks me out.

"Wait," I remember. "I was supposed to bring Stacie a macchiato." Jen disappears behind the counter and starts working that machine.

"You want something?"

"Do me one of the same," I say, digging into my pocket to find my phone, I should give a call Stacie to let her know I'll be on my way shortly. My pockets are empty—no phone. Maybe I dropped it in the car.

Jen hands me my coffees when I hear a siren.

"Jesus, another one? Wonder what's on fire up there," one of Jen's baristas mutters, and my head whips around to her.

"Another? What's going on?" I demand, my voice shrill with sudden panic.

"Already had two fire trucks going up the mountain earlier," she says.

"This last one was an ambulance," a customer sitting by the window pipes up, but I'm barely listening, I'm already running out the door, ignoring Jen's cries behind me.

I'm buckled in, and firing up the engine, when I spot

the phone in the cup holder. It's not mine, it looks like Stacie's, with a few missed calls from Ben.

I turn up the road to the campground and call him back, my heart beating in my throat.

I watched as the two women got in the car.

Watched the bitch take the passenger seat as the other one, with the blue knit hat, got behind the wheel. I thought I might've missed another opportunity, but then I watched them turn left toward the campground instead of right, toward town.

I watched as they carried those cans into that old trailer, and an idea began to form.

The old gas can I'd found in the cabin, still half full, might come in handy. I tried not to think about the collateral damage since the bitch is never alone, but I felt my time running out. This might be the perfect opportunity, and it would look like a horrible accident.

With the can in the trunk of my car, I turned back for one last look at the view below. It looked like the gods might be on my side, when I saw the other one get in her SUV.

Ben

"What is your emergency?"

"Fire and explosion...up at the campground...on

528," I bark into the phone, already out of breath. In the distance, I can see smoke and fire coming from where the trailers are parked.

"Is anyone hurt?" the woman asks, and it takes me a second before I can answer.

"Possibly two," I choke out, unable to even fathom it.

My lungs are burning by the time I hit the campground. I get closer to see the Deville, this side of it ripped open, and what was still standing fully engulfed in flames. I have to force down the bile surging up.

"Isla!…Stacie?" I call their names as I run closer, hearing little other than the roar of the fire.

"Sir?" The tentative voice sounds on the other end of the line. "Sir? They're on their way, only a few minutes out."

I still have the damn phone plastered to my ear, like a fucking lifeline, as I rush around the other backside of the trailer, forced to keep my distance due to the heat of the fire. There's no goddamn way into the trailer, and whoever was in there, would be dead by now.

"I've gotta go," I manage, ending the call when I can hear sirens in the distance.

For a moment I just stand there, scanning the debris scattered around, some of it still burning. Toward the front, from what I can see, the larger window is on the ground, blackened. Only a few feet away, I spot something covered by a charred piece of siding—something that has me gasp in a lungful of smoke.

Immediately I start hacking, but I can't bring myself to drag my eyes away from the ratty, rolled up jeans legs and the baggy ass, just visible under the edge of the panel. Exactly the way Isla likes to wear them. I reach the still smoldering piece of siding, covering the upper half of the body.

Grabbing onto the edge, I don't care that it's burning the skin off my palm, as I flip the panel up and off.

Most of the clothes are burned off her back, exposing dark patches on the skin where fire touched. Her head is covered by some kind of cloth, a towel maybe, and the body is still and unmoving. Frantically, I look around for a second body, but can't see anything.

My sight is blurry: from the heat, the smoke, and the tears. I can barely make out the fire truck as it races closer, firemen jumping out the minute it comes to a halt.

"Over here…" I try to call out, but end up having to point down at the ground, where I need a second to clue in on the slight movement. Her hand—her hand is moving.

"Sir—step back please, sir. Give us some room to work." The bulky fireman shoves me out of the way and I land on my ass in the snow. Numb.

"There could be someone else…in there," I point at the trailer but am not surprised when the same fireman gives me a slight shake of the head.

I'd forgotten I was holding my phone when it starts buzzing in my hand. Trying to decipher the name on the screen, I quickly hit answer.

"Stacie…" Her name comes out on a sob.

"Ben?"

Isla?

But that means that…

CHAPTER 24

Isla

"Family of Anastasia Gustafson?"

Ben is on his feet before the woman in scrubs has a chance to finish her sentence.

I'm not sure how long we've been here exactly, but it feels like the middle of the night.

-

I can still see the look on Ben's face when I pulled in behind a fire truck and watched him barrel toward me. I didn't have a chance to get out before he yanked open the door and pulled me half-out, holding me like he wanted to absorb me.

"Ben. Baby, talk to me, I'm scared. Is anyone hurt? Why is there an ambulance? What's going on?" I rambled, one question after another, my panic only increasing as his grip on me tightened with every one.

"Anastasia," he whispered, the sound raw and slicing me to the core.

"Is she…?"

"I don't know," he said defeatedly when I couldn't finish the question. "I thought she was…I thought it was you." He buried his face in my neck and I could smell the smoke in his hair.

"Where's Mak? Uncle Al?"

"At the pond, I told him to stay with her." He tilted back to look at me. "Nobody is alone at any time. No one."

"Sir, we need to check you out." An EMT was standing behind him, giving me a kind nod, but I felt Ben's arms tighten.

"Promise me," he hissed.

"I promise, but, sweetheart, let them have a look," I told him gently, pushing him back a little.

"My sister?"

"Sir, she's in the ambulance, about to head out to Southwest Memorial. They're taking good care of her."

Ben let himself be checked out when I looked at what remained of the Deville. Not much more than a metal frame on wheels.

We had a brief argument when Ben tried to get into the driver's seat of Stacie's car, insisting he could drive, despite the burn on his hand. Since I still had the keys, it was a moot point, and we swung by the pond to pick up my uncle and Ben's niece. Atsa had luckily stuck around with Mak and we loaded him in the back. I'd drop him off with Jen; I didn't want to leave him there alone.

That resulted in another brief argument, because Ben didn't want to stop at all, but I convinced him it would be best. It only took a minute, since Jen saw me pull up and had come running out. Without asking questions, she simply gave me a tight hug, took Atsa by the collar, and headed inside.

I saw the looks my uncle and Ben exchanged when I got back behind the wheel. Not sure what that is, between law enforcement people; they seem able to communicate things without words. I know some message was relayed when Uncle Al's mouth became a firm stripe and a muscle in his jaw started twitching.

I wasn't sure I even wanted to know, there was enough chaos and confusion in my head, and pain in my heart. Especially listening to the gut-wrenching sobs from Mak in backseat, when Ben told her that her mom had been hurt pretty badly.

-

"Yes. Talk to me." Ben is in the woman's space, scaring the shit out of her.

"Ben, give her room, honey," I try gently, as a sleeping Mak shifts in my lap. She had clung to Ben all day, while we were waiting, but when Neil and another man showed up to talk to him, he handed her to me. She stayed plastered against me, even after Ben came back and whispered with my uncle in the far corner of the waiting room. I still didn't want to know. Or maybe I just didn't want to have confirmed what I already suspected. My heart couldn't take it. Finally, a few hours ago, Mak fell asleep on my lap.

"Anastasia is out of surgery," the woman shares when Ben takes a grudging step back.

"Stacie," he mumbles. "She prefers Stacie."

"Okay," she says, nodding kindly. "Stacie is in recovery. We were able to remove some shrapnel from her back, but she had a piece of metal embedded in one of her kidneys. We weren't able to save the kidney. In addition, she suffered a depressed skull fracture and we had to remove a shard of her skull. We're monitoring for swelling of her brain. In addition, she has third-degree burns on sixty percent of her body. The deepest burns were on her back, and we debrided as much of the dead skin as we could. At some point in the future we'll be using grafts to help grow new. The biggest danger right now is infection, and we're doing everything we can to prevent that. She will definitely be facing more surgeries down the road. Given the extent of her injuries, she's considered critical and will be kept in an induced coma until her condition improves."

"Can I see her?" Ben asks, his voice thick with unshed tears and my heart hurts.

"Go to him," I hear my uncle's voice beside me, as he gingerly lifts Mak from my lap and settles her on his.

I walk up to Ben and wrap my arms around him from behind, plastering myself to his back.

"I'm sorry, sir. Once she's ready to be moved to the ICU, you may be able to visit her for a few minutes. I promise to keep you updated, but perhaps you should consider heading home and catching some sleep." With a friendly nod to Uncle Al, she turns and leaves the room.

Ben doesn't move for what seems like a long time, until he finally turns around, grabs me under the arms and half-carries, half-drags me to the love seat on the far wall. There he sinks down, pulls me on top of him and buries his face in my neck.

The silence in the room is complete as I feel the heat of his silent tears burn my skin.

"I can't lose her, too."

Ben's whispered plea draws a sob from my chest. I can't find the words to give him comfort, so I just pull a little closer, burrow a little deeper, to try and soothe him. My own eyes are blurred with tears as I catch a glimpse of Uncle Al, smiling sadly in our direction.

"The doc is right," my uncle says gently. "We should go back and get some rest."

"I can't leave," Ben says, grief lacing his voice as he

raises his head.

"Ben—Son—trust me, I understand, but look at this sleeping little girl? When she wakes up, she's going to need you most of all. Whatever happens, she's going to look to you to find her strength."

-

"Where's Mom?"

I turn around at Mak's sleepy voice. Uncle Al is behind me, carrying her down the hall to her bedroom. We left Ben outside, with the two men that were apparently waiting for him. One of them I saw briefly earlier in the day, with Neil at the hospital, but the other I've never seen before.

"She's still sleeping at the hospital, baby," I soothe, stroking the hair from her face. "We're going to get some sleep, too. Uncle Al was just taking you to your room." I watch as tears fill her eyes.

"Can I sleep with you and Uncle Ben?"

My heart breaks at the fear in that little voice.

"Of course you can, sweetheart. Do you need Uncle Al to carry you?"

"I can walk," she says, putting on a brave face as he lowers her to her feet. I grab her hand tightly in mine and smile at my uncle.

"Night." He tags the back of my head and presses his lips to my forehead.

"Night, my girl. You look after this one for a bit," he says, with a wink in Mak's direction. "I'll take care of your man. Try to get some sleep."

I give Mak an old shirt of mine to put on and help her in bed. Then I strip down to my underwear and tank, before joining her under the covers. She instinctively crawls to me, and I try to keep my crying silent, as I press her head to my chest and listen to her breathing even out with sleep.

Ben

"Sorry to meet under these circumstances."

I nod as I shake the hand of the man, Neil introduced as Gus Flemming. Same guy, Damian had tried to set me up with.

"Me, too."

"How's your sister?" he asks and I almost flinch.

"Don't know," I manage through gritted teeth. "Was wheeled right into surgery and I'm about to lose my shit."

"Hold it in check, I'm sure they'll let you know when they have something to report."

From anyone else, a platitude like that would have me blow, but Gus makes it sound like an order as he holds a firm grip on my hand, and oddly enough, it helps.

"Won't keep you long," he continues, releasing my hand with a final squeeze. "Neil's already got me up-to-date on what he's been looking into for you, and Damian filled me in as much as he could with what he found out through official channels. We'll have a look at the scene, see what we can find that wasn't trampled over by emergency personnel, and maybe check out your place as well. Give us a call when you leave here and we'll meet you at your place."

With a firm clap on my shoulder, he turns on his heels and heads for the lobby.

"He's something, right?" Neil, who's been quiet the entire exchange, points out. "Been with him since my deployment ended. He's like a father figure to me."

I could see that. Although the guy is probably not older than me by much, he seems to have the ability to make you feel he's got your back. And I need everyone at my fucking back just about now.

"I'm so fucking sorry I didn't get to you sooner this morning," the younger man says, and it's clear I'm not the only one carrying that particular load. "Could've probably…"

"Shut up," I cut him off sharply. "I've been saying shit like that to myself all fucking day long. Don't you drown under that kind of useless guilt. Only one who should carry that burden; it isn't me, and it sure as shit isn't you. Focus on finding that deranged bitch."

Neil nods and starts walking in the same direction where Gus has already disappeared.

"Thanks," I call after him. He stops and turns around.

"Go back to your family, man. We've got this."

-

"So what's the plan?"

Al's waiting for me in the great room, a bottle of scotch and two glasses ready on the coffee table.

Gus Flemming was at the house as promised, when we got here. Don't remember the other guy's name, Jim or Joe, or something. Looked ex-military or maybe former law enforcement. I wasn't really paying attention to introductions.

According to what they'd been able to find out, the fire had been arson. Not that I hadn't figured that already, but it was still good to have it confirmed. It looked like the door had been braced shut with a picnic table, which was then doused in gasoline and set aflame. According to the fire chief, my sister likely tried to escape by kicking the larger window out. The heat of the fire had been intense enough to ignite the small propane tank, and the explosion possibly threw Stacie clear of the trailer. The sheriff's office is treating it as arson and attempted murder.

"Flemming has a guy liaising with law enforcement, and he says he has a few guys with an eye on the house," I tell Al, as I sit down beside him and accept the glass he offers me. "My friend, Damian Gomez, the FBI agent I told you about, is pulling all the strings on this one. He's handling the assault on those old folks in Durango. If Damian trusts Flemming, who is former law enforcement himself, then I trust him, too."

"Good enough for me," Al says, tossing the last of his drink back. "Another?" He holds up the bottle and I follow suit, throwing the scotch back like a shot before I hold out my glass for a refill.

"The girls sleeping?" I ask, looking around.

"Both in your bed."

"Good," I mumble, my lips on the rim of my glass. "Fuck, what a day."

"You can say that again," Al says, his large paw landing on my shoulder, giving it a firm squeeze. "We should turn in. I'm staying here. I'm keeping my gun on my body, and I've got your back. Try and get some rest."

I watch as the old man walks out of the room, leaving me to sip the last of my scotch. Grabbing both empty glasses and the bottle, I deposit them on the counter in the kitchen, turning off lights, and checking doors and windows as I go.

When I walk into the bedroom, I halt as I take in the tangled mess in our bed. Mak is clinging to Isla's sleeping form like a monkey, her limbs literally wrapped around Isla's body and her face buried under her chin. I can't believe Isla is able to sleep like that, and as soon as I shed some of my clothes, I try to crawl between the two. I manage to untangle my niece, only to have her cling to me, still sleeping, and I tug Isla close on my other side.

I need that, feeling both their breaths tickling my skin and both their heartbeats beating against my body. I close my eyes and try to let myself drift off, as I hope with all my heart that somewhere in a hospital bed, another breath is taken and another heart keeps beating.

CHAPTER 25

Ben

"Okay, I think I'm ready now."

I turn around and watch Isla walk down the hall toward me.

"Ready for what, babe?"

When I woke up this morning I was surprised I'd even slept. I managed to sneak out of bed, without waking the girls, grabbed my phone from the nightstand—no calls—and made a beeline for the coffee maker. It already had a full pot, courtesy of Al, who was sitting at the counter.

"I've been thinking," he said, when I took my first hit of caffeine. "The fire and explosion were intentional, but your sister? I'm pretty sure that was an accident. I want to bet the target was my niece."

"I would agree."

The old man stared silently into his cup, before raising his eyes.

"Need you on the ball, Son. She's all I've got left." His voice was thick with emotion, and he had to clear his throat to continue. "Ginnie—she doesn't know who I am, and there's little left of her I recognize. I've already made my peace with that loss. But, boy, something happens to my girl, I swear it'll be the death of me. And I'll welcome it."

All I could do was reach over and squeeze his shoulder. I heard him; I got what he was saying. You can't control what is in the past, but you sure as hell can try to get a bead on what's ahead.

I called the hospital right there, needing to know how my sister had gotten through the night. As soon as I was told she was stable, I shifted my focus ahead. So I called Neil.

That's who I just saw out the door.

I open my arms and Isla walks right in.

"Did you sleep?" she asks, apparently forgetting her earlier question as her eyes scan my face. I kiss her good morning before answering.

"I snuck in between you two," I admit, smiling down at her. "I slept. Is Makenna…?"

"She's still asleep. I left the door open so I can hear her and she can hear us when she wakes."

"Stacie's stable," I tell her. "I called earlier; she got through the night without any incidents."

"Are we heading to the hospital?"

"I'm not sure," I answer honestly, and I watch surprise register on her face. "I was just showing Neil out."

"I thought I heard him." She nods, as if to bolster herself. "Which brings me back to what I said earlier. I'm ready to know what happened. I want to know everything, and I know you've been keeping stuff from me. I've heard the whispers; I've seen the glances. I know you've let my uncle in, and I understand why, but I need to know what we're up against as well." She closes her eyes briefly and breathes in audibly through her nose, before looking up at me. "Cause as I see it, what happened yesterday shouldn't have happened to Stacie—it was supposed to happen to me."

Isla

The girl is killing me.

Before I had a chance to get what I was looking for from Ben, Mak came tearing out of the bedroom, with panic in her eyes. Ben scooped her up and calmly reassured her that her mom was doing okay.

"Get yourself a coffee," he said to me over her shoulder. "I've got her." And disappeared back into our bedroom with her.

When they resurface fifteen minutes later, Mak is dressed, it looks like her face has been washed, and she's clinging to her uncle's hand.

"Hop up, girl." Uncle Al pulls out a stool for her and Ben swings her up. "Why don't I get us some breakfast going, while these two," he waves his hand between Ben and I, "get themselves ready for the day."

"I'm not really hungry," she says in a tiny little voice.

"Nonsense. You just wait until you get a whiff of my famous scrambled eggs with liver and onion. You won't ever want anything else for breakfast again."

I can't hold back the chuckle when I see Mak's face simply blanch. He used to tease me like that all the time.

"He's kidding," I whisper in her ear. She's starting to look really panicked when he dives into the fridge.

"Maybe I'll just have oatmeal," she whispers, looking for a rescue from Ben.

"You'd rather have oatmeal than liver?" Al turns to face her. "How about those oatmeal pancakes Isla was talking about. Think we should give those a try?" That earns him a smile and an enthusiastic nod.

Ben kisses her head, grabs my hand, and drags me down the hall. In the bedroom, he leads me to the side of the bed and pats the mattress.

"Sit, Pixie."

So I do. I sit down clasping my hands in my lap, because despite the fact I've asked for what is coming, I don't know if I'm ready to hear it. Ben sits down beside me, looking at me, and I know he's waiting for me.

"Tell me," I whisper.

In his deep, raspy voice, he lays out the parts of the past few days I was in the dark on. The video, with Ben's assurances it wasn't his hairy ass featured. Then he tells me about the violent attack on the couple he had visited in Durango—Jahnee's parents.

I have to swallow hard when he informs me the man did not survive, and her mother just barely. My heart aches for that woman, already dying of cancer, only to have your own flesh and blood turn violent against you. The irony is bitter. I can only hope her suffering won't be long and that she may still find some peace in death.

Finally he fills me in on both the official findings of arson and the measures put in place for our—or rather, my—safety.

"Are you sure it was her?" I ask, but then I shake my head. I know better. Deep in my gut, I know. "Never mind that." I hold up my hand when Ben starts to answer. "That was supposed to be me."

"Don't go there, Isla," Ben cuts me off. "If you're trying to take responsibility, you're gonna have to get in line." He cups my face in his big hands. "Trust me on that." I try to read his eyes and see nothing but sincerity there.

It makes me feel only marginally better, but there's part of me that wonders if I maybe should've known about the video before. I can't help think that, as a woman, I might've seen the aggression in that, whereas the men likely waved it off as only an annoyance.

"So what now?" I want to know.

"Now we're going to lay low. There's a chance she thinks she's accomplished what she wanted and will try to connect with me at some point. I'd like to keep her thinking she was successful, which means keeping you out of sight, just in case she's watching."

"What the hell does she think is going to happen? That she can just walk up to you and you'll declare your undying love for her?" I snap, suddenly angry at the situation.

"I don't know, it's hard to try out what someone, who's clearly out of their mind, is thinking, but I promise you that everything is being done to locate her before we find out." Ben tries to soothe me, but I'm still bristling. "Neil's boss, Gus, that's the guy from the hospital last night, is technically working for the FBI on this. It helps that both Damian, and Gus, have strong ties to local law enforcement."

"And Neil this morning?"

"Alarm system. He took some measurements and is coming back this afternoon to install it."

I slump my shoulders. Here I was, thinking this would be our haven, our sanctuary, and instead it sounds like it's becoming our prison. Ben drapes his arm around my shoulders and tugs me close.

"I need to know you and Mak are safe when I'm not

here."

"What about you? What about you being safe? Or Stacie? Have you thought about that?"

"There's extra security at the hospital. Stacie is taken care of. As for me, she's not out to hurt me—she's out to have me."

I look up at the most beautiful, gruff-looking face, with the warmest, ice blue eyes I've ever seen.

"I know," I confirm with a calm I don't feel. "That's what scares me."

-

"When can I see Mom?"

I look up from my computer, where I'm playing around with some edits.

"I'm not sure, sweetheart," I tell Mak honestly.

She's been so patient all morning, with just a minimal explanation as to why we were stuck inside. Thank God for Netflix and family movies. I just don't know what to tell her. The guys, Neil, Ben, and my uncle, are all outside laying out something called a perimeter protection system. Not sure what it is, but it's supposed to alert us to anyone coming within fifty yards of the house.

"Want to help me put some dinner together? Maybe when your uncle comes in, he can give you a better answer."

I know Ben ended up telling Mak a little. Just that there is a person out there who is out to hurt the people he loves, and that is why we have to stay inside. She seemed to take it in stride and allowed me to distract her with the big screen TV for a little.

Atsa had passed up on being Mak's shadow the moment the guys went outside. He's been out all afternoon as well after Uncle Al picked him up from Jen's.

"Okay," Mak says, getting up from the couch and following me into the kitchen. "But can we make tacos? It's Tuesday." I grin at her poor attempt at an innocent look.

"We're gonna have to make our own tortillas though, because I don't have any ready-made."

"You know how?"

"Sure do. It's pretty easy, I'll show you."

That's how we stay busy, and distracted, the next hour and a half until we hear the front door open.

"Whatever you're cooking, I'm staying for dinner," Neil says, the first to walk into the kitchen, with a big smile on his face.

"We've got enough," Mak says, a little blush on her cheeks from hanging over the stove, or maybe not. It would appear Neil's charm works on any age.

"Did you cook?" he asks her, and she eagerly nods her head. "Well, in that case, sign me up for a double serving."

"Must you flirt with everything that sports twin x-chromosomes?" Ben walks in, shaking his head at Neil.

"Actually," he answers, with his index finger up. "Interesting bit of trivia for you; did you know there are men with two x-chromosomes and women with a y-chromosome?"

I chuckle as I watch Mak's eyes grow big and bounce between the two men.

"I don't even want to know," Ben says, raising his hands. "All I know is I need you to back away from my niece."

Ben

It's the look in Mak's eyes that has me fold.

We've just finished eating when she hits me with the request to see her mother. Although I'm able to tell her Stacie seems to be stable, as per my last call to the hospital, I can see it's not enough.

"Okay, honey," I give in. "I'll see what I can do."

It takes a bit of logistic maneuvering, but in the end Neil offers to stay with Al and Isla, when I bundle Mak in the Toyota. She's uncommonly quiet during the drive, and normally I'd welcome the lack of chatter, but at this time it just makes me uncomfortable.

"What's going through your head, girl?" I finally ask her. I quickly glance over at her profile and notice her lip is quivering. "Honey? You can tell me."

"What will she look like?" The quiver sounds through in her voice, and now I'm questioning whether this was a good idea.

I swerve off the road, stop on the shoulder, and put the car in park. Turning my body toward her, I reach out and brush at the single tear running down her cheek.

"I know she'll have to grow back that pretty hair of hers," I start carefully. "And she'll probably have a lot of bandages and maybe even some wires and tubes coming from her body, but the thing you need to remember is that underneath all that, it's still your mom. Her outside may not look the same but, baby, I promise you, the size of her heart, the light in her soul, and most importantly, her love for you have not changed. Not even a bit."

"Promise?" Her chin wobbles even harder, and I wrap both arms around her, tucking her head under my chin.

"Cross my heart, Makenna. Cross my heart."

-

"Sorry, sir, there's no kids allowed in the ICU."

I glare at the gray-haired nurse at the desk, but her gaze doesn't falter, and I know I'm in for a battle.

"What do you mean there's no kids allowed in ICU? This is her mother, you can't be telling me she can't see her only parent?"

"Sir," the old hag hisses, as she leans closer. "The ICU is no place for children, besides, her mother is not exactly looking her best." She tries, but fails miserably, to keep her volume low so Mak, who's standing by my side, won't hear. I take in a deep breath, attempting not to lose my temper in front of my niece, before I answer.

"You're absolutely right, it is no place for children. Problem is, her *mother* is in there, which makes it the absolute right place for my niece to be. Secondly, if you think for one second that her imagination is not far worse than the reality of what her *mother* might look like, you are delusional."

In the end, I failed as well. My voice clearly had raised enough to draw the attention of the doctor, who'd been in the operating room with Stacie yesterday.

"What seems to be the problem?" she asks, walking up to the desk, with a gentle smile for Mak and a stern look to me, before she turns her attention to the nurse. "Carol?"

"I'm trying to explain no kids are allowed in the ICU."

"I'm afraid that's true," the doctor says with an apologetic smile, before dropping her eyes to Mak, who is burrowing into my side. Then she leans over the counter and says to the nurse, under her breath, "I'm afraid Mr. Sparrow in room 302 has soiled himself. Could you please…?"

Carol takes in a sharp breath, flicks her eyes back and forth between me and the other woman, and finally with a big huff, gets up and stomps down the hall.

"Better come with me, quick," the doctor holds out a hand to Mak. "Let's go see your mom before the gatekeeper gets back."

Mak looks at me and I give her a little nod, before she accepts the hand offered.

-

"*Thank you,*" I mouth to the doctor when she moves to the door. She took her time to explain to Mak exactly what all the beeping machines, tubes, and hoses were for. It helped her get over her first shock of seeing Stacie, or what is supposed to be Stacie, lying in that bed.

There's little recognizable, between the bandages and the swelling.

"You're right, Uncle Ben," Mak suddenly says, standing beside Stacie's bed, running her fingers over the hand that is not covered in wrappings. "Look."

She carefully turns her mother's hand over and points to the little four-leaf clover my sister had tattooed on the inside of her wrist, in her college days.

My eyes burn when Mak leans over and gently kisses the only recognizable part of her mother.

That stupid little clover.

CHAPTER 26

Isla

"Are you awake?"

"I am now," I groan into my pillow as Ben's hand slides down between my legs.

I'm rolled halfway on my stomach, and his warm body is pressing up against me from behind, his deft fingers quickly finding my softening core.

"Need inside you, Pixie." The low rasp of his voice and the feeling of his thick erection against my ass, triggers an involuntary shudder to run through my body, leaving my nipples instantly alert. With only the rough pad of his finger dragging over my clit, I throw my head back against his shoulder and moan deeply as the slow burn of a lazy orgasm washes over me.

My body had clearly been ready for his touch after a long week of sharing our bed with Mak.

Last night was the first time, since the explosion, Mak didn't ask to sleep with us. Ben and I had exchanged a look, but we didn't say a thing when she walked into what had been her mother's room and crawled into her bed.

"I miss her smell," was the only thing Mak had said in explanation as she burrowed under the covers. When we checked on her a few hours after, on our way to bed, she'd been fast asleep. Still, we left the door open so we could hear her during the night.

A quick glance tells me our bedroom door is now

firmly shut; Ben must've closed it at some point.

"You ready for me, baby?"

Instead of answering him, I roll on my back and pull my sleep shirt up and over my head. Right away, he repositions, dropping his hips in the cradle of mine.

My eyes focus on his face hovering over me. The still sleep-swollen eyes. The creases in his brow and along his nose and mouth. The strong, slightly parted lips. An interesting face, an arresting face, even, but what makes it truly beautiful is the expression on it when he looks at me. My hand reaches up to scrape along his scruffy jaw.

"Gonna love you now, Isla," he warns me with his lips almost touching mine. I can taste the mint of toothpaste on his breath and briefly worry about my own. Ben, clearly unconcerned, cuts off any possible protest by slipping his tongue in my mouth at the same time his cock finds my entrance and powers deep. He drowns my loud groan with his kiss.

-

"The old woman died?"

Ben is pacing back and forth down the hallway, and I'm in the great room, trying hard to distract Mak from his telephone conversation, but it's not easy. Her head pops up and she zooms in on her uncle at those words. I see him wince when he spots her looking, and he throws me an apologetic glance before disappearing into our bedroom.

The house is not small, but under these circumstances, it's starting to feel even more confined than living in the trailer did. It's not just the four of us either; it's Neil, Damian, Gus and most of the other guys I've come to know over the past week, who could drop in at any time.

We're all getting frustrated. Snappy and irritable at

being cooped up day after day. Even with a large contingent of law enforcement looking for her, they haven't been able to come up with a thing.

I know I've snapped at both Ben and Uncle Al enough, and this morning I even snapped at poor Mak. She came running from the bedroom, Atsa of course right behind her, and the two of them barreled into me. I was just coming out of the laundry room with yet another load of laundry, freshly washed and folded, and dropped the basket on impact. Clothes and towels all over the damn floor, which I hadn't mopped in days, because with all the feet tracking through it, why bother. I made her cry, only to promptly burst into tears myself.

"What old woman?" Mak asks softly.

"I think they're talking about someone your uncle met, who was very ill, but I can't be sure."

She doesn't ask more, just nods and dives back into the computer game I downloaded for her on my laptop. I get up off the couch and join my uncle in the kitchen.

"Something's gotta give," I hiss at him on my way to the coffee pot.

"One of the hardest parts of the job—this was. The waiting, not being able to actively do something, anything, to help things along. Racking your brain to try and figure out what you might be missing. It consumes you." His arm catches me around the neck when I try to move past him, and he gives me a quick hug. "Patience, my girl. You think it's bad for you? It's nothing compared what your man is dealing with. He's so torn; I'm starting to see the cracks on the outside. He's got some crazy chick from his past, who almost killed his sister, and is targeting his woman. He wants to be there for Stacie, but he's afraid to leave you for too long. And more than anything, he wants to chase down that bitch, so everyone can breathe again." He grabs my shoulders and gives me a light shake. "But he can't do any of that. Not until something breaks, and something will, I promise you that. In the meantime, you're going to have to reel it in. Whatever you need to do to relieve some of that pressure building on him, do it. I love you, my girl, and you know it, but that man is feeling nothin' but guilt right now in every damn direction, and you're only adding to it."

I can't remember a time when I've felt more ashamed. I barely manage a nod when my uncle finally releases his hold on my shoulders. I literally slink out of the kitchen, straight down the hall and into the bedroom. That's where I find Ben, lying on his back on the bed, his arm flung over his eyes, and his phone still in his hand. He doesn't even move when I crawl up on the bed and wrap myself around him. The only acknowledgement is his free arm sneaking around my body and pulling me in even tighter.

"Love you, Ben." My voice is muffled by his sweater.

"Me too, Pixie. Me too," he says, but his voice sounds exhausted, so I lift my head. His eyes peek out from under his arm and I smile.

"Talk to me."

Ben

Talk to me.
Easier said then done.
The death of Dorothy Banks weighs heavily on me. It

feels like another on a growing list of strikes against me on the balance sheet. I don't blame her. She was already dying, but then to have to watch your husband die, and at the hands of your own flesh and blood, would be too much. Her death, so shortly after the attack, is perhaps a blessing. What do I know?

"Her last memories before she died will be the most horrific ones a parent can experience," I start, watching as understanding dawns in Isla's gaze. "I know I wasn't the one beating her or her husband to a pulp, but I might as well have been. This woman is like a guided missile, and anywhere I turn, anyone I touch, just becomes another target. The fucking irony is, I'm one who launched it."

"I'm sorry," she mutters and I'm glad she's not telling me it's not my fault. I don't think I could hear that right now, because I fucking need someone to blame, and I'm the most likely candidate.

"We can't find her, Isla. Every day is another damn dead end and it would be so easy to get lulled into thinking that she's gone to ground permanently, but that would be stupid." I blow out a deep breath before I continue. "They found her car in the parking lot at the Ute Mountain Casino in Towaoc, just south of Cortez, yesterday morning, but no trace of her. She wasn't in the casino, isn't staying at any hotels, and no one's seen her. Damian is checking with Cortez Cab, who runs shuttle taxis from the casino, to see if they picked anyone up there in the past couple of days who fits her description, but I'm not holding my breath. For all we know, she's long gone, but the kicker is we can't be sure."

"No she isn't," Isla counters firmly, surprising me. "She's not gone. Why would she be? From the start, she's had one goal and that hasn't been met yet. Nothing she does is rational, but it doesn't mean she's stupid, just that she's unpredictable." She swings her legs off the edge of the bed and sits up, letting her eyes drift to the window. I can see the wheels turning. "I think she's not that far, keeping an eye on her objective—you. Probably thinking she cleared the way by getting rid of me, and is waiting for the right time to lay claim to you. She's not in a rush, she's been waiting for over a decade." She smiles a little when she turns to face me. "You guys are looking for a hardened criminal, when you should be looking for a jealous and possessive—not to mention bat-shit crazy—woman."

"How'd you get so fucking smart?" I growl, pulling her down on top of me. She grins, a wicked little gleam in her eyes.

"Always been that way," she smarts off. "Which is why I know the one sure way to draw her out in the open."

My hands on her ass freeze in their lazy explorations when I clue in on what she's suggesting.

"Fuck no," I say sharply, rolling her off me and jumping off the bed. I turn and tower over her. "Hell. The fuck. *No.*"

-

"It's actually a good idea," Neil says a few hours later. *Fucking traitor.* "We can have her covered from every angle. Especially if we contain her movements to just routine stuff in Dolores. The grocery store, the coffee shop; places she'd normally go."

"I'm right here, you know?" Isla pipes up beside me. "Don't be talking over my head like I'm some prop you're moving around."

I chuckle at her fire, but in the next moment the smile is wiped off my face, when Neil opens his mouth again.

"Oh, honey, trust me. I know you're no prop," the slick bastard coos. "And trust me, you wouldn't feel that way either if I were *moving* you around." Then he attempts to blind her with his smile. Throwing on the high beams with his '*aw shucks*' attitude, when he's nothing but a lecherous wolf in surfer boy disguise. It takes everything out of me not to knock out some of those shiny, white fucking teeth.

"Not a good time to poke the bear," Isla warns Neil, laughing softly.

"I think unless you want to keep everyone locked down for God knows how long, or you're aiming to move to Bolivia, this may be your only route to go." This from Al, who's been quietly sitting off to the side. The one person I thought would perhaps be even more dead set against this whole *bait* idea.

"I agree," Gus puts his two cents in.

"We'll keep her safe, my friend," Damian says over speakerphone. He's back in Durango, but called in on this meeting.

"I can't believe this shit," I mumble, dropping my head in my hands. "You've all lost your fucking minds. She's got the biggest target on her back."

I feel Isla shift beside me when she slides off her stool and steps between my legs. Her small hands cup my jaw and lift my head, as she leans close enough for our noses to touch.

"That's exactly why," she whispers.

"You're killing me, Pixie," I mumble, for her ears only, as the rest of the group starts discussing strategy.

The two of us oddly removed in our private little bubble. "You're asking me to—" Her fingers press on my lips, cutting of my words.

"No, honey. This is not you alone—not this time. This is all of us making that decision and sharing that responsibility."

-

I watch as Gus's big Yukon rumbles down the snow-covered drive. He and Neil had stayed for dinner and we just finalized plans for tomorrow. *Fucking tomorrow*.

I walk over to the lookout point, while Atsa is off sniffing around and doing his business before we turn in for the night. It's a clear night; crisp cold air with little wind and no clouds. The light of the moon gives everything a blue hue: the trees, the snow, and the ice covering McPhee reservoir. It would be a nice night to go out on snowmobiles. The four-wheelers do well when you stick to the path, but less so when you try to take them into the soft snow. Maybe next winter we'll invest in a couple of snowmobiles.

Seems like a luxury to be thinking about next winter. With Stacie still critical, and now Isla sticking her neck way the hell out, I don't know what tomorrow will look like, let alone next winter.

I tuck my hands in my pockets and turn back to the house, the crunch of my boots in the snow loud in quiet around us. I whistle through my teeth for Atsa, as I make my way to the door.

"Come on, boy!" I follow up when he still hasn't surfaced. I hear a few sharp barks, and then the crunch of something coming through the underbrush behind me.

Just as I turn around to look, the dog bursts out of the

trees, panting like he's just run a marathon.

Close. That was so close.

Lucky I've taken to carrying bear spray on me after a close encounter with that mountain lion a few weeks ago. Apparently it works well on dogs, too.

I had to come back out here—had to see him.

I heard the explosion, saw the ambulance rush away. I was standing right where he was standing just now, looking out over the campground. I'd seen the way he hugged that woman who drove up, the one I'd mistaken for the mother of that little girl. But it had been her—that deceitful bitch had purposely misled me. I could see it clear as day when this woman came no higher than his chin, where the other woman was quite a bit taller. But she'd been driving her car, she'd been wearing the blue hat, I was so sure...

I took off then. Got as far as the casino parking lot, when my stupid car started to sputter. The next two hours I spent playing slots, or at least pretending to. I was invisible there for a little bit, until an older guy sat down beside me.

"Hi, there," he said, pulling his stool a little closer. "Swear I come here every night, and I know I ain't never seen you around. I'd remember a pretty face like yours." The way his eyes roamed up and down my body repulsed me. The stench of days' old sweat wafted off him and his breath stunk like the bottom of a dumpster. I'd been about to tell him off when a waitress walked up.

"What can I get ya, Martin?" she asked him, and he

turned around to me.

"What's your poison, gorgeous?"

It was on my tongue to brush him off, but I was afraid that might draw more attention than just playing along.

"Screwdriver," I mumbled, keeping my head down.

I'd put up with his stench and his company, until I could figure out what my next move was going to be. I was never one to pass up on an opportunity, so I took the drinks he offered, suffered the noxious odors and finally, I let him take me to his home. When he was done taking what he wanted, I took what I needed: a shower, his keys, and his truck. I left him with his life—I think.

I had to come back. After all I've been through, all I've done, I deserve to have it all.

But I'm going straight for the prize now.

CHAPTER 27

Isla

"How have you been? How's Ben's sister? Do you know anything yet?"

The questions are fired off staccato as Jen rushes toward me when I walk through the door of The Pony Express.

I've talked to her a few times, over the last little while, since dumping Atsa on her doorstep. Last time I saw her, too. My uncle had gone and picked him up the morning after and had given her a minimum of information, so she'd called me right after he left.

I told her all I knew, which Ben hadn't been happy with initially, but I argued that since she already knew the entire background story, she'd only be unduly worried if we didn't let her know what was going on. He made me have her promise not to spill a word to anyone, to which she'd snorted.

"Who the hell would I be telling it to?"

Jen had kindly offered to go to the hospital and sit with Stacie, but I explained only family was allowed in the ICU.

I find myself engulfed in a tight hug before I'm dragged to the back, through the kitchen, and into her small office.

"You know you've just given about half a dozen men a heart attack, right?" I scold Jen, thinking about my protection detail that she knew about. "Not like I didn't tell you about them when I called this morning."

Jen makes her eyes wide in fake innocence. She knew. She did this on purpose.

"Now don't you mess with my little bit of fun," she pouts, her hands on her hips when the innocent look clearly has no effect on me. "How often do you think I get a chance to leave an indelible impression on a real live, hard-bodied, fully equipped, living, breathing man—let alone six?"

"Drama queen," I accuse her, but she just laughs me off.

"I just wish I could've seen their faces," she says, with a mischievous glint in her eyes.

"Everything okay in here?" A huge, imposing, and unfairly beautiful native man ducks his head in the office.

"All good, sorry about that. Thanks, Caleb," I apologize on Jen's behalf, who is still staring at the doorway where the man disappeared again. "Your mouth is open," I point out, startling Jen back to the present.

"Who—in all that is fucking holy—was *that*?" I wince at the shriek-like quality of her voice, which I'm sure has traveled to the farthest corners of the shop.

"First of all, I don't think you're supposed to say *fucking* and *holy* in one and the same sentence," I bring up. "And to answer your question; that's Caleb who works with GFI investigations, along with his brother Malachi. There's also Joe, and I think you've met Neil."

"There's two of them?" she gushes. "Those names are enough to pucker up my nips. Please tell me at least one of them is single?" She looks at me hopefully, despite the fact she has me giggle out loud. Didn't think I'd be laughing at any time today, so I'm grateful for that touch of brevity.

"You're nuts. And I'm sorry, from what I understand, every last one of these guys is married. Besides, they are all outdoorsy types like Ben. You wouldn't last long." She feigns shock at my words, but she knows damn well it's the truth. Jen may like the rugged look, but she sure doesn't like the rugged life.

I finally answer her initial questions; I update her on Stacie's condition—stable and without infection, so far—and explain why I'm suddenly out and about as opposed to locked away.

"I don't want you to get hurt," she says, her face drawn with concern.

"Trust me, I don't want to get hurt either," I inform her. "But sitting locked up in a house, on the side of a mountain, is giving that woman more control over our lives than she deserves to have. I'm done with that. Now," I promptly change the subject. "What's happening with the book?"

For the next twenty minutes, we go over marketing plans, Internet sales, and planned projects, and I'm struck once again, with Jen's keen business sense. Something I do not possess. Which really does make us a great team.

I'm actually smiling when I leave a little later, with one of Jen's froufrou drinks in my hand, and the crazy stalker situation all but forgotten. Although when I get into Ben's Toyota, I can't help looking around to see if I can spot any of the guys, who are supposed to keep eyes on me at all times. I can't see a single one. It makes me nervous, even though I've been assured that even if I don't see them, they will be there.

As much as it makes me nervous, I'm nowhere near the wreck I'm sure Ben is by now. He was not a happy camper this morning when I left. If she were actually watching, she'd be less likely to make a move if she spotted him around.

Uncle Al, Mak, and Ben stayed behind with the dog.

We haven't really done a good grocery haul since before Christmas, so I figure I'd make my time in the crosshairs count by filling up two carts. Probably overkill, but it can never hurt to be stocked up. I even saunter into the small clothing section where I spotted some cute leggings. Mak might like those. She doesn't like girly things, but leggings aren't really girly. They're more sporty, but the cute daisy pattern makes them pretty as well. Maybe she'll hate them, but she needs some more clothes, since she'll be with us indefinitely, and we don't exactly have her favorite stores in Dolores. This'll have to do for now.

Aside from the daisy pattern, they also have a pair that is covered in dog paw prints, which I'm pretty sure she'll go for. I toss a couple of long-sleeved T-shirts and a zippered hoodie, in what I think is her size, in the cart as well.

Throughout my shopping spree, I try not to think about eyes on me, but am still reassured when I see Caleb casually pass by one aisle over. He's really quite stunning and I'd love to get him in front of my camera one day. Wishful thinking.

I'm lost in thought and don't see it coming, so when I'm hit from behind, my knees buckle and I go down.

Ben

"Your turn, Uncle Ben."

I can't believe Al taught her how to play blackjack. Not *go fish*, not *crazy eights*, but straight up blackjack.

She cornered me the moment I came out of the bedroom this morning, and Al just laughed at me from the kitchen. I'd allowed her to distract me for a little while, but then I went to see Isla off. After I watched her drive away, it was harder to keep my mind on the game.

I turn away from the window and look at my niece.

"I think I'm gonna take a break, Makenna. Maybe Uncle Al will play. I'm going to let Atsa out." I point at the dog whimpering by the front door. I flick off the switch inside the laundry room that controls the perimeter sensors before I open the front door and let him out.

The fresh air feels good. I watch as Atsa lopes off into the trees and saunter over to the shed myself to grab some more firewood. The stack by the front door has dwindled down to just a handful of logs. Unfortunately, whatever I'd moved up from the campground was running low as well, and I load the last of it on the wheelbarrow. Probably wouldn't be a bad idea to cut up those big logs that are left by the trailer, down below. Bring the chainsaw back up here to clear some deadwood from the clearing, just up from the house. Nothing better than some old-fashioned, physical labor to kill time, and hopefully get my mind off Isla.

I've just finished stacking the last of the wood by the

front door when I hear Atsa start barking. Putting my fingers in my mouth, I whistle for him. With my eyes trained in the direction the sound is coming from, somewhere on the other side of the drive, I whistle again. This time louder. The barking stops, and then starts again, coming in this direction. Just as the dog's big, lumbering body comes tearing out of the trees, a rabbit darts across the drive ahead of him.

"Atsa!" I yell, trying to get the dog's attention. A quick glance in my direction before he refocuses on his escaping prey.

"Atsa, HERE!"

Like throwing the brakes on, all four of his legs lock up, and he almost dives face first into the snow, before looking at me woefully as the rabbit scoots behind the shed. Lead-footed, he turns in my direction, and with his head down low in defeat, makes his way over. Damn dog.

Behind me the front door opens and Al sticks his head out.

"Everything okay?" he says, stepping to the side as I point Atsa inside.

"Chasing a bunny. Keep him inside, okay? I'm just going to run down to cut up the last of the wood there, and I'll bring back the chainsaw. We're running low, but there's some dead trees up by the clearing that are dry enough to burn easy."

"Need any help?"

"Nah, I'm good, if you don't mind keeping an eye on Mak."

With Isla in the Toyota, I'm stuck taking the ATV down. It's not going hold anywhere near what I could load in the back of the SUV, but I'll just make a few trips. Not like I have anything better to do. I just need to stay busy.

It takes ten minutes of tinkering with the damn chainsaw before I can get it started. It's fucking loud. So loud, I don't hear the ringing of my phone, but I can feel it vibrate in my pocket. Letting the saw idle—I don't want to risk not being able to start it up again—I set it on the snow and pull out my phone.

"Neil?" My ears are still ringing and I can barely hear the voice on the other end. "You there?"

"It's me. Just wanted to let you know it's all quiet," Neil answers on a chuckle. Undoubtedly he can hear the anxiety in my voice. "She's fine. She's in the grocery store with Caleb close behind her. Shouldn't be too much longer before we're heading back."

"Nothing?" I ask, even though the answer is already clear from his concise report.

"No sign of her. We can try again tomorrow," he says, ending the call.

Fuck that. Do this again? I tuck my phone back in my pocket and bend over to pick up the saw.

Two more of those big logs to go and I can start hauling it up to the house.

Al

"When's Uncle Ben going to be back?"

I look up at the little girl, who reminds me so much of my Isla when she was a child. Sharp as a tack, inquisitive, and more tomboy than girl, just like my girl was. Still is.

The dog, who'd gone to lie in his bed by the fireplace

earlier, was sitting at her feet, staring out the window.

I could hear the sharp whine of the chainsaw earlier, but I can't hear much now. Haven't heard it for a bit. Old instincts die hard and the hair on the back of my neck stands up straight.

"I'm sure he'll be up soon. He's probably loading the wood. I'll go see if he's coming up the drive." I keep my voice calm, smiling at her as I scoot back from the table, where I was teaching her to play poker. Isla was only twelve when she could con me into thinking she had a royal flush in her hands, when all she had was a couple of pairs. I folded many a good hand based on that poker face many a professional gambler would be jealous of. But only when playing poker, any other time, the girl was like an open book.

Just like this one, looking up at me with big, scared eyes. She feels it too, something heavy in the sudden silence. Heavy and ominous.

"Stay here, honey. I'm just going step outside. I won't go far off the front steps, okay?" I assure her, as I pull on my coat and put on my boots. She's standing in the hallway, the big dog protectively pressed against her side. His ears are up and alert. "Atsa will stay with you."

I'm surprised to find it's started snowing when I step outside. There's no wind, but it's plenty cold enough so my breath comes out in a little stream of fog.

The snow may have something to do with the heavy silence, but still it's odd not to hear a thing. No sounds at all. I walk away from the house a few steps, and try to listen closer, hoping perhaps for a thud of a piece of wood thrown on the ATV I heard Ben take down earlier. Or maybe the whir of an engine.

Nothing.

I want to walk over to the rock, so I can see the campground below, but I promised Mak I wouldn't go far. Something is off. Something is way off.

With a sudden sense of urgency, I turn back to the house. I need to get to Mak, to a phone.

My hand is already on the door when I hear something: a low hum, an engine, and then the crunch of wheels on the snow. I turn to look at where the road up meets the level ground of the driveway, expecting the four-wheeler to come into view.

It's not.

CHAPTER 28

Ben

The first thing I notice is the smell.

A strange combination of freshly turned soil, mold, and fresh wood shavings; not entirely unpleasant.

But the sight when I manage to crack open my eyes, is, *unpleasant*.

The last thing I remember is going to pick up the saw. Nothing else, no sound, no warning. Judging by my throbbing head, I got clocked good.

I try to let my eyes adjust to the limited light coming in through the small, dirty windows, but I keep my focus on the shape in front of me. The more I see clearly, the more disturbed I am.

"There you are."

Even the voice is revolting. I can barely recognize the syrupy, breathy sound. Although there must've been something about the woman in front of me I once found, at least somewhat, attractive.

Whatever that might have been is now gone.

I remember thinking it was odd there weren't any more current photos of her at her mother's place. This woman is a caricature of the young pretty blonde in the picture I saw on the fireplace mantel, or even the grainy image Neil had dug up and handed out copies of this morning. I'm sure underneath that elaborate, almost clownesque makeup job, she's still there, but I'm having a hard time finding her.

"Jahnee." Her face lights up when I say her name, and a slight shiver runs down my spine.

I'm lying on a bed, in what looks to be the bedroom in a small cabin, my arms and legs tied to the solid bedposts with very little movement available to me.

I can see her sitting through the open door at a small, Formica kitchen table, her long, talon-like nails tapping on the hard surface. She's dressed in some flimsy dressing gown that she left half-open. That's got to be cold. I swear the temperature in here is not much above the outside one, even though there's a small wood stove burning against the far wall behind her.

What's most disturbing, and yet almost mesmerizing, is her other hand, dipped between her widespread legs, her fingers playing in the clearly wet curls there. It's like passing an accident on the road, you want to look away but you find yourself drawn.

"Where am I?" I ask, my voice raspier than normal, and I'm surprised to see she can hear me from there, when I force my gaze back up to her face. She smiles and suddenly I recognize the girl she once was, but the very next moment her words chill my blood.

"Home," she coos. "You're finally home."

Isla

I land hard.

A sharp jab shoots up both knees, when they hit the ground. The cart in front of me keeps rolling and I vaguely register it bumping into the shelves. I'm still hanging on to the second cart, the one I was dragging alongside me.

"Jason!" I hear a woman yelling behind me, but before I can even turn around, strong hands slip under my arms and lift me straight onto my feet.

"You okay?" The voice, smooth like dark chocolate, belongs to Caleb. The man doesn't say much, but when he does speak, he has all your attention.

He turns me to face him, while his hands distractedly brush at my coat. That's when I see the little boy being scolded by what appears to be his mother. There are tears streaming down the poor kid's face.

"I'm okay," I call out, as much to Caleb, as for the mother's ears. "Really, I'm fine."

The woman marches up, pulling the reluctant kid, who's maybe six or seven years old, along with her.

"Apologize to the lady, Jason." She gives the boy a little shake.

"Sorry," he mumbles through his sniffles.

"It's fun, isn't it?" I tell the boy with a wink. "I used to do exactly that when I was a kid, until I learned going fast is really only fun when you have brakes." Caleb chuckles behind me, and I don't really know if what I say will stick with young Jason, but my Aunt Kate always said you can't pass up on a teaching moment. This seemed like a good one.

"You done shopping now?" Caleb asks, his big hand still steady on my upper arm.

"I think I am." I take a step away and he drops his hold. "Even if she had eyes on me, she wouldn't make a move now."

"Can't count on that. For all anyone knows, I'm just a fellow shopper jumping at the chance to pick a pretty girl up off the floor. Plenty of damsels in distress need rescuing at the local food market." The slight smile that follows—more like a tilt of the mouth—is nevertheless potent as hell. What's with these guys?

"Grocery store hero?" I joke, causing his smile to deepen as he shrugs.

"More like clean up in aisle five."

It's my turn to laugh, as I pick up the few cans that have rolled off the shelves.

"Grab your carts and let's get out of here," he says, all business again, before disappearing down the aisle.

-

I'm loading the last of my bags in the back of the SUV, when I hear my name called. Young Phil McCracken is behind the wheel of his rig, waiting for the light to turn across the road. I lift my arm and wave, but instead of waving back, he leans out the window and yells something I can't quite make out. I put my hand behind my ear, a universal sign I haven't heard a damn thing.

"Did…father call you yet?" This time I hear enough and I shake my head. I haven't heard from the old curmudgeon, but it could be my uncle knows something.

"No," I yell across the road, just as the light turns and the rig starts moving. With a flick of his hand that holds the middle between a wave and a dismissal, Phil drives off.

I shake the snow, that's starting to come down good, from my head and arms and climb up behind the wheel.

As I make my way out of Dolores and up the mountain, I'm lost in thought, finding I'm both relieved and disappointed that nothing happened. When my phone rings in the deep dark recesses of my purse, we hadn't set mine up on the car system yet. I pull over on the shoulder to dig it up. Not the kind of weather conditions to be attempting to do anything but keep your eyes on the road when you drive.

"Hello?"

"Ms. Ferris? I'm calling from Southwestern Memorial. We wanted to let you know there's been a change in Ms. Gustafson condition." My heart shoots up in my throat.

"A change? What change?"

"We've started bringing her out of her coma early this morning and she's starting to respond."

"Have you called Ben? Her brother, Mr. Gustafson? He should be listed as primary contact."

"There's no answer at that number. We've tried a few times," the woman says, and that anxiety I thought I felt moments ago, is nothing compared to the sheer panic seizing me now.

"We'll be in touch," I mumble in the phone before ending the call, and taking a deep breath in before I steer the car back on the road. The woman probably thinks we're a heartless bunch, not caring about Stacie. She'd be wrong, but the truth is, I have a feeling that even though Stacie has turned a corner, the rest of us may have just slipped further down the rabbit hole.

I'm surprised to find Uncle Al coming down the steps as I pull into the drive, and I don't like the look on his face.

"Get inside and lock the door," he says, the second he pulls the door open.

"Why? What's going on?"

"I don't know yet, but I need you to get inside," he

bites off through gritted teeth, basically pulling me out of the car and taking the keys from my hand.

"Where's Ben?"

"Goddammit, girl! Would you just do as I say?"

I'm shocked into compliance. I'm quaking on the inside, and no less so now that my uncle, who hardly ever raised his voice at me, just yelled at me. Loudly.

The front door opens before I reach it and all I see is Mak's pale little face peeking through the opening. I slip inside and close the door behind me, when I'm tackled by Mak, who wraps her skinny arms around my middle, and buries her face in my coat.

"Where's Uncle Ben?" Her wobbly little voice slams home the fear already crawling over my skin.

"I don't know," I whisper.

I'm not sure how long we stand there, my back against the door and Mak clinging to my front, when I notice Atsa whimper. Shortly after the crunch of wheels on the snow can be heard outside, and I shove away from the door and yank it open, making a grab for Atsa's collar when he tries to slip through. A large SUV and a pickup truck are pulling up behind the Toyota. Gus and Neil get out of the vehicles and join my uncle, who gestures at the campground. It's Neil who spots me in the doorway, holding on to the dog on one side and Mak plastered against my other. All three heads turn in my direction and they slowly make their way over.

"Inside, Isla," my uncle orders in a warning voice.

"Where is he?" I counter, not budging, staring my uncle down.

"Let's talk inside." This from Gus, who gently, but firmly, puts a hand behind my neck as he leans close.

"Please."

-

The general mood in the great room is gloomy. Mak and I, snuggled together on the couch, are flanked by Uncle Al and Gus, who's talking in a low voice on his phone. Neil is at the dining room table, tapping away on a large laptop he hauled out of his truck.

"I've gotta do something," I announce, kissing Mak on the head before I hand her off to Uncle Al, who wraps the sniffling girl in his arms.

In the kitchen, I start yet another pot of coffee before I turn to the breakfast dishes still in the sink. We have a dishwasher, but I don't think we've used it more than two, maybe three, times since we moved in. Much more economic to do them by hand. Besides, sticking your hands in warm water is always good therapy.

The thoughts in my head are tumbling around as I try to cling on to something Gus said earlier. He suggested that if Ben had been this woman's obsession, it's unlikely she would harm him any more than she already had.

Oh God, I hope so.

Caleb took Atsa down to the trailer earlier, on a leash so he couldn't take off. Since the snow has been falling steadily for a few hours now, the only thing they could find was a wide swath, which looked like it had been made by a sled. Caleb thought she might have used it to transport Ben to a waiting vehicle. The trail stopped just on the other side of the gate to the road and some vague tire impressions could be seen leaving.

There was no question at this point that she somehow managed to snatch Ben. Atsa sniffed out his phone, lying in the snow, not far from a length of wood that had some blood on it. The thought of Ben injured made me nauseous. My uncle had tried to keep Mak distracted, while the guys had been updating me in the kitchen earlier.

I'm not sure what everyone is up to now, but I don't doubt they're doing the best they can, and I'm leaving them to it. I just had to stop asking questions, when I noticed how upset it was making poor Makenna.

It's hard sitting still with just your thoughts for company, and I look over at Mak whose eyes are glued to me.

"Wanna help me make some sandwiches, sweetheart?" I ask her, looking to offer some semblance of normalcy in this emotional chaos.

It's not until after we've made lunch and fed the guys, and managed to eat a little ourselves, that I remember the call from the hospital. I catch my uncle's eye, while Mak is momentarily distracted by a show on Netflix, and nudge my head in the direction of our bedroom.

"What's up?" he says, closing the door behind him after he follows me in. Before I have a chance to answer, he has me wrapped against his teddy bear body, and I fight to keep the tears at bay, feeling like that twelve year old again. "It's gonna be okay, girl. You're man's been in much hotter water than this, trust me. Either he'll find his way out, or we'll find him."

"I know. It's not that," I say, taking a step back from his embrace. "With everything going on, I totally forgot that the hospital called earlier. They couldn't get hold of Ben and called me when I was on my way home. Stacie—they started weaning her off some meds—she's apparently showing signs of waking up."

"That's great news."

"I know. I was rushing home, so I could tell Ben. I'm sure he would've taken Mak to see her. I don't know what to do, Uncle Al." I watch as my uncle walks to the window and stares out in the waning light, running a hand through his hair. The next second, he turns to me with a big smile on my face.

"Listen, I'm going nuts sitting around with my finger up my ass, too. If it's not too late, why don't I take Mak down to the hospital? I'll keep my phone on, anything happens you can get hold of me, but it may be best for everyone? What do you think?"

What I think is that my uncle rocks, and I let him know as much when I wrap my arms around his neck and give him a resounding kiss.

"But what if they give you a hard time getting in, or even letting her in?" I voice my concerns, knowing Ben had encountered a battle when he'd brought Mak in before.

Uncle Al just grins and winks at me.

"Don't you worry, girl. It may not be obvious to you, but I haven't completely lost my touch yet."

Ben

I must have passed out, because this time when I manage to open my eyes a crack, I'm met with darkness. My arms hurt when I test my restraints, probably from being pulled on. I'm not exactly in particularly bad physical shape, but right now I can feel my age in every fiber of my body.

A body that, until now, I hadn't realized was naked. That's not something that would normally bother me much in any kind of company, but lying here, spread-eagled with my bag of tricks flopping in the wind, I'm feeling a tad exposed.

The door is closed. That much I can make out, and I'm listening for any sounds on the other side. There's nothing.

Could be it's the middle of the night. Sure feels that way. Time to get my bearings.

With my fingertips, I can touch the underside of the knots in the ropes tied around my wrists, but there's not enough slack in the rope for me to work them. I pull up with my leg, to test the hold there, but all it does is tighten the noose she has around my ankle.

Despite the cold air in here, sweat is starting to drip down my forehead as I give short little jerks on the ropes at my feet, hoping I can create enough leeway, even on one side. My head feels like it's about to explode but I can't afford to waste any time. I don't know what she's up to. Whether she's planning to hurt Isla.

I yank on the restraints with a little more force, ignoring the burn as the rope scrapes my skin bloody, when the door flies open, crashing against the wall.

"I'm not gonna let you go," she smiles, backlit in the doorway, holding up a syringe.

Now I have a whole new reason to get loose and I try furiously. I even snap at her hand when she gets too close, but that results in backhand across my face that has me seeing stars. That is, stars on top of the stars I was already seeing, and suddenly the room spins out of control, and I can just turn my head to the side before my stomach turns inside out.

She doesn't hesitate either; the moment I start yacking up whatever's left of breakfast, I feel a sharp stab in my neck. Heat radiates out from my neck down to the tips of my fingers and toes. The last I manage to do is turn my head, so I can look at her as darkness starts filling in from the outside until there's nothing.

CHAPTER 29

Isla

"*Still sleeping.*"

The whispered voice outside the bedroom door, that just clicked shut, belongs to my uncle. A soft conversation can be heard moving down the hallway, but I can't distinguish any words.

It must be early morning, judging by the soft light coming in the window, and just for a moment I let myself linger on the edge of awareness, where the pain of reality isn't so sharp. Unfortunately, my bladder won't let me linger too long and I roll over to swing my legs from the bed. A tiny groan, from the small form beside me, yanks me firmly back to the brutal truth.

Last night she ended up in bed with me. I'm not quite sure whether it was her or me who needed to stay close, but we ended up clinging onto each other regardless. I never expected to sleep, but emotional exhaustion eventually took over, and I can't remember much beyond actually crawling under the covers.

Sadly, Uncle Al never got to take Mak to see her mother. I ended up calling ahead and was told even though she was starting to move her extremities, she had not woken up yet, and it was too late for a visit. We're supposed to call back this morning.

I look over at the little girl and am grateful she's still sleeping, because the rush of feelings that assaults me when I spot Ben's toothbrush on the edge of the sink, is too much brutal reality. I manage to pee and wipe the sleep, and tears, from my face with a wet washcloth before I slip back in the bedroom to grab some clothes. Mak is sitting up straight in bed, her eyes wide and fixed on me.

"Morning, baby," I coo gently, padding over to the bed and sitting on the edge. I reach my hand out to stroke the back of my fingers over her sleep-creased cheek. There's no answer, just those big blue eyes playing out every emotion. "Do you want to hop in the shower? Or I can draw you a nice bath in the big tub?" A large whoosh of air is released from between her lips and she swallows audibly.

"Mom?"

"Gonna call the hospital right now, baby," I assure her.

"Uncle Ben?"

Son of a fucking bitch. That one hurt, so I grind my teeth and swear up a storm until it subsides. I've done enough crying in front of her.

"Honey, the only reason your uncle isn't here, with the people who matter most to him in the whole world, is because we haven't found him yet. But I promise you, we will. I'll go out and look for him myself today."

I'm not sure how my uncle or any of the other chest-pounding males in my house feel about that, but I don't care. Not when an eight-year-old girl with big eyes, is looking at me as if I have all the answers.

I don't, but I'm damn well going to find them.

-

I lied.

I knew exactly how the guys were going to react to

my announcement I was going out looking today.

I'm thinking the only thing preventing me from being tied down, or locked up in my room right now, is because I was smart enough to wait until Uncle Al took Mak down to Cortez. Although I have to admit, Neil looks about ready to handcuff me to the dining room table himself.

"I'll take one of those radios," I say, pointing at the row of chargers now living on my kitchen counter. "I'll check in every ten minutes, but you've got to admit, I know this mountain better than you guys do."

"Who's saying he's still on this mountain?" Gus points out and for a moment, I have no answer.

"I am," I finally say. "I can feel he's close."

I fully expect to be dismissed outright for saying something that I can't possibly know for sure. Except; I do. I can feel it in my bones. Surprisingly, the three sets of eyes looking back at me don't hold any ridicule, just curiosity. Caleb is the one who speaks up.

"Where do you feel it? Your heart or your gut?"

"Gut," is my immediate response. My heart is a little overwhelmed right now, my gut is the only thing I trust.

"Good enough for me," Gus says dryly, looking at the other two men in turn before focusing on me. "Take the four-wheeler, stick to the paths and roads. Check in every fifteen minutes by radio, and if you find something—*any fucking thing*—you radio it in. Got that, Sugar?"

The pet name was surely thrown in there to soften up the steel-edged tone in which he relayed his message. No wonder he was able to keep all these men, some bigger than him, in check.

"Got it," I mumble back, some of my own bluster deflated.

Ten minutes later I've got it back, as I zoom off on my four-wheeler, bundled up like I'm ready to explore the Arctic Circle with the radio and my phone tucked in my pocket.

I don't really have a plan, but I'm letting my instinct lead me. Caleb took off up the mountain, taking Atsa with him on the leash again, and Gus and Neil were staying back, waiting for word from Damian. He'd called this morning about a possible lead in Towaoc he was looking into.

I took the road down to the campground, hoping that with my photographer's eye, I might spot something the others overlooked. Fat chance of that, since they'd gone over every square inch yesterday already, but it's as good a place as any to start.

I'm trying to imagine what it's like to be so blinded by want for someone, that you lose all grip on reality. That you'd go so far as to approach anyone standing in your way of getting what you want, like an obstacle in need of removal, by whatever means.

I can't. I just can't imagine it no matter how much I love Ben.

I drive around the campground, stopping every now and then to look up the mountain, to see if anything catches my eye, but nothing does.

As I'm turning out of the campground to go up the road, my phone starts buzzing in my pocket. I almost drop it; my damn fingers are so frozen.

"Hello?"

"This Al's little girl?" If I weren't freezing half to death, looking for a madwoman who has my guy, I might've chuckled at the description. As it is, I don't want to be shooting the breeze with Phil McCracken.

"Hey, Phil. Yes, it is, but I'm in the middle of something. Can I call you back?" The cold is making my teeth chatter.

"Stupid fuckers probably froze their asses up there already," the old grump mutters. I'm confused and more than a little irritated, but I still ask.

"Up here? Who are you talking about?" I bite.

"Tried to explain huntin' season was over, but they wasn't lookin' to hunt."

"Phil, I have no idea what you're talking about." I was about to hang up on his ass and get myself inside to warm up for a bit.

"The boy 'n me, we've got ourselves a little cabin up your ways. On the east side of the road. Used it for huntin' for years. I don't go alone, and with the boy being busy hauling loads, we ain't been up there in a while. Figure I could catch some rent on it this huntin' season and tacked a note on the board at the Food Market. Some couple called, wanting it for the winter. Said her and the husband were wantin' a romantic place to get away to on the weekends. Didn't matter I explained to her there ain't nothing romantic about that cabin. She wanted it."

"She?" The cold all but forgotten, a niggle of fearful excitement is ballooning into something much bigger. "Phil, you said she?"

"Yes, damn city girl, too. That's why I'm calling, maybe one of yous can check in on them? Ain't seen her around since she came to pick up the key and directions, and dropped a wad of cash. Forgot to ask for her number before she took off, was too busy countin'. Must've been a looker once—"

My mind is churning, still trying to process the information, when I interrupt him.

"Did she leave a name?"

"She might've. Can't quite recall. She was driving a city car though. One of them Chryslers? Shit for the birds, those. Specially in these mountains. Damn thing was white, too."

-

I cut the engine and pull out the radio when I reach an old pickup, pulled off to side, at the end of the narrow trail. It looks old enough to have been sitting here for years, except for the layer of snow covering it. It looks too fresh, and not nearly as thick as the snow on the rocks on the opposite side.

"Gus, are you there?"

There's just a crackle of static in response. I already tried my cell phone but I have zero reception on this side.

"Gus?" I try again, only to be met with the same result.

Just like about a dozen other times on my trip down this trail, I wonder if perhaps I should've gone home first. And every time I convinced myself that I technically hadn't seen anything worthwhile mentioning yet. That, and the gnawing in my gut, drove me to keep going.

Until now.

The truck is something, which is why I'm trying to raise Gus now, except I'm afraid maybe I'm out of range.

"Caleb, can you hear me?" I try the other man, who's supposed to be somewhere on the other side of the road, with my dog.

First there's only the static, but then I hear a click and a voice.

"Where—you?"

"Caleb! I'm on a trail, just below the top of the ridge, on the east side of the road into town. I found a truck." The last words I whisper, realizing a bit belated that someone might hear me.

"—ay there—wait—oming." His voice is broken up, but I get the gist of it.

I'm not sure how long it is I'm waiting, but with every second that ticks away, thoughts of Ben, of what she might be doing to him, become louder in my head. The what-ifs are driving me nuts, until I decide just to move a little bit up the hill. Just a bit of exploration. Get the lay of the land, so to speak. There may be nothing up there, but then again, it might just be my world.

I freeze when I hear a rustle in the brush to my left, only to let out a sigh of relief when a rabbit scoots out from under a fallen tree limb. I find a narrow path, running between the rocks along the trail, and although the base feels solid, there's enough fresh snow on top to make it pretty tough going. It's mostly uphill and my leg muscles are starting to burn, so when I spot a sturdy branch that will double well as a walking stick, I snatch it up.

Much easier like this, and I have to admit, it feels good to have something solid in my hand.

I almost charge out of a thick copse of trees when I notice the smell—wood burning—and I stop in my tracks. In a small clearing, just up ahead, is a dilapidated log cabin. There's a woodpile stacked against the side, though, and clearly smoke coming out of the stone chimney.

Sneaking up behind the thick trunk of a tree, I have a

pretty clear view of what looks to be the front of the place. So now what? I can't go barging in there. I have no idea what I'll find. I don't even know if Ben is even in there.

As the cold I've been ignoring starts crawling up my body from my toes, I realize I've bitten off way more than I can ever hope to chew.

I'm still contemplating my own inadequacy when I hear a loud crash from inside, followed by an unholy scream.

One that propels me into action.

Ben

I'm fucking groggy as shit.

Floating in and out of consciousness for God knows how long. I wouldn't be surprised if she shot me up with a large dose of Rohypnol. It's used as a date rape drug, often ingested, but when injected can bring down a large animal.

Guess that's what I am. It's certainly what I feel like, fucking naked and tied up to a bed, not even able to step outside for a leak. At some point I must've pissed myself, judging from the smell. I can only pray I don't get the runs or I'll be in deep shit. Pun most certainly not intended.

I'm trying to let my senses tell me what's happening around me, without opening my eyes. I don't want to alert her to the fact I'm awake, only to hit me up with another load of that drug. I also don't want to puke all over myself, which I almost did when sunlight hit my retinas.

She definitely hit me hard.

For the past little while, I've heard her shuffle around, mumbling, and occasionally the floor would creak on the other side of the bed. I couldn't see her, but I could hear her, smell her, and sense her eyes violating my body. I had to fight the urge to shiver with revulsion.

But she's in the other room now. I can hear what sounds like a can opener and then something being dumped in a pot. Then there's a heavy metal scrape and a dull thud, followed by another metal scrape. Adding wood to the stove, I figure. The smell of warm food, just a little later, confirms it.

Every time I think her back is turned, my fingers pick away at the knot on my right wrist. It's slow and tedious, and at any time I expect to be caught, but I'm making progress.

"Oh, my baby, did you soil yourself?"

I try not to move when I hear her moving closer.

"You did, didn't you?" she coos, now only steps away. "Look at you. Momma's gonna have to clean you up. Good thing I warmed up some water for the dishes."

I follow her voice as she moves away again, and this time I try to peek through slightly opened eyelids. The light immediately has my stomach surge up, but I grind my teeth and manage to hold it together, as I watch her fill a bowl with water from a pot on the little stove and grab a rag from the sink.

Fucking hell. She intends to wash me. I close my eyes again

With everything in me I want to stop her, but when she's almost to the bed I have an idea.

"Bed's wet," I slur on purpose, hoping she doesn't realize I'm more alert than I appear.

"So it is," she purrs. "I'll fix that as soon as I fix you."

I keep my breathing as steady as I can, even as the wet glide of a rag between my legs and over my limp junk makes me want to hurl. She's thorough and she's slow, and by the time she's done I feel like I've taken it up the ass.

But then I feel her hand on my ankle, as she loosens the bindings on one side. Then she starts working on the other. I take another peek from under my eyelids to see her back halfway turned, and the fingers on my right hand pluck furiously at the knot.

"Roll over, so I can get the sheet and wash your backside."

Oh hell no.

The moment she leans over, and puts her hand on my far hip, helping me roll, I sharply pull up my right knee, knocking her off balance. She stumbles back and trips, landing on her ass, while I frantically work the last loop free on my wrist. I finally yank it free just as she scrambles to her feet and charges me, screaming like a banshee.

I get a good swing in, but she's like a rabid dog, using her claws and teeth on me. I only have limited movement to evade her, and am running out of steam quickly when the front door slams open.

"Get off him!" I know that voice, even through the thick throb pounding through my entire body at this point, I recognize that voice and it fucking terrifies me.

I can handle pain, I can handle the contemplation of my own demise, but I cannot handle Isla in the path of danger.

"Get oudo'ere…" comes tumbling out of my mouth,

barely identifiable, as I watch the crazy bitch swing around.

Her head drops between her shoulders like a fucking animal readying for attack, and she charges straight for Isla, catching her in the chest and plowing her straight outside.

I struggle against my ankle restraints and frantically pull at the remaining knot on my left wrist. From outside, I can hear the noise of a struggle, and what sounds like the snarl of a dog.

The last thing I hear is the sharp reverberation of a gunshot, before I lose my balance, tumble off the edge of the mattress, and everything goes dark.

CHAPTER 30

Isla

"What the fuck were you thinking?"

Caleb's once velvety, dark chocolate voice is now edged with cold steel.

I wasn't thinking; I was reacting.

Despite my uncle's many warnings that one day my impulsive nature would get me in trouble, at forty, I'd still not been able to get a handle on it. Truth is, I like being impulsive. I like to think I'm being adventurous. Although, at this particular moment with my lungs still struggling for air, I'm pretty positive I could do without this kind of adventure.

I sure as hell didn't expect a screeching amazon barreling straight for me when I flung the door open. I only got a quick glance behind her to see Ben trussed up on the bed—blood caked to his face and a wild look in his eyes—before I was knocked straight off my feet by a five foot ten human battering ram.

She flattened me out on my back in the snow with embarrassing ease, knocking the wind out of me. Before I could catch my breath, before I even had a chance to react, her hands were wrapping around my neck.

I fought.

I clawed, I punched, I tried to kick at the snarling, spit-slinging, inhumanly strong she-woman pushing me down in the snow, but when I started seeing little stars dancing in front of my eyes, I wondered if this would be it. My next thought was that Uncle Al would be really pissed if he had to bury me too, and that idea alone gave me renewed energy to fight.

The next thing I know, there's snarling of a different kind, when a giant, black and white ball of fur, with sharp teeth, comes out of nowhere and knocks the woman clear off me. A loud gunshot rings out and suddenly all noise stops.

That's when I hear the voice.

"*Not much,*" I try, but not much sound comes out and talking hurts like a mother.

You'd expect to feel cold, lying in the snow, but my body is feeling oddly warm.

"Did she stick you?" he asks, and I feel his hands on my body, looking for holes I presume, although at this point I can't be sure of anything.

"*I don't...*"

Ben

"I just spent a day and a half tied to a damn bed already. You wanna prolong the torture?"

I'm fuming when the nurse tries to push me back on the bed and threatens me with restraints if I don't lie down.

I think I remember Isla kicking open the door and standing there, wide-legged and fierce, with the blow up of snow swirling around her five foot frame as my pint-sized avenger. My cavalry. Can't remember a damn thing after.

"Can you please find me someone who *does* know something?" I grind out to the nurse, who doesn't look very sympathetic. "Please, my wife may be hurt."

The little involuntary hitch in my words apparently does the trick, because her face softens as she nods and scoots out the door. The wife thing—I'm going to make that happen as soon as I can fucking see her face.

Minutes later, I'm up and swinging my legs out of bed, again, when Al walks in. My eyes immediately search beyond him, but no Isla. I'm not liking the look on his face as he walks up to the foot of the bed and just stares.

"God, tell me she's okay," I choke out. It's been a long time since I've used that name without following it up with a juicy curse, but not this time. This time it sounds more like a prayer.

"You better be callin' on him," Al says, his face stern. "You should see the marks that woman left on my girl. I swear she's turning what little remains of my dark hair gray. Won't stop asking for you, even as the doctor tells her she needs to stop talking to give her voice a rest. Bruising clear around her throat and gashes so deep some of them needed stitches." The old man runs a shaky hand through his hair, more shaken than he initially let on.

The relief I feel is quickly replaced with anger.

"Where is she?" I demand, ignoring the spinning room as I try to get my feet under me.

"Right here, you fool," her raw whisper sounds from the doorway, where she's standing with a grinning Neil behind her.

I'm being kept overnight for observation because of a concussion and the drug still floating around my system. The gash on my scalp has been stitched up and they treated and bandaged the scrapes on my ankles and wrists. All that would heal, as will the marks and injuries Isla sustained, but it's going to be a long time before I'll be able to get over the guilt I feel.

With Isla tucked in beside me, despite the nurse's objections, Al and Gus get us up to speed. I can't believe my sister is waking up. Mak was in here earlier, crying when she saw both Isla and me bandaged up. Poor kid. I almost choked up when she threw herself in my arms. For once, Neil's cocky charm came in handy when he expertly coaxed her out of the room with the promise of unhealthy candy and violent video games on his laptop.

"She was treated for dog bites and is on her way to Durango where she'll be held in the hospital psychiatric ward for assessment. The DA can figure out what to do with her there," Gus says.

"I heard a shot," I point out.

"Yeah, Caleb fired in the air. Your damn animal was about to tear the woman's throat out. It was the only way he could get the dog's attention away from her."

"*Where is...*" Isla starts, but I cut her off with my hand on her mouth. Something I've had to do a few times to keep her quiet. Her glance is scorching when I look down at her.

"Pixie..." I growl softly to which she rolls her eyes.

"Told them to drop the mutt at the coffee shop," Al says, looking at his niece. "Jen will look after him."

"*Not a mutt...*" she mumbles behind my hand.

"I swear, woman, I'm going to slap duct tape on that mouth if you don't keep it zipped."

I'm pretty sure I won't have sex for the next five years, but at least she stays quiet after that.

Apparently, despite the poor radio connection, Caleb hadn't been that far from where Isla was. Basically just in the woods on the other side of the road. He'd picked up just enough to know she was east of where he was, and with Atsa's help was able to pick up her trail quickly. The dog had torn free of his leash when it spotted Isla being attacked. They'd found me hanging off the side of the bed, still tethered by my legs and one arm, which had almost been twisted out of its socket. I feel that, although I can't remember much of my trip down to a waiting ambulance in the same sled Jahnee had apparently used to get me up to the cabin.

Isla had briefly blacked out from lack of oxygen, but had been able to walk back to the trail with just a little help.

"That is one seriously whacked woman," Gus points out, when he gets ready to leave. "Did you see the gallery she had on the living room wall?"

"Can't say I had an opportunity to take in the sights, no," I answer rather sardonically.

"Might be best," he says, with a quick glimpse at the woman by my side, before returning his gaze to me. "They've probably been taken down for evidence by now anyway."

With a two-fingered salute and a chin lift, he turns, just as a doctor walks in. Gus slips by him out the door and immediately Al gets up as well.

"I'll go see if I can get some news on your sister and

find Mak." He walks over to the bed and leans down, giving his niece a kiss on the forehead. "You keep that motor-mouth in check, will ya?" As he walks out of the door we can hear him mutter, *"Damn girl will be the death of me yet."*

"Is it Ms. or Mrs. Ferris?" the snot-nosed doctor, who barely looks old enough to be wearing laced shoes, asks Isla.

"It's Ms.—for now," I answer for her, since she's not supposed to be talking and this dumbass is asking her questions.

"Right," he sputters, looking at the chart in his hands. "Well, I'm an OBGYN resident and am supposed to ask Ms. Ferris some questions."

"That'll be hard, because Ms. Ferris was told not to strain her voice, since someone tried to strangle her today." I can hear my voice rising as frustration takes over, but Isla's small hand on my chest calms me. Enough for something to register.

OBGYN?

"I apologize, I'll do my best to ask only yes or no questions, although with the first one, that might a problem," he says, looking nervously at me, before turning to Isla.

"When was your last period?"

Isla

Ohmygod. Ohmygod.

"Breathe, Pixie," Ben's deep voice penetrates my

panicked inner chant.

I try, but I end up coughing, which hurts my throat like you wouldn't believe and tears spring to my eyes. Somewhere in the background I hear the click of a door closing, and the next thing I know is Ben's face looming over mine.

"You okay, baby?"

"*Baby...*" I rasp between coughs. I watch as the worry melts off his face and is replaced by a shit-eating grin.

"So it seems," he says, clearly not feeling my level of sheer panic, and I promptly burst into uncontrolled sobs. "Shhh," he hushes, rolling on his back and taking me with him, somehow managing to keep both of us from rolling off the narrow bed.

"*Too much...*" I mumble against his chest when the tears slow down, still feeling utterly overwhelmed. It is all a bit much to take in one sitting; although it's becoming quite clear Ben and I aren't destined to live a nice, steady, predictable life.

There was a time, before Ben, when I would dream of some excitement, but I have to admit at this point, I've had about all the excitement I can handle.

"Never too much. Not with you," he whispers in my hair and my sobs start all over again.

I managed to keep it together for twenty-four of the most harrowing hours of my life, tracked down my man, was almost killed by a lunatic, was saved by the best dog in the world, only to find out I'm having that baby I was told I'd probably never have.

I just started to come to terms with it, too. At least I thought I was.

A baby.

How am I going to raise a baby on the side of a mountain? If I can't keep track of my grown ass man, who the hell decided it was a good idea to put me in charge of a child?

Ohmygod. I'm going to have to give birth. But first I'm going to be big as a whale. What if something is wrong? We're not exactly spring chickens, aren't there things that can go wrong?

"That's why he says they'll monitor closely," Ben says, making it clear that my quiet private meltdown wasn't quite as private, *or* quiet, as I thought it was.

"I don't think I can do this," I admit, looking up at him, more than a little pissed when I see him smile.

"I don't think you have much of a choice at this point."

"A little less of the cocky would be good," I snap, hurting my throat in the process, but it only makes his grin bigger. He puts his mouth close to my ear.

"Can't recall you complaining about that when I was planting my kid in you."

I'm about to hit him when a woman in scrubs pushes a machine into the room.

"Ready?" she asks with a bright smile.

"You bet," Ben says, with all the confidence in the world as he scoots off the bed, despite my protests, and sits down on the chair beside it. My efforts to still his hands are pointless as he helpfully pulls up my shirt.

Only a few minutes later, our hands are tightly entwined as we get a first glimpse of our nugget, aptly named by Ben with his overt appreciation for fast food.

"This little one measures at about eighteen weeks. Do you want to know what it is?"

"You can see that?" Ben asks.

"Sure can."

Ben looks at me and then both of us turn to the woman.

"Yes," Ben says, just as I say, "No." But one glance at the crestfallen look on his face when he turns to me with his mouth open, and I change my mind.

"Oh fine."

Ben

"Hey, Sis."

I smile despite the shock to my system the sight of Stacie's bandaged body gives me. One of her eyes is covered under the thick padding and the other is half-opened. It's looking straight at me though.

Mak is with Isla in my room, and I was able to bribe Al into wheeling me in a chair to the ICU. That nurse, Carol, was manning the desk but she took one look at me, then at Al, and threw her hands in the air, before purposely turning her back. Al chuckled behind me.

"Guessing you had a run in with her, too?" I conclude.

"Sure did. Told me she *figured* we all belonged to the same family. Damn battle-axe missed her calling as drill sergeant."

I reach out and carefully stroke my sister's fingers that seem lost against the white blankets.

"You're hurt," she croaks. The observation, along with the sound of her voice, dislodges a sound that is half-cough, half-sob, from my throat.

"You still win," I whisper, bending down to kiss her fingers. "I'm sorry."

"Not your fault," she says, and when I put my forehead to the mattress to hide my emotions, she lifts her hand and lets her fingers trail over my hair.

We stay quiet like that for a while, when Stacie clears her throat.

"You thirsty?" I ask, lifting my head. I spot a cup of water on her nightstand and carefully bend the straw to her lips.

"Where's Mak?" she wants to know, her one eye scanning as much of the room as she can.

"Isla's taking care of her in my room." A little smile tugs at Stacie's lips. "It's good practice for Isla," I add quietly, so only she can hear. I watch as her eye pops open and the small smile gets a little bigger.

CHAPTER 31

Isla

"Can I bring Mom a few cookies?"

Mak is pressing the Hershey's Kisses in the hazelnut cookies we just rolled. It's the third load. We've got two trays cooling, two trays in the oven, and two more in production. Ben thinks I've gone crazy, but I have this need to stuff my freezer to capacity with all the things I might not feel up to or have time for once this baby is here. Even if it is still months away, I have to make up for the eighteen weeks of prep time I missed out on.

I turn to her, smiling. "Absolutely, if you think she's allowed?"

"She was eating a sandwich yesterday," she says, shrugging her shoulders.

"Well good, then pack a few up." I wipe the dishwater from my hands and pull a box of zipper bags from the drawer, handing them to her. "And fill a bag for the nurses' station, too."

Ben was released two days ago with orders to rest. Which, to me, means your feet up and napping when you can. However, in Ben's world it means driving off on his ATV, my traitorous uncle following behind on mine, to go haul some dead wood from the clearing. My concerns were laughed off, which necessitated me to bake cookies or do some target practice on their asses. Since my baking skills are far superior to my shooting abilities—I have no wish to put this little bean in any danger—I quadrupled my recipe.

We are baking twelve dozen cookies; hence there are more than enough to share.

"They're back," Mak says, her gaze going out the window and mine follows automatically. I can hear the buzz of the engines and Atsa's excited bark, just moments before they come into view.

I blow out a deep sigh, releasing tension I didn't realize I was holding, and toss my towel on the counter. Mak is already up and running for the door and I follow behind, only marginally slower.

The moment she opens the door, Atsa comes bounding inside, shaking snow everywhere.

"I just cleaned that floor, puppy," I grumble, grabbing a dirty towel from the laundry room and mopping up the mess. I should've waited, because I'm still on my knees, wiping, when both men come walking in, stomping the snow off their boots all around me.

"Oops," Uncle Al says when I look up, giving both my dirtiest look, although Ben just smirks.

"Where's the wood?"

"Dumped it by the shed," my uncle clarifies to Mak. "We're taking a break."

I get to my feet and dart into the laundry room, to get rid of the wet towel, when I feel someone push inside behind me, closing the door.

Ben's cold body wraps around me from behind and wet hands sneak under my flannel shirt.

"Dammit, Ben, that's cold!" I blurt out when his frozen fingers touch my stomach.

"Don't think I fucked you here, yet."

I whip around and try to shove him off me, to no avail, clearly. I lift up on tiptoes and stick my face close to his.

"My uncle and your niece are right outside the door," I hiss, not quite believing his gall.

"So?" he fires back, a smoldering fire in his eyes.

"So, there's no way I'm letting you in my pants when they're standing right outside," I stage whisper.

"They're in the kitchen by now. You can smell whatever it is you're baking clear across to the shed. Why did you think Al was in such a hurry to get inside? Guaranteed he's in the kitchen already, stuffing his face."

"Tonight," I promise, trying hard to keep a straight mind, while his hands continue to stroke and knead my skin.

"Now," he rumbles, slipping those big paws down the back of my pants and giving my ass cheeks a good squeeze.

The ice blue of his eyes darkens as he lowers his head, and I'm almost hypnotized by the widening of his pupils, and his lips, when they touch mine, are still cool from the outside. His tongue, though, is hot in contrast, as he licks along the seam of my mouth, teasing me to open. The fire his kiss ignites is immediate. My hands, which had been planted flat in his chest to ward him off, now claw into his sweater, as he ravages my mouth.

We've snuggled, we've pecked, but we haven't really kissed, or touched since before Ben was hit over the head. And even before that we'd had Mak in our bed every night since the explosion. I crave his touch, but I don't want to sneak around in the laundry room.

"Ben..." I mumble against his lips when he tries to

shove my pants down. "Ben, please, hold up." This time his hands still as he pulls his head back. For a short while we just stare at each other, my eyes pleading and his getting stormier by the second. Until finally his hands drop away from my body and he hangs his head.

"Grabbing a shower," he bites off, before he opens the door and walks out.

I'm frustrated, too, I want to call after him, but what's the point in that, it's not like he doesn't know that.

When I walk into the kitchen, Uncle Al shoots me a smile before turning to Mak, who is back to unwrapping Kisses.

"You know what?" he says, turning to Mak. "I think I saw some elk tracks up on the edge of the clearing. Did you know that we have a pretty decent herd here on the mountain? They tend to be shy in the summer, especially with the cattle invading their space, but in the winter they'll show themselves from time to time." Now he turns to me with a smile. "First time I took Isla to go find them, she wasn't much older than you are, and we ended up smack in the middle of the herd. We were looking so hard in one direction, we didn't see a bunch of them come up behind us and suddenly they were just there. Remember that, girl?" he asks with a grin. I smile back, because I do remember. I remember almost peeing my pants from fear and from sheer excitement.

"She peed her pants," he informs Mak, who suddenly smiles big.

Okay, so maybe I did wet myself, a little. Not every day you have a close encounter with a bunch of animals with antlers the size of a Buick, that look nothing like the Bambi you'd imagined. I shrug my shoulders at Mak, who giggles.

"How's about you and me go see if we can find us some elk?" The girl looks up at him with big eyes.

"But Uncle Ben was going to take me to see Mom," she says.

"We're not going long. Your uncle is having a nice, relaxing shower first anyway." My sneaky uncle throws me a wink before leading Mak out of the kitchen.

Five minutes later, after shoving Atsa back out the door with them, I sneak into the bedroom, listening to the water running in the shower. I strip out of my clothes quickly before stepping into the bathroom, where Ben's large silhouette is outlined behind the mottled glass shower door.

His back is toward me, one hand leaning high up on the tile wall, the other moving lazily between his legs. My body responds instantly with a tightening of my nipples and a surge of heat through my core. He doesn't seem to hear my sharp intake of breath at the sheer beauty of him, over the drone of the water.

Ben

I still my movements when I hear the door slide open, but before I can turn my head, small hands slip over my wet skin. From the low of my back, around to my stomach, and lower, to where my fist is still wrapped around my painful erection. One of her hands slips lower, cupping my balls, as the other curves around my cock at the root, right behind my own.

I can't help it. I jerk at the sensation that triggers a distasteful memory, before I feel my body shutting down. I make a fast grab for her wrists.

"Stop," I whisper. "I need to see you."

Without a word, she releases her hold, slipping between the wall and me, as she looks up with eyes that hold a clear question.

"I need to know it's you," I try to explain, without spelling it out. She blinks a couple of times before her eyes grow big with understanding. Then her eyes turn to slits as angry determination washes over her face, and holding my gaze, she lowers herself to her knees.

"Baby…"

"Shhh." She purses her lips as she leans forward and kisses the tip of what's left of my erection. "Keep your eyes on me," she instructs, as she runs her tongue around the crown before sucking it between her lips.

So goddamn beautiful, with the water running down her face, clinging to her eyelashes, and the tip of her small nose. Those deep pink lips stretch wide as she slides the heat of her mouth over my quickly recovering cock, holding my eyes with hers. I finally let go of her wrists and brace myself with both hands against the wall behind her as her soft hands gently explore.

"*Fuck*," I hiss when she swallows, her mouth massaging my length from root to tip.

All I see is Isla.

All I feel is Isla.

Her small fist wraps around me, working my cock in tandem with the strong suction of her mouth, and this time no one else is touching me. Just her. Just my Pixie.

Almost without warning, I can feel the pinpricks at the

base of my spine spreading into a full body tingle, the instant before my balls tighten, and the first spurt surges out of me. My jaw drops as a low groan rumbles through my chest, but my eyes never let go of hers.

She takes everything I give her and when I'm spent, barely able to stay standing, I feel clean—untainted.

"Love you," I rumble, as I grab her under her arms and pull her up, pressing her against the tiles with my body. "Love you so fucking much it hurts."

"I want to hurt *her,*" my little Pixie spews venomously, and I can't hold back a chuckle, dropping my head in the soft spot between her neck and shoulder. I inhale her deeply and am surprised when my dick shows signs of renewed life.

"How long before they get back?" I mutter against her skin, as my hand slides up her side to cup her breast, lifting it up for my lips.

"Ahhhh," she moans as I take most of her small breast inside my mouth and suck deep. "Too soon," she manages breathlessly.

"We'll have to be quick then."

In one move I bend down to lift her, hook my arms underneath her knees, and brace her against the wall, spreading her wide open. Sliding my cock along the crease of her pussy I can feel how wet she is. Sucking me off turns her on as much as it does me. I poise myself at her entrance, and with a single thrust, drive myself deep inside her.

"Hold on," I warn her. She slips her arms around my neck and clings on as I fuck her fast and furious against the wall.

The feel of her nails digging into my neck, the sound

of slapping wet skin, and the guttural little sounds she makes drive me crazy. I'm fast barreling toward my second orgasm, when she hasn't come once yet. I slip my hand between our bodies and easily find her distended clit, right where our bodies are joined. All it takes is a few fast flicks, and then firm deep pressure from my thumb, to feel her inner walls clamp and pulsate around me. I follow right behind her.

"Not sure that's what the doctor meant when he said for you to take it easy," she mumbles, when I gently lower her legs, making sure they're firmly underneath her before letting go.

"Bullshit," I counter. "You're my best medicine."

-

"Don't take off your stuff," I tell Mak when she comes running in just as I step into the hallway.

They were gone for quite a while. Had I known, I would've maybe tried for a third round, but in bed this time. Don't think my knees would've handled another go against the wall.

"Guess what?" I look down into my niece's upturned smiling face.

"I give up," I joke, raising my hands in surrender.

"I saw an elk!"

"You did? That's pretty cool." I keep her talking as I get dressed to go outside myself.

"I want to take a picture, so I can show the kids at school. Otherwise they won't believe me. Do you think next time Isla can come with her camera?"

I smile at the ongoing chatter until I realize I have no clue when she's supposed to go back to school. Or where. In the next day or two, Stacie will likely be transported to

Durango Mercy Regional where she will be undergoing the first of a series of graft surgeries, and of course Mak will stay with us.

Isla walks into the hallway to see us off, and with Mak still chatting away as she goes outside, I quickly pull Isla aside.

"Mak has to go to school."

"I know," she says, cool as pie. "She mentioned something this morning. Maybe call the school from the hospital, see if Stacie feels up to talking to them. I'll look into to finding her a school here. We'll also need to pick up the rest of her stuff in Albuquerque. Do something about her place there. Her job. I've started a list."

"Uncle Ben!" Mak shouts from outside. "Are you coming?"

"Better go, honey," Isla says, grabbing my coat and pulling me down for a kiss. "Tell Stacie I'll see her tomorrow."

She's not coming with me today, because Al is leaving tomorrow. I think Isla secretly would love him to stay around permanently, but as long as his wife is alive in nursing care in Flagstaff, that's just not an option.

It'll be quiet without the old guy around.

Isla

"That girl tuckers me out," Uncle Al mutters when I walk into the kitchen. "If you don't mind, I'm gonna lie down for ten minutes."

As soon as he disappears in his bedroom, I go in

search of my computer, which I find on the narrow table under the TV. It's been since before Christmas that I've done any work on my edits and I feel like being creative.

With Atsa asleep in his bed by the fireplace, I curl up on the couch, flip open my laptop and sign on. Immediately my email notifications pop up; fourteen new emails. I scroll through them; discarding most since they're newsletters or advertising, but there's one that catches my eye.

Julie Winton.

I hesitate briefly, wondering if I should simply send it on to Neil, but curiosity wins and I click on the name.

MINE

There's just that one word, plus an attachment.

The image is one of a room I saw only a brief glimpse of, before I was tossed on my back in the snow. The wall depicted looks like a gallery, or perhaps a shrine is a better description. In the center is my own photo, the one I took of Ben overlooking the reservoir, the one she reportedly bought from the gallery. All around it are a host of others, mostly grainy images of Ben: some alone, but also some with me, taken from a distance, with one thing in common; her face glued or superimposed on mine.

Even more disturbing are the other shots, showing Ben, naked, tied to the bed, and clearly out of it.

CHAPTER 32

Ben

"Son of a bitch, Neil. How in hell did that get through?"

I'm furious. I come home from spending a few hours at the hospital with my sister, thinking it's safe to leave my girl at home, only to find her in a ball on our bed, crying her eyes out. It doesn't matter that by her own explanation it was only "*pregnancy hormones,*" or that she was crying because she couldn't have "*another go at that bitch.*" What matters is that she was upset because of an email that never should've reached her.

"I'm sorry man. I closed down the tracking program as soon as the woman was in FBI custody. She must've had that email lined up to go out from her phone, but without reception, it got stuck in her outbox. The phone was dead when they took it as evidence from the cabin. They must have charged it up to examine it at the FBI offices, and as soon as it found a signal, it would've automatically sent off whatever was in the outbox."

I hate that he makes sense. I want to hang onto my anger, but I have to admit I can't really blame anyone for this unfortunate fuck up.

"Got it," I grumble. I could probably be a bit more gracious but Neil doesn't seem to hold a grudge.

"I'm still sorry," he says, with a lot more meaning than I'm comfortable with. Living through that shit and having any memory of it was bad enough; having every-fucking-body get a gander at your naked, helpless self is beyond humiliating. *Son of a bitch.*

"Yeah," I blow him off. "Anyway, you got any more news? I haven't talked to Damian yet, but I figure your nosey ass probably knows whether that psych assessment has come back yet."

"Funny you should mention that," he says, chuckling. "Nothing's official yet, but I may have accidentally tripped over the hospital transcripts of a forty-three-year-old, caucasian female with paranoid schizophrenia in an acute stage of psychosis. Further hospitalization is recommended to attempt to control symptoms with a variety of treatment options."

"In other words, she'll be found unfit to stand trial," I conclude.

"Likely," Neil agrees before he offers, "but, she'll be behind bars either way."

"Nah. They'll drug her up until she can barely function and declare her healed. She could be out in months; forget to take her meds and end up just as bat-shit crazy as she is now."

It's the truth. I've heard stories of people who've done unspeakable things, who avoid prison by reason of insanity and before you know it, they're back on the streets. I never thought much about it, I only had myself to worry about, but the prospect terrifies me now.

I have Isla and our child to worry about.

"We'll keep track of her," Neil says, immediately understanding. "I'll personally keep track of her. I promise."

"I'd appreciate that."

I end the call and pour myself another glass of scotch when I hear footsteps behind me.

"Got another one of those?" Al asks, pulling out the stool beside me.

"You bet." I get up to grab a second tumbler and pour him a good two-finger measure. I can hear the sound of laughter coming from our bedroom, where Isla and Mak are cuddled up with her laptop, watching some comedy on Netflix.

"Couldn't help overhear part of that," Al says after taking a sip from his drink. "Need me to stick around?" I turn around in my seat and clap a hand on his shoulder.

"Thanks," I tell him sincerely. "But there's no way to tell what's going to happen. Only thing sure is that she's locked away for the foreseeable future. You've gotta go see to your wife and trust me that I'll take care of mine."

"Yours?" He pulls up one eyebrow.

"She will be. Soon."

"No need to rush things, Son."

"Gonna be fifty next year, old man, I'd hardly call it rushing." I know Isla had wanted to keep the pregnancy quiet for a bit so the two of us could get used to the idea first, but her uncle deserves to know. "Besides," I add. "No child of mine will be born without my name."

It's deadly quiet. Al's glass is suspended somewhere halfway to his mouth as he gapes at me, the wheels turning behind his eyes. Suddenly he slams the glass down on the counter and I'm surprised it doesn't shatter on impact. Without taking his eyes off me, I see him take in a deep breath.

"Isla! Get your ass out here, girl!" he bellows suddenly and I can't stop the bark of laughter.

"What?" The dog jumps up in confusion as Isla comes running from the hallway, Mak padding in behind her. She takes one look at her uncle staring at me with something close to murder in his eyes and then she turns her gaze to me, with much the same expression on *her* face. "What's going on?"

"You were going to send me on my merry way without telling me you're pregnant?" It's almost humorous, seeing her mouth open and close like a fish as she reaches for an appropriate answer.

"You're having a baby?" This from Mak, who is the only other person who seems to be happy with the news. Must be a familial thing.

"You told him," Isla hisses at me.

"I had to," I explain, looking from one to the other, before I settle on Mak. "Yes, honey. We're having a baby."

"Yay!"

"Ben!"

"Son of a bitch!"

The last was Al who looks ready to feed me his fist, yet the person who worries me most is my Pixie, who appears hungry for blood.

"I had to," I repeat, keeping my gaze fixed on her. "Because he didn't want me to rush into marrying you, and I wasn't going to ask you without his blessing."

It all makes perfect sense to me, and to an enthusiastically nodding Mak, but the other two seem less convinced. Time to bring out the big guns. Or the ring.

One of the reasons I was so pissed off about finding Isla in tears was because I'd planned to ask her tonight, with her uncle still here, but the timing was clearly off.

Mak helped me pick out a ring this afternoon, after we left the hospital, and she'd been as excited as I was.

I slip off the stool, take a step closer to Isla, put my hands on her waist and lift her up, swinging her around so I can sit her down on the edge of the counter. Before she has a chance to react, I pull the box out of my pocket and flip it open.

"Marry me."

Isla

Seriously?

That doesn't even remotely sound like a question, let alone a proposal.

Something in my face must've given him a clue, because his face softens as he grabs my hand with his free one.

"You know I don't do words, Pixie, but you've got to know by now how meaningless my life would be if I didn't have you to share it with. You were a surprise when I met you, and you've been a surprise every day since." He pauses, checking me out like he's gauging his level of success, when Uncle Al pipes up.

"Girl, just say yes. Put me out of my misery. If I have to listen to this man bungle through this wedding proposal any further, I might actually have a stroke." Then he turns his attention to Ben. "And you're about as smooth as low grit sandpaper. You need some game."

I almost laugh, watching Ben's face fall, but then I spot Mak's hopeful little face, looking at her uncle like he hung the moon, and I melt. Because I recognize it. Sometimes I look at Ben the same way. He's bossy, can be overbearing, and he certainly has the ability to irk me, but he also believes in me, makes me feel safe, and loves me without reservation. My uncle is wrong; he's not bungling his proposal, because his intentions are right there, plain as day on his face.

I place my hands on each side of his rugged face and kiss him sweetly.

"Of course," I whisper against his lips, smiling when I hear Mak let out a *whoop*.

-

Still, it's bittersweet when Mak and I furiously wave goodbye to my uncle walking through security at the airport. Ben stands off to the side, his hands in his pockets, only lifting his chin slightly when Uncle Al looks at us one last time before disappearing.

He'll be back. In April, he said, when he can drive without the risk of snow.

"Should plan your wedding then," he suggested with a big grin.

"We can do that," Ben answered for both of us, which resulted in another discussion around the importance of communication, or rather the lack thereof. I was feeling a might left out to say the least. A significant oversight, since I'd be the one walking down the aisle, the size of a truck by then. This baby is due early June.

I argued to wait until after the baby is born to get married, but nobody else agreed with me. Then Ben promised that he couldn't imagine me any more beautiful than round with his child, and I finally gave in.

Last night, the two men had talked about Ben's retro

trailer ideas while I sat curled up in the corner of the couch, just listening to them talk as I twirled the pretty blue moonstone ring on my finger. Ben's choice was perfect and indicative of how well he really knows me. I'm simply not a diamond kind of girl, and when he told me the moonstone reminded him of the first time we kissed out on the dock, he had me burst out in tears. Even Uncle Al grudgingly nodded his approval.

Happy times.

Even while saying goodbye, because he'll be back.

We dropped Atsa off at Jen's again this morning, who is getting much too attached to our big, hairy, and very lovable mountain dog and stopped in at the hospital on the way to Durango, to see Stacie. Her transportation to Mercy Regional is scheduled for tomorrow. Ben suggested we all see Uncle Al off, and drive straight through to Albuquerque, with the trailer hitched to the SUV.

The plan is to pick up as much as we can haul back of Mak and Stacie's stuff, and pack the rest into storage. With Stacie looking forward to months of rehabilitation and at this point unable to see where the future will lead; she, along with Ben, decided that mainly for her peace of mind, she'd give up her little bungalow. We'll spend one or two nights to get that sorted and then we'll pack up the trailer and head back.

We'll stop in Durango, this time at Mercy to see how Stacie has settled in and to give her the few things she's requested from her home, and then it's back to Dolores.

It's not going to be easy, a lot of driving back and forth to Durango to see Stacie while she's recovering at first. Then once the bulk of her surgeries are done, we should be able to bring her home, hopefully sooner than later. Home with us, because her road to recovery is really only just starting.

The emotional lash back will undoubtedly come. Not just half her body, but also half of Stacie's beautiful face is marred by burns and will likely be scarred, even after grafting. Although there's a lot that can be done with plastic surgery these days, she will never look the way she did before.

Ben's biggest concern is her emotional well-being. Of course she is in a tremendous amount of pain still, but it's obvious she is already retreating. Except when Mak is there; she comes alive when she sees her daughter.

"Can we stop at Sonic?" Mak pipes up from the back seat when we get back into the car.

"You guys have a serious addiction to fast food," I observe.

"But I've never actually been to one," she argues. "Every time we'd drive by one at home, Mom would tell me next time."

I peek sideways at Ben, who's looking at his niece in the rearview mirror before turning his hangdog eyes on me. When I turn around to check on Mak, her eyes hold the same pitiful expression.

"Oh for Pete's sake, fine. Let's do drive-thru," I give in, rolling my eyes.

Mak squeals in the back seat and Ben reaches over and squeezes my knee, his signature shit-eating grin on his face.

The worst part?

I may have developed a pregnancy addiction to mozzarella sticks dipped in peanut butter fudge shake.

To Ben and Mak's delight, we hit every Sonic Drive-thru in Albuquerque while there, and I keep telling myself it's because we have no time to put together a proper meal. All lies.

"What's wrong?" Ben asks me when we're driving back home. He must've heard my deep sigh. Would be hard not to, since I may have put a little umph into it.

"I wish we had a Sonic closer by," I complain, to Ben's hilarity.

"We may have created a monster, Makenna," he says over his shoulder, and I hear her soft giggle from the backseat.

"Guess she doesn't know they have one in Cortez," his niece answers, snorting.

Oh no. Correction; by the time April comes around, I'll be the size of a blimp.

It doesn't stop the grin from spreading.

CHAPTER 33

Ben

March

"Mak, hand me that edging brush, will ya?"

I'm teetering at the top of the ladder, trying to get this bedroom painted.

The original slate gray wouldn't do for the baby, Isla decreed. So despite the fact we just painted it a couple of months ago, here I am again, slapping on a sunflower yellow. Perfectly non-gender specific, according to my fiancée, who's insisted we at least keep the gender to ourselves, since I already spilled the beans on the pregnancy itself.

I couldn't care less, and I'm willing to bet neither would the baby, but she's adamant that this is a happy color that will be soothing and uplifting. Very well. I am not about to argue with my furiously mood-swinging Pixie. Especially given my niece is in full support of the color change. Since she's the one living here, at least for the next few months, and I want her to feel at home, I don't grumble—much.

"Want to start pulling down the tape around the doorframe?"

I don't even get an answer; I just hear the ripping off of tape as Mak enthusiastically dives into her task.

"Careful, you don't just toss it on the floor, kiddo,

there could be wet paint on it. Stuff it in that garbage bag."

"Ohmygod." I turn to find Isla in the doorway, her hands clapped over her mouth. Eyes big and shiny as she looks around the room.

She's glorious. Still her own person, with today's ensemble of an old pair of my sweats, cut off below the knee, showing the bottom of a pair of daisy leggings and topped off by her favorite Converse high tops. A white tank is stretched tight over her bulging belly and a man-sized flannel shirt hangs open over top. Her hair has grown out a little, yet is still short and spiky, but it's her face that makes the whole thing work. Fine-boned like a china doll, with a small narrow nose and big eyes. Happiness stretches her lips from an almost dainty cupid's bow to a wide open-mouthed smile, and despite the age lines and faint wrinkles, she still looks like a young girl to me.

My own contradiction on feet, and I love her.

From the very first moment she aimed that smile at me, she showed me an alternate universe from the one I'd been living in for years. One much brighter with color and light. She introduced me to a full range of emotions, from beautiful to downright painful, but all very real. I wasn't lying when I said every day with her is a surprise and her quirky wardrobe choices are just external manifestations of the vibrancy she gives my world.

"Isn't it pretty?" Mak chirps happily.

"It's perfect," my girl sighs, as she looks at me in that way that makes me feel larger than life. And not just because I'm standing at the top of a ladder.

"Almost done. Just let me finish this edge up, then Mak and I will shove the furniture back in place. We've got time."

I know she's worried about bringing Stacie home.

My sister has undergone three surgeries in the past six weeks, the last one two weeks ago on her arm, where an earlier infection created even more damage than the burns had. All in all, she came away relatively lucky, with visible damage contained to one side of her body. We'd all been worried about her face, but were assured that she would be able to hide most of those injuries with her hair. The burns were limited to one side of her face, and the graft running down from cheekbone down to the jaw and back to the ear, is still swollen. Right now it pulls on the corner of her eye a bit, making it droop, but once the swelling goes down, that will hopefully be minimized.

She's coming home this afternoon. She's still going to have to make regular trips to the burn clinic, and we have a physical therapist lined up, right here in Dolores, to work with her. It'll be a few weeks yet before she can drive herself, and in the meantime either Isla or I will drive her.

"Do you think I should put on a dress?" Mak comes into the laundry room where I'm rinsing out the paint trays.

"A dress? Do you even own one?" I ask, a little perplexed at that particular question from that particular mouth, but I feel immediately guilty for being flippant when I see the dejected look on her face.

"Mom bought if for me last year. I've never worn it."

I turn, pick her up, and set her on the washer, leaning my hands on either side of her. She's pretty tall for her age, all arms and legs, but she weighs nothing.

"Why do you want to wear a dress?" I ask, dipping

my head low to catch her downcast eyes. "I thought you hated dresses?"

"But Mom bought it for me," she says with a shrug. "Maybe it'll make her happy if I wear it."

My heart squeezes. Stacie has been struggling emotionally, something I thought she was hiding phenomenally well around Mak. Apparently not as well as we'd thought. I take her face in my hands and tilt it up.

"Wear the dress if it makes you feel better, kiddo. But what I know about your mom, she doesn't really care all that much about what you have on. She cares more about how *you* feel. And I'm pretty sure she doesn't want you to change who you are to make her feel better."

"But she's sad. Her eyes don't smile anymore," Mak says, her eyes brimming with tears. Damn kid is breaking my heart.

"She's been stuck in a hospital room for months. It's hard to find things to smile about when life goes on around you but you're not part of it." I kiss her forehead when the first tears start rolling. "It may take her a little time, but I know your mother; once she can smell the fresh air, feel the heat of the sun, and hug the one person who means more to her than anything else in the whole world, she will remember how to smile. I promise you." I hug her little body close and the way her skinny arms try to wrap around me, chokes me up.

I'm not a particularly demonstrative person, not with anyone other than Isla, and I may have been missing something. It's so easy to misjudge someone by what they represent on the outside, and Mak may show a rough and tumble tomboy, but that doesn't mean she needs less affection. Maybe it just means she doesn't know how to ask for it.

So I hug her a little tighter and kiss the top of her head as I let her cry out her worries and her fears.

"I love you, Makenna," I gently tell her, her short hair tickling my cheek. "You're perfect just as you are."

Isla

He's killing me.

I didn't mean to eavesdrop. I just grabbed the sheets off the bed in the other bedroom, where Stacie will be staying, and was going to wash them when I heard talking from the laundry room.

Mak comes skipping out of the laundry room, her cheeks wet with tears but a big sunny smile on her face when she spots me.

"I'm gonna put my daisy leggings on, too," she announces, as she darts past me down the hall.

"You heard," Ben's deep raspy voice comes from the doorway. All I can do is nod. "Never realized how much alike you two are. For two people not related by blood, there are some uncanny similarities." I smile at his words. There's some truth in that. I see a kindred spirit of sorts in the almost nine-year-old-girl.

"We're both children of single beautiful mothers. I lost mine; she almost lost hers. We're both much tougher on the outside than we are on the inside. And we both had strong male role models step up to the plate when we needed someone. I'd say we have plenty in common."

"I'll say," Ben says dropping a brief kiss on my lips.

"I'll do better," he mumbles, and although I want to tell him he's doing amazing already, I keep my mouth shut. I don't want to depreciate his intentions. So instead I lift up on tiptoes and kiss him back.

-

"If you'd like, you can get these filled at the hospital pharmacy downstairs," the nurse says, handing Ben a stack of prescription slips for Stacie.

"Dismissed," he mumbles, as he slips by me out the door.

Stacie was sitting next to her bed, wearing a pair of the soft sweats we bought for her and a long sleeved T-shirt. Mak, however, had wanted to make a special stop for her mom and handed Stacie the bag with the Rose Pedal logo on the side.

"What did you get me, baby?" Stacie asks, one side of her mouth pulling up in a smile as she looks at a nervously twiddling Mak.

"Open it."

"Mak wanted to make sure you had something pretty to wear home," I explain to Stacie gently, when she pulls out the soft, floral, knit lounge pants and soft pink, oversized hoodie, and looks up confused.

"It's beautiful," she tells her daughter, whose look of relief is almost comical. "I'd love to wear it home."

"I can quickly help you," the nurse jumps in. "If you would excuse us?" She turns to Mak and me.

"Actually," Stacie pipes up. "Why don't you give us a minute instead?"

"But—" the younger woman protests, but Stacie holds her gaze firm, until she slinks from the room.

"You guys ready for this?" Stacie asks, a world of

insecurity in her voice. Mak is oblivious and excitedly starts pulling tags from the clothes, but I know exactly what she's asking.

"You bet," I answer, putting my words into action as I reach out and help her get out of her shirt. First her good arm, and then I lift it carefully over her head, where the hair is slowly starting to grow back. Finally we strip it carefully down the still bandaged arm, where she just received the final grafts a few weeks ago.

The damage to her beautiful body brings tears to my eyes, but I quickly blink them away. Stacie's eyes are flicking between her daughter and me, clearly waiting for a reaction. Any reaction. I realize that aside from medical personnel, we are the first ones to see the extent of her injuries.

I conjure up what I hope is an encouraging smile, but it's Mak who turns this into a pivotal moment when she turns to her mom, ready with the pink hoodie in her hand.

"Here, Mom. Put your head through," she says, leaning over her mother, not giving the deep red ridges on her torso a second glance. "It's got bat sleeves," she explains to Stacie. "All you have to do is slip your hands through the cuffs. See how easy that is?" Mak's chatter easily breaks through the heavy air of anticipation as her mother clearly braces for a shocked reaction. I love the little girl, even more than I already did, when she doesn't even pause as she pulls the hoodie down to cover the scars on Stacie's body. "It looks pretty on you, Mom." She smiles proudly at her mother, who swallows hard and simply nods.

"Perfect choice, Mak."

She turns her pleased smile on me at the compliment.

"Now the pants."

With a little help, we get Stacie on her feet, and Mak takes care of gently stripping the simple gray sweats and replacing them with the pretty, soft, palazzo style pants she picked out.

"Does it pinch anywhere?" she asks her mom.

"No. It's perfect, baby." The smile on her face reaches her shiny eyes for the first time in months, as we carefully lower her back down in the wheelchair.

"I'll just go grab the car," Ben says a bit later when we reach the lobby. Hospital policy requires a nurse to bring the patient to the door, so the young nurse is pushing Stacie's chair. "Be right back."

"Okay, I'm going to find a bathroom quick, before we get on the road," I announce. Pregnancy makes for very frequent bladder emergencies and with an almost two-hour drive ahead of us, I don't want to be caught by surprise. "Need to go to the bathroom, Mak?" I ask.

"I'm okay."

Leaving Mak with Stacie and the nurse, I backtrack down the hall to where I'd spotted a public bathroom earlier. I dive through the door, my head low as I concentrate on holding it in. The bathroom seems empty, and as soon as I close the stall door, I yank my pants down and let go with a groan of relief.

I flush, put my clothes back in order, and am just unlocking the door when I hear the footsteps of someone else entering the bathroom. I don't even look up when I make my way to the sink to wash my hands—I don't want to keep anyone waiting—so when a low husky voice speaks right behind me, I jump.

"Who is she?"

Whipping around, my breath catches in my throat when I see a face I don't think I'll ever be able to forget, nor the glint of a knife in her hand.

"You?—How?—" I stammer, instinctively covering my pregnancy with my hands. Her eyes follow my movements and widen slightly at the significant bump of my belly.

"Who's she?" she repeats, her larger frame leaning forward, crowding me into the little alcove by the sink. My eyes dart over her shoulder to the door she's blocking.

"Who?"

"The woman in the wheelchair?"

"Ben's sister," I admit. I'll say anything to keep her from focusing on my baby. I watch as a range of emotions plays out on her face, before her eyes squint and move back down to my belly, and up. "That was supposed to be you," she hisses.

"I know," I whisper, praying for someone, anyone, to come through that door. "What are you doing here?"

"I've watched him. Watched you and him for weeks. You always park in the lower parking lot, right by the rock garden. I've seen you from my window." Her voice, low and almost seductive, takes on a harsher edge, becoming almost shrill as she talks. "I've seen you kiss, right below the room where you had me locked up. Do you know how hard it's been to pretend? Do you know how patient I've had to be?" Spittle starts flying from her mouth as her face morphs into something barely recognizable as human.

I vaguely register a call for 'code yellow' over the hospital intercom as the woman in front of me steps closer. There's nowhere for me to go, with the wall at my back and the sink biting in my hip, I'm stuck.

"Jahnee," I plead, hoping the use of her name will call on a healthier part of her mind. "How did you find me?"

"Watching and waiting. Today was the day. I knew it when I saw you flaunt your victory over me, but you didn't honestly think I'd just let you walk away with my man and my baby, did you?"

I barely manage to turn my stomach to the wall when she jabs at me with, what I can now see, is a butter knife.

"You were always first," I try. I'll say anything to get her to back off. "You were his lover first, you carried his baby first. I'm sorry...I didn't know." The moment I mention her baby, the twisted expression on her face seems to melt away as her eyes float away, perhaps reliving some distant memories.

"I wanted it to be his so badly," she says, her voice dropping to a whisper. "He would've made a much better daddy than the sick bastard, who left me lying on a bathroom floor, with his dirty cum still dripping out of me."

I feel for her in that moment. Despite the horrible things she's done, the damage she's unleashed in her own life and in others', I feel for her. In a moment of compassion, I reach out my hand to her, but the moment my fingers touch her skin, she reels back and hauls me across the face.

"Mine!" she shrieks, raising the hand wielding the knife above her head. It may just be a butter knife but I imagine it can do enough damage, so I drop down to the floor and instinctively curl myself around my baby.

Ben

I leave the engine running on the Toyota as I rush inside to load up my girls and take them home.

Stacie is sitting in the wheelchair, with Mak and the nurse by her side.

"Where's Isla?"

"Bathroom," Mak clarifies, pointing down the hall.

"Okay, let's go ahead and get you two loaded up," I decide, holding the door open for the nurse to push Stacie's chair through, just as a code comes over the hospital intercom. The young woman briefly pauses, listening, before rolling my sister to the passenger side of the SUV. We manage to strap her in, using some of her clothes as padding so the seatbelt doesn't rub her injuries, and I carefully close the door.

I follow the nurse inside to look for Isla, when the overhead sound system repeats the code yellow.

"Hey," I call out, stopping the nurse who's already walking away with the empty wheelchair, an unsettled feeling in the pit of my stomach. "What's a code yellow?"

"Missing patient," she says. "It doesn't happen often, usually someone elderly, confused with dementia or Alzheimers. But sometimes one slips from the psychiatric ward."

Something suddenly snaps home.

"Bathroom!" I grab the nurse by the shoulders, almost shaking her.

CHAPTER 34

Ben

"What do you mean, she's dead?"

I step back to let Neil in.

"They found her first thing this morning. She'd managed to do a lot of damage with a shard from a mirror in the bathroom."

"*Jesus*," I hiss, running my hand through hair that is in dire need of a cut.

"What?" Isla's voice sounds behind me. "Oh hey, Neil? What brings you here?" she asks, wedging beside me as she slips her arm around my waist.

It's been two weeks since we brought Stacie home. Two weeks since I barged into a hospital bathroom to find two women on the floor, bloodied and crying. I'd been frantic as I examined Isla for the source of the blood. She directed me to Jahnee, who was sitting on the floor against the opposite wall, a cut on the inside of one wrist bleeding profusely, and a blood-stained butter knife clasped in the other hand.

She'd been weeping pitifully as she was strapped onto a waiting stretcher and couldn't look me in the eye.

"Hey, beautiful," Neil greets Isla, while darting me a questioning glance.

"Neil has some disturbing news, Pixie," I tell her, dropping my arm around her shoulders and tucking her close as she lifts her face up to me. "Apparently they found Jahnee this morning." I don't have to explain anything; understanding is instantly visible on her face. Still, her words surprise me.

"Good," she says, closing her eyes and nodding firmly. "I hope she finds peace."

Isla had recounted every word that was exchanged in that bathroom. The knowledge that the baby Jahnee lost had not been mine, had already given me the sense of peace I wasn't even aware I needed.

"Well, don't just stand there," she says, waving Neil in. "Come on in. You can be our guinea pig. Mak and I are teaching Stacie to bake." She slips out from under my arm and leads toward the kitchen

"Should I be worried?" Neil asks under his breath as he passes me.

"My sister's kitchen skills are killer." I try hard to keep a straight face, but Neil's worried expression is too much, and I'm laughing as I follow him inside.

Stacie flinches when she sees the unexpected guest walk into the kitchen, but kudos to Neil for not reacting to her dramatically changed appearance from last time he saw her. He simply leans down and kisses her cheek, as he does with Mak. Easy as the guy himself.

My sister has become quite comfortable around us in the last weeks, no longer trying to hide her scars. I contribute it to my niece and Isla, who treat Stacie no different than they would've before. I'm the one who's having a harder time treating her as before. I've been more protective, more careful of her feelings, and most of the time it just seems easier to avoid interaction at all.

Until a couple of days ago, when the girls were talking about the wedding. Our wedding.

I was prepared to haul Isla off to Vegas to do the deed. No muss, no fuss. So when Isla asked Stacie to be her maid of honor, my ears perked up and my protective instincts jumped to attention.

"I would love to be your maid of honor," I heard my sister exclaim.

"Perfect!" Isla clapped her hands. "Mak and I were looking online yesterday and we found the perfect dress for you. If you like it of course," she quickly adds.

"She doesn't have to wear a dress," I jumped in. "Why doesn't everyone just wear what they feel comfortable in? We don't need to get all gussied up, do we?"

Three pairs of eyes turned in my direction, all burning holes through me.

"What? Since when do we stand on protocol?" I defended myself.

"Since your wife-to-be and my daughter clearly know me well enough to realize that I wouldn't pass up on a chance to wear a pretty dress. Unless, perhaps, you think I shouldn't?" Stacie snapped and I wanted to sink down a hole when I saw the hurt in her eyes.

Fuck me. My forty-ninth birthday just weeks away and I still hadn't learned a goddamn thing.

In two steps I stood in front of her, pulled her out of the chair and wrapped her gingerly in my arms.

"I think you should do whatever makes you happy. You're always beautiful, but when you're happy, you are breathtaking."

"Good save," Isla stage whispered, making Makenna giggle.

Clearly I've been dramatically outnumbered, which is

why I don't mind at all throwing another set of balls in the vice that has been firmly clamped over mine. Namely Neil's.

"Neil came to sample your baking," I say with a grin in my sister's direction, who immediately narrows her eyes, before diving down to pull a fine-looking pie from the oven.

Now, I've learned not to get fooled by looks alone, but in contrast to previous experiences with Stacie's pies, this one actually smells good.

She cuts a healthy wedge, and hands it to Neil who, with his puppy dog enthusiasm, dives right in. I wait for the inevitable grab for a glass of water or something to wash the taste down, but to my surprise, he forks another piece in his mouth. And then another.

"Hot dang, this is good pie," he says around a mouthful. "And I should know, I lived in Gus's guest house for a while and his wife, Emma, is a master pie baker. For a while, I was their resident taste tester. Best job ever," he mutters, as he shoves in another forkful.

The smile on my sister's face is big as she turns to me with an eyebrow raised.

"Fine," I say, my hands up defensively. "I'll have a taste." Stacie's mouth falls open and Mak busts out laughing.

"Are you shitting me?" my perfect little sister slings at me. "You give me grief over my cooking and baking for years, but now that someone else likes what I have to offer, you suddenly want to have some? Forget it."

With determination, she cuts the remaining pie into four pieces, loads another slice on Neil's plate, hands a plate to Mak and one to Isla, keeping the last one for herself. She demonstratively shoves half of her slice in her mouth at once.

"You're a pain in my ass, you know that?" I tell my sister with a roll of my eyes.

"Well, I hope so," she counters with a half grin, crumbs falling from her mouth. "I work hard enough at it."

Isla

I don't know why I'm nervous.

Maybe it's because I'm wearing a dress. Not just my only secondhand sundress, but an actual girly dress with three-quarter sleeves of lace. *Lace!*

If not for Stacie pointing out how perfect it would look with my brand new, baby blue Converse high tops, I probably would've passed on it. It's a simple dress. The simplest we could find in the store. Technically, it's just a strapless, Empire waisted dress of the softest flowing material. A deep scoop neck showcasing my pregnancy boobs. Something I know will make Ben happy to have on display, since I actually have some cleavage now. The skirt is gathered high, right underneath my breasts, leaving the rest flowing freely around my big baby bump and my ever-widening caboose in the back. Pear-shape anyone? The three-quarter sleeves belong to a long lace vest coat that closes with a single clasp between my breasts and falls open from there, creating the prettiest frame for my unhideable, advanced pregnancy bulge.

I let Mak go to town on my hair, with baby's breath

and what looks like dill, making my head look—and smell—like a salad. She loved it, and I didn't have the heart to say anything other than that I do, too. Stacie tried to contain her giggles as she helped me put on some makeup. She lost that battle when Uncle Al came to get me and announced something smelled good, and was making him hungry for salmon.

But standing outside in the doorway to the front deck, which Ben and my uncle finished this past week, seeing my husband-to-be waiting for me on the lookout point, the dog by his side, I find myself suddenly nervous.

What was supposed to be a small intimate wedding has morphed into a sizable gathering. Damian is here, serving as Ben's best man, and some of Ben's old crew are here, too. I recognize his old boss, Joe Francisi, as well as Barnes; I just don't remember his first name. Then of course there's Jen who came together with Ryan DeGroot. And even our lawyer, Nicholas Flynn, who's been leaving messages for Stacie since Ben mentioned she might be settling in town.

Then there is an entire contingent of GFI operatives with whom we've become quite close, who all brought their wives.

Just like that, I've gone from a solitary, somewhat searching soul, to someone with a home, a community—a family.

"You look beautiful," Ben says smiling, when I finally reach him after only tripping three times on those damn long skirts. He leans in to kiss my cheek. "And you smell fucking fantastic," he mumbles in my ear, and I can't help myself, I burst out laughing.

The actual wedding is brief, practical. The vows we

exchange are simple; yet hold every truth and emotion. The first kiss as husband and wife a scorcher, burning many a retina in the crowd. And the party that follows is the most fun I've had in a long time.

For the first time we reap the full benefits of the great room, easily housing the thirty some people we have here. The moment is perfect, when Ben pulls me in front of the fireplace and calls the guests to quiet, once everyone is provided with a glass of champagne. I'm holding my own glass, filled with only a single sip, so I can take part in the toast I know Ben is about to make.

"In case it's escaped your attention," he announces in his deep rasp, which carries surprisingly throughout the room. "We're expecting." Loud catcalls and whistles go up and I can't stop a blush from heating my cheeks. "My *wife* and I have known for a while, but decided to wait sharing the gender with friends and family until we could officially reveal the perpetuation of a family name that seemed doomed to die with me." He pauses for dramatic effect, even though everyone is already smiling and chuckling, before he concludes. "It's a boy."

The evening is a bit of a blur after that, with congratulations, hugs and kisses, lots of laughter, and the boisterous hum of life within the walls of our home.

But what will stay with me until I let go of my last breath is when, after the last guest has left, Ben grabs a quilt and leads me back outside. He sits me down on the rock, in between his legs, and wraps his arms around me, covering my belly with his big hands. His big body is curved around me as he rests his chin on my shoulder.

It's a clear night, after a crisp but beautiful early spring day. I don't feel the cold, not with Ben's body and the quilt to warm me. The moonlight bounces off the water of the reservoir and stars dot the sky.

"You gave me this," he says, his breath caressing my cheek. "A place on top of the world. A beautiful view that goes on forever. A future I can hold in my hands. And a life I want to grow old in."

EPILOGUE

Ben

Last week of May

"I think we should head to the hospital."

As she did the previous three times I made that suggestion, Isla waves me off impatiently.

It's just after four in the morning, and my wife has been puking her guts out for the past two hours. Every time I've tried to pick her up off the floor to try and get her in bed, a new wave surges up, and she's bent over the toilet again.

"It's just the flu," she says. Again.

Sure, Stacie mentioned that Mak had been down with a stomach bug for a couple of days this week, but we haven't seen them since we were over at their new place, down in Dolores, the week before last. I doubt a stomach bug would incubate that long.

Again, Isla lifts up on her knees and bends herself over the toilet bowl. By now all she's bringing up is bile. I wet the washcloth under the tap and wipe her mouth and face.

"Oops," she says, looking down where I can feel warm liquid touching my knees.

"Was that...?"

"My water," she says, looking a bit sheepish.

"Dammit, Pixie," I growl. "Could've been at the

hospital already." I get to my feet, and grabbing the trashcan, I toss the lid aside and shove it in Isla's hands. "Hold on to that. I've gotta get some clothes on you."

Five minutes later I have Atsa locked in the house and my wife bundled up in the SUV. I dial my sister on handsfree as Isla sticks her head in the trashcan again.

"It's time?" is the first thing out of Stacie's mouth. Poor Isla retches in response.

"Water broke a couple of minutes ago, can you call Al? He's going to want to catch a flight. And I locked Atsa in the house, depending on how long this is going to take, could you make sure someone lets him out at some point?"

"Got it. Good luck, guys! We'll see you soon."

"Not fair." Isla's voice echoes around the inside of the trashcan. "You're not even flustered," she tells me.

Little does she know that I'm so terrified right now, I'm afraid I'm going to shit my pants. Fine pair we make.

"You've got this," I encourage her when she starts gagging again, this time ending on a deep moan, but she seems beyond speech now.

Every now and then I flick my gaze to where she is now slumped in the passenger seat, groaning with every bump in the road we hit. I'm doing my best not to get us in an accident as I barrel down the road to Cortez.

"Isla?" She doesn't even respond to her name, as she starts tugging on the sweats I just put on her at home. "Babe, what are you doing?"

We're almost in the hospital parking lot and my wife is stripping off her pants, grunting like something primeval.

I don't even look at her now; I just focus on not

hitting the portico over the emergency entrance of the hospital. I slam the car in park, unclip my belt and lean over, just in time to catch my son, who comes shooting out of Isla like a goddamn projectile.

Isla screams, the baby screams, and I'm pretty fucking sure I'm screaming too as I pound my free hand on the car horn for help.

-

"Oh my God," Stacie gushes as she storms into the room, Mak right on her heels, and zooms right in on the bundle in my arms. "He's so precious. Gimme," she says, holding out her arms and wiggling her fingers.

"Buzz off," I growl, not ready yet to let go. Not sure I'll ever be.

"Ignore him," Isla says from the bed. She's way too damn perky after giving me a goddamn heart attack. "He's grumpy because I birthed all over his precious car. Oh, and I might've spilled a bucket of puke on his leather seats, too," she snickers, the other two girls falling right in with her, giggling away.

"See, bud?" I tell my boy; counting my blessings he's got the right set of chromosomes. "That's why we have to stick close, you and me."

"What's his name?" Mak asks, sitting down on the armrest of the chair. I can't resist the reverent look on her face as she takes in her little cousin.

"You ask the right question," I tell her, throwing a dirty look at my sister, who responds by sticking out her tongue. "Why don't you sit here?" I get up off the chair and wait for Mak to settle in properly. Then I put the baby in her waiting arms.

"His name is Noah James Albert Gustafson," Isla

says, tears in her eyes as she watches Mak press a little kiss to Noah's forehead. Mine are getting cloudy, too.

"That's quite the mouthful for such a little guy," Stacie says, doing a bit of sniffling herself.

"Eight pounds eleven ounces," I announce proudly.

"Ouch," my sister says, looking sympathetically at Isla, who winces at the memory.

Part of me is happy I was too busy trying not to get us killed, so I was spared watching my wife expel our bruiser of a boy from her body.

"Your dad, my uncle, and his own name," Isla explains to Stacie.

"It's perfect," she answers.

"He's perfect," Mak whispers.

This is perfect, I think.

Isla

First week of August

It's hot as a whorehouse on dollar day.

The campground is packed. I'm carting around in the golf cart with Noah in a harness on my chest, since Ben won't let me drive my ATV with the baby, and I have three more washrooms to stock with TP.

I would love to have a shower sometime this century, but between a perpetually hungry baby who is rapidly depleting the extra boobage I gained in pregnancy, and the height of season for vacationers, I truly don't even have time to fart.

And I was so looking forward to today.

I've finally convinced Stacie to let me photograph her. She'd been skeptical at first, when I talked to her about maybe doing a book for the Children's Burn Foundation. I showed her the royalty report Jen sent me on the sales of my coffee table book and it went a long way in convincing her. It was selling and the income I was generating from that and the website, was turning out to make for a nice little nest egg.

I'm proud of Stacie, of how she's been able to adjust to living with the visible scars of violence. I'm especially proud of the way she's used her experience as a jumping board to get involved with the Children's Burn Foundation. And I'm not adverse to playing up to her sense of pride, in order to get what I want; a chance to show the world, but Stacie herself in particular, that true beauty can't hide behind scars and deformations.

By the time I get back to the storage shed by our old trailer, Ben is waiting for me.

"Give me my boy," he growls, sticking his face in little Noah's neck, and blowing loud raspberries on the soft skin. All to Noah's great hilarity. I may be handy to have around for nutritional value, but Daddy is the cat's meow. Noah never smiles bigger than when Ben walks into view.

"I don't have time," I tell him. "I have to try and feed him, and get him down for a nap. Would love to at least drag a wet wash cloth over all my dingy spots, and stuff a banana in my face, all before your sister shows for her shoot." I lean my weary forehead to Ben's sticky chest. His large hand wraps around the back of my head as I listen to the rumble of his voice.

"I'll take him now. I'll feed him a bottle from the fridge and get him down for a nap, while you eat the sandwich I made you, and have a shower while you pump. In that order," he instructs me.

I lift my face and smile in teary gratitude.

"Love you," I whisper.

"Back atcha." He winks, dropping a kiss on my mouth. "Go on. Get yourself together before you make my sister look like the beautiful creature she is."

~.THE END.~

ACKNOWLEDGEMENTS:

First of all, I'd like to thank my fabulous co-author KT Dove, who actually provided the inspiration for Freeze Frame after getting a taste of Shutter Speed. Her ideas were so fabulous, we decided to collaborate on this project. Love you, lady!!

Next I'd like to thank Joanne Thompson and Karen Hrdlicka who were invaluable in the process of getting this book ready for the readers. There isn't an editor more 'in tune', or a proofreader sharper. Love you, my lovelies!

My PA Natalie Weston who works her tush off every day to keep me sane and get the word out there. I love you hard, Nat!
Our fabulous betas; Sam, Pam, Catherine, Deb, Nancy, Debbie and Chris—thank you so much for taking the time to make sure our words flow and our story makes sense. Love all of you!
The Barks & Bites group, in particular January and Rachel, who pimp and promote like crazy! You know I adore you!!

The bloggers who spend so much time out of their day promoting and reviewing. Especially those bloggers who are willing to give everyone a chance to shine. You are at the core of this Indie industry and we appreciate you so much!

A big loving thanks our families who put up with us while we disappear into our stories and forget about real life playing out around us.

And finally you, the readers; thank you is not enough. There are no words to explain how much it means to have you read our words, meet our characters and get drawn into our stories. We put a little of us (or sometimes a lot!) in each book we write, and your feedback is the best compliment we can receive.

ABOUT THE AUTHORS

Freya Barker inspires with her stories about 'real' people, perhaps less than perfect, each struggling to find their own slice of happy. She is the author of the Cedar Tree Series and the Portland, ME, novels.

Freya is the recipient of the RomCon "Reader's Choice" Award for best first book, "Slim To None," and was a 2016 Kindle Book Awards finalist for "From Dust". She currently has two complete series and three anthologies published, and is working on two new series; La Plata County FBI—ROCK POINT, and Northern Lights. She continues to spin story after story with an endless supply of bruised and dented characters, vying for attention!

Stay in touch!

https://www.freyabarker.com
https://www.goodreads.com/FreyaBarker
https://www.facebook.com/FreyaBarkerWrites
https://twitter.com/freya_barker
or sign up for my newsletter:
http://bit.ly/1DmiBub

KT Dove grew up, and still lives, in the Midwest. At an early age she developed a love of reading, driving the local librarians crazy, and would plan plot lines and stories for her favorite characters. KT received degrees in English, Speech/Drama, and Education. And yet instead of becoming an English teacher as planned, she opted for an unexpected HEA.

Now married, a mother and still an avid reader, she stumbled upon the Indie author movement and became involved on several levels. Never in her wildest imagination would she have thought she would co-author a book. With the support of her family, she took the plunge, adding writing to an already busy literary existence.
She wouldn't have it any other way.

Stay in touch!

https://www.facebook.com/KTDove/
https://www.goodreads.com/author/show/16344207.K_T_Dove

ALSO BY FREYA BARKER

CEDAR TREE Series

Book #1
SLIM TO NONE

Book #2
HUNDRED TO ONE

Book #3
AGAINST ME

Book #4
CLEAN LINES

Book #5
UPPER HAND

Book #6
LIKE ARROWS

Book #7
HEAD START

PORTLAND, ME, Novels

Book #1
FROM DUST

Book #2
CRUEL WATER

Book #3
THROUGH FIRE

Book #4
STILL WATER

SNAPSHOT Novels

Book #1
SHUTTER SPEED

Printed in Great Britain
by Amazon